Alice Hoffman

HERE ON EARTH

VINTAGE

Published by Vintage 2002

18

Copyright © Alice Hoffman 1997

First published in Great Britain in 1997 by
Chatto & Windus

Vintage edition 1998

Vintage
Random House, 20 Vauxhall Bridge Road,
London SW1V 2SA

www.randomhouse.co.uk

Addresses for companies within
The Random House Group Limited can be found at:
www.randomhouse.co.uk/offices.htm

The Random House Group Limited Reg. No. 954009

A CIP catalogue record for this book
is available from the British Library

ISBN 9780099750819

Penguin Random House is committed to a sustainable future for
our business, our readers and our planet. This book is made from
Forest Stewardship Council® certified paper.

Printed and bound in Great Britain by Clays Ltd, St Ives plc

To E.B.

For countless kindnesses
and twenty years of generosity and support
the author wishes to thank Elaine Markson.

PART ONE

ONE

TONIGHT, THE HAY IN THE FIELDS IS already brittle with frost, especially to the west of Fox Hill, where the pastures shine like stars. In October, darkness begins to settle by four-thirty and although the leaves have turned scarlet and gold, in the dark everything is a shadow of itself, gray with a purple edge. At this time of year, these woods are best avoided, or so the local boys say. Even the bravest among them wouldn't dare stray from the High Road after soccer practice at Firemen's Field, and those who are old enough to stand beside the murky waters of Olive Tree Lake and pry kisses from their girlfriends still walk home quickly. If the truth be told, some of them run. A person could get lost up here. After enough wrong turns he might find himself in the Marshes, and once he was there, a man could wander forever among the minnows and the reeds, his soul struggling to find its way long after his bones had been discovered and buried on the crest of the hill, where wild blueberries grow.

People from out of town might be tempted to laugh at boys who believed in such things; they might go so far as to call them fools. And yet there are grown men who have lived in Jenkintown all their lives, and are afraid of very little in this world, who will not cross the hill after dark. Even the fire fighters down at the station on Main Street, courageous volunteers who have twice been commended for heroism by the governor himself, are always relieved to discover that the fire bells are tolling for flames on Richdale or Seventh Street—any location that's not the hill is one worth getting to fast.

The town founder himself, Aaron Jenkins, a seventeen-year-old boy from Warwick, England, was the first to realize that some localities are accompanied by bad luck. Jenkins built his house in the Marshes in the year 1663. One October night, when the tide froze solid and refused to go back to sea, he received a message in his dreams that he must flee immediately or be trapped in the ice himself. He left what little he owned and ran over the hill, even though there was a terrible storm, with thunder just above his head and hailstones the size of apples. In his journal, exhibited in the reading room at the library, Aaron Jenkins vows that a thousand foxes followed on his heels. All the same, he didn't stop until he reached what is now the town square, where he built a new home, a neat, one-roomed house that is currently a visitors' center where tourists from New York and Boston can pick up maps.

Those foxes who chased after Aaron Jenkins are all but gone now. Still, some of the older residents in the village can recall the days when there were foxes in every inch of the woods. You'd see them slipping into the henhouses, or searching for catfish out by Olive Tree Lake. Some people insist that every time a dog was abandoned, the foxes would befriend the stray, and a breed of odd reddish dogs with coarse coats came from these unions. Indeed, such dogs were once plentiful in these parts, back when farms lined Route 22 and so many orchards circled the village that on some crisp October afternoons the whole world smelled like pie.

Twenty-five years ago, there were still hundreds of foxes in the woods. They would gather and raise their voices every evening at twilight, at such a regular hour people in the village could set their watches by the sound. Then one dreadful season the hunting ban was lifted, and people went crazy; they'd shoot at anything that moved. Most folks still regret what went on; they truly do. For one thing, the rabbits in these parts are now so fearless you're likely to see them sitting on the steps to the library, right in the middle of the day. You'll catch them in your garden, helping themselves to your finest lettuce and beans. You'll spy them in the parking lot behind the hardware store, comfortable as can be on a hot afternoon, resting in the shadow left by your car. They're pests, there's no doubt about that, and even the most gracious ladies on the library committee find themselves setting out poison every now and then.

There are so many rabbits along the back road to Fox Hill that even cautious drivers risk running over one. This, of course, is simply one more reason to avoid the hill. March Murray, who was raised here, agrees that it's best to stay away, and she has done exactly that for nineteen years. All this time she has lived in California, where the light is so lemon-colored and clear it is almost possible to forget there are other places in the world; these woods for instance, where one could easily mistake day for night on an October afternoon, where the rain falls in such drenching sheets no birds can take flight. It is exactly such a day, when the sky is the color of stone and the rain is so cold it stings the skin, that March returns home, and although coming back was not in her plans, she is definitely here of her own free will.

The simple act of returning, however, doesn't mean she's a

local girl right off, that she would, for instance, still know every shopowner in town by name as she once did. In the time she's been away, March has certainly forgotten what rain can do to an unpaved road. She used to walk this way every day, but the ditches are much deeper than she remembers, and as they drive over branches tossed down by the storm, there is an awful sound, like the crunching of bones or a heart breaking. The rental car has begun to lurch; it strains all the way uphill and sputters each time they have to traverse a deep puddle.

"We're going to get stuck," March's daughter, Gwen, announces. Always the voice of doom.

"No, we won't," March insists.

Perhaps if March hadn't been so intent on proving her point, they wouldn't have. But she steps down hard on the gas, in a hurry as usual, and as soon as she does, the car shoots forward into the deepest ditch of all, where it sinks, then stalls out.

Gwen lets out a groan. They are hubcap-deep in muddy water and two miles from anywhere. "I can't believe you did that," she says to her mother.

Gwen is fifteen and has recently chopped off most of her hair and dyed it black. She's pretty anyway, in spite of all her sabotage. Her voice has a froggy quality from the packs of cigarettes she secretly smokes, a tone she puts to good use when complaining. "Now we'll never get out of here."

March can feel her nerves frayed down to dust. They've been traveling since dawn, from San Francisco to Logan, then up from Boston in this rental car. Their last stop, to see to the arrangements at the funeral parlor, has just about done her in. When March gets a glimpse of herself in the rearview mirror, she frowns. Worse than usual. She has always had very little appreciation for what others might consider her best features—her generous mouth, her dark eyes, her thick hair, which she has colored for years to hide the white streaks which appeared when she was little more than a girl.

All March sees when she gazes at her reflection is that she's pale and drawn and nineteen years older than she was when she left.

"We'll get out of here," she tells her daughter. "Have no fear." But when she turns the key the engine grunts, then dies.

"I told you," Gwen mutters under her breath.

Without the windshield wipers switched on, it's impossible to see anything. The rain sounds like music from a distant planet. March leans her head back against the car seat and closes her eyes. She doesn't have to see to know that directly to her left are the fields of Guardian Farm and the stone walls where she used to balance, arms out, ready for anything. She truly believed that she carried her own fate in the palm of her hand, as if destiny was nothing more than a green marble or a robin's egg, a trinket any silly girl could scoop up and keep. She believed that all you wanted, you would eventually receive, and that fate was a force which worked with, not against you.

March tries the engine again. "Come on, baby," she says. This road is not a place where she wants to be stuck. She knows the nearest neighbor too well, and his is a door she doesn't plan to knock upon. She pumps the gas and gives it her all and there it is at last: the ignition catches.

Gwen throws her arms around her mother's neck, and for now they both forget all the fighting they've been doing, and the reasons why March insisted on dragging Gwen along instead of leaving her at home with Richard. So a mother doesn't trust a daughter? Is that a federal offense? Exhibit A: birth control pills at the bottom of Gwen's backpack wedged between the Kleenex and a Snickers candy bar. Exhibit B: pot and rolling papers in her night table drawer. And C of course, the most definitive evidence of all: the dreamy look on any fifteen-year-old girl's face. C for cause and effect. C for ceaseless trouble, and for cry all night, and for cool as ice to your mother no matter what or when. How could Gwen guess that March knows fifteen inside out; that she knows, for instance, whatever feels most urgent and unavoidable to you at that age can follow you forever, if you turn and run.

"The sooner we get out of here, the better," Gwen informs her mother. She's dying for a cigarette, but she'll simply have to control herself. Not exactly what she's best at.

March steps on the gas, but the wheels spin them deeper and deeper into the mud. There's no longer any hope of going forward; in fact, they won't be going anywhere at all without the help of a tow truck.

"Damn it," March says.

Gwen doesn't like the way her mother sounds. She doesn't like the whole situation. It's easy to see why tourists don't usually come here, and why the maps in the visitors' center are yellow with age. In these woods, autumn brings out ghosts. You may not see them or hear them, but they're with you all the same. You'll know they're present when your heart begins to beat too fast. You'll know when you look over your shoulder and the fact that there's no one directly behind you doesn't convince you that someone's not there.

Gwen reaches over and locks her door. There aren't even any streetlights out here, not for miles. If you didn't know where you were going, you'd be lost. But, of course, Gwen's mother knows the way. She grew up here. She must know.

"Now what do we do?" Gwen asks.

March takes the keys from the ignition. "Now," she tells her daughter, "we walk."

"Through the woods?" Gwen's froggy voice cracks in two.

Paying her daughter no mind, March gets out of the car and finds herself shin-deep in water. Sloshing through the puddle, she goes around to the trunk for her suitcase and Gwen's backpack. She'd forgotten how cold and sweet the air is in October. She'd forgotten how disturbing real darkness can be. It's impossible to see more than a foot in front of your own face and the rain is the kind that smacks at you, as if you'd been a bad girl and hadn't yet been punished enough.

"I'm not walking through this." Gwen has gotten out, but she's huddled beside the car. The mascara she applied so carefully while she waited for her mother behind the funeral parlor is now running down her face in thick, black lines.

March isn't going to argue; she knows that doesn't work, and in all honesty, simple logic never convinced her of anything when she was Gwen's age. People tried to tell her she'd better behave, she'd better take it slow and think twice, but she never heard a single word they said.

March grabs her suitcase, then locks up the car. "You decide what you want to do. If you want to wait here, okay. I'm walking to the house."

"All right," Gwen allows. "Fine. I'll go with you, if that's what you want."

Gwen gets her backpack. No way is she staying out here all alone. Not for a million bucks. Now she understands why her mother, as well as her father—who also grew up here, right down the road—never come back. The reason they're finally visiting is actually pretty horrible; if Gwen allowed herself, she'd have a mini-breakdown right now. She's shivering so badly that her teeth are actually chattering. Wait till she calls Minnie Gilbert, her best friend, to tell her: *My teeth were chattering like a skeleton hanging on a rope, and I couldn't even have a goddamn cigarette because there I was, right next to my mother. All for the funeral of some old woman I'm not even related to.*

"Are you okay?" March asks as they make their way down the road.

"Perfect," Gwen says.

Thursday is the day of the funeral and Gwen may faint, especially if she wears her tight black dress, which is scrunched into a ball at the very bottom of her backpack. Judith Dale was the housekeeper who raised March—whose mother had died when March was little more than a baby—and although Mrs. Dale came out to visit in California once a year, Gwen can no longer picture her face. Maybe she's blocking it out, maybe she doesn't want to think about nasty things like death and getting old and being stuck in a horrible place like this with one's mother.

"Do you think the casket will be open?" Gwen asks. Finally, the rain is easing up.

"I doubt it," March says. After all, Judith Dale was one of the most private people March has ever known. You could tell Judith anything, you could pour out your soul, and it wouldn't be until much later, perhaps even years afterwards, that you'd realize she'd never told you anything about herself and that you didn't even know what her favorite dessert was, let alone who she loved and what she believed in.

Now that the rain is ending, they can hear things in the woods. Mice, probably. Raccoons come to drink from the puddles.

"Mom," Gwen says when something flies overhead.

"It's nothing," March assures her. "An owl."

Not long ago there were mountain lions roaming these woods, and black bears, who came down to the orchards to eat their fill in October. There were moose who would charge anything that moved. Even when March was a girl, the sky was still so clear children in town were often disappointed to discover they couldn't reach up and pull the stars right out of the sky.

"Are we almost there?" Gwen asks. Her idea of exercise, after all, is to ride on the back of someone's Honda.

It is now dusk, that odd and unreliable hour when you see things which don't exist, at least not in present time. It is almost possible for March to catch sight of the ladder her brother, Alan, left beside those sugar maples. That dark shape in the woods may be the bucket Judith Dale used to collect blueberries. And there, by the stone wall, is the boy March once loved. Unless she is very much mistaken, he has begun to follow her. If she slows down, he'll be beside her; if she's not careful, he'll stay for good.

"Why are you running?" Gwen complains. She's out of breath, trying her best to keep up with her mother.

"I'm not running," March insists. All the same, she gives her daughter a list of reasons to hurry: Call for the rental car to be towed. Phone Richard and let him know his worries were for nothing—they're fine and have arrived in one piece. Contact the Judge to set up a time when they can go over Judith's estate. Call Ken Helm, who's always done odd jobs for the family, and have him check out the house to see if repairs are needed. Surely, there are squirrels in the attic, as there always were at this time of year.

Gwen's good boots are caked with mud and she's freezing. "I can see why you and Dad never come back here. It's disgusting."

March's shoulders hurt from carrying her suitcase, or maybe it's just tension in her neck. This old dirt road is all uphill. Probably she should have taken Route 22 and made a left at what people in town call the devil's corner. If Richard hadn't been in the middle of a term and had come with her, she might have gone that way, but she's not ready to face that piece of road with only Gwen for company. Not yet. She has told both Richard and herself that the past is the past—what happened once doesn't matter anymore—but if this were true, would she feel as though someone had just run an ice cube down her skin in a straight line?

"I think I see the house," Gwen announces.

Ken Helm, the handyman, was the one who found Mrs. Dale. He knocked at the door after delivering the bricks needed to repair the chimney early on Monday evening, when the sky was the color of a velvet ribbon falling over the hills. At first he'd thought no one was home, but then the wind had come up and pushed the door open, and there Judith was, in the chair by the fireplace, no longer with us. March's father's old friend and partner, Bill Justice, known throughout the commonwealth as the Judge, told March all of this when he phoned the next morning. At least there were no hospital stays, no pain, no heroic measures. And yet this information brings March no comfort, especially because she believes that Bill Justice, who has been an attorney for fifty years and a judge for thirty of those years, was covering the mouthpiece of his telephone in an attempt to conceal the fact that he was crying.

"That's definitely a chimney." Gwen squints against the darkness. "I see it now. And there's a gate."

On the plane ride here, March had fallen asleep, something she dreads when traveling, since she's always logy and disoriented after napping. In her dreams, she saw her father, who has been dead for nearly twenty-five years. In March's dream, Henry Murray was standing in the doorway to their living room, wearing the sweater that March had loved best, the brown wool one with deep pockets, where he always kept peppermint drops. He and Bill Justice were the only lawyers in the village, and although they were partners they participated in the most friendly of feuds concerning which was the more popular.

"Do you want Murray or do you want Justice?" Bill used to joke, and maybe he had to, since Henry Murray was everyone's favorite. Children would beg for a peppermint drop each time he walked into town, and they'd follow behind, asking for a second and a third. When he died suddenly, while working late at his office, every boy and girl in the village reported smelling mint in the night air, as if something sweet had passed them right by.

Every time she thinks of her father, March experiences a sharp pain in her side. It is astounding to consider how many losses a single individual can sustain. Richard has no family left at all, except for March and Gwen, and March has little more—only her brother, Alan, from whom she's so estranged it no longer makes sense to consider him blood, which is doubly true for Alan's son, a boy she's never even met.

"So this is it," Gwen says.

They are standing at the gate.

March puts her suitcase down to take a good look.

"I can't believe you ever lived here," Gwen says. "Yikes."

In the dark, the house looks tilted and old. The section that burned down—the original kitchen and dining areas—has been rebuilt as a modest addition. March lived in this house until she was twenty-one. Hers is the window above the porch roof, the one with the black shutters which need to be set back onto their hinges. That was where she spent most of her time in those last years. Waiting at the window.

Is she surprised to find that she is thinking of Hollis now that she sees that window once again? She was only seventeen when he left, but she'd already been in love with him for most of her life. That terrible winter when he went away, when the sky was always the color of ashes and the chestnut tree in the front yard was encased in ice, she began to find white strands threaded through her hair.

Tonight, in that same yard where the chestnut tree still grows, there is something jostling the quince bushes. Gwen moves as close to her mother as she can get; she's ice, inside and out.

"Mom?"

If Gwen sounds frightened, that's because she is. This is not what she expected when she agreed to come east with her mother for the funeral. She figured she'd miss a week of school; she planned to sleep until noon every day and eat nothing but candy bars and cereal, full-out enjoying the break from real life. Now, on this dark night, she feels much too far from home. Who is this woman beside her, with the long dark hair and the sad countenance? Gwen, who's brave enough—or foolhardy enough—to argue with security guards when she's picked up for shoplifting at the Palo Alto Shopping Center, is actually shaking now. What has she let herself in for? How possible would it be to turn and run for home?

"Look," March says to her daughter. "It's only some rabbits."

Sure enough, several brown rabbits are beneath the hedge of quince. The largest of them comes out, as if to do battle with March and Gwen, as if the entire hill belonged to a creature small enough to fit in a large sunbonnet or a cast-iron pot.

"Scat," March tells the rabbit. "Go on." When it doesn't move she rattles her suitcase, and off goes the rabbit, into the woods. "See?" she tells her daughter. "No problem."

But Gwen is far from convinced about this place. "Should we go in?" She is whispering, her voice a raspy, breakable thing.

"We'll have to sleep on the porch if we don't."

They both have to laugh at this; it's not too dark to see that the gutters have sloshed torrents of water over the porch. Not a place you'd want to spend the night, unless you were a centipede, or some other creepy-crawly. March reaches beneath the mailbox, and there is the extra key, wedged underneath, as always.

"You definitely lived here," Gwen says.

March used to see this same sky every morning; she used to take these porch steps two at a time, always in a hurry, always wanting more. From where they stand, March can see Judith's garden and instantly, she feels comforted. In spite of everything, some things remain constant. The garden is exactly as it was when March was a child. The spearmint still thrives in weedy bunches, and the scallions, with their sharp bitter scent, haven't been the least affected by the chilly weather. The last of the season's cabbages are nestled against the fence, as they always were in October, in neat, tidy rows, like well-behaved green toads.

Maybe she'll regret coming back, but right now there is nowhere on earth that could feel more familiar. There, in the lower yard, March can make out the orchard, her favorite place of all. The apple trees are twisted, like little old men, their backs turned to the wind. March used to climb these trees every afternoon at this time of year, grabbing at McIntoshes and Macouns, turning the stem of each apple exactly eight times as she recited the alphabet, the way girls do to learn the identity of their true love, making sure to pull the twig free only after she'd reached the first letter of his name.

T W O

HE ARRIVED LIKE A BUNDLE OF MAIL,
on a gray and windy day. March remembers it
perfectly well: It was a Saturday and her father
had been away for nearly a week, at a conference
in Boston. For much of that time March had been
slightly ill, with a low-grade fever and sniffles,
and Mrs. Dale had kept her supplied with orange
juice and mint tea. March had woken late that
day, something she rarely did at the age of eleven,
when it seemed that the whole world was right
out in front of her, waiting and ready for her
alone.

On that Saturday, March's brother, Alan,

normally the late sleeper in the family, was already in the kitchen drinking coffee when March traipsed in, searching for breakfast. Alan, who was ten years older than March, had graduated from Boston University, but he hadn't done well. He'd registered to audit a few courses at Derry Law School, still hoping to follow his father in his profession, something he would never manage to do.

"We've got a boy," Alan said.

"No we don't." Even at eleven, March knew that her brother was a braggart, and was careful not to believe much of what he said.

"Really," Alan insisted. He had just begun dating Julie, the girl he would later marry, and was more good-natured than usual. He didn't call March an idiot or a moron the way he usually did, or refer to her by her given name, Marcheline, for spite. "Dad brought him back from Boston. He found him wandering the streets or something."

"Yeah, right," March had said. "Liar."

"Want to make a bet?" Alan said. "How about your allowance for the rest of your life?"

Judith Dale came in with a basket of laundry she had taken off the line. She wore her hair caught up in those days, and she favored slacks and cardigans, along with peace and quiet.

"People can't just get people," March said. "Can they?" She always turned to Judith to back her up, but now Judith shrugged. She was hazy about details, but she admitted she had made up the guest bedroom with clean sheets and a quilt that was usually stored in the attic.

March went to the window, but she couldn't see a thing. Alan came up behind her, eating a piece of buttered toast and flicking the crumbs from his chest.

"He's right there," Alan said, pointing toward the orchard.

And true enough, there he was, just beyond the gate. He was thirteen and skinny, with long, dark hair that hadn't been washed for weeks.

"What a prize," Alan said, with his usual disdain.

The boy must have felt himself being watched, because he suddenly turned and glared at the window. The clouds were thin and wispy that day, blown about by the wind.

When March waved, the boy was so surprised that he just stood there, blinking. March would have laughed at his discomfort if she hadn't realized, all at once, that she did not want to stop looking at him.

"Do we get to keep him forever?" March could sense, deep inside, that it was better to whisper.

"God, I hope not," Alan said.

Out in the orchard, the boy continued to stare at her. The grass hadn't yet been mowed that season and all the daffodils were closed up tight, to protect themselves from unpredictable weather.

"I'll take him," March volunteered.

"Get serious," Alan had said, but when he walked away March stayed precisely where she was.

"I am serious," she said out loud, although there was no longer anyone who could hear her. Nearly thirty years later she can still recall the way those words felt in her mouth, how delicious they were, how absolutely sweet. "From now on, he's mine."

Everything she knew about him, she learned from Judith Dale. He'd been an orphan in Boston, so poor he'd eaten nothing but crackers and whatever else he could steal. Few people would give him the time of day, let alone a dollar for his supper, but March's kindhearted father had brought him home.

"And that's all we know?" They were sitting out on the porch on a fine, blue day, filling up the bird feeders Judith liked to hang from the chestnut tree. "What about his parents? His religion? Does he have brothers and sisters? Are we sure he's thirteen?"

"You are so nosy," Judith said. "His name is Hollis and he's here to stay. That's all you need to know."

At first, the new boy wouldn't eat dinner—not even when there were lamb chops and asparagus, then strawberries for dessert. He wouldn't look anyone in the eye, including Henry Murray, whom he obviously respected, for Mr. Murray was the one person to whom Hollis didn't talk back. He was certainly fresh enough to most people, but in an edgy, self-contained fashion. It was the way he looked at you that could make you nervous. It was everything he didn't say.

After three months, Hollis was still avoiding them all. The less he revealed, the more interesting March found him. She kept wishing she'd run into him, but when she did—once when he was throwing rocks at some invisible target beyond the orchard, and again when they all but crashed into each other in the hall one night en route to the bathroom—she was completely mute in his presence. Since March had always been a great one for talking, this behavior was particularly puzzling.

"Speak up," Judith Dale would have to tell March whenever Hollis was near, but March couldn't oblige. She even took to drinking rainwater, which she had overheard Mrs. Hartwig, a matron who worked in the school cafeteria, vow was a sure cure for a tongue-tied child.

Still, Hollis and March hadn't spoken, not even to ask the other for bread and butter at suppertime. And then one day in the summer, she got her wish. It was July, March believes, or maybe the first week of August. At any rate, it was brutally hot and had been for ages. March had been going barefoot and the soles of her feet were black. She was pouring a glass of Judith's mint iced tea for herself when she saw the dragonfly pass by overhead. It was larger than the ones you usually saw skimming over the flat surface of Olive Tree Lake, and so blue March had to blink. She followed the dragonfly into the living room, where it perched on the drapes, and there was Hollis, in her father's chair, reading one of Henry Murray's textbooks, a complicated treatise which concerned homicide.

"I want to catch that dragonfly," March said.

Hollis stared at her. His eyes were absolutely black. "Well, good for you," he finally answered.

The dragonfly was beating its iridescent wings against the fabric of the drapes.

"You have to help me." March was amazed at how sure of herself she sounded, and maybe Hollis was as well, because he put his book down and came over to help.

In a panic, the dragonfly tried to get away; it banged into the window glass, and then, truly desperate, twisted itself into the long strands of March's hair. March could feel the dragonfly, almost weightless; she could still feel it after Hollis had plucked it from her tangled hair. Hollis shoved the window open and let the dragonfly outside, where it disappeared immediately, as if swallowed by the sky.

"Now are you happy?" Hollis asked March.

He smelled quite strongly of soap, since Mrs. Dale had insisted he take a shower each day, but also of some other scorching scent, which March would later come to believe was anger.

"No. But I will be soon," March told him. She took him into the kitchen and got out two tubs of pistachio ice cream. They consumed a pint apiece, and by the time they were done they were shivering, even though the heat was as sweltering as ever. March can still remember how cold her tongue felt, from all that ice cream.

"You'd better stay away from him," Alan warned March. He relayed some ugly rumors: That Hollis had murdered someone and had then been released into their father's custody. That his mother was a prostitute who'd been murdered herself. That March had better lock away what few valuables she had—a silver comb left to her by her mother, and a gold-plated charm bracelet—since Hollis was most definitely a thief.

March knew it was jealousy that drove her brother. When

Henry Murray introduced Hollis as his son, Alan always turned pale. Alan had never gotten along with his father, and had disappointed him in every way, and now he'd been replaced by someone who hadn't known what shampoo was and still didn't have the faintest idea of how to behave in company. At dinner parties or on holidays, Hollis would sit there reading from one of those miserable law texts, and he wouldn't answer when spoken to; the only people he paid any attention to were Henry Murray and March.

"Why don't you go someplace where you're wanted?" Alan asked Hollis.

"Why don't you shut up?" Hollis said right back, and he didn't even bother to look at Alan, who was eight years older and a full-grown man, despite his foolish ways.

Alan took every opportunity to humiliate Hollis. In public, he treated Hollis as though he were a servant; at home he made certain the boy knew he was an outcast. Often, Alan would sneak into Hollis's room, where he'd do as much damage as possible. He poured calves' blood into Hollis's bureau drawers, ruining Hollis's limited wardrobe, knowing full well Hollis would rather wear the same clothes every day than admit defeat. He left a pile of cow manure in the closet, and by the time Hollis figured out where the stench was coming from, everything Henry Murray had given him, the books and the lamps and the blankets, had been contaminated by the smell.

The kinder Henry Murray was to Hollis, the more bitter Alan grew. During that first winter when Hollis was with them, Henry Murray came home from a conference in New York with gifts for all. He presented March with a thin gold necklace and both boys with beautiful pocketknives, made of steel and mother-of-pearl. Alan had botched his classes at the law school, and now the fact that he and this creature he'd had foisted upon him were being treated equally, like brothers in fact, sent him sulking. By the time they sat down for dinner that night, Alan was steaming with rage.

"He's too young for a knife," Alan told his father. "You'd never let me have one at his age. He can't be trusted with it."

"You'll be fine," Henry Murray said warmly, ignoring Alan in order to address Hollis, who sat to his left.

"God, you are blind," Alan proclaimed. It was Judith Dale's day off, but she had left them their dinner. They were having roast chicken and potatoes and green beans, but now Alan pushed his plate away, upsetting his water glass. "No one in his right mind would give him a weapon. You have to be crazy."

If there was one thing Henry Murray couldn't stand, it was a man who was not fair, and that was what his son seemed to be. Hollis said nothing in his own defense, and that's what March couldn't bear to see: The way he wouldn't meet anyone's eyes. The way he seemed to fold up inside himself, going farther and farther inside, until the part of him having dinner at their table was only the smallest corner of his soul.

"Shut up, Alan," March said. "You're the one who's crazy."

March was sitting to her father's right, and he now put his hand on her arm. "I don't want you to talk like that," he told her. "Not to Alan. Not to anyone."

Hollis still hadn't touched his food. He was staring at his plate, but March had the sense that he was watching everything. "You're just jealous," she told Alan.

Alan gave a short trumpeting laugh. He nodded toward Hollis. "Of that?"

Henry Murray put down his knife and his fork. "Leave the table," he said.

"Me?" Alan truly was shocked. "You want me to leave?"

"Come back when you can act decently," Henry Murray said, and it was clear, from his tone, that he didn't expect such an occurrence anytime soon, certainly not that evening.

Alan got up so hastily that his chair fell with a clatter behind him, sideways on the floor. March had been staring at Hollis all this time, so she noticed that he now proceeded to eat his supper. He cut his food carefully; he looked back at her and didn't even blink. March was possessed by the giddiest feeling. She would make Hollis laugh; she would see if she could. She crossed her eyes and stuck her tongue out at him.

"What do you think you're doing?" her father said to her.

March hadn't imagined her father catching her. "Nothing," she quickly told him.

When she looked at Hollis, she saw that if she hadn't gotten a laugh out of him, then at least she'd gotten a grin.

"She wasn't doing anything," Hollis agreed.

"That's good to hear." Henry Murray finally turned his attention to his food. "One rude child is more than enough."

Alan should have been too grown-up for games of revenge, he should have set his mind to finding a job or studying for his classes, but after that dinner he went after Hollis wholeheartedly. He waited for the time to be right, and at last, on a cold winter day, when a beautiful light snow was falling, Alan and some of his cronies captured Hollis on the path which led to Olive Tree Lake. Staked out long enough to have ice form around their nostrils, fueled by six-packs of beer, these friends of Alan's were ready to beat someone senseless. They tackled Hollis and spat in his face. They held him down and took turns hitting and kicking him, usually in the ribs, carefully aiming with their fists and their boots.

The horizon was gray that day, and crows were circling in the sky. Alan and his friends hit Hollis until his nose and mouth gushed with blood. They wanted him to call for them to stop, to beg for mercy, to cry, but he did none of these things. He closed his eyes, so that he wouldn't accidentally be blinded by one of their punches. He cursed them so deeply inside his mind that his expression revealed nothing. There was blood seeping into the snow, and from the other side of the lake came a droning sound, as Mr. Judson, who owned so much land up there, rode his snowmobile through the woods.

Finally, when they had tired of beating him, Alan and his friends tied Hollis to a tree, where he stayed until dark, never once calling out. When he didn't show up for dinner, Alan took the opportunity to call him irresponsible and thoughtless. When he still hadn't shown up at nine, March went looking for him. By the time she found him, Hollis was burning with fury and embarrassment. March cut the ropes with the mother-of-pearl pocketknife she knew he kept in his pocket, while Hollis kept his face averted.

"Don't feel sorry for me," he said when she was through.

There were bloody, red marks on his wrists where they'd tied the knots too tight.

"I don't," March had said, and that was the truth. Even then, it was Alan she'd felt sorry for; for Hollis she felt something entirely different from pity. "I know Alan did this. Tell on him. I'll say I saw it all."

"But you didn't," Hollis said. He wiped the blood from his face with the back of his hands, then rubbed snow on his cheeks and hands. His coat had been ripped off, and now he tore at his shirt-sleeve. "You didn't see this either." He motioned for her to hand back the knife; he took it in his left hand. Quickly, deeply, he cut a long gash up his right arm.

"Stop that!" March said.

Ignoring the wound he'd inflicted, Hollis stood up and threw the ropes Alan and his friends had tied him with as far as he could, so that they disappeared into a distant drift of snow. After that, they walked back home, a trail of blood behind them. Halfway home, Hollis's teeth started chattering, even though his coat was thrown over his shoulders; when they reached the front door and were at last safely inside the warm hallway, he collapsed.

Henry Murray drove them to St. Bridget's Hospital, where

twenty-three stitches were needed to close up the gash in Hollis's arm.

"Who did this?" Henry Murray demanded to know as he and March sat in the waiting room. "Was it Alan?"

March stared at the floor and could not bring herself to answer, and this response her father took to be a definitive yes.

That night, Henry Murray informed Alan that if he wished to continue living in his house, he would have to treat Hollis with respect. Moreover, he would have to write a letter of apology, and, out of his own funds, he would have to pay for the hospital bill, along with a new coat, since Hollis's had been ruined. Alan's knife, of course, was confiscated, in spite of his many denials.

"Don't add liar to your list of credentials," Henry Murray said, and after that Alan stopped proclaiming his innocence.

That night, March couldn't sleep. She went to the kitchen for a glass of milk, and on her way back to her room, she stood outside Hollis's door, then knocked and pushed the door open. He was in bed, but not yet asleep. March stepped inside and closed the door behind her. She could see by the moonlight reflecting off the snow in the yard. Hollis's arm was bound with white cloth.

"You know why I had to cut my right arm?" Hollis asked. He had carefully thought it out while tied to the tree. "So no one would think I did it to myself."

"How did you make yourself do it?" March asked. She sat on the bed to get a better look at his arm. "Didn't it hurt?"

"That's a stupid question."

Hollis had that mean edge in his voice, and March might have turned and left, if she hadn't then realized that he was crying. She stretched out beside him, her head on the pillow, while he cried. She stayed there a long time, watching him, and that was how she found out just how much it hurt.

She remained with him until he fell asleep, and although they never spoke of that night, or the fact that she had been there beside him in bed, they became allied in all things. Whenever some schoolmate wanted March to come visit, or if her father insisted she spend time with girls her age—his partner's daughter, Susanna, for instance—March suffered through the social engagement, counting the minutes until she could be with Hollis. Sometimes she made excuses, she said she was feverish or sick to her stomach, and she ran all the way home to Fox Hill.

She especially remembers the summer when her father died, when she was fourteen. At night the moon seemed huge, the silver moon of August that rises when the hermit thrush begin to appear in gardens. That year, the peepers in the woods had gone wild. They called from the far-off shores of Olive Tree Lake and from every puddle in the yard. They clambered into the garden, where Judith's mint grew, and sang all night long, a muddy refrain that made it difficult to sleep. Whenever March closed her eyes, she heard the peepers, like a living pulse, the background of hot August nights so black and deep they carry you far from peaceful rest and dreams.

Hollis would already be out there, on the flat part of the roof, whenever she climbed through her window. They had to be quiet, so as not to wake anyone. They kissed with their eyes closed at first, as if that would make for more silence and secrecy. March told no one, not Mrs. Dale whom she'd always confided in, or pesky Susanna Justice who always demanded to be apprised of the most intimate details of everything. It was the sort of summer when it was not possible to notice the existence of anyone other than yourself and the one you loved, and so March was doubly stunned when Alan woke her one morning, shaking her by the shoulder, announcing that their father had died.

Although Henry Murray had drawn up hundreds of wills for his clients, he hadn't redrafted his own since before March was born. Alan, therefore, inherited all of Fox Hill. Mrs. Dale stayed on, of course, and March's expenses were all paid for, but Hollis was sent to live in the attic. Now Alan had his chance to do as he pleased, and he began by writing up a weekly bill which charged Hollis for board and lodging. It took Hollis two years straight after high school before he could pay Alan Murray back, but he did it. He worked at the bakery on Main Street, putting in a full day before noon, and then headed over to the Olympia racetrack, where he learned that a man had a chance to double his money if he was willing to wager what he already had. On evenings and weekends, he drove a truck for the Department of Public Works, spreading salt on the roads in winter, cutting down branches and gathering trash from Route 22 when the weather was fine.

The weather happened to be exceptionally fine on the day that he left. March would soon graduate from high school, and she remembers that while she and Judith Dale were talking about her future, which seemed completely wide open back then, they had decided to clean the windows, the better to see the gorgeous blue sky. No matter how many possibilities March came up with—college, travel, a job in Boston—all futures included Hollis, that much was certain.

When Hollis came in to announce he had quit all his jobs, he felt he had never before been free. He had worked off his debt to Alan with the help of a gelding named Sandpaper who had run a race with twenty-five-to-one odds at the Olympia track, and who had amazed all bettors, including Hollis, by managing to win. Now, he could walk away, clean and clear, ready to start over. It was the most important day in Hollis's life: the moment he'd been working toward ever since Henry Murray had died, but March didn't realize this. Lately, Hollis had been working so much she'd gotten used to missing him; she'd begun to look elsewhere for companionship. She was going next door to the Coopers' for dinner; she'd become friendly with the daughter, pale red-haired Belinda, and was thinking about nothing more than what she might wear that evening. Her blue dress came to mind, and so she didn't have room to pay as much attention to Hollis as she might have.

"Would you rather be there with them or here with me?" Hollis demanded to know.

His question had taken her by surprise as she was choosing a pair of earrings from her jewelry case, and she answered too slowly—she must have, because he grabbed her, something he'd never done before.

"Stop it," she said to him. He'd always been jealous of her friendship with the Coopers, but she'd never paid much attention, until now. He was twisting her wrist; as soon as she shook free, she backed away. "Leave me alone," she said.

March had never spoken to him this way, and her irritation came as a shock to both of them. It was just that he wanted so much from her; she never had a minute to think.

"Are you making a choice?" Hollis said to her then.

"No," March had spat back, not considering how easily hurt he could be. "You are."

It is always a mistake to tell someone, *Don't you dare walk out that door,* and a far worse mistake to actually cross the threshold and walk out on someone you love. Ever since that day, March has wondered what she could have done differently: Stayed home from the Coopers'? Thrown her arms around him? Admitted that all day long she'd been planning her future with him? Halfway through dinner, she sensed how wrong she'd been; she left and ran all the way home, but it was already too late.

After he'd gone, she waited upstairs at her window, day after day, week after week. There were no letters, not even a postcard, and by the time March graduated from high school, she no longer bothered to walk down the drive to check the mailbox. Still, each spring the doves who nested in the chestnut tree in the yard returned, and March took that as a sign of Hollis's loyalty and his love. The girls she'd gone to school with went off to college, or took jobs in the village, or married boys they loved, but March stayed by her window, and before she knew it the pane of glass had become her universe, the empty road her fate.

After three years, she no longer recognized herself when she looked in the mirror. She wasn't certain how it had happened, but she no longer seemed young. At last, on the morning of her twenty-first birthday, March Murray did not go to her window. She never found out whether or not the doves returned that year to nest in the chestnut tree. She didn't hear the peepers call that spring or smell the mint which grew beside the door. Instead, she packed her suitcase and waited while Mrs. Dale called for a taxi to take her to the airport. Alan had lent March the money for a round-trip ticket to California, but while she was waiting to board, March went into the rest room and tore the return section of the ticket into pieces, then tossed it into the trash.

March had spent a lifetime up in her bedroom, waiting for Hollis, trying to figure out what she'd done wrong. She's spent another lifetime since as a wife and a mother; she is a completely different person now. Here she is, making up the beds in this cold, empty house on Fox Hill where she hasn't been for so long. Her hands are quick as she pulls the clean bed linen over the mattress. It was a young girl who came to this bed, one who cried easily and counted stars instead of sheep on nights when she couldn't sleep. March doesn't cry now; she's far too busy for anything like that. Still, there are mornings when she wakes with tears in her eyes. That's when she knows she's been dreaming about him. And although she never remembers her dreams, there's always the scent of grass on her pillow, as if the past were something that could come back to you, if you only wished hard enough, if you were brave enough to call out his name.

THREE

EVERY EVENING AT THIS TIME, HOLLIS
checks the perimeters of his property. He can do
it on foot or in his truck, he can do it blindfolded,
if need be. Like any poor relation, he knows precisely what belongs to him. Even those blueberries are his, although it gives him some deep,
bitter pleasure to watch the squirrels and raccoons enjoy the fruit. They can eat their fill, as far
as Hollis is concerned, without ever once having
to beg, as he used to each and every day.

Hollis has long believed that the past can only
hurt you if you let it. If you stop to consider all
that was done and undone. Best not to dwell

on what went wrong. Even better—don't think at all. There are days when Hollis actually manages to do so, relying instead on instinct and habit. Of course, there are evenings such as this, when he can't stop thinking. He knows March Murray is coming back for the funeral; she may already be here, up in her old room where the shadows fall across the floor at this hour. At times when he can't block out his thoughts, Hollis tries to rearrange his perspective. He goes over all he owns, which now includes not only all of Guardian Farm and Fox Hill, but most of Main Street as well. He has land down in Florida, along the west coast and in Orlando and down in the Keys. He is also co-owner of a racetrack outside of Fort Lauderdale, and the best part about all this is, he never even has to return to that state where he spent so much miserable time; he gets all his checks in the mail.

This year Hollis will be forty-two and he's done all right for a beggar who looked so ragged that the Coopers' caretaker threatened to call the police the first time he saw him. He's done just fine for a boy who left Fox Hill with fifty-seven dollars in his pockets. All that he owns should be enough. Hollis has squared the debts owed him, he should be satisfied, but he's not even close. He's starving for something, and even though he forces himself to eat three meals a day, he keeps losing weight, as if he were devouring his own flesh.

He's not going to think about what's bothering him; he simply refuses to get farther inside his own head. Instead, he'll see to the old pony that belonged to his son, which has come down with colic. There are the usual measures—keep the pony standing and feed it mineral oil—but Hollis always blows a little salt into each of the afflicted animal's nostrils as well. It's a trick he learned years ago at the tracks down in Florida, one of the few tactics he'd dare to reveal. An old wives' tale, scoff the regulars down at the Lyon Cafe, but those who have tried Hollis's salt remedy haven't been unhappy with the results.

Well, nobody ever said Hollis was stupid. That's never been the complaint. Still, his presence is something most men down at the Lyon would prefer to do without. Hollis is the richest man in town, and probably in the county as well; he contributes generously to the Policemen's Association and the Firemen's Fund, and a ward at St. Bridget's Hospital has been named in his honor, but that doesn't mean anyone wants to socialize with him, or that Hollis doesn't notice that the town elders only court him when they need a new roof for the library or funds for a stoplight.

One thing wealth buys in a town this size is respect. Other men might flinch when Hollis joins them at their table, but they don't dare suggest he find another seat. They talk to him courteously, all the while wondering why the hell he doesn't just go home. He doesn't even drink, he only sits there, with a Coke or a ginger ale, for reasons the regulars are still trying to figure out. Jack Harvey, who specializes in air-conditioning and heat installation, insists that Hollis's motive, when he joins them at their table, is to ensure he'll be ready to snatch up their souls if they have one drink too many. Whenever Hollis finally leaves, and a cold wind blasts through the door as it slams shut behind him, then his neighbors are brave enough to refer to him as the devil. Mr. Death, that's what they call him when his back is turned, and they drink a toast to his departure.

It's the women in town who turn to look when Hollis walks by. They pity him, they really do. He lost not only his wife but their boy, Coop, who was sick every day of his life, as weak as paste and in need of constant nursing from the start. It's lonely for a man to live like that, and the women in town know who among them have gone home with Hollis over the years. They're not always the prettiest or the youngest. They're women who know the score, who won't make demands, who may have a husband who works nights or a boyfriend in the next state. They're the ones who know that Hollis isn't about to give them anything they want or need, but who still can't turn him down. He's been hurt, that's what the women who have slept with him say, and he needs someone. They don't have to mention that getting older has only served to make Hollis even more handsome than he was back in high school, when they would never have had a chance with him, when he wouldn't look at anyone but March Murray.

Tonight, Hollis searches through the cabinets for the canister of salt, then reaches for his jacket, which is so worn the fabric is past repairing. The same is true of the house; it has begun to come apart, and this pleases Hollis. He hasn't had the place painted in fifteen years, hasn't repaired the roof, which leaks in twenty-six spots when the rain comes down hard. The destruction of the house which once belonged to the Coopers is a small, but enjoyable, satisfaction. Hollis likes to find cobwebs in the parlor where Mr. Cooper used to smoke his cigars. Annabeth Cooper's perennial garden, of which she was always so proud, has been destroyed by Japanese beetles and mildew. In Richard Cooper's bedroom you can hear the raccoons, who are living in the walls, and in Belinda's old room the edges of the marble mantel have disintegrated into dust. The Wedgwood, so elegant at parties, is currently being used for the dogs and is now so chipped no one would imagine this china came from London in wooden crates, and that each bowl and plate had been wrapped in a swathe of white cotton.

Hollis slams through the side door, ignoring the sleepy red dogs, who all rise to their feet to follow, working out of instinct, just as surely as Hollis does. These dogs are strays, the ones people say are descended from mongrels abandoned to breed with foxes over a hundred years ago. Whatever their lineage, the dogs look evil, with their coarse coats and yellow eyes; their piercing yelps often frighten off deliverymen and letter carriers. The dogs are sensitive to Hollis, however. They know his moods, and when he pauses to take a deep breath and look at the sky, they push against each other and whine. They're anxious when Hollis slows down, but Hollis is merely appreciating what's around him. He's always favored October, with its gloomy, cold core, and he can never get

enough of looking over his land. Why shouldn't he stop to appreciate all that he once envied and now owns? He gave up everything
for this land, so he might as well stand here and feel that it's his.

The year when Henry Murray brought Hollis home, there
were more than fifty racehorses at Guardian Farm. Hollis had no
interest in horses, and doesn't to this day, but March was fasci-
nated, not only with the Coopers' horses but with their wealth.
Her father gave most of what he earned away and much of the
work he did after hours was pro bono. Even though Henry Murray
was an esteemed member of the community, March had only one
pair of new shoes a year whereas Susie Justice, for instance, had
four or five. At that point, March cared more about shoes than she
did about the welfare of the poor, and maybe that's why she was interested in the Coopers' horses: each one was worth more money
than her father would ever manage to earn.

Hollis remembers that he and March hid on the far side of a
stone wall so that March could count the horses. It was a hot,
windy day and March had to keep grabbing at her long, dark hair
so it wouldn't fly into her eyes. The wind echoed, like a drumbeat
or a warning, and everything smelled like grass. Mr. Cooper's
horses were hardly the same species as the bony haybags found in
backyards along Route 22. These horses had run at Belmont and at
Saratoga; they were so fast they could outrace the storm clouds
that came down from Fox Hill.

As soon as Hollis married Belinda, he sold off nearly all the
horses, and now there are only three in a barn large enough to
house dozens: his son Coop's lazy, old pony; the ancient work-
horse, Geronimo, who used to pull bales of hay into the fields for
the thoroughbreds; and Tarot, Belinda's horse, who killed two of
his riders before they took him off the track. Hollis hates them all.
He hates the sound and smell of horses; he hates the stupid ones,
who shy at garter snakes and pools of rainwater, and he hates the
smart ones, like Tarot, even more. Right now, as he nears the barn,

Hollis can hear the pony whimpering. It's a faint, small sound, but it sets Hollis in mind of how horrible a horse's scream is. Before he can stop himself from thinking, he sees a white horse fall to its knees. It falls like snow, like a drift which can cover you completely. Well, Hollis isn't about to dwell on that. He turns off all consciousness when it comes to the years he was away. Some people might say three years isn't that long to be gone, but Hollis knows it's time enough to have a hole form inside you. It's exactly the right amount of time to leave you empty, forever after, no matter who you once were or what you once might have been.

Tarot is in the first stall, which has been his home since the day he came to the Farm. A bay thoroughbred, dark as mahogany, he would have brought more at auction than any of the horses Hollis disposed of, if his reputation hadn't been so notorious. Breeders up and down the east coast still refer to Tarot when they want to call up a horse whose potential is chewed to pieces, a champion who went so haywire he might as well have been sold for dog food. Even though he would behave for Belinda, people in the village still talk about the times when Tarot escaped. Some of the shopkeepers—Sam Deveroux, who owns the hardware shop, for instance, and Mimi Frank, who styles hair at the Bon Bon—insist that Tarot breathed out fire when he ran through the town. They swear there was one warm evening in May when he singed all the lilacs on Main Street. To this day, the flowers that bloom on these bushes carry the scent of sulfur; they've been known to burn a child's hand, if one is foolish enough to grab for a bunch of the blossoms.

People in town wonder why Hollis bothers to keep a worthless old racehorse around. The women like to think it's a mark of respect for Belinda, who loved the horse so, but the men joke it's simply because Hollis refuses to take a low price for his property. Neither assessment is correct. Hollis retains the horse because he is a waste, just as Hollis himself is. Every night they face off, and each time they do, they despise each other a little more. This feud doesn't mean that Hollis would ever get rid of Tarot. All in all, you don't take the only creature mean enough to be your equal out behind the barn so you can shoot him in the head.

"Hey, buddy," Hollis whispers as he approaches Tarot's stall. As usual, the thoroughbred looks right through him. "Fuck you too." Hollis is always astounded by how damned haughty a horse can be. "Double fuck you."

On that day when he and March first came here, they were caught by Jimmy Parrish, who now uses a cane and spends all his evenings at the Lyon Cafe, spouting racetrack statistics and boring people silly. Back then, Jim was the foreman at Guardian Farm, and he took his job seriously. It was a dog who gave them away, one of Annabeth Cooper's stupid poodles, who yapped like crazy and led Jimmy Parrish right to the stone wall where they were hiding.

The Coopers weren't friendly with people in the village and *No Trespassing* signs lined the perimeters of their property. Even their parties, given all summer long, had guests imported from New York and Boston, although local people were always well aware when Annabeth Cooper threw one of her bashes. Truckloads of roses would be delivered from Boston, and so much champagne was served that the bees got drunk and wandered into houses all over the village, buzzing like crazy, but too giddy and confused to sting.

Hollis and March knew they weren't wanted at the Coopers', but they came to count horses anyway. Hollis can still hear the wind the way it was on the day they were caught. He hears it in his dreams, and when he walks across the pastures he now owns. It was impossible to make out what March was saying over the roar of the wind, but Hollis could see her foot was caught between two stones. Annabeth Cooper's poodle was snapping; it had surprisingly large teeth for a dog of its type, and it must have struck flesh, because March's hand was bleeding.

"I'm phoning the police," Jimmy Parrish had shouted, loud enough for them to hear.

March was wearing a white shirt which billowed out like a flag in the wind. She knew that Hollis had had several run-ins with the police. He'd been caught taking some magazines he couldn't afford at the pharmacy, and the owner of the liquor store had ratted on him when he tried to buy a six-pack of beer. He was a city boy, brought to Fox Hill with his city ways intact, and March didn't hold it against him. Still, one more strike and he might just be out.

"Go," March mouthed to him. "Go on," she insisted.

Afraid of the police, spooked by the wind, Hollis turned and ran. Hollis was a good runner, but there's not a day that goes by when he doesn't wonder what might have happened if he hadn't been so fast, if he'd been caught, or if he'd simply stayed where he was. What if he and March had spent that day up at Olive Tree Lake instead of spying at the Farm? Is this how fates are made and futures cast? An idle choice, a windy day, a dog that can't mind its own business?

Some people know the exact moment when they've lost everything. They can look back and see it plain as day and for the life of them they can't understand why they didn't spot the situation as it was happening. Why didn't Hollis stop running? Why didn't he stay by her side? He waited for March for what seemed like forever, on the rutted back road which led from the Farm to Fox Hill. As the afternoon went on the wind died down, but the blood rushing in Hollis's own head had replaced the sound. His head was pounding, and the more time that passed, the worse his headache became. Finally, the sky turned inky. The peepers were calling and the moon was climbing into the sky by the time March appeared.

She was holding a handful of roses cut from Annabeth Cooper's own garden; Unity and Double Delight and Peace were all clutched to her chest as she ran toward him. That's what Hollis saw first, pink roses in the dark night. All at once he felt like crying, and he might have done so, if March hadn't started talking right away. It wasn't that he was listening to what she said—certainly he didn't want to hear how smart Richard Cooper was, or that his sister, Belinda, was so kindhearted she kept an opossum as a pet, feeding it bread softened in warm milk, allowing it to sleep on the quilt at the foot of her bed, even though Mrs. Cooper had forbade any animals but her poodles in the house. No, he didn't need to hear those details, because he knew what had happened from the look on March's face. In a single afternoon, all because of a stupid dog and a stone wall, it had happened. He had lost her.

As soon as Guardian Farm legally became his, Hollis cut down all of Annabeth Cooper's roses. They used to grow by the split-rail fence, and they're a lot more stubborn than Hollis would have imagined. Every year or so he has to take a sickle and hack away at the branches which insist on growing back. This past spring he found a red rose on the ground beneath the fence, and it was just as startling to him as a pool of blood would have been. He kicked the flower beneath a hedge of evergreens, and yet he continued to see it from the corner of his eye. He saw that rose long after it had already wilted, and died.

Tonight, however, it's not roses he's thinking of. It's revenge. Once you get a taste of getting back at someone, it sticks with you. It makes you count up all your assets and your enemy's losses, again and again, even though the figures have remained the same for years. Of course, it's hardest to calculate the worth of a human being. Hollis's adopted nephew, Hank, for instance, is usually an asset, but tonight he's a total loss. He was supposed to make certain Coop's pony stayed on its feet, but he's fallen asleep in a rocking chair, and the pony is down on its knees, moaning in a pile of hay.

"Good nap?" Hollis says.

Hank immediately gets up, stumbling over one of his own boots. He's grown more than six inches in the past year; he's six three and still growing and he always feels clumsy and much too tall. His coloring is fair, like his father, Alan's, with hair the color of straw and a ruddiness that rises into his face whenever he's embarrassed.

"Shit," Hank says, although there's no need for him to curse himself. Hollis will do that for him.

"What the hell were you thinking?" Hollis asks. "Or have you given up thinking?"

"Sorry," Hank says, for all the good it will do. He never does anything right, at least not in Hollis's eyes.

Hank has been thrown off all day; he's been thinking, all right, but what's on his mind is Judith Dale, who used to take care of him and Coop. She used to cook dinner every evening after Belinda died; she fixed corn fritters and curried turkey soup, pumpkin custard and wild grape pie. You simply couldn't stop eating when Mrs. Dale made you something; you wished for a triple stomach, like that of a cow, so you could keep on shoveling it in and asking for more. Now, Hank and Hollis mostly have bologna-and-cheese sandwiches and things out of cans—soups and chilies that don't taste like much unless you add half a shaker of salt. Mrs. Dale wouldn't have tolerated a diet like that. She believed in homemade things. Every year, on Hank's birthday, she would bake a chocolate cake. Even after Coop died, when Hollis told her they didn't need her anymore and she went back to live in the house on Fox Hill, she sent Hank a chocolate cake once a year, and he always ate every bit.

In the past few years, Hank has made certain to stop by Fox Hill every few weeks and check on Mrs. Dale. Just ten days ago, he'd gone over and cleaned out her gutters, even though she insisted she could easily hire Ken Helm from the village to do the job. Afterwards, she'd given Hank a piece of cranberry-orange pie at her kitchen table. No one could turn down one of Mrs. Dale's desserts, and she often brought pies out to the old house in the Marshes, the one people said was built by the town founder, Aaron Jenkins. She carted bags of groceries out to the Marshes as well, and heavy woolen blankets and clean gloves and socks. She brought out matches and soap, and sweaters she found at the rummage sale held once a month at Town Hall.

She saw to just about every item a person might need to exist in this world, at least when it came to physical matters. But she never trod on emotional territory, and wouldn't think to give counsel unless directly asked. She never, for instance, suggested that Hank go out to the Marshes himself. She never said, "Go see your father." She may have thought about it, she may have even been convinced that unless Hank went out to that ramshackle place, where the reeds were taller than a full-grown man, his life would forever be lacking, but she never said more than "Lemon or milk?" after she'd poured his tea, and she always hugged him close when it came time for him to leave.

Hank didn't even know Judith Dale had passed on until this afternoon. He had stopped at the hardware store on Main Street and was standing in the pet department, looking for mineral oil for Coop's ailing pony, when he overheard someone in the next aisle discussing Judith Dale's funeral. Immediately, Hank felt something behind his eyes go all hot, but he didn't cry. He stood there in the pet department until he didn't feel dizzy anymore; then he went to the register, paid, and left.

Tonight, while he should have been taking care of the pony, he was thinking instead of the look on Judith Dale's face when she told him that Coop had died. It was a winter night, cold and filled with ashy starlight. Hank was out feeding the dogs; as he walked back to the house he could hear his own footsteps on the frozen earth. Judith Dale was waiting for him, holding the screen door open, and a stream of yellow light swept across the ground. She put her hand on Hank's shoulder, and to his great surprise he saw that she had to reach up to do so. "We've lost him," Mrs. Dale said, and in that instant Hank realized he had never before seen real grief.

This is the reason he's forgotten his chores now, all these years later—an oversight not usually in his nature. He's been too preoccupied with wondering what happens when you lose someone. His mother, for instance, who died when he was so young he doesn't even remember her. His father, as well, whom he'd prefer not to remember. Hollis and Belinda's son, Coop, who died at the age of twelve, and never found out what happened at the end of *Treasure Island*, the book Mrs. Dale had been reading to him in the last month of his life.

Hollis is slipping a rope around the pony's neck, doing Hank's job himself, and although the pony is stubborn and rolls its eyes, it gets to its feet when the rope is tugged. Hollis spills out some salt into the palm of his hand, then blows it into the pony's nostrils. The single character trait shared by father and son was their dislike of horses. Coop was allergic to animals and broke out in hives if he got close to anything with a tail. It was Belinda who insisted the boy needed a pony, and it's Hank who's set on keeping this pathetic creature in memory of the boy.

"Sorry about falling asleep," Hank says. "It won't happen again."

"Give me one good reason, and I'll get rid of this thing," Hollis says of the pony.

Hank nods. He knows Hollis means what he says. Hank keeps his mouth shut and his thoughts to himself, as he always has. He's used to Hollis's ways, just as Hollis is used to him, after all these years.

"You heard about Mrs. Dale?" Hollis asks now.

Hank nods again. You've got to tread carefully with Hollis. You've got to watch what you say.

They've walked outside together, into a starry night that's unusually clear and cold for this time of year. All that rain which fell earlier will freeze tonight, so that the ground will give them some trouble tomorrow when they go to bury Judith Dale. Mrs. Dale was a good woman, Hollis will grant her that. A busybody and a pain in the neck, but she never judged what she didn't understand and that, Hollis knows, is rare. Unlike Alan and the boys in the village, she treated him fairly, but that doesn't mean he has to moan and bellyache down at the funeral parlor. Ashes to ashes, that's all there is. If you can't change a fact of life, then be smart enough to walk away from it, that's always been Hollis's motto. Walk away fast.

"If you want to go to the funeral, that's your business," Hollis tells his nephew.

"Thanks," Hank says. "I might."

If Hollis did go to the service it would be for one reason alone. March Murray. Instead, he's going to wait for her to come to him. It will happen, he knows that much. He's gotten everything else that was ever denied him, all that's left now is March. He has never loved anyone else, and he never will. He thought he couldn't live without her, and in a way he was right. It's a half life he's been living, one where you go through the motions without any of it mattering. He simply has to give it more time, that's all. People who think you can't will certain things into being with the power of your pride are fools, plain as that. She's already back in town. It's only a matter of time before she's back with him, and for that, Hollis can wait a while longer.

Tonight, he'll go to bed in the spare room off the kitchen, since he can't stand to enter the bedroom where he slept when he was married. In the morning, while people in town are getting dressed for the funeral service, while March Murray is brushing her long dark hair, Hollis will fix himself black coffee, as always. He'll begin the chores he does routinely—paying the bills, speaking with his lawyer, making certain rents are collected and debts are paid. At noon, when his neighbors have left the chapel to gather at the cemetery beyond the golf course, off Route 22, he'll walk the boundaries of his property to make certain none of the fences are down and no one has trespassed. He'll do this, as he does every single day, and he won't stop until he's completely exhausted, knowing full well that if he ever did stop, if he ever really looked around him, every single inch of this acreage he owns would serve to remind him of all that went wrong.

FOUR

ON THE DAY OF JUDITH DALE'S FU-
neral, the sky is as gray as soapstone. Mothers in

town fix their children oatmeal for breakfast and

insist that wool mittens and socks be retrieved

from dresser drawers. The doors of the library

squeak when they're pushed open, the way they

always do when the weather begins to change.

Over on the corner of Elm Street and Main, the

bakery must have loaves of the cinnamon bread

they're so famous for in the oven, because the

scent is everywhere; it's as if someone had tossed

dough over the whole town. This is the sort of day

best spent in bed, but March and Gwen are

dressed and ready to go at eight-thirty when Susanna Justice, March's oldest friend, comes to fetch them in her red pickup truck, apologizing for the dog hair her Labrador retrievers have left on the seat, bemoaning the fact that March and Gwen will have to scrunch together in order to fit.

"Listen, I don't know what I'd do without you," March says, and she tells the saga of the rental car, which has already been towed back to town. "You are a true friend. I'm grateful."

The surprising thing is, March means it, and she never thought herself capable of such sentiments when she and Susie were girls. They were thrown together because their fathers were partners, but they hated each other all the same. For two years solid they refused to speak even the simplest phrases to each other, not even "Pass the sweet potato pie" at Thanksgiving dinner. Now, of course, neither can remember exactly why they'd constructed their wall of silence.

"It was because you were an idiot," Susie says as she does her best to clear out the cab of her pickup. Aside from the dog hair, there are files and stray bits of paper and dozens of maps.

"Actually it was because you were a know-it-all," March shoots back. "And you still are."

They both have to laugh at this. Susanna is a reporter for the local newspaper, *The Bugle*, and in fact, she does know everything that's going on in town. She knows not only how much old Mr. Judson got for his land up at Olive Tree Lake, but also that he refused to sell to Hollis at an even better price, although he allowed Hollis to take him out to dinner in Boston and send him a crate of vintage Chablis. Not that she would ever mention this bit of business to March; nor the fact that half a dozen women in town are so crazy for Hollis they would walk out on their husbands or boyfriends and abandon their real lives if only they were asked.

Why, Susanna Justice has acquired more information than most people would have room for in their heads. She knows what the school committee budget will be next year, and that the animal control guy, Bud Horace, is too much of a softy to pick up stray dogs. In all of this jumble, there are plenty of facts she could have done without knowing. Who died last night at St. Bridget's Hospital, whose husband gets nasty when he has too much to drink at the Lyon Cafe, who was found in a parked car at the rest area on Route 22, with a gun between the seats and a suicide note taped to the glove compartment.

"Honey, all you have to do is squeeze me and I give out worthless information," Susie always says.

She even knows when the sales take place at Laughton's Lingerie Shop (every January and July, second Saturday of the month) and how much the jelly doughnuts cost at the Bluebird Coffee Shop (fifty cents). She's always learning something new, and it has recently come to her attention that Ed Milton, the chief of police, kisses with his eyes closed and looks like an angel when he sleeps. Some information, however, she's been aware of all her life; it's old news. For example—that her old friend March Murray wouldn't know good luck if it came up and slapped her in the face.

"You think you're so hot living out in Palo Alto. Well, for your information, Eileen Singleton is retiring on Tuesday after forty-three years of work at the library."

"Oh, gosh," March says. "Stop the presses." She winds her long hair into a knot, which is kept in place with a silver comb, one that she cast herself. She and Susie are wearing similar silver bracelets, among the first March ever dared to try. What started out as a hobby has become more and more rewarding, both financially and artistically.

"That's nothing," Susie says, brushing at the dog hair stuck to the one dress she owns that's sober enough to wear to a funeral. Susie has cropped blond hair and gray-blue eyes and black is definitely not her color, dog hair or no. "You want real news? Mr. and Mrs. Morrisey are pleased to announce the engagement of their daughter, Jane—remember that bitch?—to some guy they don't think much of who's got a job with the DPW in Gloucester and is really cute. I saw him at the engagement party and double wow. He probably will be a problem. Halfway through the party, he asked me for my phone number. Everyone has to invite me to everything, you know, if they want a mention in *The Bugle*."

"That's because you're a superior being," March says.

"As are you," Susie says. "Hence our friendship."

Gwen, who's been listening in and who now struggles to climb into the cab of the pickup in her extremely short skirt, cannot believe how ridiculous her mother and Susanna Justice are when they get together. Susie comes out to California once or twice a year, and they're just as stupid on the west coast as they are right here. "You are both so mature," she says disdainfully.

Gwen's tiny black dress isn't the only reason Susanna Justice and March shut up and stare. Gwen is wearing gloopy black mascara and has moussed her hair so that it spikes up in the front, like a little bed of nails. Wait till she tells her friend Minnie: *There I was, trapped like a rat, with the two of them giving me fashion attitude. I couldn't get away, I was trapped, I tell you, trapped in a way no human being should ever be.*

"You're letting her go like that?" Susie asks March.

"Letting her?" People who haven't had children have the oddest ideas.

"Can we just go to the funeral and get this over with?" Gwen says in her froggy voice. Before coming outside, she sneaked a cigarette in the bathroom, then doused herself with some Jean Naté she found in the medicine cabinet which she thinks has gotten rid of the scent of smoke.

"Oh, yeah, definitely," Susie says, getting in behind the wheel. "Let's not let Judith's funeral take up too much of your precious time."

"Exactly," Gwen says. She's flipped down the visor in order to get a glimpse of herself in the mirror. She wishes for two things: bigger eyes and a thinner face. She can't abide her own reflection, so how could anyone else? Maybe her mother and that stupid Susie aren't so wrong when they judge her. Cutting her hair was certainly a mistake, she sees that now. Her look is so wrong it's almost a joke. She'd like to be the human equivalent of an Afghan hound. Instead, what she sees is a beagle looking back at her.

"Do you mind?" March says.

Scrunched in next to Gwen, March has to struggle to push the visor back up so it won't jab either of them in the eye as they ride along the bumpy back road. This day is going to be awful. It's the sort of day you wouldn't mind losing completely, even if it meant your life would be twenty-four hours shorter.

"I can't believe Judith is really dead," March says. "She took care of everyone and never complained. I can't think of a single selfish thing she ever did. Not ever. She was the greatest."

"She was something, all right," Susie concurs.

March might have called Susie on a statement like that, but the road has become so bumpy Susie is concentrating on navigating past the ruts. And anyway, Susie always took pride in being cryptic. *What is that supposed to mean?* March was always saying when they were younger and thrown together for the day, and Susie would always look at her as if March were crazy and any implications sprang from March's own unreliable imagination.

"This is where my rental car died," March says as they approach the deepest of the ruts.

"Then hold on," Susie says, and for old time's sake she floors the gas pedal for a real roller-coaster ride.

"You guys are nuts," Gwen shouts, but Susie and March, supposedly older and wiser, pay no attention to her. For a little while at least, as they shake and rattle over the bumps, they manage to forget today's destination. They forget how long it's been since they've walked down this road, arm in arm. They were fierce and fearless girls back then, in their jeans and boots and sweaters, and March, for one, was absolutely confident of what her future would bring: total happiness and true love, that's what she wanted. Nothing more or less would do, just as no other place would ever be home; nowhere but the hill would ever be as comfortable or as beautiful or as real.

Susanna Justice suddenly steps on the brakes, hard, so they're all snapped back by the force of their seat belts.

"Do you believe that goddamn thing?" Susie says, as a rabbit runs right in front of them.

This landscape is definitely real, if nothing more. From the minute March woke this morning, in the old bed where she'd slept for thousands of nights, she knew coming back had been a mistake. She opened her eyes, and already she was thinking of Hollis. When she saw the lattice of frost on the inside of her windowpanes it was exactly as if she never had left. Her room was always the chilliest in the house. Often, she would find that the tumbler of water she'd left beside her bed had frozen solid. She remembers how she would hold the glass up and breathe on the ice until it melted into streams that spelled out Hollis's name.

The first thing she did today, after she pulled on her navy-blue dress and a black sweater, was go downstairs in her bare feet and try to phone Richard. From where she stood, by the telephone table, she could see Gwen, asleep on the couch in the little sewing room. She could see through the oval window, past the garden and the trees. Her heart was racing, that was the silly thing. She had begun to make a bargain with herself, the kind that women who are in love with the wrong man always resort to: If Richard answered by the fifth ring, she would be all right. She would be perfectly safe, and safety, after all, was what she had opted for, even though she was back here looking out at the apple trees she used to climb. And then she'd realized how early it was in California, only a little past three a.m., and she'd hung up quickly, but she'd been all right without talking to him; she'd made tea in one of Judith's pretty ceramic pots and in no time she was fine.

Or so she had thought. Now that she's face-to-face with the pastures of Guardian Farm her skin feels cold. She wishes she had brought along gloves and a heavy woolen scarf. At this moment, she'd prefer to be a million miles away.

"Don't worry," Susie says. She's noticed the distress on her friend's face. "He won't show up at the funeral. Take my word for it. He's still refusing to do whatever it is he should."

March gives Susie a look which she hopes will silence her, but it's too late.

"Who are we talking about?" Gwen asks.

Gwen always does that—listens when you don't want her to, ignores you whenever there's something you want her to hear.

"No one," March tells her.

"A figment of our imagination," Susie insists on adding. "Or some of us, anyway."

"Yeah, right," Gwen says tartly. "Like I know what you mean."

"She means she's a know-it-all," March says, but inside she's thinking, *Lucky for me that you don't understand. Lucky for you.*

They've left plenty of time to get to the service, and yet somehow they've managed to be late. The parking lot is already crowded when they pull in, and why shouldn't it be? Judith Dale had a lot of friends, from the library, where she'd been a member of the board for ages, and from the garden club, which did so much to beautify the town, and from St. Bridget's as well, where she volunteered in the children's ward two nights a week, reading stories and playing games of Candyland.

March remembers wondering why it was that Mrs. Dale didn't have children of her own. She'd asked her once, when it was late at night and she'd been sick with a fever and Mrs. Dale had been sitting up with her, spoon-feeding her rice pudding and endless cups of tea.

"That's not what was intended for me," Mrs. Dale had told her.

What Mrs. Dale had meant by that, March never quite understood. Was it God she was referring to, or the hand of fate, or the choices she herself had made, perhaps a long time ago? At any rate, there were sides of Mrs. Dale which were secret, and sides which were not. She liked rain, and children, and going off by herself on holidays from which she brought back small tokens as gifts: pretty matches, hair combs, mints with pink and green candy shells. She believed in home cooking and in the supreme beauty of yellow roses, six dozen of which March has ordered for this service. The scent of roses is sweet and ripe and sorrowful, making March dizzy as she goes to sit in the front row of the chapel, between Gwen and her father's old law partner, Susie's father, the Judge.

The Judge is tall, six foot four, and so imposing that some people say there are criminals who confess at the mere sight of him. But today, he seems a shakier version of himself; he will be seventy-two next month and his age shows, in his large hands, which tremble, in his pallor and his faded blue eyes. He keeps one hand on March's, but for whose comfort, even the Judge isn't certain.

Since there's not room in the pew for everyone, Louise Justice, the Judge's wife, is sitting directly behind them. Every once in a while she leans forward and pats March or the Judge on the shoulder.

"This is such a shock," she whispers, again and again.

Judith Dale left instructions for the service to be simple, just as the marker she chose for herself is to be a plain gray stone. Gwen had no idea how depressing such a service could be. She is sitting up straight, studying the closed coffin. She actually seems frozen in place, her skin white as ice. With her spiky hair and her excess of mascara, she looks fairly ghoulish. Several people who have come up to give March their condolences have avoided Gwen completely, or have shaken her cold hand without saying a word.

Now, while Harriet Laughton is giving the final address, on behalf of Judith Dale's friends on the board of the library, Gwen leans close to her mother. For one brief moment, March thinks her daughter wants a hug.

"I'm going to be sick," Gwen whispers.

"No," March says, even though the scent of roses and the heat inside the chapel are cloying. "You won't be."

"I'm not kidding," Gwen insists. It's the smell of death that's getting to her. It's the very idea. "Oh, boy," she says, sounding scared.

March and Gwen make their way out of the pew; then March circles an arm around her daughter and guides her into the aisle, toward the door. She can hear a murmur of concern: the voices of Judith Dale's friends, kindhearted volunteers from the library and the hospital.

"You just need fresh air," March tells Gwen.

Gwen nods and gulps, but she feels like she may not make it. She manages a dash for the door, and when she races past Hank—who is in the last row, along with Ken Helm, who considered Mrs. Dale one of his favorite customers, and Mimi Frank, who cut Mrs. Dale's hair—he looks up in time to see Gwen slipping out of the chapel, quick as a shadow. It's not often you see someone you don't know in the village, and Hank has the sudden urge to get out of his pew and follow this girl. She looks so distressed, and she's beautiful besides, but Hank isn't the sort to storm out of a funeral service. He stays where he is, seated beside one of the vases of yellow roses March ordered from the Lucky Day Florist on Main Street. He's wearing his one good white shirt, a pair of black jeans he hopes don't look too beat-up, and his boots, which he polished last night. He borrowed a tie from Hollis, who has a closetful of expensive clothes; he combed his hair twice.

All the same, Hank has a shivery feeling under his skin, in spite of how overheated the chapel has become, and when the service is over, he's one of the first to leave. This way, so quick to be out the door, he's more likely to get another look at the girl. And he does—she's over on the curb, so dizzy that she needs to keep one hand on the fender of the hearse, for balance. Three crows are flying above the parking lot, making a horrible racket. The sky is so flat and gray Gwen has the urge to put her arms over her head for protection, just in case stones should begin to fall from the clouds.

Six strong men—Ken Helm, the Judge, Dr. Henderson, Mr. Laughton, Sam Deveroux from the hardware store, and Jack Harvey, who installed an air conditioner for Mrs. Dale last summer—help to carry the coffin from the chapel. Just seeing them struggle with its weight brings tears to Gwen's eyes. Here she is, with her short skirt and her hair all spiked up, looking like a perfect fool, completely unprepared for real life. Well, ready or not doesn't matter. Something is about to happen. Gwen can feel it. Time itself has changed; it's become electrified, with every second standing on end.

Gwen can see her mother now, in the doorway of the chapel, a look of heartbreak on her face. Here comes the coffin, carried even closer. This is not the sort of thing that usually affects Gwen; she has a talent for blocking out bad news. All she has to do is shut her eyes and count to a hundred, but she's not closing her eyes now. Oh, how she wishes she had stayed at home. How easy it would have been to go on thinking about nothing, to ignore death and fate and the possibility that a life can easily be shaken to its core. That is how you know you've left childhood behind—when you wish for time to go backward. But it's too late for that. Whether Gwen likes it or not, she's here, under this gray and mournful sky, and her eyes are open wide.

FIVE

AFTER THE CEMETARY, AND THE BUFFET
supper at Harriet Laughton's house—where
March is called *poor dear* at least a dozen times,
and Gwen is asked so often whether something is
wrong with her eyes that she finally goes into the
Laughtons' powder room to remove her mascara
with a white washcloth—March phones Ken
Helm, who always says no job is so odd he can't
get it done, and asks if he'll drive them back to the
hill.

"Not that way," March all but shouts when she
realizes Ken intends to take Route 22.

"Gee whiz, Mom." Gwen can't believe how

touchy her mother has become. "What's the difference?"

"About two bucks," Ken Helm says, deadpan as always. "That back road is one slow shortcut." Ken stares into the woods. "Make a tree sound and its fruit will be sound. Make a tree rotten and its fruit will be rotten."

Intrigued, Gwen leans forward. "Meaning?"

"We're all responsible for ourselves, aren't we?" Ken takes the bumps in the road easily. "And what we harvest."

"Are you trying to tell us that orchard of Mrs. Dale's needs work?" Gwen asks. "Is that your point?"

"No," March says. "He's letting us know that you pay for what you get. Two dollars more, for instance, for the back road."

"That's it," Ken says. "Matthew 12:33."

It's twilight when they reach the house, which means it's still a sunny afternoon in Palo Alto. Richard is probably in his office, on the far side of the quad. Sunlight streams in from the west at this time of day; the windows are so high Richard has to use an iron rod in order to pull down the shades. He needs to take care at this hour; the specimens he keeps lined up on the window ledge are susceptible to light damage.

The house on Fox Hill is cold when they get inside, but before March bothers with checking on the heat or lighting a fire, she goes to phone Richard. She's still wearing her jacket; her purse strap is draped over her shoulder as she dials. She feels a little desperate, perhaps even more than a little.

"How about some tea?" she calls to Gwen.

"Fine," Gwen says, throwing herself into the easy chair patterned with roses.

"No, I mean, you make it. Please."

March simply wants her daughter out of the room. She wants to be alone with her husband and be told that she continues to be the same exact woman she was when she kissed him goodbye at the airport. She wants to hear him say it out loud, because at this moment, standing here in this house, she doesn't feel the same. If she weren't such a rational creature, she'd think the night air was calling to her; she'd believe there were still peepers in those muddy puddles, even though this isn't their season. Her heart is beating in a different rhythm here; faster, a dangerous pace.

Richard had visited her during those years when she was waiting for Hollis, but she never made anything of it back then. She'd been friendly with his sister, Belinda, and Richard was the sort of kind, slightly dazed person to whom charity came naturally. He rescued lost dogs and stopped for hitchhikers, so it made perfect sense that he'd come to call on March, bringing candy and books, as if getting over Hollis was not unlike recuperating from some horrible illness.

March might have never noticed that Richard was courting her, in his own mild way, if not for the night of Alan and Julie's wedding. The wedding was held on New Year's Eve, the year March was nineteen, and by then March could barely feel anything. She could stick a pin in her finger and not even bleed. She could go without eating for days and not feel hunger. She could stay up all night with no need for sleep. The only indication that she was alive at all was that the new shoes Mrs. Dale had insisted she buy hurt her toes.

On the night of the wedding, March was alive enough to overhear many of their guests whisper their opinion of her. What a sorry thing she was, that's what they were saying. Wasting away, growing old before her time. Only nineteen and look at her, so pale and gray she was little more than a ghost. Look at her hair, with all those white strands. Look at the way her hands had begun to shake. To console herself, March drank five glasses of Mrs. Dale's champagne-laced cranberry punch, then gave in and danced with Richard. Richard was so tall that March couldn't look him in the eye as they danced, and perhaps that was best, since she would have been extremely surprised to discover how ardent his expression had become.

Then a senior at Harvard, Richard spent his days at classes and his evenings doing good deeds, volunteering at a shelter—where he folded laundry and mopped floors—and tutoring freshmen students who were overwhelmed by their class work. If not for March, he wouldn't have returned to Jenkintown at all, since he and his father were no longer speaking. That he came back so often, March had convinced herself, was simply because she was another one of his projects. But on the night of Alan's wedding, as she danced with him, she realized this wasn't the case. It was the way he held his arms around her and the slow sound of his breathing which informed her that pity was not Richard's motivation. Actually, it never had been.

After Alan's wedding, Richard began to appear several times a week. He brought March boxes of apricots and books from the library. He presented her with potted tulips from Holland and fancy Vermont maple syrup. Often, when Mrs. Dale had the night off, Richard insisted on coming to the house to cook dinner. Alan's new wife, Julie, who couldn't fix anything more complicated than a grilled cheese sandwich, acted as his assistant, dicing peppers and carrots, stopping only long enough to take March aside and whisper that she'd be crazy to let Richard Cooper get away from her now.

March watched Richard sometimes, as he sat in the living room and read from one of his textbooks, and he looked so familiar and comfortable that she felt like weeping. She allowed him to kiss her, and she kissed him back, but when she went up to her bedroom and stood at her window to watch the road below, it wasn't Richard she was looking for.

"You probably shouldn't come here anymore," she finally told him one day when the air outside had turned meek, the way it often does before a storm. "I'll never be in love with you."

She thought he'd be hurt when she said this, but instead Richard took her hands in his. He was going off to Stanford, for graduate work, and he wanted March to go with him. He'd had a last bitter argument with his father, which concerned Mr. Cooper's interests in a logging company that was destroying a species of wood spider so tiny it was invisible to the naked eye. In fact, the fight was about greed and love, the sort of brutal argument that can get you written out of your father's will and drive you three thousand miles away.

Richard had nothing to lose by asking March to marry him, and he wasn't destroyed when she said no. He was a biologist, after all, with a specialty in entomology, and he knew what reversals often happened in a single life cycle. He sat beneath a palm tree outside his rented apartment in Palo Alto and wrote to March every week, and she wrote back from her bedroom on the second floor. She informed him that the leaves were changing, and that his sister Belinda no longer seemed interested in anything but her horse, and that the hunting ban had been lifted on the hill, so that shotguns could be heard all day long. She told him much more than she would have imagined, and revealed herself in many ways, although she did not write that she often woke from sleep with tears in her eyes, or that she sometimes heard Hollis's voice inside her own head.

After she finally stopped waiting for Hollis, Richard was there, right on time, when she arrived in San Francisco. In fact he'd gotten to the airport two hours early, and had been awake since dawn. That first night in California, March slept in his bed. It is the bed they still have; the headboard is more than a hundred years old. Richard found it in a junk shop in Menlo Park, but actually it's quite a good piece, fashioned of golden oak. March has often wondered why anyone would have ever gotten rid of such a wonderful bed; if, perhaps, the previous owner had died or if he'd loved someone so completely he couldn't bear to sleep in the same bed once she'd gone.

Richard is stretched out on that bed when March phones, his thin, angular frame completely relaxed. Though it's late in the day in California, he's just getting around to reading the morning paper. He appreciates the topsy-turvy in life; he's always believed, for instance, that mutation is good for a species. If he'd been someone who was easily convinced by statistics, rather than a man who rejoiced in the odd and unprecedented, he would never have gone after March in the first place.

"I'm so glad you're there," March says when he picks up the phone.

Richard laughs. "Well, I can't say the same for you."

"It's awful here," March says. "That's for sure."

"That's why we left," Richard reminds her. "Did you see your brother?"

"He wasn't at the funeral, and I don't have the heart to go looking for him. Although, I guess I really should." Then out of March's mouth comes a thought she's been thinking all day: "Hollis wasn't there either."

She can hear Richard breathing; it's almost as if he's in the same room. She shouldn't have mentioned Hollis.

"I didn't ask about him," Richard says, "did I?"

After March had married Richard and soon after she discovered she was pregnant, Judith Dale finally told her that Hollis had come back. He had been living above the Lyon Cafe for some time, spending a great deal of money, impressing everyone in town with his new financial status. March remembers how she sat there in the backyard after that call from Judith; her chair was beside the lemon tree, and her feet, which had swollen with her pregnancy, were soaking in a basin of cool water. She dialed Jenkintown information, then phoned the Lyon, and she did it all quickly, before she could stop and think. When she asked for Hollis, she was told he didn't have a phone, although the bartender who answered was willing to go upstairs to get him. She waited, completely unaware of the scent of lemons. She didn't notice that there wasn't a cloud in the sky.

It took exactly twelve minutes for the bartender to retrieve Hollis from his rented rooms. As soon as she heard his voice, March panicked. She listened to him say *Hello* twice, and then she hung up. After that, she was nervous every time the phone rang. Had he guessed his caller was March? Had he cared? All through her pregnancy she felt sick to her stomach and trapped in some deep, irrevocable way. When her doctor informed her that her blood pressure was elevated and she needed to spend at least six hours in bed, on her left side, she wasn't surprised. She was affixed to this place and to her own body; anchored by flesh, blood, and her own exhaustion, she dared not fight her condition. She slept away mornings and afternoons, so dreamy she didn't hear the birds in the trees or Richard's voice when he tried to rouse her from sleep.

On the day when Hollis phoned her, March had just woken from a nap, and at first she thought she was still dreaming. *March*, he said. That's all he said at first, her name, and she had to sit down before she could listen to more. *Why did you leave?* he asked. *Why did you do this to us?*

Don't be mean, that's what she said to him, forgetting where and who she was, at least for the moment.

You're the mean one, he'd said to her. *It's you*.

They spoke every night after that, hushed and secret calls, conversations so passionate their words burned. March was seven months pregnant, but that didn't keep her from calling him. For some reason, she thought it could go on and on that way, but then he made it clear that he wanted her to come back to him. He'd fly out and get her or messenger a first-class ticket. March looked out at her lemon tree. She could feel the baby inside of her moving, and that's when she knew she couldn't go. Hollis, however, seemed incapable of understanding that she was too far along in her pregnancy to pack a suitcase and leave.

If you wanted to, you would, he kept saying. *If you loved me, you'd do it.*

Each night he sounded more bitter. Each night, his disappointment grew. Finally, March called the Lyon to discover that Hollis had moved out. After Gwen was born, March was so distracted, in such a milky trance, that she was able to keep herself from thinking about him. By the time she admitted to herself how much she wanted him, he had married Belinda and it was too late to do anything other than sit beside the lemon tree and cry, then go and wash her face before the baby woke from her nap.

"I'll be home before you know it," March tells Richard now.

It's the oddest thing—she feels as though she is lying, and she's not. He's so far away, that's the problem. She's more connected to whatever is close by—the teakettle whistling in the kitchen, the first star in the sky.

"Five days tops," she says. "We'll go over the estate, pack up the house, and we're gone."

It takes Richard a long time to answer, as if the distance between them has somehow slipped them into different time warps.

"I don't know." Richard is stretched out on his bed, but he might as well be floating through space. "I worry about you being there."

"Well, don't." March can barely hear him now. It must be the connection, or the disparity between a starry night and a bright afternoon. "I love you," she tells her husband, but her voice sounds wavery, as if she needed to convince either him or herself.

After March hangs up the phone, a dog somewhere on the other side of Fox Hill begins to howl. Looking out the window, it's possible to view a vista that appears to reach on without end;

it's as if she can look across the darkness into another universe.

"Did you want milk and sugar?" Gwen calls from the kitchen, where she's fixing the pot of tea. When there's no answer she goes to the doorway and sees her mother with her coat still on, standing by the phone. "Mom?"

"You know what?" March says. "I'm too tired for tea. You have it. I'm going to bed."

Not that she could sleep if she tried. Not in this house. When March goes to her room, she sees the same quilt, fashioned of red and white squares, that was on her bed when she used to think about Hollis. It was as if his image had been implanted inside her eyelids; she carried him with her night or day, eyes opened or closed. She thought about Hollis so much you'd guess there'd be nothing left to think, but here she is, doing it all over again.

It started with all that kissing out on the roof, on hot nights when they couldn't sleep. In the morning, they'd always pretend nothing had happened. They avoided each other or were overly polite; sometimes, they did manage to forget for an hour or two, long enough to go swimming at Olive Tree Lake, where they raced against each other in the deep water for hours, as though they were nothing more than friends.

When Henry Murray died, at his desk, in his office on Main Street, everything in the house went black for two weeks. All the mirrors were covered with old sheets, and the door was left open so visitors could stop and pay their respects. March mostly remembers sitting in a corner and watching neighbors arrive with bouquets of lilies and platters of food. Once, Hollis sat down beside her. He didn't own a suit, and was wearing jeans and a white shirt; when he tried to take March's hand, she pulled away from him. Hollis took up so much space, and at that moment, March had no room for him. But with Hollis it was all or nothing, always. He was sulky and nasty-tempered for days afterwards, leaving March to feel guilty—about what exactly, she was never quite sure.

She should have learned her lesson then; it was so easy to wound him and so very difficult to make amends. She didn't search him out to apologize for slighting him until several days later, when the house had cleared out. But when she knocked on his door, he didn't answer; his belongings were no longer in the bedroom closet or stored in the oak dresser. Alan had decided that Hollis had best move up to the attic, seeing as how he wasn't a member of the family—he was really, Alan reminded Hollis, nothing at all—and that was where March found him. He was sitting on his bed, under the eaves, where a spider was hard at work on its web. The air was close up here, and filtered through a haze of dust, so that everything you looked at seemed silvery and swirling.

"What do you want?" Hollis said. He had a hard, annoyed tone, and he gave her one of his stares, a mean, superior look that could make almost anyone feel like an idiot.

It was best not to talk to Hollis when he got like this. March sat down on a wooden stool and picked up a book from a box of her father's lawbooks that was being stored up here. *Criminal Procedure*. She wondered if criminals had the same talent she did: to appear to be doing one thing—leafing through an old, dusty book—while you were really doing something else completely inside your mind. In March's case, she was imagining that she was kissing Hollis as she sat there and dust floated by.

There was a sharp, stinging odor in the attic, as if a trail of sulfur had been poured over the wide pine floorboards. It was probably the scent of fury, which, in Hollis's case, was often overpowering. The heat had a heavy, yellow cast, and it was oddly exhausting. Hollis lay down on his metal bed and turned his face toward the wall. There were squirrels nesting on the other side of the plaster; their feet skittered back and forth, like drumbeats inside the eaves.

"Go away," Hollis said. "Get lost."

March knew he could be cruel, she'd seen it herself. In a fight he was particularly dangerous because his own blood didn't frighten him; he didn't care if he got hurt. Boys at school had learned this the hard way; even those far stronger than Hollis were amazed at how much punishment he could take. Alan had given up physically harassing him; sticks and stones were nothing to Hollis, broken bones still less. It was humiliation that did the trick. The supper eaten at the kitchen counter. The bed in the attic. Anything secondhand, second-rate, run-down, charitably donated.

"Fine," March said after he told her to go. She was genuinely amazed by the cool authority of her own voice. "Your loss."

March felt as if she were outside of herself, perched somewhere in the rafters of the attic, watching calmly as her earthly form flung the heavy lawbook on the floor. A cloud of dust rose between them. She would have done anything for Hollis at that moment. Thrown herself out the window. Relinquished every possession. Slit her wrists. But she certainly wasn't about to let him know.

Hollis turned to look at her as she headed toward the door. When it seemed that, indeed, she truly was leaving, he stood up, confused. "Wait," he said.

It was probably ninety degrees outside, and much stuffier up in that attic. March thought about that night when she'd watched him cry himself to sleep. She thought about all of their kisses. A single leaf fell from the chestnut tree in the yard, and March swore she could hear it, falling and falling. When Hollis came over to her, March could feel how hot he was. She was only fourteen, but she knew what she wanted. She wanted him to look at her that way.

"Don't be mean to me," he said.

March laughed. He always said that. "You're the mean one."

"No, I'm not. It's you."

She knew what was going to happen if she stayed, and yet she couldn't imagine leaving. That was when she began to wonder if the scent of sulfur wasn't fury but desire, and if, perhaps, it might not be rising from her own skin. She'll never know how she had the nerve to kiss him the way she did. This wasn't anything like what they'd been doing on the roof on nights when they sneaked out their windows. Those kisses were shy, tentative things, and this was everything; this was what was deep inside. As soon as she kissed him like that, Hollis could tell how far she was willing to go. He didn't have to be a mind reader to divine that. It was the way she leaned her head back; it was the way she closed her eyes. She thought she was so smart, keeping all her secrets safe, but in a single instant she revealed every one.

Hollis locked the door and they went to his bed, which hadn't yet been made up with sheets. When he got on top of her, March heard herself say *Oh* as if she meant to tell him something, but her voice sounded peculiar and he wasn't listening anyway. He knew how to kiss, he really did; he knew how to touch you in ways that made you feel like crying, and caused you to want him even more. He must have had the ability to make a girl lose her reason completely, because there they were, in the attic, with Mrs. Dale cooking chicken cutlets for dinner in the kitchen and Alan drinking a beer out on the porch, and March wasn't stopping him when he pulled down her jeans. A truck delivering some fencing Alan had ordered turned into the driveway, but March didn't understand what the deliveryman was calling out. She couldn't understand anything, except how hot she was inside. His fingers were burning her up when he reached into her underpants; he seemed to be going right through her, but she must have been crazy, she was crazy by then, because she never once thought to tell him to stop.

Alan was still talking with the deliveryman from the hardware store when Hollis pulled his zipper down. March grabbed her long hair away from her face. There was a wasp hitting against the window, and all that dust, and outside the fencing was being tossed down from the truck. She knew this would happen, back when she was standing in the doorway. She knew once you'd started something with Hollis, you'd better be ready to go all the way.

All the same, March had a nervous feeling in the center of her stomach; she was starting to have pins and needles in her legs, as she always did when she was frightened.

"Maybe we shouldn't."

When she closed her eyes and turned away, she could feel him. All that heat, right next to her. "You know we're going to." He was whispering, but his voice sounded thick. "You know we will."

Of course, he was right, and she knew it. She went to the attic every night after that, and now she wonders how they managed to keep their secret. Sometimes they'd do it with their clothes on, hurried and silent, and he'd cover her mouth so she couldn't make a sound. *Don't say anything,* he'd whisper in her ear, when they heard someone downstairs, Judith Dale on her way to the bathroom, or Alan coming home late from a date. *Don't move,* he'd say, and he'd make love to her that way, forbidding her to shift her body, not even an arm or a leg, until she was so overcome with desire she thought she would faint.

That winter, they grew even more daring, and March sometimes didn't get back to her own bed until six or seven. By then the house was already growing light and she had to run through the halls or be found out. Whenever Mrs. Dale wondered about noises in the night, March blamed the squirrels nesting in the wall, or the family of raccoons who had come inside for the winter. Or perhaps it was the wind—that might explain the moaning Mrs. Dale heard, as if someone's heart was about to break. They were shameless; they did it three times a night, and there were days when March was so exhausted she'd fall asleep in class. At noon, she was often so tired she would put her head on the table in the cafeteria and miss lunch completely. Belinda Cooper, who went to a girls' boarding school in Connecticut and was only home on weekends, was completely puzzled when March would come over to visit, only to curl up at the foot of the bed, where she would sleep for hours. Of course it was Susanna Justice, who had inherited her father's talent for judgment, who finally figured it out.

"I don't believe it," Susie said after taking a good look at the dreamy expression on March's face. "'You're doing it with him, aren't you? Now I know you're insane."

Susie went with March to a doctor she'd heard about in Boston for birth control pills. The girls said they were going shopping, and in fact, both made certain to hurriedly buy a pair of shoes before starting for home.

"I wish it was anyone but him," Susie had said. "I wish you weren't so stupid."

They were waiting for their bus across from South Station. The girls had been on hiatus from despising each other, but March could tell they'd be back to hating each other before the afternoon was through.

"Well, maybe love is blind," March said archly.

"Maybe you are too," Susie slung back.

To this day, Susie doesn't understand why March fell in love with Hollis. Susie has always demanded hard evidence and documentation, and there is no explanation for something such as love, considering what grief it can bring. Now, for instance, what would compel March to go up the crooked old stairs to the attic? There's nothing but junk on the other side of the door, boxes of it, and yet she can't seem to stay away. The explanation she gives herself is one Susanna Justice would never accept. It is simply that March has discovered that when she kneels beside that old metal bed, she can feel the wind rattling the roof; she can still hear every leaf as it falls from the chestnut tree to the cold ground below.

S I X

BILL JUSTICE DRIVES OVER TO FOX HILL
after lunch, if anyone could consider crackers and
tea a proper lunch. His old Saab grunts and acts
ornery whenever the ditches are too mucky, but
Bill Justice just keeps going, and so does the Saab.
When he gets to the house, he parks and gets out;
the smell of woodsmoke immediately brings tears
to his eyes. Bill wipes at his face with his big,
gnarled hands. For a moment, he's completely
disoriented. What day is this? He can't quite recall. What is it he'll find when he walks through
the door? He can't figure that either.

Bill is known to be a rational man, one

who loves logic and facts. He can weigh murky, emotionally charged information—rage and love, for instance; divorce and hit and runs—and come up with a fitting legal solution. Who gets the children, who keeps the house, how many years is enough time served, what constitutes a crime of passion. However, at this moment, standing in front of the house on Fox Hill, everything seems like a puzzle. And then someone waves to him from the window and he realizes it's March's daughter. That's it. March is the one who lit the fire in the fireplace. She's waiting for him to go over Judith's estate.

"It's that judge guy," Gwen calls to her mother.

Gwen has been standing by the window, fogging up the glass with her breath and feeling as trapped as a fly in pudding. Being here is beyond nowhere. This morning she had to help her mother begin to sort through Mrs. Dale's belongings, and the whole time Gwen was carrying boxes up from the cellar she'd been wishing she could teleport home. She has tried to call her best friend, Minnie, three times, but the line is always busy. *This is beyond purgatory.* That's what she planned to tell Minnie, if Minnie ever shut up long enough for her to get a call through. *It's worse than hell. It's hell times two.*

"He's got a briefcase with him," she tells her mother, who's in the kitchen fixing coffee.

The Judge has one hand over his eyes and he's staring at the house. He walks toward the gate, then takes a step back.

"He's kind of stumbling around," Gwen reports.

"The Judge doesn't stumble," March informs her daughter as she brings the coffeepot and two china cups over to the dining room table. She comes to stand next to Gwen at the window, then waves to the Judge. He waves back and swings the gate open.

"I'll bet he was great-looking when he was young," Gwen decides.

March snorts.

"What?" Gwen asks.

"When are you going to understand—you can't rate people by the way they look." The funny thing is, March never realized how handsome Bill Justice was, but now she remembers that her father used to tease him about their women clients being the only ones who preferred Bill. "Anyway, he's over seventy."

"Well, I bet he was cute," Gwen insists. "He's still not too bad. For somebody ancient."

"A perfect day for October," the Judge says as he comes inside. "Unfortunate that we have to use it to tend to such sad business."

He kisses March's cheek, then takes off his overcoat. He seems a little bewildered when he sees the cardboard boxes filled with Judith's belongings that are strewn across the dining room table.

"I thought I should go through everything," March explains.

"Of course you should." The Judge sits down and accepts some coffee.

"You can't believe some of the things I've found already." March holds up a blue ribbon. "Alan's. From some debating team he was on."

"Alan," the Judge says sadly. "There's a man who ruined his life."

Gwen has been looking out the window, idly eating Pepperidge Farm Mint Milanos from the bag. Now, she shifts her attention.

"How ruined?" she asks the Judge. "Completely ruined? Totally ruined?"

"Gwen!" March says. She turns to the Judge. "She's never even met him. Do you think I should bring her to visit him?"

"He wouldn't see you. He wouldn't open the door." The Judge notices a silk scarf in one of the boxes; when he narrows his eyes he realizes that the blobs of orange are lilies, like the ones which grow in his own yard. "How long do you plan on staying?" he asks March.

Gwen stops chewing so she can hear the answer. Her whole life depends on this.

"I thought a week." March looks around at the accumulation of a lifetime. "But there's so much to do. And so much of what's left in the house was Alan's or mine. I found all my sweaters, every one I ever wore, from kindergarten on up, folded into two boxes in the attic."

"Richard should have come with you," the Judge says.

"Oh, no." March pours more coffee. For some reason, just the mention of Richard's name makes her feel flushed, as if she'd already betrayed him, somehow. It was going up to the attic, that was the problem. She keeps seeing dust, out of the corner of her eye. She keeps hearing the door shut, the way it used to when she and Hollis sneaked up there; she keeps feeling the way she did whenever he was near. "Richard had classes. Midquarter exams. He couldn't leave."

"I don't care what he had. He shouldn't have let you come back alone."

Gwen puts down the bag of cookies. This judge guy is more interesting than she would have imagined.

"Cookie?" March offers the Judge, hoping to change the subject.

Bill Justice takes two bites of a Mint Milano, and when there's only a small piece left, he whistles.

"Sister," he calls.

March and Gwen look at each other, confused.

The Judge whistles again and holds out the piece of cookie, and then, all of a sudden, he gets a pained expression. His whole face falls.

"Where's the dog?" he asks, and when March looks blank he tosses the cookie bit on the table. "Shit," he mutters. "Where's the damned dog?"

The Judge rises to his feet and heads for the door. He's already pulling on his overcoat when March and Gwen reach him.

"Judith got a dog last winter," the Judge says. His breathing sounds off and he's having trouble finding his car keys. "A West Highland terrier."

"A West Highland terrier?" March feels a bit dazed.

"A little white dog," the Judge says, impatient. "Have you seen her?"

Now that it's mentioned, March remembers Judith saying something about a dog she got for Christmas. Judith had been planning to come out to California for Thanksgiving, and she worried about putting the dog in the kennel.

"There was something out on the porch last night," Gwen pipes up, but when her mother and Bill Justice look at her, expectantly, she feels silly. "But it was a rabbit."

"I didn't remember there was a dog," March says. "There was no sign of it when we got here."

"Oh, fuck," the Judge says.

March gets goose bumps from the sound of those words coming from Bill Justice. It is so unlike him to speak in that manner, that she feels she has done something terrible, perhaps even criminal, in forgetting Judith's dog.

The Judge opens the hall closet and takes out a leash neither March nor Gwen noticed when hanging up their coats; then he goes outside without bothering to say goodbye.

"It probably died because of us," Gwen says. Her voice sounds sad, but also accusatory, as if the whole thing were really March's fault.

March grabs a sweater. "Look around the yard," she tells her daughter. "I'm going with the Judge."

Bill Justice is already backing out of the driveway, but March runs over and taps on the window. When he stops, she gets into the Saab and they drive slowly along the road, windows open, calling over and over again for Sister, the little white dog.

"I wasn't thinking," March says as they drive too fast over the bumps. Or perhaps the problem was that she was thinking too much about subjects she shouldn't have allowed past the first circle of her mind. Just as before, Hollis is taking up too much room. "I was so upset about Judith."

Instead of listening to her excuses, the Judge is peering into the bushes as he drives. At the turnoff, they head for the village, driving so slowly that other cars honk, then pass them by. They keep the windows open and continue to whistle and call out. They try the main roads, and most of the back roads; they drive past the schoolyard and the park and St. Bridget's Hospital. The Judge stops to phone Bud Horace, the animal control officer, from the pay phone outside the Red Apple market, but Bud has no reports of a white dog being sighted. At last, the Judge decides to look down by the Marshes. The sky is already purple; the first few stars have appeared, suddenly, as if someone had thrown a handful of silver across the edge of the world.

"Hard to believe this is where Alan wound up." The Judge shakes his head. They drive along the salty blacktop, then turn down a dirt path.

"Sometimes I forget I have a brother," March admits.

"Well, you've got one," the Judge says. "And that's where he lives."

There is a ramshackle house at the very edge of the Marshes; it's fashioned out of wooden shingles that are the color of a dove's wings. Most people say it's the Founder's house, and that Aaron Jenkins built it with his own two hands, although others remember stories of a fisherman who lived down here at the turn of the century, a nasty fellow who set out eel traps and refused to speak when greeted by anyone from the village.

"It's parkland," the Judge tells March, "but the town council lets him stay. Once or twice a year someone from social services comes over, but he won't open the door for them. The ladies on the library committee pay for his expenses. Judith was the one who started that, and she usually brought him his groceries. She tried to check on him once a week or so."

"I had no idea. She never talked about him."

March looks out at the thick grass and the reeds. She has always blamed Alan for driving Hollis off, with his cruelty and his jealousy. Now she wonders if she herself wasn't guilty of the same exact sin she has always blamed on her brother. Perhaps she also has carried a grudge too long.

"Well," March says, "with Judith gone, Alan can sell the house and Fox Hill and have enough money to take care of himself. That was his one good deed—allowing Judith to live there."

"He wasn't the one who let her live there." The Judge watches, closely gauging March's reaction. "It was Hollis."

Well, there you have it—she truly didn't know who owned Fox Hill. She has turned to the Judge, riveted.

"Alan sold the place right after Julie died; he was desperate for money, he was drinking it all up, and he got a nice offer from some corporation based in Florida. That corporation turned out to be Hollis. I was coming over to tell you today. You've been left all of Judith's personal effects, but Hollis owns the house."

The Judge clears his throat. He has always disliked Hollis, but not for the reasons other people might have, because of his mean streak. The Judge, after all, has seen men at their worst and at their best in his courtroom. As far as he can tell, the problem with Hollis is that he has always blamed others for what's wrong with his life. He never takes any responsibility, and a man like that, the Judge knows, simply cannot be saved. Truth is, he wouldn't want to be.

"It appears that Hollis got everything he wanted," the Judge says now.

"It does look that way," March says.

"Well, let's hope so, at any rate. Let's hope he's satisfied."

The Judge stops the car to call out his window for the dog; then he puts the car in park and gets out. March gets out too. She's shaken by the proximity of the past. There is her brother, on the other side of these reeds. There is Hollis, beyond the hilltop and the trees, the owner of the house where she grew up and now sleeps, the owner of everything the eye can see. He was so poor and neglected when he came to them that he did not know it wasn't necessary to stand by the back door, like a dog, to get his dinner.

"Sit at the table," March remembers Judith Dale telling him, and he sat there mute, staring at lamb chops and lettuce and apple pie as if he had no business to dream such things, let alone have them for supper.

The water in the Marshes is rising with the tide; it seems purple and starry as well—an inverted sky.

"Not a soul," the Judge says.

They don't call out their windows on the ride back. They don't bother to speak. The Judge takes the shortcut back to Fox Hill, avoiding the village and Route 22, which means zigzagging past the cemetery. He hadn't been thinking of how this course might affect them, but the choice is clearly a mistake. Less than twenty-four hours ago, they were here to bury Judith. How is it that even grown men, old men who should be content with all that they've had, still want more? How is it that death always seems impossible, a trick of nature one should somehow be able to set in reverse? The Judge feels a sharp pain up and down his left arm, never a good sign.

"I think we should stop," March says as they approach the cemetery.

March truly surprises him sometimes. In the past, Bill Justice viewed her as spoiled; the selfish little girl her father could never say no to. But with March, you never can tell. Tonight, for instance, her impulse to visit Judith's grave is one hundred percent on target.

The Judge nods and drives through the iron gates, then along the narrow road which leads to the newest burial section. Scarlet leaves drop from the maples, adding to the carpet already on the ground. Now the sky is purple through and through; there are no other visitors, not at this hour. After they get out of the car and approach the grave, March can feel shivers along her skin.

It's cold here. Too cold to be left all alone. Later in the week, March will bring a pot of asters to plant, the wild variety which return year after year. She will, however, avoid the older section of the cemetery; she knows too many who have been buried there, more, in fact, than she knows among the residents living down in the village.

The wind has begun to pick up, blowing the fallen leaves into little whirlwinds. How is it, March wonders, that life happens this way? Is it really possible to be a child one moment, asking for candy and a hand to hold, and then, in what seems like seconds, to be a grown woman walking through a cemetery on such a dark and bitter night? She's confused being back here; she's seeing shadows. It makes perfect sense that she doubts her own vision when she spies something beside Judith Dale's grave.

March closes her eyes; she's dizzy, it's true, but when she looks again, she's certain something is there. All at once she feels a pressure inside her chest, like a fist which prevents her from breathing. At this instant, she could believe in ghosts, but when she concentrates she sees it's no billowy mist that covers Judith's grave. It's no specter returned. It's an animal at rest, a shaggy creature with leaves matted into its fur. March tugs on the Judge's coat sleeve.

"The dog," she says. "Hey," she cries to the terrier. She claps her hands and whistles.

The dog sits up, ears twitching. It's little and so dirty all of its fur has turned a muddy gray shade. It has been waiting here for a long time, it hasn't eaten for days, and it's not about to be disturbed from its vigil by strangers. As March approaches, the terrier growls, low down in its throat.

March stops, startled by such a small dog's depth of feeling.

"It's all right." The Judge has come up beside March. "Sister," he calls. "Here, girl."

At the sound of his voice, the dog leaps up and runs to him. The terrier is filthy, but the Judge bends down and picks it up.

"You silly thing," he says.

The dog's tail wags like mad against the Judge's overcoat. It's clearly in ecstasy to be held in his arms, and it yaps with what little voice it has left, since it has been howling each and every night.

For all they know, this dog has been following the body of its mistress from the time she was first taken from the house. It may have been waiting in the alley beside the funeral parlor, pursuing the hearse down Route 22. This small creature is not at all confused about what it wants, unlike men and women, who have the ability to conceal their deepest desires. Men and women, after all, can hide their love away. Men don't chase after cars. Women don't throw themselves upon cement doorsteps, curled up in a heap, until somebody opens the door and finally lets them inside.

Among men and women, those in love do not always announce themselves, with declarations and vows. But they are the ones who weep when you're gone. Who miss you every single night, especially when the sky is so deep and beautiful, and the ground so very cold. On this night, the Judge cries more quietly than it would ever seem possible for a man of his size. He keeps his face averted, buried against the dog's fur. March doesn't even realize he's weeping, until a sob escapes. And that is how she finally knows that Bill Justice loved Judith. He loved her for thirty-five years, which for some people is as good as a lifetime. He loved her the way no one else ever has, and yet, in spite of that, he's only entitled to grieve privately, in the dark. At least he has a right to that, and March wouldn't think of intruding. She'll stand beside him, in silence, beneath a sky that is now perfectly black, until he's ready to drive her home.

SEVEN

AT TWILIGHT, FOX HILL IS THE MOST
beautiful place on earth, with its long, blue views
of Guardian Farm and its twisted black trees.
Hank comes here often at this time, accompanied
by the dogs, who are unusually subdued at this
hour, as if they knew that bickering and snapping would be a crime against the silence down
below.

Most of the time, Hank considers himself to
be too obvious and too tall, but here on the hill,
he is small and extremely well aware of his own
insignificance. What is the difference between
himself and a single blade of grass? The grass,

as he sees it, is worth a thousand times more than he is, since it serves a purpose, and hard as he's tried Hank has never been able to figure a single reason for his existence. All he's ever been is a problem, a burden—but there must be a reason for this life that he has, there's got to be. After all, he is here, just as surely as the fields he walks across. He is breathing this sweet, October air.

Sometimes, when he stops thinking of himself as Hollis's adopted nephew and his father's only son, Hank has the sense that there might be something worthwhile inside of him. It is possible that no one perceives the world the way he does, or views this landscape with the clarity with which he sees. This alone would be a reason for him to exist. When he thinks about the idea of his own singular vision, the world suddenly seems filled with endless possibilities, and he wonders if this is what hawks experience at the moment of flight. Expectation, that's what it is. The kind you feel when you're seventeen, and the air is cold and fresh, and the dogs lie down beside you in the grass, and everything is quiet, the way it always is right before something is about to happen.

The evening star rises into the dark blue night. But this star is only the beginning, like opening the cover of a book but not yet turning the first page. Below, in the pastures, there used to be dozens of horses, including the thoroughbred named Tarot's Deck of Fortune, who was once entered in both the Preakness and the Belmont Stakes in a single year. Hank found a photograph forgotten in the barn, crammed between two stalls. When he saw the image of Tarot, draped in blue and white silks, Hank actually cried. He wished he had lived at the Farm in Mr. Cooper's time. He's heard from some of the older residents of the village that the ground used to shake when the horses ran together. You could feel it all the way in town; the floors of the bakery and the hardware store used to vibrate so badly several residents were convinced that the village was prone to earthquakes.

Of all the racehorses once boarded here, Tarot is the only one left. Belinda used to spoil him terribly; she'd feed him sugar cubes and whisper in his ear. She always rode at the end of the day, when the sky was halfway between black and indigo, like ink spreading out on a page. Tarot still gets restless at this hour; he paces when he's down in the pasture, and if he's in his stall, he kicks, and that's when you'd better beware.

Jimmy Parrish—who knows his horses if nothing else—has told Hank that before Tarot went crazy, Mr. Cooper had been offered five hundred thousand cash for him by a consortium in Atlanta. Even now, Tarot is still beautiful. He's old, twenty-two, but few people would guess to look at him. Of course, he hasn't been ridden for so many years that he's even more headstrong than ever. The dogs are terrified of him, especially since last spring, when he kicked a pup who was too curious for its own good, snapping its spine, so that Hollis had to shoot the thing, to relieve the poor creature from its misery.

Probably, Hank should be over at a friend's house at this hour, instead of coming up here to the hill. The funny thing is, the kids at school think he's rich. They probably assume he's at some fancy dinner party, or down in Boston, at the opera or something. A real laugh, although Hank can understand why they'd be misled. Hollis is rich, but that surely doesn't mean the wealth extends to Hank. The reality is, Hank is as poor as any orphan. He owns nothing; even the clothes on his back were paid for by Hollis. The kids at school are certain that Hank chooses to wear old boots to be cool, and that he's simply not interested in going out with them to the bowling alley on Friday nights because he's got better things to do, but the mortifying fact is, he has no cash to spend.

He's a great guy, of course, he's got a million friends. If he ran for student body president today, he'd probably win. It's not his fault that he's always too busy for social events. Like tonight, for instance, there's a party at Willie Simon's house. Willie's parents are in the Bahamas and he's got the key to their liquor cabinet and all the prettiest girls will be there. And yet, in spite of an invitation, Hank is here, on Fox Hill, thinking about horses and fate. He's concentrating so deeply that it takes a minute before he realizes he's not imagining someone walking down the road. It's a girl in a black ski jacket. Hank gets to his feet to see her more clearly and convince himself she's not a mirage.

It doesn't take long for Hank to realize this is the girl he saw at Mrs. Dale's funeral. She's small, but she has a tough sort of posture. She stops and takes out a crumpled pack of cigarettes, shakes one out, and lights it. Hank has the sense that he's doing something bad watching her like this. She's really pretty, but that's not what's getting to him. He feels like he knows this girl. He experienced the same thing at the funeral parlor; it's as if he'd been waiting for her before he ever saw her. She was so upset after the service; she seemed to be crying, but as soon as people began filing out the door, she acted as if nothing was wrong. That was what got to Hank, that she wouldn't let anyone witness her pain. It's exactly what he's been doing all his life.

Now, he wonders if he should announce himself, cough or holler; or maybe he should turn heel and get out of there fast. But he's too interested to leave. Beside him, the dogs are jittery, so Hank holds up his hand as a signal, forbidding them to bark.

Down on the dirt road, Gwen paces back and forth while she smokes, so she won't freeze. Beneath her T-shirt and the ski jacket she's worn only twice before on trips to Big Bear, her arms are covered with goose bumps. She's got on two pairs of wool socks, and some old boots she found in the hall closet, but it isn't enough. She's simply not used to the cold. And this is only October, it's mild as far as people around here are concerned. Well then, in Gwen's estimation, people around here are crazy. Let them live in New England and pull on long underwear and gloves and go about their business, all the while pretending they aren't freezing their asses. Maybe there's a reason for that. Maybe this kind of weather does something for you, if you ever get used to it—it purifies you and gets right down to the bone, leaving only the parts that can face up to hardship.

In spite of the cold, Gwen is relieved to be out of that dreadful old house. Since they've arrived, they don't seem to be going anywhere fast. Gwen's mother is spending all her time sorting through Mrs. Dale's belongings, dividing them into what should be thrown out, given away, or kept. March doesn't seem to be sleeping at night, a fact Gwen knows because she herself is sleeping in the little sewing room and can hear her mother searching around in the attic, or in the kitchen at odd hours, fixing tea. Only last night, Gwen woke to see her mother on the stairway landing, looking out the window, concentrating so hard you'd think the most important thing in the world was out there.

And then there's the dog. Gwen's mother waits on the dog, as if she's doing some sort of penance for forgetting it in the first place. She feeds the raggedy thing canned tuna fish and cooked chicken, in spite of the fact that the dog has twice tried to bite. The stupid beast sits by the front door and howls, and when Gwen is forced to take it for a walk after supper, the awful creature will not follow unless Gwen tugs and curses and, finally, begs it to come along nicely.

Last night, when she called her friend Minnie to complain and decompress, Minnie wasn't home. Her mother said she was sleeping at Pepita Anderson's house, but that's nothing more than a code all the girls use, a fake friend, a disembodied name given to parents when you want to be out all night. *The old Pepita excuse*, Gwen planned to tease Minnie, if she ever got to talk to her. *Well, I hope you enjoyed yourself. I hope you had a whole bunch of fun, because I sure am not having any.* If she were home, Gwen would probably be over at the Shopping Center; at least she could spend some money and feel better. Here, when she wants to get away from her mother there are only these silver fields, and the fading light, and the woods filled with things that are probably watching her—raccoons and weasels, and hopefully nothing more.

As she walks along this empty road, Gwen realizes that nobody knows her. No one could begin to imagine what it's like to be her. Ever since she got here, she's been desperate to get back to California, but if she's really going to be honest, what is she going back to? She's a loser, that's the truth. She hates school, she hates all her friends, except for Minnie—who, when you come right down to it, is even more of a loser—she hates her last two boyfriends, both of whom she had sex with for reasons she can't remember anymore. Admittedly, the sex was nothing. She'd heard so much about it, but it turned out she was floating outside her body while she did all those things. It wasn't love, that's for sure. It was all so nothing. If a nuclear bomb fell from the sky, would it really matter? Wouldn't it be better to be blown away, completely and utterly, before she screws up the rest of her life?

She started to think like this at the funeral parlor, and she's been morbid ever since, going over weird concepts. What, for instance, will she do with the rest of her life? Now that she's here, with no outside stimulus—no TV, telephone, mall, pot, boy—who is she really? Why can't she go back to being the way she was before she came here, when she barely thought at all?

Gwen puts out her cigarette on the road, crushing the embers beneath her boot. She leans on a rickety wooden fence, and reaches into her pocket for a scarf. But before she can loop the fabric around her throat, she begins to feel a tingling sensation on the back of her neck. It's as if someone was breathing on her; either she's going crazy, or someone is right there behind her. She might have turned and run home without stopping to see what sort of creature breathed out such warm air, if she hadn't then heard a noise, one so small it resembled a question mark. Even before she turns and sees Tarot, Gwen feels as if she's entered into a dream. This night, with its dark and silver edges, this horse on the other side of the fence who has come to her without being called. And perhaps that is why she has no second thoughts as she slips through the railings and goes into the pasture; it's a dream, and it's hers, and she's desperate to see what happens next.

Up on the hill, Hank grabs one of the youngest dogs, who's begun to yelp, and gives it a shake. He wants to see this, and he doesn't want some idiot dog to announce his presence. Hank tries to be responsible in most things, and usually he is. He knows he should climb down the hill, fast, and stop this girl. If she stays in the pasture, she could get hurt. Tarot has charged at much lesser things—at the wind, for instance, at butterflies and bees. But Tarot seems completely hypnotized, maybe because the girl is so beautiful against the blue-black sky, or maybe Hank is the one who's been hypnotized. In fact, the only time Gwen has even seen a real live horse has been at county fairs. She doesn't even think to be afraid. She's comfortable enough to stand beside Tarot and talk to him when most grown men would run. That's what she's doing down there in the field, where frost coats the soles of her borrowed boots. She's telling this evil old horse that he's gorgeous, and he seems to like what he's hearing. He steps closer to Gwen, carefully, slowly, as if to hear more of whatever she has to say.

It is very odd, indeed, to see the horse everyone called a killer trail along, mild as can be, as the girl heads toward the rotten stump Hank should have pulled last spring. It had been a huge maple tree, before lightning split it in two. Ken Helm took it down, in exchange for the wood, and Hank was supposed to come here with some dynamite and get rid of what was left. Now, he's glad he forgot. What remains of that old maple is the perfect height for this girl to get onto so she can throw herself onto Tarot's back. When she nearly falls off, she gives Tarot a little slap, which, in other circumstances, would have sent him racing.

"Stand still," she tells him. "You big cutie."

Although Gwen knows nothing about horses, she's right about

his size. Tarot is sixteen hands high, which is even bigger when you're up on his back, looking down at the ground.

"Be a good boy," she tells him.

For his part, Tarot seems too shocked to move. If this girl does get hurt, Hank will have to live with it. A broken leg, a crumpled spine would be his fault. And yet, he does nothing to stop her. The muscles in his arm have tightened; his pulse is going fast. He keeps a hand on the yelpy dog, willing to shake it like a dust mop if the dog dares to bark and startle Tarot.

Gwen is leaning forward, her hands holding on to the horse's mane. She's afraid that if she blinks this will all disappear and she'll wake in her bed to find she never even left the house; she never borrowed these boots, or walked along the road, or found this beautiful horse. If this is a dream, she wants to go on sleeping. She doesn't make a sound; that's how much she wants this to be real. And as he watches from the highest point on Fox Hill, Hank wants it for her just as badly. In this pasture, in the dark, Gwen's life has made a major turn, something as rare as planets leaving their orbits to crash into each other and fill up the night. In a place she never wanted to be, on a night that will be cold enough to freeze the apples on the trees, she is no longer alone.

EIGHT

THE COWARD SITS ON A HARD-BACKED
chair, wearing gloves and boots, since the old
house where he lives hasn't got a bit of heat. He
does not deserve heat, he knows that. He deserves exactly what he's got, which is nothing, in
spades. He's not quite fifty, but most people
would guess he's twenty years older than that. His
skin is sallow and pockmarked. His long hair and
beard are gray. He's thin as a twig, and as crooked
as one too. When he happens to catch sight of
himself in the reflection of his battered coffeepot,
he always gets a good laugh. He is what he

appears to be, there's no hiding that. His inside is affecting his outside, like a rotten piece of fruit.

Years ago, when the Coward was a boy, he was on the debating team at the local high school. He had a slick quality, which always helps in an argument, and was often applauded for his speaking voice. Words, however, are nothing to him now. There are weeks when he doesn't talk to anyone. He doesn't complain to the fleas who live in his mattress; he doesn't bother to shoo the flies away from his morning cereal—that is, when he remembers to eat. He has ruined his life, and although he can't blame it all on drink, drinking has become his whole universe. Sometimes, he doesn't bother to get out of bed before he starts. It's just as easy to lie there and reach for the bottle; he doesn't even have to open his eyes.

This morning some woman was knocking at his door. She must not have known that the Coward's philosophy of life makes him temperamentally unfit for human contact, although he did appreciate Judith Dale's visits. When he heard the stranger out on his porch, the Coward knew it wasn't Judith, since she is dead, and there's no one else he allows to visit. He crawled to the window on his belly so he could peek outside. The woman out there had long, dark hair; in spite of a heavy, woolen coat, she looked as if she were freezing. She was ill at ease, and kept glancing over her shoulder. She knocked several times, and when there was no answer she called out "Alan" in a clear, pretty voice which startled the Coward. That name—which he never uses anymore and would never sign on a piece of paper, even if offered a hundred dollars cash—made him cover his ears and count to a thousand. Luckily, by the time he was done, the woman had left.

If she'd really wanted to see him, of course, she could have merely pushed the door open, since the Coward never bothers to lock it. Probably, his caller had heard his dreadful history. Not even the charlatan at last summer's circus fair outside Town Hall would read his fortune. That's how bad his past has been, and his future looks no better. People used to say the Coward fed his dog gunpowder, to make it more vicious, and this was the reason everyone avoided the Marshes. But that dog died years ago, of arthritis and old age, and the Marshes are still unknown territory for most local residents. Anyone who goes there goes at his own risk.

Of course, twelve-year-old boys are always looking for trouble, and teenagers need their thrills. Sometimes there are groups daring enough to make their way through the muck and the reeds. They pitch winter apples and stones at the roof of his house, defying the Coward to come chase them away, but he never does, and he never will. Even on nights when stones are thrown, the Marshes are silent, and that silence is scary enough to chase off most unwanted visitors.

To the children in the village, who whisper the Coward's story at slumber parties, his is a cautionary tale about what can happen to spoiled boys who think they have everything. Greedy, thoughtless habits take you down a road you can't get off, even when you've seen the error of your ways. Before you know it, you've grown up to be a man who doesn't give a damn about anyone but himself, and then your fortune is your own affair, and hopeless is probably the best you can ask for.

The Coward knows all this—it's the reason he has never fought for his son. He doesn't deserve the boy any more than he deserves heat or light or hope. If the Coward happens to be out wandering on a starless night, he avoids Fox Hill, and if he ever comes within a mile of Guardian Farm's property lines he begins to shake and he's unable to stop until he's safe in his house with a drink halfway down his throat.

Although he can barely remember it now—his memory is foggy, and he's thankful for that—there was an occasion when he went to search out his son. One look, that was all he wanted. A minute; a single word. It was pathetic, really, and he knew it even at the time. He crept up to the schoolyard for a peek at Hank, but five years had passed since he'd last seen the boy and among all those children out for recess, the Coward could not tell which one was his. Unlike the common duck, which can distinguish its young from another's in a crowded pond or stream, unlike a swan, who will kill for the sake of its hatchling, the Coward had forgotten his own son's features. This, of course, only made him despise himself more. He is, after all, called the Coward for good reason.

In the past years, his single companion was his old dog, whom he still misses—a wretched boxer someone had set out to drown in a burlap bag. The drowning was somehow bungled, and when the Coward dragged the bag out of the marsh at low tide, there was one dead puppy inside, and another live one who was, from that moment on, forever grateful. Not that the Coward didn't try to dissuade the misguided beast. He could throw a frying pan at the poor dog's head, and it would insist upon licking his hand. He wishes he still had that dog, although he is convinced it was the stupidest creature on earth, foolish enough to misjudge its own master and believe him worthy of loyalty.

Though it now seems ridiculous, the Coward once considered himself lucky. He had inherited all his father owned, and was free to do as he pleased. The only dark spot in his life had been Hollis, and he always resented his father for bringing this false brother home. But Hollis, who had recently returned to the village, was nothing to Alan anymore. Why, Alan could pass him on the street and not even feel compelled to acknowledge Hollis's existence. He had, after all, far better things to think about. His marriage, for one. Julie, the woman who had become his wife, was said to be the sweetest girl in town. There was something peaceful about her, as if snow had settled inside her soul. Often, she slept fourteen hours straight, and when she woke there was a smile on her lips. Their son took after her—Hank rarely cried as an infant, and as a toddler he put himself to bed when he was tired, climbing into his own crib.

On the day the fire started, the Coward was out in a hammock beneath the chestnut tree. It was Mrs. Dale's day off, so Julie was fixing dinner, which, like all her meals, would surely turn out to be a well-intentioned disaster. Hank, who was three, was sitting on the floor, playing with measuring cups. The child was there when the Coward walked through the kitchen on his way to the yard, and he was probably still there when the fire leapt from the rear burner of the stove, attaching itself to the curtains, and then to the wood countertop, and finally to the pink dress that Julie was wearing, a pretty cotton shift the Coward had bought her in Boston.

In minutes, the smoke was so thick that people standing on the steps of the library in the village could see it; by the time the fire fighters arrived, sparks were shooting into the sky. The fire fighters worked like mad that day, desperate to stop the flames before they spread through the woods; they were far too busy to notice Alan Murray standing at the gate, so close to the blaze that he was covered with soot. The air was brutal, a burning, black soup, and yet Alan had been standing there long enough to have his eyebrows singed off. He was crying tears that were so scalding they burned little holes in his face, the scars of which, like pinpricks or small pox, have never faded away.

The heat and the flames had paralyzed Alan. His wife and his child were trapped in that house, but he could no more go inside and search for them than he could jump up and land on the moon. Ken Helm, who was one of the volunteers, was the first to notice Alan, and it was Ken who realized there were still people left inside. Alan was crying beside the purple clematis, which had grown by the garden gate for as long as anyone could remember, but had now burned to ashes, and he didn't stop crying when they brought Hank out. Someone had been left behind in that burning house, and although it was Julie's body that was taken from the wreckage, that someone who'd been lost turned out to be Alan himself.

People in town started talking about him at the funeral, as he tore out his hair and called for his wife. They whispered when he lost his money, spending wildly—rebuilding the house, conned into dreadful business deals, practically giving it away. They talked when night after night he had to be carried out of the Lyon Cafe, and when he had to sell Fox Hill to pay off all he had borrowed. Some people say that Hollis bailed him out by covering his debts and buying the hill at a fair price, but Alan knows Hollis never intended to be kind. He bought Fox Hill anonymously, through his lawyer, well aware that Alan would never have sold to him. At any rate, due to extreme carelessness, the money from the sale of Fox Hill disappeared fast. Alan and his boy were often tossed out of rented apartments; Alan tended to fall asleep while smoking, and once he would have burned himself alive, and perhaps been glad of it, if Hank, then four, hadn't thrown water on the smoldering easy chair where his father slept.

At last, Alan took his son to live in the Marshes, to this house people say the Founder built, a shack really, nothing more. Hank was often discovered wandering alone, his clothes filthy and coated with mud. People who didn't even know him would insist on taking the child to the Bluebird Coffee Shop, where they'd buy him big bowls of macaroni and cheese or thick tomato soup. Hank always ate each meal as though it were his last, wolfing down his food, even when it was hot enough to burn his tongue. Clearly, if the board of the library hadn't appropriated clothes for him at every flea market and rummage sale, this child would have gone around town naked. That's how drunk Alan was by then; that's how pathetic he'd become.

Hollis went out to the Marshes for the first and last time on a Sunday afternoon that year when Hank was four, plowing through the mud in Mr. Cooper's old pickup, which he continues to drive to this day. Now that Hollis was married to Belinda, he owned more acreage than any other man in the county; he must have wanted to gloat over his victory, but he never got the chance. He found Alan passed out on the floor. That day he brought Hank with him when he returned to Guardian Farm, and the boy has been with him ever since. People say Hollis is good to Hank, or so the Coward has heard, and that makes perfect sense. No doubt Hollis has some idea of the pain his mercy causes the Coward. No doubt at all.

There are times, of course, when the Coward wonders what their lives might have been like if he had treated Hollis, if not like a brother, then like a human being. When he starts to think about what might have been, that's when the Coward begins to drink gin, his favorite liquid in all the world. So transparent and empty, just like the rest of his life. The one remnant of a schedule which remains in his life is his Friday routine, for that is the day when he takes the single journey that matters to him—across the Marshes, down Route 22, to the liquor store on the edge of town. He goes after dark, always, and all he needs to do is sign an X on the account page. It took a while, but he finally figured out why Mike Howard was letting him have all this booze on credit, when he's never gotten paid back. Of course, he thought when it hit him. Naturally. Hollis would gladly foot the bill for arsenic as well, if that had been his pleasure.

On clear days, the Coward sits on the sagging porch of his old house and considers everything in the Marshes that could kill you, if quick suicide was what you were after. You could, for instance, eat the thin, poisonous pods of milkweed stalks or ingest the bitter leaves of the mallows. You could reach down and pluck one of the orange mushrooms that not even the ants will go near. But the end results would be nasty, and messy as well. Gin, however slow, doesn't make you foam at the mouth like the mushrooms would. There are many ways to accomplish what the Coward's after, but liquor is the most civilized method. In fact, it's the last piece of civilization in his life.

At night, when people in the village are fast asleep, he still hears the sound of fire. It's a sound from hell, all twisted and hot. You get thirsty when you hear a sound like that in your dreams. You get terribly thirsty and there's not a damned thing you can do about it, except to take the same route every Friday and make certain not to answer your door. You never know who you'll find out there on your own porch; it may be someone who believes it's a righteous person's duty to convince the Coward he has to stop drinking and turn his life around, when it's abundantly clear he's never going to do that. He's here for good; for better or, more likely, for worse, all the rest of his days.

NINE

SINCE HER RETURN TO FOX HILL, ALL March has accomplished is an orderly mess. There are currently twenty-five boxes in the kitchen, all labeled to go to the Library Association's booth at the Harvest Fair, which is always held in the basement of Town Hall. Most of the objects March has packed, she knew by heart: The cake pans Mrs. Dale seemed to collect, dozens of them. The lace curtains, the throw pillows, the ceramic candlesticks from England. March's father's lawbooks have already been donated to Derry Law School, carted there by Ken Helm, who's been running all March's errands, since she decided not to replace her rental car. Eight silver place settings, brought out only on holidays, have been mailed home to California, where they will most likely never be used.

Judith, who didn't care much for jewelry, had only three good pieces: A gold necklace, which March has given to Harriet Laughton, one of Judith's dear friends. A pair of heavy gold earrings, rarely worn, has been presented to St. Bridget's Hospital, to be auctioned off to the highest bidder at the next fund-raising drive. The lovely, square-cut emerald Judith never took off, March now wears on her right hand. Luckily, March found the emerald in an envelope stuffed into a night table drawer she was clearing out. March studied that ring so often, as Mrs. Dale folded laundry or planted mint or tucked her in at night, that she cannot help but wonder if the emerald has affected her career choice. The jewelry she fashions is simple in design; as with this ring, the overall effect often depends on small, but perfect, stones. She favors green and blue in her work: topaz and tiny sapphires, crystals and aquamarines, Chinese jade and emeralds, of course, although none has appealed to her as much as the stone she now wears.

Today, while March works on organizing the house, Judith's little dog sits by the window, waiting for rabbits. Each time the dog spies one, out in the orchard or calmly chewing mint by the back door, it goes completely berserk.

"Will you stop that?" March complains, because whenever the dog barks, she's startled all over again.

Aside from the dog, the house is amazingly quiet. There's no TV switched on, no radio, no sound of traffic. And there's definitely no Gwen. March had expected she'd have to argue constantly with her daughter; she'd imagined Gwen would want to sleep until noon or one, when she'd rise only to throw herself in an easy chair to complain, grouse, whine, and threaten, all the while eating cookies or frozen pizza, spreading crumbs on the rug and talking about teenage suicide statistics.

None of this has happened. When March wakes in the morning, Gwen is already gone, her bed in the sewing room neatly made, her cereal dish washed and drying on the dish rack that March will have to pack up today. She's been out for a walk, Gwen explains when she returns later in the day; she's been running, getting herself in shape. March wouldn't believe a word of it—Gwen is usually the most sedentary creature on earth; getting off the couch to search for the remote is often the most movement she manages to accomplish—but there's a rosy cast to the girl's skin when she comes back to the house, and a fine film of sweat on her forehead, all of which seems proof of her honesty.

With no distractions—no Gwen, no car, no one other than Susie calling on the phone—March should be done clearing out the house, but the work is going slowly, as if each trinket and kitchen utensil, every sweater and scarf were stuck in molasses. Now and then, March comes across some item which truly surprises her, and then she gets completely sidetracked. This morning, for instance, she found a box of matches from a restaurant called the Blue Dolphin, a small, family-run place down by Lamb's Cove, less than ten miles away. Seeing those matches, she remembered a night nearly thirty years earlier, an evening Mrs. Dale had off, but because taking care of children is not a job that's easily compartmentalized, as soon as Judith came home she went upstairs to check on March.

When she came to sit on the edge of March's bed, Judith Dale smelled of garlic and cologne, a combined scent that was both lemony and pungent. She had appeared so dreamy and young that March had scrambled to her knees to get a better look. Mrs. Dale's hair was curled, from the damp salt air at Lamb's Cove. She'd shown March this box of matches, with its smiling dolphin logo; she'd said this restaurant had the best shrimp scampi and the most fabulous cheesecake, and some grown-up drink called a mimosa that March has had a fondness for ever since hearing its beautiful name. Now, March realizes it was love that made the menu so special, and that Mrs. Dale's dinner partner that night was probably Bill Justice.

Though March is trying to divest, she has kept the box of matches, just as she has held on to one of her brother's blue ribbons from his high school debating team. She went out to the Marshes to visit him, but, exactly as the Judge had warned, Alan wouldn't open the door. In all honesty, she was relieved. What would she say to him after all these years? Why presume that she knows him? If you're disconnected from someone for a long enough time, does blood still commit you to one another? Does history, or fate? Alan is not the only one March has attempted to contact. Twice, she has phoned Hollis. She's embarrassed about it, she's mortified, yet she couldn't seem to stop herself. Both times she called, she felt completely possessed—some demon held the receiver, and dialed, and waited, and then, thank goodness, hung up. If she was giving herself a test, she has failed. Now that she's gone this far, she wants to keep calling. His voice is deeper than she remembers, and much more interesting than it should be.

"Take my advice," Susanna Justice had recommended when they went out to the bowling alley, which serves the best burgers, last night. "Go home before anything happens."

March had vowed she wouldn't tell Susie about the calls, but as soon as Gwen wandered off with two local girls Susie had introduced her to, March admitted she'd been phoning him.

"It's nothing," March vowed. "It's like a game."

"There are no games," Susie had insisted. "Other than Monopoly."

Susie is a big fan of Richard Cooper's, and she always has been. She's told herself that if she could find a man as good as Richard, she'd marry him tomorrow. But of course, she may have found exactly that in Ed Milton, the new police chief, and what does she go and do but cancel a date with him in order to have dinner with March at the bowling alley. As they dined, they had a perfect view of Gwen and the two girls from town, whose mothers March and Susie went to school with about a million years ago. The girls rolled one gutter ball after another, and from the look on Gwen's face, she was the only one who cared.

"Hollis is bad news, and he always has been," Susie said. How Hollis manages to get his way in this town never fails to amaze her, but he knows who to charm and who to pay off, and in the end, if he wants something—whether it's business zoning at the end of Main Street or the DPW to plow his properties first—he gets it. "You're going to be sucked in all over again."

"He's a whirlpool, is that what you're saying?" March had laughed. "Don't worry so much. I'm married, remember?"

"I remember," Susie had said, pointedly.

"Don't say the rest of that," March had warned.

"Fine."

"Because I do too, Susie. I remember real well."

Today, to spite Susanna or to prove something to herself, she phones Richard three times. But Richard is busy and distracted, and really, all he wants to know is when she's coming home.

"The end of the week," March promises, but already she's thinking she'd like to stay for Founder's Day, which celebrates the night when Aaron Jenkins ran over Fox Hill more than three hundred years earlier.

Gwen has heard all about Founder's Day from the girls who have befriended her, and now when they go for sodas at the Bluebird Coffee Shop, Lori and Chris assume the Founder's celebration is the reason Gwen is so intent on staying in Jenkintown. Those girls would never guess that Gwen rises before dawn so she can visit the horse down the road. They think she doesn't meet them in the evenings because she's afraid to walk across Fox Hill in the dark, but in fact, she has better things to do. She's down in the pasture when darkness falls, feeding a beautiful old horse some fallen apples and the sugar cubes she steals from the coffee shop.

Gwen has no idea that the man who owns the fence she sneaks under, who owns the grass beneath her feet and the horse whose mane she likes to braid, always knows when someone has trespassed. Hollis has found a piece of frayed rope, a makeshift rein he supposes, kept beside the tree stump. He has seen footprints in the frost. He never likes anyone on his property—what's his is his, after all—although when he first saw these signs he thought March might be his trespasser, and he felt truly exhilarated. He felt the way he used to when he'd play cards down in Florida and bluffed someone into letting him win.

Ever since March arrived, he has been keenly aware of her proximity. He goes to stand outside in the dark, cold morning with the knowledge that she is just down the road. Whenever he drives into town he is mindful that he could run into her anywhere—at the hardware store or waiting for a red light to change on Main Street. However it finally happens, she must come to him. That's the way it has to be; that's the way it will be. This is the reason Hollis is biding his time, no matter how difficult this is for him; it's why he stands there in the morning with his desire locked inside of him rather than rushing to knock on her front door. He's not some beggar. He's not some fool. It's the night that causes him problems; that is the time when he can no longer bear the way he feels. That's when he drives over to the hill. He makes sure to cut his lights and engine before she can notice his presence; he parks there and watches the house, the way he has, every now and again, for all these years.

Hollis no longer believes March is the trespasser who is wandering through his pastures. Whoever does leaves cigarette butts on the road and candy wrappers in the weeds. She's careless and thoughtless, nothing like March; a teenager probably, with some silly notion that fenced beasts should be set loose. Hollis is even surer of his theory when he notices that Hank has a flushed, distant look to him when he comes in for supper. On this day, Hank seems to be hurrying with his chores and he turns down an offer of food—a dead giveaway that something's wrong.

"Someone's been riding Tarot," Hollis says.

Hank is at the refrigerator, getting himself a can of soda; a pinkish tint spreads across the back of his neck as soon as Hollis mentions the horse. Bingo.

"Know anything about it?"

Hank opens his soda and waits for his pulse to slow down. "Nope," he says.

"Really?" Hollis's voice sounds flat; he doesn't give much away.

"Want me to check it out?" Hank doesn't even know why he's lying, except that he feels Hollis will ruin this for him if he finds out about the girl. He knows he owes Hollis. The fact that he's here at all, eating three meals a day at this kitchen table, is a measure of Hollis's charity. And yet he keeps his secret. He has, in fact, been watching the girl every evening, and each time he does, he falls for her a little bit more. What he feels for her is tearing him apart and keeping him together and, it appears, it is also turning him into a liar. "I can hang out tonight, and see if anybody shows up."

Hollis finishes his dinner—a bologna and cheese sandwich and a bag of chips—and brings his plate to the sink. "I'm impressed," he says coldly. "I didn't think you could lie right to my face."

"I don't know who she is." The one time Hank is dishonest, and he's caught—well, it figures. "That really is the truth."

"I'm not surprised, since you don't seem to know much of anything." Hollis washes his plate and stacks it on the drainboard. "Does she come from the village? From Route 22?"

Hank shakes his head. "From over the hill."

"Then I've got news for you," Hollis says. If Hank were paying more attention to Hollis's tone, he'd hear something rare—Hollis is actually pleased. "I know who she is."

They go up to the hill together. Twilight is coming earlier, and the dusk is no longer purple, but is instead that inky blue which is always a sign of colder weather to come. When they get to the very top, which looks out over all the pastures below, Hollis crouches down. Everything he sees, he owns. There's only one thing left, and he's about to get that too.

"I'll bet your little friend is staying at the house on Fox Hill."

There's something strange in Hollis's voice, but Hank is too wound up to notice. Hank nods at the road; sure enough, here comes the girl. "That's her."

She's wearing her black ski jacket and tight black jeans and heavy boots that make a clumping noise. This girl may be March's daughter, but she didn't inherit much from March, at least not in Hollis's opinion. She's nowhere near as pretty, and she's stupid as well. There she goes, ducking under the fence, heading for the old stump, where she searches for the rope Hollis confiscated and now has in his pocket. It's Richard she resembles, and maybe that's why Hollis feels such immediate distaste. Here is the reason March would not come back to him. Frankly, Hollis isn't impressed.

Gwen seems puzzled when she can't find the rope, but she climbs onto the stump anyway, then whistles.

"Jesus Christ." Hollis snorts. "She thinks she's calling a fucking dog. Look at her."

Down in the pasture, Gwen is unaware that she's being watched, but for some reason she feels nervous. This is her secret, and she doesn't want to share it. She needs to come up with a good excuse to stay on here. She'll say she's heard the high school in Jenkintown is great, so much better than the one she's been attending, or she's been involved with drugs back at home. She's already decided—she's not going back to where she was a major nothing, inside and out. Tonight, it's even colder than usual, but Gwen's made sure to wear the leather gloves she found in one of those boxes her mother is packing. She claps her hands and whistles again and the horse appears from the woods and trots right to her, as he always does. She leans close and whispers a greeting, while the horse, supremely pleased at being told how wonderful he is, noses for the carrots she keeps in her coat pockets.

Up on the hill, Hollis rises to his feet. He watches the girl pull herself onto the horse with no reins and no saddle and no idea, it would seem, of any danger.

"Well, there she is," he says. "March Murray's daughter. That makes her your cousin."

Cruelty never loses its flavor, at least not for Hollis. The look on Hank's face is exactly what Hollis expected: pure confusion.

"That's what she is to you," Hollis goes on. "Your first cousin."

They go down the hill in the dark. What is Hank supposed to do now? Stop thinking about her twenty-four hours a day because they are somehow related? Well, he can't do that. He's not going to do that.

"Get off," Hollis calls when they get to the fence.

Gwen and the horse, who have been walking through the meadow, stop dead when they hear his voice.

"Right now," Hollis shouts.

Startled, Gwen quickly swings her legs over and gets down. The horse hovers behind her.

Hollis tosses the rope to the girl. "Put it around his neck and lead him out." He swings open the gate.

As far as Gwen is concerned this guy has a lot of nerve to boss her around, but the horse seems to belong to him, so she does as she's told.

"That's dangerous," Hank says. "She can't lead Tarot."

Gwen shoots Hank a look of what she hopes is contempt, but says nothing. He's gorgeous, she sees that—she'd have to be dead not to. If she was at a mall with her friends back home, they'd probably follow him anywhere. But it's different here, and Gwen feels as if something major were at stake.

"Take him down the road, then into the barn. It's too cold to keep him out all night anymore."

Now that her ability has been put in question by the boy, Gwen ignores the way the older, bossy guy is ordering her around. She's dealt with bullies before, and she knows you can't win an argument with his type. She leads the horse down the road, and Tarot follows, mild as milk, all the way back to Guardian Farm. The air is silvery and sharp; Gwen is shivering, but she wouldn't think of complaining, not about the cold and not about how far they have to walk to reach the Farm.

All the dogs begin to bark when they reach the driveway.

"If you want to ride this horse, that's fine," Hollis says. "But make sure you use the right equipment, and put him back in his stall when you're done."

Hank is shocked by this magnanimity, it's not at all like Hollis but he isn't about to ask any questions. Gwen is trying her best to keep her euphoria in check. It will be just as if the horse really belonged to her.

"Show her where to put him," Hollis tells Hank.

Gwen follows Hank to the barn, and waits while he opens the door to the first stall.

"He's hard to get in there," Hank warns. "He broke one of the dogs' backs last year, so watch out."

Gwen pats the horse, and Tarot goes into his stall, as calm as any lamb.

"How did you do that?" Hank asks, following her out of the barn.

"Wouldn't you like to know." Gwen uses her snippiest tone.

"That's why I asked," Hank says, confused. "I would like to know."

Gwen laughs. "Are you for real?"

She's ready to laugh again, but then she sees the way he's looking at her. He's extremely real, she sees that now, and he's not like anyone she's ever met before. Most people are so guarded, but what he feels is right there in his face. He's not hiding his interest in her, and what Gwen doesn't know is that he couldn't hide it even if he tried.

"Let's go," Hollis says. He's in the truck with the engine running, that same old pickup of Mr. Cooper's Hollis refuses to get rid of, though he could surely afford far better. "I'll give you a ride home." Hank and Gwen both approach the truck, which gives Hollis a chuckle. This boy's got it bad. "You don't need a ride home," Hollis tells Hank, who's hanging around this girl like a lovesick pup, and is left to mope in the driveway when they make the turn onto the road.

The truck smells like gasoline and it rattles when it goes over inclines and through ditches. All the way to Fox Hill, Hollis asks Gwen questions. She figures it's like an interview. After all, she'll be responsible for his horse. No, she doesn't know how long they're staying, and her father isn't with them, he's a professor with too many deadlines to be here, and all her mother's been doing is looking through mementos from the past.

The way Hollis sees it, this girl is going to assist in keeping March in town until they're together again. She's going to be his little helper, and she won't even know it. She wants that old horse? Fine. Let her have it, if that's what it takes to get March to stay.

When they get to the top of the hill, and the house is in sight, Hollis pulls over. "I'd appreciate it if you gave your mother a message from me," he says, in that strange, inhuman voice he's got.

"Sure," Gwen says. This guy gives her the creeps, but she supposes that the least she can do in return for riding his horse is to deliver his stupid message.

"Tell her I've been waiting." Hollis nods at his own words. Sometimes he feels as though he's been waiting forever, as if it were his occupation or his trade.

"You being?"

"She'll know. Just tell her."

Gwen nods and opens the rusty truck door. She doesn't like this guy one bit, plus she's freezing; once she's out of the car she races up to the house.

"Don't tell me you've been running all this time," March says when Gwen comes through the door. She's been worried sick and has already called Lori's and Chris's moms, and has had to hash over old times from their school days even though all she wanted to know was whether or not they'd seen Gwen.

"Actually, I've been riding."

"Don't get funny with me."

"Down the street. At that farm place. There's a horse I've been riding."

March has been sitting on the rag rug in front of the fire, sorting through old picture postcards her father mailed home from business trips. Now, she stands to face her daughter.

"You've been going there? Without permission?"

"I got permission." Gwen doesn't know why her mother has to be so upset about this. "The guy over there said I can ride whenever I want."

"Oh, really." March has the funniest feeling along the backs of her knees, of all places. It's as though she has pins and needles, only worse. She felt certain he would never come to her, he has too much pride for that. She told herself all she had to do to be safe was avoid him, but maybe that isn't the case.

"He told me to say he's been waiting."

Gwen watches her mother carefully. After all, March could forbid her to go see Tarot—she knows the horse's name now, and it suits him—and then she'd have to have a major temper tantrum, which she's really in no mood for. But for once, March doesn't seem concerned about possible dangers.

"Did he say anything else?" March asks.

"Yes, and all of it was boring."

For as many questions as March asks, Gwen does nothing more than shrug; finally she excuses herself and goes up to bed. Sister is at the door, scratching to be let out, refusing to be ignored, so March goes to the closet for the leash and clips it on. "Don't you dare bite me," she warns the dog, when it curls its lip.

By now, the moon is in the center of the sky. She made her choice years ago, didn't she? She left and didn't come back, not even when he called her, and yet here she is, on this dark night; here, and noplace else. There are still bullet holes in some of the apple trees in the orchard from the time open hunting was declared, the year that Hollis left. Six hundred and fifty-two foxes were killed in a single season. Boys hung fox tails from the handlebars of their bicycles and Hal Perry, who owns the Lyon Cafe, offered a free draft and a photograph taken and hung on the wall to anyone who brought in two pelts in the same day. Every once in a while, a fox is sighted and people get all fired up; the story always gets printed up in *The Bugle,* and for a night or two, the rabbits may tremble, but the very next evening they're back, fearless as ever.

Tonight, for instance, there's a rabbit calmly chewing chives, who doesn't budge when March comes out of the house. Sister starts barking and tugs at the leash. When the dog realizes it can't get to the rabbit, it sits down and whines. The dog sounds pitiful, and so March, who's been cooped up all day and now feels light-headed just thinking about Hollis, does something she really shouldn't. She reaches down and unclasps Sister's leash. Sister looks up at March, then takes off after the rabbit, who darts into a thicket of wild raspberries.

Looking up, March feels as though she's never seen the moon before, or at least, not for a very long time. She walks along the road a bit, but it's only when she reaches the crest of the hill that she sees a truck pulled over onto the side of the road. March holds the dog's leash in one hand. She can still hear Sister running after the rabbit. She can hear branches snapping in the woods.

Hollis would never sit in a beat-up old truck with the headlights turned out. He would never come to her like this. He'd wait for her; he always did. It must be a stranger parked there, and knowing she's being watched makes March turn and hurry back into the yard. Sister is already up on the porch, yipping to be let in. It won't be until tomorrow that March will find the rabbit on the far side of the garden, its neck bitten through by the terrier's sharp teeth. That's when she'll have the nerve to walk up and inspect the roadside, but of course in the morning the truck will be gone, and there won't be a single sign to show that he's ever been here, except for the tire tracks which lead directly to Guardian Farm.

PART TWO

TEN

ON FOUNDER'S DAY THE WIND RISES UP
from the Marshes and shakes the leaves from the
trees. The night is so black it seems to Gwen that
if she reaches into the air she'll wind up with a
fistful of coal dust. She let Lori and Chris talk her
into going to the dance at the high school, and
now her mom and Susie Justice have driven her
over to Lori's house, even though Gwen would
much rather be down at the barn; blustery
weather like this makes Tarot nervous, and now
she'll be worrying about him all night long.

Actually, she has a good excuse to stay home;
her teachers have sent a huge manila folder

full of school work she has to make up, since she's been absent for two weeks. But Gwen's mom seemed so excited that Gwen was doing something as normal as going to a school dance, what could she do? Gwen has to act the good girl and do as she's told if she wants to achieve her goal: stay in town and buy Tarot. This objective has caused her to go easy on the eye makeup and spiked-up hair; it's the reason why she's heading into the windy night with two girls she's not even sure she likes very much, en route to a high school she doesn't even attend.

"My father's in there," Chris says casually as they pass the Lyon Cafe, which is overflowing with people in various stages of inebriation. "Drunk as a skunk."

Chris is seriously pretty, with a rope of blond hair and creamy, pale skin, but now she goes right up to the window and makes a supremely goofy face. Lori and Gwen both peer in through the glass as well, and that's when Gwen sees that Hollis is inside. Only Hollis isn't at the bar, where there's a party atmosphere and bowls of plum pudding, supposedly the Founder's favorite treat. He's over at the last table, drinking a Coke, speaking to no one. He glances up, and maybe he sees the girls peering in the window, but if he does he looks right through them. Seeing him from this distance, Gwen realizes that he really is handsome, surprisingly so, because there's definitely something peculiar about him; Gwen is always relieved to find he's not around when she goes to get Tarot. He seems cold-blooded, somehow; someone you'd want to avoid.

"Let's get out of here," Gwen says.

"Definitely," Lori agrees.

They stagger through the night, tilting into the wind, their coats blowing out behind them; they can't help but laugh at the effort it takes to walk two blocks.

"Oh, God, look at us," Lori cries after they've reached the high school and have gone to the girls' room to comb their hair. It takes a while before they're ready to present themselves to the world at large, and Gwen decides to put on mascara and eyeliner, although in her opinion, nothing will make her look good compared to beautiful Chris and trendy Lori, who is wearing a short red velvet dress and silver beads threaded through her dark braids.

The gym has been hung with crepe paper, like something out of the fifties, and it's so noisy you have to yell to be heard.

"I can't believe it," Chris says. "Hank's actually here."

Gwen looks toward the refreshment table and there he is, with a group of the boys who are clearly the most popular, since they all look so pleased with themselves. All except for Hank, who appears to be rather anxious, and who is wearing a new white shirt he got at the discount shop in the basement of the Red Apple supermarket and boots he spent over an hour polishing.

"He never comes to these things," Chris confides. "He's always working or something."

At first, Gwen and Hank avoided each other whenever they ran into each other at the barn, but they don't do that anymore; now, they actually talk. Usually, it's impossible for Gwen to let down her guard, but it was too hard not to be nice to Hank. He said they were related somehow, which made it okay for her not to be nasty. Though she'd never admit this, Gwen feels good just being around him, and this is not the way she ordinarily feels when confronted with human life forms. But all that may change. Hank may prove himself to be nothing more than another jerk, after all. Here he comes, and Gwen is fairly certain that Chris is the one he's after.

"I didn't know you were going to be here." He's walked right up to Gwen, and either he's nervous or he's choking, because he keeps putting his hand into his collar, as though he needed more air.

Gwen glares at him fiercely. What is his comment supposed to mean? That she doesn't belong here?

"I thought you hated people." Hank goes for a joke, but it falls flat. Gwen blinks her heavily mascaraed eyes and looks blank.

"Well, anyway," Hank says—what the hell, he has nothing to lose—"you look great."

Chris and Lori elbow each other, and then they elbow Gwen too, who suddenly seems to be dead on her feet. She looks like hell, with her horrible haircut, a pair of black jeans, and an old white sweater she borrowed from her mother. What is wrong with Hank? Is he stupid or blind or what? No one says things like that, especially not if they mean it, and from the way Hank is staring at her, he appears to be sincere.

"Thanks," Gwen says. "So do you."

She must be out of her mind. She has never been this civil in her entire life. She'd never say a thing like that to a guy, and certainly not in front of her friends. But here she is, smiling, agreeing when he asks her to dance. As soon as he circles his arms around her, she feels like she's having a heart attack. She doesn't even know if this is possible for someone her age, but by the end of the dance she's certain that she'd better take a break.

"I have to go outside," she tells Hank, and who can guess what he thinks, although he follows her through the door and stands there watching while she takes a few deep breaths of fresh air.

They've both left their coats inside the gym, but they don't notice the low temperature or the wind from the Marshes. The weird thing is, Gwen had sex with her last two boyfriends on their first dates, if fucking someone in his father's car can be considered a date. She's always been wild, she's never given a damn, and she's the one who's currently a wreck. Her hands are sweating, and her heart continues to go crazy; she's in the middle of thinking she might as well give up, just leave the dance and walk home by herself, when he kisses her. He kisses her for a really long time, and even though her heart is still pounding, she no longer feels she is suffering from some sort of attack. She's seen the way he looks at her when she comes to take Tarot out to the field; all along she's been wondering if he was attracted to her or if he was merely an idiot. She's genuinely shocked by the depth of her pleasure now that she knows the answer.

"Do you want to go back inside?" Hank asks.

They can hear music playing and there's a wash of light when Lori and Chris open the door and call out for Gwen. Gwen shakes her head no; she doesn't want to go back. She waits on the bleachers while Hank goes in for their coats.

"I told your friends you were sick," Hank says when he comes back.

"Good one," Gwen says. "Not that they'll believe it."

They walk back to Fox Hill together, taking the long way, but that's all right with them. They can't wait to be on a dark, empty road and out of the village, which is so crowded for the Founder's Day celebration. They pass right by Dimitri's, the restaurant where March and Susanna Justice are having dinner, but they skitter by like leaves, and even though March is looking out the window, she doesn't see them.

"Did we really order all this?" March asks when more food arrives.

Their waitress, Regina, has already brought over lasagna and baked stuffed shells, and now she's delivering the crab-and-mushroom pizza they ordered.

"We're pigs," Susie says, and she asks for a second bottle of wine.

Although March would never have placed her, she and Susie went to school with Regina, who recognized March as soon as she walked through the door.

"I don't remember anyone," March says when Regina has gone off for their wine.

"Yeah, well, you had one person on your mind and he took up a lot of space."

Now March recalls why she hated Susie when they were kids.

"You're judging me. It must run in the family."

"I'm not at all. Okay, I used to, but I'm not anymore. I'm only saying that you were in a Hollis-induced fog." Susie sprinkles Parmesan cheese onto a piece of pizza. "You never seemed to notice that my father was over at your house constantly."

For several days, March and Susie have been dodging around this subject, on the phone and in person; it's definitely not a comfortable topic for either of them.

"He was always at Fox Hill, allegedly on business." Susie sighs. "Why do you think I hated you?"

"I thought I hated you." March sticks out her tongue and Susie laughs, but then Susie looks sad and she pushes her plate away. "You knew about them all the way back then?" March asks.

"I knew right after your father died. My dad kept going over there, every single night, for weeks. Maybe he was in love with her for ages before that, who knows? Maybe they'd already been lovers for years. But I knew because one night I saw him when he came home from your house. It was about ten o'clock and I was supposed to be in bed, but I was looking out the window. My mom was downstairs listening to the radio; she was used to him being out late. He turned off the headlights of his car; then he got out and he walked over to the roses, which were especially beautiful that year, and he ducked his head to smell them, and I knew. He looked like someone else entirely, standing there. He looked like someone who was in love with a woman he couldn't have. I cried myself to sleep, because I knew."

"No wonder we hated each other," March says. She reaches across the table and takes Susie's hand.

"All I can say is, I'm glad my mother never found out." Susie squeezes March's hand, then withdraws it so she can get a Kleenex out of her purse. "I've really tried not to be angry at him, but I don't think I could have been so generous if my mother had known."

"Have you ever talked to him about it?"

"Him? My father?" Susie wipes her eyes, then blows her nose. "Are you crazy? You don't talk to my father, you listen."

Regina brings over desserts—on the house: chocolate mousse with sugar cookies wedged in along the side of the bowl, and a helping of plum pudding, in honor of the Founder. Regina sits down with them for a minute to talk about old times and discuss her pet project—the Harvest Fair down at Town Hall. Somehow, before Regina goes back to work, March finds herself announcing that she would consider running a booth that will raise funds for the children's section of the library.

"Why did you do that?" Susie asks, when they've gotten their coats and paid their bill—with a thirty percent tip for Regina. They've left behind half-portions of everything they ordered, and are stuffed all the same. "You won't still be here for the Harvest Fair. If you want my opinion, you should go home right now."

"Well, thanks," March says as they go outside.

The wind has died down a bit, but it's still a raw night.

"When you come back to a town like this, people think you're staying," Susie says.

March wraps her scarf around her throat. "I don't care what people think."

"Okay, forget people. How about Richard?"

"Who?" March teases.

"You're deranged." Susie links her arm through March's. "You'd better get serious."

"I've been serious for so long I can't stand it." If she hadn't been so serious, would she have agreed to come back to him, even though she was in the seventh month of her pregnancy? By then, she'd already lined up a babysitter and a diaper service; she had registered in a new mothers' exercise class. Could she have booked a flight to Logan anyway? Could she have tried? "I need a break from my life, that's what I've realized."

This, of course, is what she's been saying to Richard—it's only a break; it's nothing, only a little time apart.

"The definition of a break is a rupture," Richard said to her, only yesterday, an answer which, of course, drove March completely crazy.

"What if Richard jumped on a plane? What if he arrived in the middle of the night and said you had to leave with him?"

"He's taking his graduate students into the field next week, and he'd never disappoint them. Even if he wasn't scheduled to do that, he wouldn't appear in the middle of the night. He wouldn't tell me what to do. Richard's not like that."

"Exactly," Susie says. "I should have married him."

They head for Susie's truck, parked down the street from the Lyon Cafe, which is all but overflowing.

"What a party," March says.

"Every drunk in town. Except for Alan. This is Hollis's turf."

"Thanks for sharing that."

March gets into Susie's truck and slams the door. Just hearing his name stirs everything up for her. It's even colder in the truck than it is out on the street. March turns up her collar; she's had too much wine with dinner, she realizes that now.

Susie comes to sit behind the wheel. "Look, if you want to kid yourself, fine. If you want to put something over on Richard, okay. But don't think you're going to fool me. You're here because of Hollis. I don't understand it, but I guess I don't have to. Maybe you need to see him, to make certain he doesn't mean anything to you."

"I'm glad that being a reporter for *The Bugle* entitles you to psychoanalyze me."

March opens the door, and without a look back, she heads off down the street. She's furious, but when she really thinks about it, she's angry because Susie is right. March is drawn to the Lyon Cafe, only a few steps away now, in hopes of seeing Hollis. Susie knows her far too well, although March herself isn't certain whether or not she'll really have the courage to act on her impulse, until Susie honks her horn, trying to get her attention. That's when March walks through the door.

When March was growing up, the Lyon was a place other people's parents went to, and only occasionally. It was an embarrassment to be a regular here, something no one wanted to admit. The draw of the Lyon certainly wasn't the decor, which is still Naugahyde and wood paneling, with three deer heads attached to the wall above the rest rooms and public telephones. You came here to get drunk, simple as that.

Tonight, the place is packed; there isn't a table to be had, so March makes her way to the bar, excusing herself politely, and when that does no good, finally pushing her way through. She signals to the bartender, and once she gets his attention, shouts her request for a glass of red wine.

It takes a while to adjust to the noise level. There's a Celtics game on the TV above the bar, and a loud, cheerful argument going on right next to her—something to do with borrowing a motorboat—which may well turn nasty as the night progresses. There's a jukebox going too, although all anyone can hear of the music are the drums and the bass, pounding. March grabs a stool when one of the guys next to her finally leaves, and at last, she can sit down and look around. Maybe Susie's wrong; March can't imagine Hollis in this drunken crowd, playing darts or debating the merit of the Celtics' back court.

Susie has come into the Lyon, and she easily makes her way to the bar, since she knows most of the people drinking here tonight. "Hey, Fred," she says to the bartender. "I'll have what she's having. What is it you're having?" she asks March. "An anxiety attack? Sheer lunacy?"

"Red wine." March grins.

"That's what I'll have," Susie tells Fred. "You know," she says to

March, "if you had your own car, I would have left you here. For spite."

"You could, you know," March says. "I'm perfectly fine. And besides, he's not even here."

"Oh, yes he is." Susie nods to a corner. "He's right there."

Be careful what you wish for, Judith used to say to March all the time. But it seems that March has already decided not to be careful. At least, not tonight.

"At the last table."

He's got his chair propped up against the wall, and although there are five other men sharing the table, he doesn't appear to be in the same universe. Certainly, he's not listening to those men. He's been watching March Murray ever since she walked through the door.

March turns away so quickly that she knocks over her glass, then has to wipe at the spilled wine with a cocktail napkin.

"It's not too late to leave," Susie urges.

March would have missed him entirely if he hadn't been pointed out to her, but now that he has been, she realizes that the difference between him and the other men at his table, most of whom are employed by the Department of Public Works, is not so much in what can be seen. Those men are also wearing old boots and jeans, and like him, they haven't bothered to remove their coats, since people who come to the Lyon like to pretend they won't be staying, even if they've settled in for the night. The difference is that the air around him seems charged, perhaps by anger, by heat and light. The difference is the way he can look at someone, the way he's staring at her right now. One look from him is more substantial than the wooden bar she's leaning her elbows upon. It's realer than the bottles of whiskey lined up behind the counter; realer than the pull of fabric as Susie tugs on her jacket.

"You don't want to finish this game," Susie shouts, because the argument next to them concerning the motorboat is getting more heated. "Let's get out of here."

At the moment, March doesn't need much convincing. She's shaking, she really is. She's putting something on the line, and she's frightened by her own actions. Wanting to see Hollis and actually being in the same room with him are two different things entirely. Now that they've decided to leave, it's not easy trying to make their way to the door. The place is packed, incredibly crowded and smoky. Susie is waylaid by Bert Murphy, the sports editor at *The Bugle,* and while Susie is enmeshed in some newspaper gossip, March looks back at the far end of the room where Hollis had been sitting, in spite of her resolve to get out of the Lyon with no damage done. But he's not there, and the effect of his absence is that her heart drops into her stomach, where it stays until she realizes that he's walking right to her.

It is sometimes possible to look at a person and see inside, although this happens so rarely it's always a shock, like a form of electricity traveling from one soul to another. It can only be glimpsed for an instant, but in that instant you can see the core of a person, even in the middle of a crowded barroom, as he comes up beside you, while the jukebox is playing a country-western song you've never heard before and will never forget. It happens quickly—seeing all that hurt and disappointment—it's as fast as a breath drawn and released. Just as fast, he closes up; you couldn't get inside Hollis for anything now. Not with a hammer or a chisel; not by begging on your knees.

"I never thought I'd see you here," Hollis says. For some reason, March can hear him perfectly above the din. "Not your kind of place, is it?"

"Maybe it is," March says. "It's not as bad as I thought it would be." She wishes she had thought to wear something other than this dreadful black sweater and an old pair of jeans; she wishes she had combed her hair. "I hear you're letting my daughter ride one of your horses."

"Is that your daughter?" Hollis acts as though he hadn't the faintest idea.

"As if you didn't know." Why is it that he still has to look so good? What gives him the right to talk to her with such arrogance, as though after all these years he continued to be the most important thing in her universe, the single shining star?

"Did she tell you I was still waiting?"

"Oh, sure." March tries to be lighthearted, but that's not the way she feels. "And I'll bet you never looked at another woman again."

People are pushing by them and there's absolutely no privacy, so when Hollis nods March follows him over to a less populated space, beneath the mounted deer heads. The only people who crowd them over here are those weaving past on their way to the rest rooms. One guy, who's quite loaded, greets Hollis and thanks him for his support on the town council, but Hollis doesn't even acknowledge the councilman's existence, and March is so distracted that if she were ever asked to identify the guy in a court of law, she wouldn't be able to. She didn't even glance at him. Standing there, she can feel the reverberation of the jukebox in her legs. Susie is right—she's crazy. She's completely deranged.

"You're the one who didn't wait," Hollis says.

Over by the door, Susie spots March and she waves like mad, but Hollis has moved closer, blocking Susie from view.

"Me?" March says. "Why didn't you write or call after you left here? Why didn't you come back for me?"

She's done it without thinking, and there's no way to take those words back. She should have said, *Screw you, I waited plenty, I waited years, and even that was too long.* Instead, she has admitted some sort of defeat; she can tell because Hollis still smiles the way he used to whenever he won.

"You went to California," Hollis reminds her. "You were the one who got married."

"You got married too," March reminds him right back.

Hollis drinks from a can of Coke, which is warm by now, not that the taste bothers him.

"That was nothing," he says.

"It was definitely something."

Hollis comes closer. "No," he tells her. "It wasn't. I got married because you wouldn't leave him. That baby was more important to you than I was."

"It wasn't like that," March begins.

"It was exactly like that." He's even closer now; March can feel the heat from his body against hers. "Or maybe I was more important but you couldn't admit it."

Susie has finally joined them; jostled by the crowd, she's taken forever to get across the room. Now, she leans against the wall and observes Hollis in what she believes to be a nonjudgmental manner.

"Fancy meeting you here," she says.

"Hey, Sue." He nods without interest. She's a bitch who's never been on his side; he doesn't intend to pretend otherwise.

"I was telling March how Alan can't come here, not even on Founder's Day, because you frequent the place."

"Oh, yeah?" Hollis gives March a look. He's extremely pleased; first March admits how much he hurt her, and now Susie reveals that she and March had been discussing him. Unless Hollis is mistaken, and he doesn't believe he is, the only reason March came to the Lyon was to look for him. She came to him.

"Where couldn't you go because of Alan? Let's see. The dump? The liquor store on Route 22?"

A bitch, just like he thought.

"Alan made his choices," Hollis says.

"That's crap." Susie is getting all self-righteous, but she can't seem to stop herself. "He decided to lose everything that was ever important to him—have it all taken away—so he could drink himself to death in a shack? Some choice."

"You feel so bad for him?" Hollis says. "Go visit him, Sue. I bet he'd love to celebrate Founder's Day with you."

"Fuck you," Susie says. Her cheeks are bright red.

"I'm shocked." Hollis shakes his head, but he's smiling. It's so easy to rile people like Susanna Justice; they're like push-button dolls.

"I mean it," Susie tells him. "Fuck you."

"Susie," March pleads. Hollis and Susie were always like this; you couldn't keep them in the same room for more than a few minutes before they started in on each other.

"I think I'll have to be the one guy in town to pass that offer by," Hollis says.

"Are you staying here?" Susie Justice asks March. "Because I'm leaving." Susie already has her keys in her hand, and she jangles them like a bell. She takes a good look at March. "You're going to stay, aren't you?"

"I'm having one more drink." March is making certain not to glance over at Hollis. "That's it."

Susie leans forward, so she can whisper. "You're insane. I hope you realize that. Be smart when you leave. Call Ken Helm for a ride. Don't do this all over again."

"She never liked you," March says as they watch Susie make her way to the door.

"Not one bit," Hollis says. "You did, though."

March looks away.

"You still do," Hollis tells her.

"Oh, really?" March laughs. She's always been surprised by his vanity and his pride. With anyone else she'd be repelled, but with Hollis emotions were so rare that whenever one showed, March couldn't help but be charmed.

"I knew you'd come back, but I thought I might be eighty before you got here, hobbling around like Jimmy Parrish," Hollis says, nodding to an old man at the bar.

What nerve, March thinks. "Believe me. I've done perfectly fine without you."

March's voice is cold; in another instant, she'll stomp away, as she sometimes did when she was a girl. Hollis must sense this, because he puts his hand on her arm.

"Well, I haven't," he says. "Not without you."

He waits till that sinks in, then lets go of her. If she's going to walk away, she's going to do it now. But instead, she goes on looking at him. And then he knows, just as he's always known. At the core, they're identical. People who didn't know the family often judged them to be brother and sister. It was their dark eyes. *Darker than midnight*, that's what people used to say to their faces. *Black as whatever hole he crawled out of*, they used to whisper when they thought Hollis couldn't hear.

As the hour grows later, the clientele of the Lyon has become more disorderly. Conversations are incoherent; misunderstandings have begun to arise. Before long, there is sure to be a brawl, as there is at every Founder's Day celebration. The bar is now filled past capacity, and people keep right on coming. There is Regina, the waitress from Dimitri's, who waves when she sees March. There's Larry Laughton and his wife, Harriet, who own the lingerie shop, and Enid Miller, who works at the library and can hush small children with a single look, and Mimi Frank, who styled so many heads today at the Bon Bon that she has a perfect right to down a few beers.

There are a dozen boys and girls that Hollis and March went to school with, all grown-up and drunk as can be, but March doesn't notice any of them. Hollis is leaning toward her—he has to in order to be heard above the din, or at least, that's what March is telling herself. Surely, he's not doing it solely to get close to her; that's all in her mind. Her extremely warped mind, since she's got everything to lose and nothing to gain. She tries to remind herself of that, the life she leads, the responsibilities she has, and yet when he says, "Let's get out of here," she nods as if she were a rational woman. She lets him grab her hand so he can lead her through the crowd.

The people they pass by are enjoying the party; they're not bothering to think of tomorrow or even today. But that doesn't mean several women who've set out to have a good time don't notice what's going on. Mary Anne Chilton elbows Janice Melnick, and over at the bar, Alison Hartwig turns away when she sees Hollis and March together and she orders another whiskey sour. These are just a few of the women who know that when Hollis drives, he keeps the windows in the truck rolled down, no matter how raw the weather. If he can't take you back to your place—if you're married, or living with someone, or if you and the kids have been forced to move back in with your mother—he'll bring you to Olive Tree Lake, and park in a spot where it's so overgrown you can't see the stars.

But any of these women would be foolish to think that being acquainted with a man's habits or having sex with him in a parked truck is the same thing as knowing him. They don't know Hollis, and they never will. They wouldn't even guess, for instance, that Hollis actually goes around and opens the door of the truck for March. He's parked on the far side of Main Street, beside the Founder's statue, which for tonight's celebration someone has dressed with an olive wreath on his stone head and a long, flowing cape tied over his granite shoulders. March touches the Founder's cold knee for luck, the way all the children in town do. She knows that she'll think about this moment when Hollis opened the door to his truck for her, over and over again. She'll remember the stars and the feel of granite. This, after all, is the instant when she did the exact right or wrong thing, depending on what happens next. Will she wonder if she was thinking straight? Will she guess the orange moon above affected her decision, or was it the cold weather, or the way he looked at her, or the wind that was shaking the trees?

You build your world around someone, and then what happens when he disappears? Where do you go—into pieces, into atoms, into the arms of another man? You go shopping, you cook dinner, you work odd hours, you make love to someone else on June nights. But you're not really there, you're someplace else where there is blue sky and a road you don't recognize. If you squint your eyes, you think you see him, in the shadows, beyond the trees. You always imagine that you see him, but he's never there. It's only his spirit, that's what's there beneath the bed when you kiss your husband, there when you send your daughter off to school. It's in your coffee cup, your bathwater, your tears. Unfinished business always comes back to haunt you, and a man who swears he'll love you forever isn't finished with you until he's done.

As they drive through town, March watches Hollis carefully; everything about him is both completely familiar and absolutely alien. When she knew him he didn't have these lines in his face, and the nervous cough he seems to have now. She thinks of the moment when she first saw him, the way he squinted his eyes in the sun, how dark his hair was, how ready he was to run. It is that boy who is beside her in the pickup truck. That boy who kisses her when they stop at a red light. March is nearly forty; beneath the drugstore tint she has those same gray streaks plaited through her hair which appeared the winter he went away, but this boy doesn't seem to mind. He wants her not only for who she is, but for who she was: The girl who never got over him. The one who knew him inside out.

The women at the Lyon can only imagine how deep Hollis's

kisses are, since he never kisses any of them, at least not on the mouth. His embrace is hot and greedy, exactly the way March remembers. When the light turns to green March pulls away. She has always considered herself a loyal sort of person, but loyal to whom? Richard knew what he was getting into when he married her. It was Hollis back then, and maybe it still is. Maybe she's no longer a woman with everything to lose. She's a girl again. She's March Murray, whose father is everyone's favorite lawyer, whose big brother is lazy and drinks too much. She's the one with dark hair and too much confidence, who does whatever she's not supposed to when no one's looking, when no one's around.

"I've been waiting a long time," Hollis says. "That much is true."

He smiles, that same predatory grin which always frightened other people, but only served to convince March that she knew him best of all. The difference between a lion and a lamb, some might suggest, is in the naming, not in the beast itself. Both are warm-blooded—isn't that a fact? Both close their eyes when they settle down to sleep for the night.

As they turn onto the rutted dirt road, Hollis has to switch on the wipers to keep wet leaves from sticking to the windshield. There are tornadoes of leaves, and fallen branches are scattered across the road. It's getting colder by the minute; it's the sort of night when pumpkins will freeze on the vine, and grapes will turn hard and become far too bitter to use for jelly or pies. It's a night when any sparrow or dove foolish enough to nest in this town for the winter will realize a mistake has been made, and survival will depend not on skill but on plain blind luck.

All over town tonight, the wind will drive women from their beds. They'll think of their first true love and search through their jewelry boxes for trinkets—gold lockets, ticket stubs, strands of hair. March would be one of those women, but instead she's here, on the road where there were once so many foxes. If truth be told, she's been here all this time, in this dark and windy place, like a ghost trapped inside the location of her memory.

Hollis pulls over beside the quince bushes, where he parked the other night when he watched March walk the dog. He turns the key in the ignition, and once he does that the wind sounds ferocious. They used to hide and do this whenever they had the chance: pretend there was no one else in the world. Hollis has his arms around her, beneath her coat. He begins to kiss her, the way he used to, but before March can respond, she hears a sound and pulls away. Someone is out on the porch.

"Shit," Hollis says. "What is she doing there?"

From this distance, Gwen looks like a girl March has never seen before. She's wearing her black jacket, but under the glow of the yellow porch light, she could be anyone. Gwen's face is flushed, but the color in her cheeks isn't from the cold. On this night, when the Founder ran over the hill, she seems to have fallen in love. She can't stop thinking about Hank—everything he said, everything he did. He held her hand all the way across the hill; before he left, he kissed her goodnight, and she can't get that kiss out of her mind. In truth, she hopes she never will.

"She's going inside," March whispers to Hollis as Gwen fumbles with the door. Once Gwen goes into the house, they wait for her to close the door, but instead she reappears with the dog. How surprisingly responsible. What bad timing.

"She's taking the dog for a walk," March says.

Hollis groans and leans his head against the seat.

March laughs, then leans close and kisses him. Who is the child here? Who is the reckless girl? She kisses him again and again, as if daring fate, as if she hadn't a care in the world.

"That's right," Hollis whispers to her, as if she were still that good girl she used to be, only too ready to please. "Give me more," he tells her.

Just then, Sister turns in the direction of the parked truck and barks, a long yip that is usually meant for rabbits. The dog is staring at the quince bushes, which March hopes can hide Hollis's truck from Gwen's view. Thankfully, Sister is on a leash, and Gwen gives the dog a tug in the other direction, back toward the house.

You have to go where you're taken, don't you? You have to follow where you're led. Don't think, don't stop, don't hesitate. Maybe this is destiny; it's the hand of fate against your skin, the love of your life. If there's a warning to be heard, March won't listen. She's like those foolish doves who have stayed on to nest in the chestnut tree this fall, and who will probably freeze to death before the New Year. She's kin to the rabbit who dared to cross Sister's path, then decided it might be best to lie silent, rather than break and run.

Hollis has his hand inside her jeans now; he's pushed her down so that her back is flat against the seat. She knows the way he likes it, as if love was a secret; or at least, that's the way he likes it with her. Other women, the ones from the Lyon, would say he prefers to get his business over with fast, and maybe it's just as well. He's so intense he can scare some women. Alison Hartwig fainted the first time Hollis fucked her, and now she calls him every day on the telephone, so she can hear his voice and imagine that he loves her before she hangs up.

All this time, March is the one Hollis has wanted. She's the one who made him miserable, and he hasn't forgotten that for a moment. Night after night, he's come here and parked in this same exact space, to stare at this house. Over and over again, he's anticipated the hour when she'd come back to him, and how good it would be to have her be the one to beg, but maybe he's waited too long. Maybe all that waiting has tainted things, and left his love with a sour taste. It's always been this way for Hollis; the more he has of something, the more he wants. Maybe he can never be satisfied, but he knows how to satisfy March; he's doing it right now, she's there at the edge as he moves his fingers inside her slowly. He doesn't stop when she tells him to, and then he stops just when she's about to come. He kisses her then, he leaves her longing for more; desperate is exactly the way he wants her.

By now, Gwen has unhooked the dog's leash and gotten herself a soda from the fridge. Maybe she's wondering why her mother's out so late, as she goes into the sewing room, where her bed is made up. Maybe she thinks she sees something, there behind the quince, when she looks through the window. On any other night, March would have worried about her daughter, alone in the house, but she can't think about that now. She's already agreeing to see Hollis tomorrow, and the next day, and the one after that. Sometimes love is like a house without any doors. It's a sky filled with so many stars it's impossible to see a single one. Out in the front yard, the mourning doves are chattering with the cold. Their pale gray feathers are no comfort in the wind, yet they stay. It's too late, after all; they made their choice at the end of summer. They'll just have to accept the consequences.

ELEVEN

EVERY WEDNESDAY AFTERNOON, AT THE
farmers' market held in the parking lot of the
library, Louise Justice buys fresh herbs. She always fixes her roast chicken the way the Judge
likes it, with sage and pepper and plenty of rosemary, for remembrance. In October, the weather
can be a tricky thing, but today it's warm and
sunny, with a wide blue sky that brings tears to
Louise's eyes. She knows everyone at the market,
and has for years. She waves at Harriet Laughton,
who's buying so much her grandchildren must be
coming up from Boston for the weekend. Funny
thing—in the sunlight Louise's own hands look

strange to her, with their brown spots and thin, papery skin. She can practically see right down to the bone.

There, on her right hand, she wears the opal her grandmother left to her, a gift she has come to believe has brought her bad luck. She's grown so convinced of this that she went down to that new lawyer in town, Janet Travis, and asked for an addendum to the will the Judge drew up for them. She wants the opal sold and the proceeds to go to the Firemen's Fund. She'll be damned if she leaves the dreadful thing to Susie.

No one in town would consider Louise to be unlucky, and she certainly would never reveal anything that might lead to this conviction. It's no one's business, is it, really? No one's but hers alone. She heads for the flats of marigolds Millie Hartwig is selling, making sure to avoid that old Jimmy Parrish, who seems to admire racehorses far more than he does human beings. Well, maybe he's got something there. When Louise was growing up, on Mount Vernon Street in Boston, she thought life was a fine and glorious thing. She believed that all her dreams would come true, and why not? She was spoiled and pretty and knew how to charm a man. She met the Judge at a Christmas party when she was sixteen and he was twenty, and aside from the times she's wanted to murder him, which are too numerous to count, she has always loved him. One man, for all these years. One man, who hasn't loved her back.

Louise has often wondered if Susie hasn't picked up on her unhappiness, for Louise's beautiful daughter has never married, and it seems she never will. Not that Susie hasn't had her share of boyfriends. You can't live in this town and not be aware that Susie has dated nearly every available man. Currently, she's seeing Ed Milton, the police chief, and of course Louise is not supposed to know about it, since Susie is a terribly private person, which is downright impossible in a town as small as this. Gossip is a strange thing; it's both silly and painful, and although people are careful not to talk in front of Louise, she has certainly felt its sting.

"Do not buy the cranberry-walnut tart."

Harriet Laughton has come up beside her.

"Too much sugar?" Louise guesses.

"Lard," Harriet informs Louise.

"I've cut out all sweets, anyway." Louise waves to Ken Helm, who does odd jobs for her and is over at the far end of the market, selling bundles of firewood. Louise and Harriet start to walk on together, but Louise spies some yarn and stops to riffle through the display basket. Soft lamb's wool, splendid stuff. She needs another skein to finish the blanket for Susie's Christmas present. Not that Susie needs her blanket to stay warm—from what Louise hears, Ed Milton is practically living at her place, buying Susie's groceries and walking her dogs. Well, good for Susie. Great for her.

"You'd never know what she was up to," Harriet says now. "From the innocent look of her."

Louise glances up and sees that Harriet is referring to March Murray, who's over at the bakery kiosk, reaching for one of the cranberry-walnut tarts. March laughs as she pays the vendor. With her dark hair loose, wearing old jeans, she looks like a girl.

"I hear they can't get enough of each other," Harriet whispers. "Just like the bad old days."

"I'm sure you've heard wrong," Louise says. She can discern a prim tone creeping into her voice. "March Murray is too smart a girl to fool around with the likes of him."

Louise sees a softening in Harriet's face, something like pity, which Louise never could stand. As if Louise didn't comprehend that love has nothing to do with intelligence or common sense. As if she was some fuddy-duddy who didn't know what was happening for all those years.

"I'm off," she tells Harriet, and she lets the yarn fall back into the basket. She'll get it next week, if it's still what she wants. "See you Thursday," she calls over her shoulder, for that is their bridge night and has been for thirty-two years. It was almost that long ago that she found out, and for all that time she has kept her mouth shut. She's done better than most well-trained prisoners of war, and in a way, she's proud of herself.

Still, October is always difficult for Louise. It was this time of year when she discovered the ring, a square emerald set in eighteen-karat gold, in the pocket of the Judge's overcoat. She remembers smiling when she opened the little plastic case from the jewelers in Boston, so sure was she that the ring was meant to be her birthday present in November. But for her birthday that year, the Judge gave her a bathrobe, peach silk, from Lord & Taylor. Nice, but no emerald. She waited then, for Christmas. She was sure the small package he placed beneath the tree contained the ring, but it was a thin, gold bracelet. Lovely, of course, but she has never worn it. That bracelet is in the back of her jewelry box, where it will remain.

Although she should get home and start dinner, Louise goes over to the bakery table. She's always had a soft spot for March Murray, that motherless child, that very foolish girl. Of course Louise has heard about March and Hollis renewing their relationship—it's all over town that they left the Lyon together on Founder's Day—but she certainly wouldn't want Harriet Laughton to be apprised that their reunion is anything more than gossip. For her part, Louise knows more about Hollis than she cares to. She was one of those people who thought Henry Murray was crazy to bring him home in the first place, since she'd been informed, via the Judge, that by the age of thirteen Hollis had been at Juvenile Hall over twenty times. His own family couldn't handle him, so what did Henry expect? Perhaps Louise's attitude concerning Hollis was a narrow one, but she still thinks she was right. No. She is certain that she was right. They should have left Hollis up in Boston, where he belonged.

"I guess you're not going to worry about calories today," Louise says as she comes up to March.

March has bought two of the tarts Harriet Laughton insists are baked with lard, and a bag of chocolate chip cookies. When she sees it's Louise beside her, March puts down her purchases so she can embrace her.

"I don't know what's wrong with me." March laughs. "I had an urge for all this." She looks beautiful in the thin sunlight; her skin is so fresh and she has that sweet, dizzy expression that women with secrets often possess.

Louise waits for March to pay for the baked goods, and that's when she sees the ring.

"Do you like it?" March has noticed Louise staring and now she holds up her hand. "It was Judith Dale's."

"Yes. I recognized it."

They are heading toward the parking lot now, and Louise simply ignores the pain in her side.

"What an incredible day," March says, staring up at the blue sky.

"Susie says you're staying longer than you'd originally planned," Louise says, tactfully, she hopes.

"There's so much to go through in that house. It's like sifting through the past."

March has always liked Louise, but now she wishes they hadn't run into each other. She doesn't want to talk to anyone. She doesn't want to think. She's going to have to tell Richard, and yet she can't. In the evenings, the phone rings and rings, but she doesn't answer. Instead, she calls his office at odd hours, when she knows he won't be there and she can leave cheerful messages. Well-meaning little reports which contain absolutely no personal information.

"That's what Susie says, there's a lot to be done." Louise will leave it at that. She doesn't need to have it all spelled out for her; she can tell what's going on from the look on March's face. She used to notice the same thing with the Judge sometimes, that identical dazed expression, half puzzled, half delirious, like a man who'd been struck by lightning and was somehow glad of it.

"Gwen has been getting her homework sent to her, but now she's after me to let her register for school here, and the craziest thing is, I'm seriously wondering if we should try it for a while."

Louise nods, although, actually, she feels like crying. She considers March to be a young woman, and she considers all young women to be fools. At twenty you're convinced you know everything, but forty is even worse; that's when you've realized no one can know everything, and yet when it comes to certain situations, you still believe yourself to be an absolute expert. When all is said and done, the weather and love are the two elements about which one can never be sure. That's what you learn at sixty, and, as it turns out, no one is ever surprised by this bit of news.

They've reached an ancient, battered Toyota parked in the last row. Louise waits while March throws open the hatchback and places her purchases inside.

"Ken Helm lent this to me. An old aunt of his used to drive it."

"Lucy Helm." Louise nods. Lucy Helm was known to be one of the worst drivers in town. People swore the old lady fell asleep at red lights.

"Maybe I'll stay around a little while longer," March says as she closes the hatchback. "If Gwen really wants to."

Poor girl, Louise thinks. The excuses one can make for love; the lies one tells.

"Well, if you need anything while you're here, all you have to do is call," Louise says.

"You're a doll."

March feels a surge of affection for Louise; she hugs her, but when March gets into the borrowed Toyota, she's shaking. She knows she's a liar. She's well aware that Gwen's infatuation with an old horse and with—according to Susie, who definitely has her sources—a boy who happens to be her first cousin is not what keeps March in Jenkintown. If anything, such variables should be driving her away. If March were her usual self, she'd be shocked at the possibility of Gwen dating a cousin. Instead, she's convinced herself it's puppy love, if that, and will quickly pass if left unchallenged.

She has to lie about what's really holding her here, even to herself. Only this morning, she lied her head off over waffles and coffee at the Bluebird's lunch counter. She actually kept a straight face while she told Susie she was trying to decide what to do next. Maybe a separation would be good for her and Richard's relationship, and although she'd been talking to Hollis on the phone, accepting that ride home from him hadn't led to anything. Why, she might even allow Gwen to sign up at the high school and finish out the semester.

Susie had sat there the entire time with her mouth puckered, as though she'd been eating lemons. For one thing, Susie had already run into Millie Hartwig, who works at the high school cafeteria, and Millie had informed Susie that March Murray's daughter had registered for classes. For another, Susie couldn't help but notice there were love bites all up and down March's neck, which March herself didn't realize until she went out to her borrowed car to drive home and caught sight of herself in the rearview mirror. After that, March got out a turtleneck sweater to wear, but even dressed in all that insulating wool she gets the chills just thinking about Hollis. She's like some foolish teenager; she can't seem to get him out of her mind no matter how hard she tries. Sometimes, he phones her at the exact moment when she's thinking of him; she carries the phone into the pantry, for privacy, and they talk for hours. Every word he says is interesting to her; she's never the first to hang up, not even when Gwen knocks on the pantry door and asks what's going on.

Liar that she's become, March doesn't tell Gwen who's on the phone, just as she doesn't admit the truth about her destination when she goes out at night. She has to stop at the pharmacy, she needs to walk for the sake of exercise, she and Susie are going to a movie, into Boston, shopping at Laughton's, to a lecture at the library. She meets him at the end of the driveway, where's he's waiting in his truck, or now that she has Ken Helm's old car, she drives herself to the old Highway Motel where Route 22 meets up with the Interstate.

She is crazy for him, exactly as she used to be. More so, because back then she was a girl who didn't know any better; she wasn't somebody's wife, somebody's mother, a grown woman who should, by this time in her life, understand the value of caution. A few nights ago, they were on the phone at two in the morning, whispering about what they'd like to be doing to each other, when Hollis suddenly decided he was coming over. March asked him not to—Gwen was asleep in the sewing room, the dog was in the hallway, stretched out by the door—but he had already hung up on her.

March locked the terrier in the pantry, where it whined all night long. She was waiting for Hollis when he arrived, and she didn't stop him from kissing her as they stood in the front hall; she didn't refuse to go up to the attic, or lock the door, or go back to that small metal bed, where they'd made love so many times before. The attic was dusty and there was evidence that mice and starlings had been living there, but March paid no attention. By the time Hollis left, it was already light, although, thankfully, this was one morning when Gwen slept late. March's lips were puffy and bruised and there were spiderwebs in her hair, but Gwen didn't seem to notice when she came into the kitchen for some orange juice.

"Where's the dog?" Gwen had asked, and only then did March remember she'd left the poor creature in the pantry. When she let Sister out, the dog backed away from March, as if it were the only one who knew what a conniver March really was.

The cranberry-walnut tart and cookies she's bought at the

farmers' market, for instance, have a devious purpose: Hollis and Hank have been invited to tea, and March, although she's no Judith Dale and wouldn't dream of baking anything herself, still wants to impress her guests. She wants it to be possible for them to all sit down in the same room and, if nothing more, be civil to one another.

"Don't have them over," Gwen said when March approached her with the idea earlier in the day. "Hank's none of your business, even if we do come from the same family."

"There's no reason to do this," Hollis told March when she went ahead and invited them over for tea. "They're kids. It doesn't matter if we accept them—they're going to do what they want—and I don't give a damn if they accept us."

Hollis isn't pleased with the effects of Hank's infatuation. Hank is even more dreamy and thoughtless than usual. He knocks over cups of coffee and steps on his own feet; he comes into the kitchen in the morning looking so rumpled and confused you'd think he was sleeping in a bale of hay. That little girl of March's has him all caught up, and it's truly pathetic to see.

"Idiot," Hollis tells him, when Hank is late for school or when he's forgotten his chores. "Take a good look at yourself."

Hollis cannot understand how a person could give up so much control. He couldn't do it; it's simply not in his nature. The idea of being told what to do, or how to feel, turns him inside out. After all these years, the greatest pleasure he has ever known was paying off his debt to Alan Murray. Hollis still keeps the itemized bill of all that he owed the Murrays in his wallet, folded neatly into quarters. This is the invoice he was presented with on the day of Henry Murray's funeral, and it charged for every day Hollis had lived with the family; the estimated cost of all meals had been tallied, along with books and clothing, even toothpaste. Each day he continued to live at Fox Hill raised Hollis's debt, until it seemed he would never pay it off, and yet, he did.

All he had planned to do when he went away was earn enough

to take March out of there, but the situation got complicated, as it always does when fast money is offered to someone who's insatiable. The plan changed daily, in terms of exactly how much he would need. First it was enough for an apartment in another town, then in Boston; then it was a house he needed to present to her, a house bigger than the one where she grew up. Finally, it was the land they had surveyed on that day when they hid behind the stone wall. Nothing less would do.

Hollis didn't even realize how much time had passed until he came back to town: The boys he'd gone to school with were men now, with wives and families. The linden trees planted around the town square the year he left, thin seedlings that needed to be propped up with posts, had become tall enough to cast shadows that covered the square entirely. If he had been able to buy the land surrounding Olive Tree Lake, he would now be the largest landowner in three counties. If anyone thinks this is meaningless, then he's never had a banker call him sir; he's never had one of the residents of town, who once helped tie a defenseless boy to a tree and leave him in the woods at dark, politely wish him a good day and move aside, quickly, to let his old hostage pass by.

Today, when he knocks on the door at Fox Hill—a silly formality, seeing that he owns the place—Hollis has nearly everything he's ever wanted, but he's in a foul mood anyway.

"Go ahead," he tells Hank when March comes to the door. "Go in."

Hank has dressed in his best clothes for the occasion, and he formally shakes March's hand.

"You look so much like Alan," March says.

Hank looks at her, confused, uncertain as to whether she's greeted him with a compliment or a curse.

"He had your color hair," March explains, suddenly nervous in the boy's presence. "But you're much taller," she adds when she sees the worried look on Hank's face.

"Oh." Hank nods, grateful to March for granting him that dissimilar feature.

"What is this supposed to be?" Hollis asks.

Sister is standing guard in the hallway, emitting a low, throaty growl.

"It's a West Highland terrier," March says. "Judith's."

"Are you telling me it's a dog?" Hollis says.

March laughs. "That's what I'm telling you."

"Well, then I have to believe it. Seeing how it comes from you." He moves toward March, and the dog growls again. "What are you looking at?" Hollis asks the terrier, who is watching him warily and snarls when spoken to.

"She seems to hate you," March teases.

"I don't mind. Let her." Hank has gone on ahead, so Hollis takes the opportunity to draw March near. "You're the one whose opinion interests me." He circles her waist and whispers, "I could show you what I mean. Let's get rid of the kids."

"Kid," March corrects. "Gwen's not here."

Hank is in the living room, stoop-shouldered beneath the low ceiling, disappointed when he's told Gwen hasn't appeared.

"You'd better watch out," Hollis suggests to the boy, after March has gone to get the tea both Hank and Hollis will politely force themselves to drink. "If you mattered to her, she'd be here." He lets the boy think that one over; maybe now Hank won't let himself be led around by the nose.

But in fact, Gwen's decision not to be at home for her mother's little get-together has nothing to do with Hank, or her desire to be with him. When she left the house early that morning, with a bunch of carrots in her pockets, she had already made up her mind that she wouldn't be home at the appointed hour. She walked quickly down the road to the Farm in the cold morning air, with no intention of being sociable with Hollis, or allowing her mother to butt into her life. Gwen likes the empty road these days; if she's quiet enough she can spy weasels running along the stone walls and field mice searching the ground for acorns. To her great surprise, Gwen likes all sorts of things she would never have thought she could tolerate.

Back in California, Gwen would sleep all day if allowed; she'd slam at her clock radio until she hit the snooze button, and be late for school four days out of five. Who was that girl? she wonders now, as she pulls on a second pair of gloves and jumps over ruts in the road. If she passed by that girl right now, she'd think, *Poor lazy know-nothing*, and she'd keep right on going. Most days, Gwen is at the barn at five-thirty, and Tarot is always waiting for her, pushing his nose up against her as soon as she enters his stall, searching for carrots and apples. Usually, she doesn't ride him; instead she brings him down to the farthest, widest pasture and lets him take off. To see him run is to witness a miracle. Every once in a while, on those days when Hank doesn't meet her down at the fields with a thermos of coffee, she does a foolish, dangerous thing. She rides Tarot at full speed, which is nothing compared to what he used to do on the track, but leaves her breathless all the same.

The other morning, when she woke at five, Gwen could not get dressed and rummage through the refrigerator for Tarot's treat, then run down the road at her usual hour. Hollis was in the hallway. She knew he was there before she leaned up on her elbows in order to peer out the door of the sewing room where she sleeps. She smelled fire, and that's the way he smells. Later, when Gwen went into the kitchen she noticed the scent of fire on her mother as well. Still, she didn't say a word. She simply went about her business, despite the lump in her throat. Sure, her mother wants to pretend nothing has happened; she wants to have everyone over for a little tea and cookies and act as if Hollis wasn't in their kitchen before dawn with his hands all over her. To hell with that, in Gwen's opinion. To hell with her.

Anyway, maybe Gwen's wrong in her assessment. Maybe her vision was cloudy and they were simply talking; they've known each other forever, after all. Still, whenever Gwen sees Hollis—which, thank goodness, is hardly ever—she always turns away and acts as though she's unaware of his presence. Even if she's standing in his field, with a horse that legally belongs to him, she turns the other way.

Mind your own business, that's what she tells herself when she starts to wonder about her mother and Hollis. *Go forward. Concentrate on your own life.* That's what she tells herself, but it isn't working. She wonders if what she feels for Hollis is hate. It's not solely on behalf of her poor, unsuspecting father that she feels this; it's the way Hollis has treated Hank. He's horrible to Hank, he bosses him around as though Hank were his servant, and Hank doesn't even seem to notice. That's what's so awful. He looks up to Hollis. He thinks the world of him.

The first time Gwen went to Hank's room, on an afternoon when Hollis had gone to Boston on business, she burst into tears. The room was so neat and tidy and devoid of possessions. It was as if Hank were a boarder, someone merely passing through, when in fact this has been his room for thirteen years. The wool blanket on his bed was threadbare and the paint on the walls was peeling. Gwen sat at the foot of the bed and wept. Hank thought it was something he'd done or said and he kept apologizing, which only made her cry more. There was such loneliness in that room, in the cracks along the ceiling and the bare walls, that Gwen was all the more aware of how lonely she herself has always been.

The strangest thing is that now that she's really, truly in love with someone, they haven't had sex. They kiss, they touch each other, but it's not the right time to do anything more, they both feel that. This is a backward universe she's in; all that she wouldn't have understood before makes sense to her now. She doesn't want her mother in on this, it's too private, too perfect, and she's certainly not going to sit and politely sip a cup of tea in the parlor while her mother interrogates Hank about what his favorite subject is at school, or whatever question parents think most reveals a boy's character.

It is, after all, Gwen's last day of freedom; she's scheduled to attend classes at the high school starting tomorrow. And so this afternoon she has trekked over to the library, where Mrs. Miller teaches her how to use the microfilm so she can look Tarot up in old newspapers. The library in Jenkintown is a wonderful place built out of local brown stone. There are two reading rooms, furnished with old leather couches and well-worn chairs. It may not be the Boston Public Library, or the main branch of the San Francisco Public Library that her father takes her to, but so far Gwen has discovered six books about horse racing and Tarot is in two of them. Back then, his full name was Blue Moon's Tarot's Deck of Fortune, called after the Blue Moon farm in Virginia, where he was sired. There is his photograph as he heads for the finish at Belmont. There he is in the colors of Guardian Farm—blue and white—in the winners' circle at Saratoga.

"You like racehorses?" some old man asks Gwen as she pages through the books. It's Jimmy Parrish, who ran the stable at Guardian and worked at Pimlico when he was a boy.

"I guess I do," Gwen admits.

Jimmy Parrish sits down across from her and begins to talk about his good old days. He's so excited Gwen smiles and lets him ramble on as she looks at photographs from great races of the past. She's not really listening until he starts to talk about Guardian Farm. If he remembers correctly, the families of the two men who were killed filed suit against Mr. Cooper, which pretty much finished the stable and wiped out the family financially. One of the men had been a jockey, the other a trainer from Louisiana, both men who knew their horses. Accidents happen, of course, but with Tarot situations always seemed premeditated. People thought the entire family was crazy when a few months after the out-of-court settlements they saw Belinda Cooper, God rest her soul, riding that racehorse as if he were nothing more dangerous than a Shetland pony.

That is when Gwen closes her book. Dust rises up from between the pages in a little gray cloud. "That's my name too," she tells Jimmy. "Cooper."

When he realizes this girl is Richard Cooper's daughter, Jimmy throws his arms around her as if she were a long-lost granddaughter. "I can't believe it's you," he cries. He actually becomes so loud and teary that the librarian, Enid Miller, comes over and informs him if he doesn't quiet down he'll have to leave, which is what Gwen and Jimmy Parrish decide to do.

"So who was Belinda to me?" Gwen asks when she and Jimmy are leaving the library. Gwen has her arms filled with books she's checked out. As they go down the stone steps of the library, she keeps her elbow out, in case Jimmy Parrish should slip on the wet leaves and need something to hold on to.

"She was your aunt. Your father's older sister. Dead nearly twelve years. And her son, who she named Cooper, has been gone for at least five. Your grandparents—the mother and father of Belinda and your dad—died in a terrible accident at the devil's corner. That's the turn where Route 22 meets up with Guardian Farm."

"Kind of a dying family," Gwen says.

"You're the last of them," Jimmy Parrish says. "No more Coopers but you."

"Yikes," Gwen says. "Does that make me unlucky?"

"I wouldn't say that," Jimmy Parrish is kind enough to tell her. "And then, of course, there's your mother's side of the family."

They have reached the Bluebird Coffee Shop. Gwen holds the door open for Jimmy, who is completely thrilled to have found a live one who is not only listening to him but actually appears interested.

"There's your mother's brother, Alan."

"I've heard about him." Gwen remembers the Judge mentioning an Alan.

"He just went to pot after his wife died."

"She died too?"

They sit down at the counter and Jimmy takes a look at the specials board, even though the specials are always the same at the Bluebird: crab cakes with mustard sauce, BLT on rye, corn chowder.

"I'll have a cup of your chowder," he informs their waitress, Alison Hartwig, whose mother will serve Gwen lunch tomorrow in the school cafeteria.

"So what's with Alan?" Gwen asks after she orders a vanilla Diet Coke.

"He's a wreck, plain and simple. No one ever sees him, and his boy, Hank, is being raised over at the Farm. I think I'll have a coffee too," Jimmy calls to Alison Hartwig. "Black."

Gwen rolls all this information around in her mind. Why has no one told her this before? This means that Hank is not simply some relative. He's her first cousin; an embarrassing, odd fact. Is it a crime to fall in love with him? Will people look at them and whisper?

"I hope you know more about racehorses than you do about your family," Jimmy Parrish says as he spoons sugar into the coffee he's been served.

"I don't," Gwen says.

She has a queasy feeling in her stomach. It sounds as if she and Hank come from the worst possible gene pool. She wishes they weren't related, that they were perfect strangers who were old enough to make their own plans, without interference from anyone.

"I've been riding that horse over at Guardian Farm. The one you were talking about. Tarot."

Jimmy Parrish has been served his chowder, but now he puts down his spoon. He looks at Gwen, hard, and shakes his head.

"You're lucky that horse isn't in his prime, or you'd already be dead."

"I don't think so," Gwen says. She puts a dollar on the counter to pay for her Coke, then grabs all her books. "I'm the one in my family who's going to live."

She walks home through the cold late-afternoon sunlight. When she gets to the dirt road, Hank is waiting for her, sitting on a stone fence.

"You didn't come to tea," he says, when Gwen perches beside him. "I had to eat all the cookies your mother put out, to be polite. She's nice."

"No, she's not." Gwen stacks her pile of books between them; her posture is stiff.

"Okay." Hank realizes he has to be careful here. She's upset about something, and he has no idea what it might be. "I was only in the house for about half an hour. She seemed nice for that amount of time."

"We're first cousins," Gwen says. "Did you know that?"

Hank leafs through the pages of one of the library books. There is a crow somewhere close by and it starts its insufferable calling.

"Did you know?" Gwen asks.

The grass in the fields is yellow now, and the squirrels are frantically collecting the last of the acorns. She can tell by looking at him: he knew. Gwen shakes her head. "You should have told me."

"It doesn't matter," Hank tells her. "That's why I didn't say anything. The way we feel is what matters."

Gwen stares straight ahead, at the maples and the oaks, then reaches to put her hand in his. Maybe some people would disapprove, but Gwen doesn't care. When Hank closes his hand around hers, that's it. They've made their bargain; they've sealed their fate. What she ever did to deserve him, Gwen will never understand.

Maybe she's a better person than she thought she was; maybe there's a reason why she would be lucky enough to find someone like Hank. They walk across the hill together, and they keep going, past the fences and the old trees, until they can see almost all of Guardian Farm, a sea of gold and green. Beyond the split-rail fence that lines the driveway, there is the piece of road that leads into Route 22.

"The devil's corner," Gwen says.

Hank laughs. "Who told you that?"

"Some guy in town."

There are several logging trucks going by on Route 22; when they honk their horns the sound echoes into the sky.

"Are you saying there's somebody else?" Hank teases since it is, at the moment, his biggest fear; the doubt Hollis placed there, for his own entertainment. "Some other guy?"

"No." Gwen grins to think he might be jealous of old Jimmy Parrish. "How about you? Is there somebody you're dying to be with?"

"You," he tells her. Exactly what she wanted to hear. "Only you," he says.

TWELVE

MARCH SITS ON THE BRAIDED RUG IN
the living room looking at a photograph of her
brother taken when he was sixteen. It was summer and Alan's hair had been bleached almost
white by the sun. He wears a polo shirt and jeans
and white sneakers and he's grinning right at the
camera. He hadn't yet failed at school, or marriage, or fatherhood. He was nothing more than a
boy who didn't know when to quit, or how to treat
people; he was fun-loving, but selfish, with a re-
grettable nasty streak. March has driven out to
the Marshes five times, and five times he has refused to answer the door. He's gone, that's what it

is. Someone lives in that shack, all right, but the boy whose photograph March examines has vanished like a handful of dust.

The clock on the mantel is ticking, the one March's father bought in Boston, the single possession she can't bring herself to pack away. She has gone through the boxes of photographs, all arranged in albums and dated with Judith Dale's neat handwriting. March will be keeping only two photographs for herself, to place into frames. One is of her and Hollis, a hazy snapshot in which they look like ragamuffins, with torn shorts and dirty knees, all dark eyes and know-it-all grins. The other is of Judith Dale skating on Olive Tree Lake on a winter day. Judith's head is tossed back, her skin is luminous; all around her the world is icy and white. Growing up, March never noticed that Judith Dale was beautiful, or that she was young, far younger in that photograph than March is right now.

Today, March is taking a pot of asters to Judith's grave. It is the perfect day for a solitary mission such as this—Hollis went to Boston on business; Gwen is safely at school. It's only Richard who holds her back, even after she's packed up the photograph albums. March spoke to him last night, finally, but he refused to understand.

"I don't think I'm clear on this," he kept repeating. "You're staying?"

It was the school, she told him, so much better for Gwen: fewer drugs, fewer temptations. Just a change, a tryout. She'd forgotten how peaceful it was here, out in the country; she'd actually been inspired to work, so could he send on a box of her tools, and the packet of semiprecious stones in her night table drawer? Gwen was so happy, after all, she was doing so well; why, she'd even begun taking care of that old horse Belinda used to ride.

"Tarot?" Richard had said. "She's spending time at the Farm?"

For those new to lying, it's easy to get caught.

"Not exactly," March had answered.

"Well, what exactly?"

March guessed that Richard had the bedroom window open as

he spoke to her, and that the scent of lemons was filling the room. She had taken special care of that tree in their garden, forsaking poppies and jade plants whenever there was a drought, using all her rationed water for that one tree.

"Richard," she had said, and for a very long time there was no response.

"You're not going to do this to us, are you?" he had finally asked.

She thinks about the sound of his voice, so far away, as she gets her gloves and coat from the closet, then takes the asters from the table in the front hall. When she goes to the door, the dog follows, blocking her way.

"Move," March tells it.

The dog looks up at the closet where its leash is kept on a shelf, then makes a noise, somewhere between a yip and a bark.

"Oh, all right," March tells the thing. "But behave."

She grabs the leash, and allows Sister to run ahead to the Toyota.

"Stay away from the flowers," March says as the dog situates itself beside the asters. "Don't eat them."

When March gets to the cemetery, there are no other cars in sight. She parks in a pile of wet, brown leaves, then clips on the dog's leash and takes the flowers.

"Don't pull," she tells Sister, who seems to know exactly where they're going.

There's a driving range which borders the cemetery, and March's father used to joke that was the reason why they couldn't keep gravediggers on the job. Man after man had gotten beaned on the head, and every one of those stray balls had been hit by Bill Justice, who continued to be a terrible golfer even though he went out to practice nearly every day, in an effort to improve his weekly game with Henry Murray. Now March wonders if the Judge only said he was going to the driving range; if, in fact, he spent those times with Judith Dale. She wonders too if her father knew—if he closed his eyes to what was going on in spite of his warm feelings for Louise.

Amazing what people will tolerate. Richard, for instance, knows the way March feels about Hollis, and yet before he hung up the phone he'd said, *Just come back. It will be all right. We'll manage.*

They have reached Judith's grave, and although the dog sits quietly, there's a tremor in its leg.

"Good girl," March croons, but the dog is shivering now.

Wet leaves have attached themselves to March's boots and to Sister's white coat. It's extremely quiet here, not even a jet overhead.

"Your favorites," March tells Judith Dale as she places the pot of flowers at the foot of the grave site, which is still bare earth.

March sits on the grass beside the grave, and the dog comes to lie beside her, so close March can feel it shivering through fabric and fur. They walk back to the car slowly, until Sister decides to chase a few scarlet leaves, the last ones that fall from a tall maple. They stop at the knoll from which March can see her father's plain gray headstone, and nearby, the headstone marking the spot where Alan's young wife was laid to rest. When they get to the car, Sister sits in the front seat. March navigates the narrow road, and then, as she's about to turn onto a larger drive, something runs in front of the car. Between the falling leaves and the asphalt there is a flash of red. March steps on the brake, hard.

Nothing but leaves and silence; March would have thought she'd imagined what passed before her, but Sister is scratching at the window, barking like mad. Then, from beneath a hedge of evergreens, the creature takes off again. It's one of the last of the foxes, a great-great-grandson of one who survived the open hunting season all those years ago. It's running as fast as it can, headed for the open fields west of the cemetery. Red lightning that doesn't look back, it's gone in the blink of an eye.

March remains there, with her foot on the brake, and Sister's barks echoing. As a little girl, March used to wait out on the front porch in the dark, hoping to see one of the foxes who were so numerous back then. She could never stay up late enough, so she came up with a plan. She'd catch one for her own and keep him in a box in the kitchen, in one of those crates they used to store potatoes and yams. She'd make certain he stayed warm under a flannel blanket, she'd feed him buttered toast and train him to dance to music, in a circle, on his toes. On some nights, she'd allow him to sleep beside her in her bed, his pointed nose on her pillow, and she'd sing him to sleep.

"Don't be silly," Judith Dale told her one summer night, when March wasn't more than seven or eight, and Mrs. Dale had discovered her out past her bedtime, poised on the porch with a fishing net, a hammer, and the vegetable crate. "You'll never catch a fox that way."

Mrs. Dale brought March to the chestnut tree, where she drew a circle in the dirt with a stick. She took some sugar cubes from her pocket, the kind she favored for her coffee and tea. She let March crush the sugar cubes, then sprinkle them around the circle.

"Spread it thin," Judith told her, and March was especially pleased that Judith clapped her hands, approving her work when it was done.

"Bullshit," Alan had responded when March informed him that she'd trap a fox by the morning. And when indeed all the sugar was found to be gone, Alan laughed out loud. "Anything could have eaten that sugar, dummy. Raccoons, stray dogs, mice. There are any number of explanations, Marcheline, and none are as stupid as yours."

But later that day, Mrs. Dale took March inside the circle and pointed out the tracks of a fox's lovely, sly paws. That's when March decided that if she couldn't keep a fox in the kitchen, she'd have one in the woods. For a very long time, she left out treats. Even after Hollis had come to live with them, she was sometimes found drawing a circle with a stick, setting out bits of sugar, or some cookies, or a fresh corn muffin she'd stolen from the pantry.

"Is that for your boyfriend?" Hollis said to her once, when she was distributing slices of apple around the circle.

"No," she said, and then she'd turned her back on him. *You're my boyfriend,* is what she was thinking, and after all this time, she's thinking it still.

When the fox disappears, March turns onto Route 22 and heads for Guardian Farm, hoping that Hollis will be back from Boston. The autumn light is sharp, and March reaches for her sunglasses. She switches on the radio and sings along to a song she didn't think she knew the words to. She has the sense that she's driving backward in time; the sky is so much smaller here than it is out west, a bowl of heaven set above their pastures and their town. She eases into the turn off Route 22 carefully, since it's a place where it's difficult to see oncoming traffic. She drives along the fields the Coopers always planted, but which are now thick with little more than wild clematis and witch hazel. There's only one tended patch, where Hank has been raising pumpkins, and that crop has done well. There are several rows of huge, fat pumpkins, still on their thick, ropy vines.

March remembers coming here with Hollis and wishing the Farm belonged to them. The house looked so much grander and more elegant back then, and Annabeth Cooper's perennial gardens were amazing, especially her rose garden, where the blooms were as big as cabbages. March used to study Richard and Belinda with real interest. How strange it was that a rich girl would wear torn sweaters and keep her hair bunched into a rubber band. How odd that Richard should cry when he discovered a worthless old crow someone had shot for sport. She found them so curious, like creatures from a distant planet; she couldn't help but be interested, and she stayed interested long after Hollis grew tired of their spying game.

It's Hollis she spies now, out by his truck, back from Boston, where he's met with one of his lawyers concerning an acquisition of more condos in Orlando. The dogs are milling around, and every once in a while he calls to them harshly, when one nips another, or when they all begin to bark, an off-key plaintive sound that carries over the hill. Still, Hollis is in a better mood than usual; he always gets this way when he buys something. For a brief time at least, he's not concerned with getting more. *There's enough for everyone,* Judith Dale always told him when he sat down at the dinner table, but anyone could tell he didn't believe her.

Hollis is wearing a gray suit made in Italy which cost more than any single item of clothing anyone in this town has ever owned. He's learned that people are foolish enough to believe what they see, so he dressed rich for his trip into Boston. He's up in the cab of the truck, in spite of his expensive suit, when March drives in. The dogs start howling and begin to circle the Toyota. In the front seat, Sister hops up to look out the window; seeing those yapping red dogs, the terrier goes berserk. If March let Sister out of the car now, it would attack the entire pack, for all the good that would do.

"Call off your hounds," March says when she gets out of the car.

"Kick them," Hollis suggests as he lifts a box out of the truck. He's gotten a new computer in Boston so he can hook up directly to his bank. He can sit at the desk in the parlor, where old Mr. Cooper smoked his cigars, and manage his finances beside a window which overlooks one of the prettiest views of his property.

March follows Hollis into the house. Just being this close to him makes her feel all jangly, as if someone has shaken her like a globe filled with snow. She can feel his energy snapping at her, charging her up, even when his attention is turned to this computer in a box.

"I'll be right back," he tells her. "Make yourself comfortable."

March hasn't been inside this house for a long time, and now that she is, she's certainly not comfortable. If anything, she's disoriented. This isn't the way she remembers the Coopers' kitchen, with its polished copper sinks and the long oak table that was always piled high with wonderful things to eat. The Coopers hired an Italian cook they called Antsy, so named because she couldn't stay still for a minute, unless she was baking something delicious. There was a housekeeper as well, a woman from the village, the mother of one of the girls from school; Alison Hartwig was the girl's name, a quiet blue-eyed girl who didn't have much to say.

The kitchen now has a spartan quality; that which isn't a necessity isn't here. Tiles that had to be ripped up when some pipes burst one terribly cold winter have never been replaced. The slate countertops are cloudy from years of thoughtless cleaning with Comet. The copper sinks have turned the color of moldy leaves. And yet the kitchen is clean. There are two coffee cups, rinsed and drying on a wooden rack; there's not a crumb on any of the counters, not a dish left out on the table.

When Hollis comes back, he goes to the sink to get himself some cool water. After he's drained the glass, he comes to stand beside March. He takes her hand and examines it.

"She used to wear this on her left hand," he says of Judith's emerald. "Like a wedding ring."

March leans in close to kiss him, but Hollis takes a step back.

"What?" March asks.

He takes her other hand, her left hand, on which she wears her wedding ring. "If you were the one who'd gone away, I would have waited. No matter how long it took."

"Well, I did until I just couldn't anymore," March says, trying to pull away.

"Wouldn't," Hollis says back.

March laughs. He used to do this to her all the time, contradict her however he could, just to get his way. Then she sees. It's no laughing matter. He's not letting go of her hand.

There is no measuring love, other than all or nothing or that space in between. This is all, she sees that in him. This is more than everything. Could she live without this, what he's offering to her? Could she turn away and settle for anything less? Another man would say, *I can't tell you what to do or what to believe.* Another man would play this as though it were a game.

"Want to know what I think?" he says to March.

She raises her chin and looks at him, even though she's afraid to find out. He seems extremely pleased with himself, as if he'd figured the answer to a difficult riddle.

"I think you were never married to him."

"Oh, really?" She tries to sound amused, but that's not how she's feeling. She's feeling as though she can't stop looking at him; she can't even try.

"Really," he says.

The white shirt he's wearing looks crisp and well pressed, but it turns out the fabric is smooth to the touch, a delicate linen that feels like silk. Hollis kisses her so deeply that her stomach lurches; if she ever had any willpower, it gives way. He's got his arms around her, so that she has her back against the sink. She can feel the cold copper against her back. Hollis pulls down the zipper of her jeans. He's calling her baby, he's telling her it's always been this way between them and it always will be. No one could ever love her the way he does, not in this lifetime, not in this world.

"Come on," Hollis says, when he's got her jeans and her underpants pulled down, as if she planned to stop him. As if she could stop herself. She knows she should tell him to wait. He has Hank living with him; how can they be sure the boy isn't already home from school? It's a bright afternoon, anyone could turn up at the door. Ken Helm with a check for the wood he's culled from land Hollis owns. Harriet Laughton collecting for the library fund.

But March doesn't tell him no. How could she? She wants him more at this moment than she's ever wanted anything: air or memory, life or breath. She wraps her legs around him, with her back pressed into that cold copper sink. She wants him to do whatever pleases him; she wants him to do it all. She's so hot that the copper behind her is growing warm to the touch; soon the metal will ping with heat, ready to burn. The way he thrusts himself inside her is incredibly greedy, but she's greedy too. That's the secret Hollis knows about her. She's no different than he is.

"You want it, don't you?" is what she thinks he's whispering to her, or maybe she's only admitting this fact to herself.

He's making love to her in a way he never did before; he's hungrier, more impassioned. March moves her hand beneath the fabric of his shirt. It's still him, that same boy. There is his heart, right in her hand. She doesn't care what anyone thinks. Let them say what they wish; let them gossip. She places both hands on the sink, palms down, to support her weight while he fucks her like this, as if the world were about to end, as if he could never get enough. The metal sink is pressing against her, cutting into her skin, so that later she will have little indentations in her flesh, and blisters, as though she's been burned.

He has his face against her neck, and she can feel all that heat inside him. She hears him say her name in a strange, garbled way, and then she's gone. She's shattered into pure energy; she's been absorbed into whatever he is, that sulfur, that heat. There is no way to measure this; no scale will do. March finds that she's crying; the heat that has owned her rises to form a single sob as she arches her head back and wraps herself around him, tighter still.

Outside, there is plenty of sunlight. Not a cloud in the sky. The dogs mill around the back door and whimper. No leaves fall from the maple trees beyond the driveway. No birds fly overhead. And even later, when the blue dusk begins to cross the horizon, it will still be a rare and nearly perfect day. Poor Sister, locked in the car for so long, barking for hours, will yelp hoarsely when March finally comes out of the house. The dog will eye March resentfully as they start down the driveway, then turn onto the back road. Halfway home, March will stop beside a stone wall where the bee balm still grows. She'll remove her wedding band to find a white circle; to hide that mark, she'll switch the emerald onto her left hand, and although she'd meant to rush home and start supper, she'll stay beside the wall for longer than she'd intended, until the road ahead is completely dark.

THIRTEEN

TONIGHT, GWEN WILL WEAR ALL BLACK,
but she certainly doesn't plan any tricks, only a
treat. She has a present for Hank, which she hopes
to give him at Chris's Halloween party. Hank is
such a serious person, finding the right gift for
him is no easy task. No CDs or tapes, no jewelry
or flashy clothes. None of that would do. Instead,
Gwen has brought along a sterling silver compass
she discovered in the attic. It's an old-fashioned
piece, and Gwen hopes it still shows true north.

She wants to be with Hank tonight. She
has been with so many boys she never gave a
damn about; selfish, spoiled guys who liked to

joke about the girls they fucked, rating each on a score of one to ten. Subzero, they laughingly called those whom, like her friend Minnie, they deemed too unattractive to bother with. And to think, Gwen actually put up with that. She stood there and listened to them tear her best friend apart and she pretended that she didn't hear or didn't care.

With Hank, it's different. It's real. And that's why she's nervous: This time, it matters.

"You look terrific," March says when Gwen comes downstairs, ready for the party.

Gwen is wearing her short black dress, but she's gone easy on the mascara and eyeliner. Instead of spiking up her hair, she's let it dry naturally, and it has a soft, pretty shape. She's desperate for Hank to think she looks good, but she still can't take a compliment and merely shrugs at her mother's approval.

"We're already late," Gwen says, ducking March's embrace when she tries to give Gwen a hug. Impatient, Gwen gets her own jacket and her mother's coat from the closet.

"You may not care if you keep your date waiting," Gwen informs her mother as they finally head for the car. "But I do."

It's the sort of chilly, spooky night when it's possible to see one's own breath in the air; perfect for Halloween.

"My date?" March says, rattled by the notion that Gwen may know more than March gives her credit for.

Gwen glares at her mother, then gets into the Toyota, which March has just bought outright from Ken Helm for six hundred dollars, borrowing the money from Hollis. Gwen slams her door to make her point. She really has had enough; she's been carrying her resentment around for some time and, like it or not, it's a heavy load.

"Are you talking about Susie?" March asks when she slides behind the wheel. She isn't ready to discuss Hollis with Gwen; it's not time, and it may never be. *I can't turn him down, I can't say no to him, I want him all the time, I always have and I always will.* Is that what she's supposed to say to her daughter? Is that the comforting tale she should tell?

"That's who you're meeting tonight?" Gwen asks, her voice even more hoarse than usual. "Susie?"

March takes too long to answer. Gwen snorts and looks out into the night.

"Just like I thought," Gwen fumes. "The truth really is an alien language to you."

"Okay," March says. "You want the truth? I'm meeting Hollis." She starts the car and pulls onto the dirt road at a speed that's too fast for the turn.

"Like I didn't know," Gwen mutters under her breath.

"It's no big deal," March insists. "We've known each other forever. We grew up together."

Gwen is feeling something weird in her throat. She can't stand for this to happen to her father, who is the nicest man she knows. All right, he's not the most conversational guy in the world unless you're talking about beetles. There have been family dinners when no one has said a word during the entire meal. But Gwen has been in the car with her father when he's stopped to watch a wood spider spin its web. She's seen him talk to a stray bear cub, when they were at Yosemite for her tenth birthday, and to this day, she would swear the bear listened.

Gwen knows that her father has been sending March cards. She found one this morning. A store-bought card that said *Thinking of you.* "I miss you every day," he had written and Gwen actually cried to see that he'd been made to embarrass himself. A man like her father, so settled in silence, had to come out and shout what he felt, and her mother still didn't seem to care.

"We're going out to dinner at Dimitri's. It's not exactly a crime." And yet March must feel it is, since she's so busy defending herself.

"Fine," Gwen says. "It's none of my business."

She knows her mother lies about where she goes. *Whatever*, Gwen thinks to herself when her mother says she has an errand to run or that she's going out with Susie. *Sure, at this time of night, my mother's going food shopping*. That's what she'd tell Minnie if the two of them still spoke on the phone. *Like I believe it. Like I believe anything she says*.

Hank knows about them too. God, how could he not? Once, he was waiting for her at the end of the driveway when she came to visit Tarot. He insisted they walk to school early, right then, and he had a funny look on his face, as if he felt sorry for her. Gwen glanced at the house then and realized the Toyota was parked there. March had spent the night, and Gwen hadn't even known. She'd just assumed her mother was still sleeping when she'd left the house at five-fifteen.

Another time, she saw them when she took Sister for a walk. They were in the driveway, parked in his truck. Gwen had looked away as quickly as she could, but she'd seen her mother kissing him. She'd seen March's head tilted back and her mouth open. After that, Gwen had run all the way back to the porch, but it was too late; she'd already witnessed too much.

"You're making a big deal out of nothing," March says as they drive toward town.

"Look, you don't have to explain anything to me. It's your life."

Gwen slinks down farther in her seat and looks out her window. The trick-or-treaters are out in full force, wandering up and down the High Road and Main Street dressed as ghosts and ballerinas and Ninjas. It's as if the children have taken over; they're everywhere, crossing streets and lawns, running through the darkness with flashlights and bags filled with candy.

"Thanks for the ride," Gwen says when they pull up to Chris's house, and she gets out before her mother can say anything more. What a relief to be walking up the path to the party. There's already a crowd inside, and a pile of coats in the front hall. The music is turned up so high that the bass vibrates through the walls and into Gwen's skin.

"Finally," both Chris and Lori shout when Gwen comes into the kitchen, where Chris's mom is mixing up a punch recipe which includes orange soda and grapefruit juice. The girls are all in black—everyone is supposed to be dressed accordingly for this event—and Chris sports a black witch's wig over her blond hair.

"You look fabulous," Lori tells Gwen.

"You think so?" Gwen says uncertainly. She has to learn to take a compliment. She has to stop being so uptight.

Chris's mom finishes the refreshments, then retires to the den, since she's promised to give them "space" for this party. As soon as she's gone, the guy Lori's started dating, Alex Mahoney, takes out a fifth of vodka and doctors the punch. Everyone's laughing about how plastered they plan to get, except for Gwen, who's too busy watching Hank come in through the back door. His face is flushed from the raw weather and there are leaves in his pale hair. He's wearing a threadbare black overcoat—one of Hollis's castoffs, no doubt—jeans, and a clean white shirt. Gwen knows him—he ironed the shirt himself; he was careful and thorough and that's why he's late. Standing here, in this crowded kitchen, she could not love him more.

"Here you go, old boy," Alex greets Hank, handing over a glass of the punch. "This should do the trick."

Hank grins, but he puts the glass on the table, and heads straight for Gwen. He bends down so he can whisper.

"You look beautiful."

"Thanks," Gwen says. She actually does it. She accepts a compliment. If she can do that, anything can happen. Tonight feels like the night of her dreams. She wraps her arms around Hank and knows that he's the one. She cannot remember being happier than when she is dancing with him, or when she perches on the arm of a couch to watch him play darts. By midnight, Gwen is ready to leave, so they can go up to Olive Tree Lake and be alone. Anyway, the group who've gotten plastered from the spiked punch are getting somewhat obnoxious. It's definitely time to leave.

"You know what we should do next?" Lori's new boyfriend, Alex, is saying. "Go down to the Marshes."

"Oooooh."

Someone is making spooky noises. A girl laughs, but it's a short, trumpeting sound.

"Seriously," Alex says. "We'll bring a few cherry bombs."

"Smoke out the Coward?" another boy guesses.

"Oh, yeah. Like you'd have the guts," Chris teases.

Several people laugh now.

"Let sleeping cowards lie," one of them suggests.

Gwen is listening to all this, disgusted, but when she turns to Hank to discuss how sophomoric these guys are, he's gone. She looks in the kitchen and in the hall. Nothing.

"Have you seen Hank?" she asks Lori, and anyone else she recognizes, but the answer is always no. Gwen has a panicked feeling. It's as if, while she wasn't looking, everything's gone wrong. She grabs her coat and heads outside. What would it mean if he left her at the party and took off? How could it be that he's already halfway down the block, black coat flapping out behind him?

Gwen runs after Hank, and when she catches up to him she hits him in the back, right between the shoulder blades.

"How could you do that to me?" she cries when he spins to face her. Gwen should be embarrassed, there are tears in her eyes, but she's not. "Is that how you treat someone you care about? You go and leave them?"

Hank's face is pale, and it's not easy to read his expression on this dark street, but all at once, Gwen realizes she's not the only one who's crying.

"What is it?" Gwen says. "What's wrong?"

"The Coward," Hank says. "The guy in the Marshes they wanted to smoke out? That's my father."

They walk through town in silence. There are a few stray trick-or-treaters ringing doorbells, but most have gone home to bed. A quarter-moon has risen, but the night is unusually dark. Hank keeps his hands in the pockets of his overcoat, and he walks fast, so that Gwen has to trot to keep up with him. Forsaking their original plans, they do not go to Olive Tree Lake—where many of the couples from the party have already trekked, looking for privacy and romance. Instead, they start for the hill.

"It's not your fault that Alan is your father," Gwen says.

Hank smiles, but he doesn't look happy. "Yeah? Then why do I feel like it is?"

"Maybe he's not as bad as everybody says."

Hank clearly doesn't want to discuss this. He speeds up his pace and they walk on in silence, an unusual and lonely condition for the two of them to find themselves in. When the house on Fox Hill is in sight, Hank backs off.

"I'm tired," he says. "I'll see you tomorrow."

So much for Gwen's perfect night. It's been ruined; it's been murdered. There is no way she's going home now.

"Go ahead, if that's what you want," she tells Hank. "I'm not afraid to check out the Marshes."

Gwen turns and takes off, not thinking of how rash her decision is; not certain, in fact, of where it is she's going.

"Hey, wait a second," Hank shouts. "Wait up. You can't go there."

But it's too late; she's in motion. Gwen is running in the direction she believes leads to the Marshes. She can hear Hank calling her, but she's too upset and angry to stop. The sound of her breathing is filling up her head and she can hear things flying from tree to tree; she hopes that they're birds and not bats. She heads east, or what she thinks of as east; she's surprisingly fast when she puts her mind to getting where she wants to go.

Gwen hears Hank calling, but she doesn't stop, not until the trees begin to thin out. The grass is taller here, and there's the smell of salt. In the moonlight, everything is silver. An owl glides over an inlet, without warning, without a sound. The silver grass moves in the wind; where Gwen walks, it's waist-high and she has to be careful to avoid the places where the mud seems deepest. People can sink so deeply into this bog they disappear forever, or at least that's what Lori has told her.

It's extremely quiet here. Sound dissolves. Why, Gwen can hear her own heartbeat. Behind her and in front of her is a sea of grass. The few trees which grow here are huge oaks, and some stringy pines. You can smell the pine if you breathe deeply. If you listen carefully, you can hear past the silence to the echo of something moving. All around are fiddler crabs, traversing the mud in the moonlight. Luckily, it's low tide, or Gwen would be sloshing through knee-deep water. Instead, she has to make her way over the crabs, tentatively, trying to avoid crushing them.

Hank comes up behind her, and grabs her with such force that Gwen almost loses her balance.

"Are you crazy?" His breathing is ragged from running. His jaw is pulsating. "You don't just wander around in the Marshes. This isn't a joke."

Gwen throws her arms around him. What will she do if she ever loses him? How would she ever survive?

"I'm sorry about your father," she whispers.

"There's the place they want to bomb," Hank says now. "His house."

Gwen steps away to look in the direction Hank nods toward. Two big, old apple trees are all she sees; that, and the moonlit grass.

"Behind the trees," Hank says.

When Gwen squints she can make out the tumbledown house. That's a porch. An old gate. A railing.

"I want to see it," she says. "Let's go closer."

"No," Hank says. "He'll hear us if we go closer."

"I don't care if he does."

Gwen looks at Hank. If he tells her not to, if he tries to boss her around, something between them will be over. She didn't realize this, but now she knows it to be true. Thankfully, he doesn't. He stays there and waits while Gwen navigates through the marsh grass and the scratchy sea lavender.

The water has begun to rise, enough so that Gwen can feel how cold it is through the soles of her boots. Funny thing, there's a garden gate in front of the house, but no fence. All you have to do is scoot around the gate, and make your way past the apple trees, then past some old blackberry bushes and over a cluster of raspberry canes. Maybe the fruit here was planted by Aaron Jenkins, the Founder, or maybe blackbirds dropped seeds down from the sky which managed to sprout in spite of the sandy soil. Either way, the bushes are now an overgrown warren, occupied by sparrows and rabbits and evil-tempered raccoons.

Gwen has to do this, go past the bushes and continue on. She refuses to be the kind of girl who gets scared off easily, whose opinion echoes her boyfriend's, who can't stand up for herself. She'll be damned if she ends up like her mother, ready to do anything, even lie, for a man. All the same, Gwen is shivering as she walks up to the house. She doesn't have to look back to know that Hank is watching her. She concentrates, trying to stop her heart from beating so fast.

As she gets closer she notices scattered glass, the remnants of windows broken by boys from town. The porch steps sag, but Gwen goes up them anyway. She looks through the window nearest the door, but it's difficult to see inside. She can make out a table and chairs, some blankets on the floor, and a little potbellied coal stove. It looks like a place where nobody lives, but he's in there. Gwen can feel his presence. He's scared, like those sparrows in the bushes who sense Gwen's proximity. He's got his eyes shut tight, and he's praying that whoever's out there will go away, which is exactly what Gwen does. But before she leaves, she reaches into her pocket. She wants him to have something, and the old compass she meant to give Hank is all she has. She places it on the threshold, then pushes the door open, only a little, but enough to smell the mildew and dust from inside.

Heading back to Hank is tougher going. The tide is coming in fast now; before long, Gwen's boots will be soaked. The leather will be ruined and she may have to throw them away, and yet she takes the time to look behind her. Unless she is mistaken, the compass is no longer on the front porch, and so she feels free to run the rest of the way; she can run until she reaches Hank at last.

FOURTEEN

EVERYONE SAW MARCH AND HOLLIS TO-
gether on Halloween night. They're common
knowledge now, discussed in the deli aisle of the
Red Apple market and in the reading room at the
library. They were sitting beside each other all
through their dinner at Dimitri's, not across from
one another like normal, civilized people. The
waitress over there, Regina Gordon, doesn't like
to tell tales, but honestly, they couldn't keep their
hands to themselves. They were practically doing
it right there at the table, and several customers
noticed when he reached his hand under her
sweater. Why they had bothered to go out to

dinner at all was a mystery to Regina, since it was clear all they wanted was each other.

Ed Milton is the one who finally informs Susanna Justice of her friend's affair. He tells Susie right after they make love, at her place, a cottage so small he can talk to her from bed while she fixes them hot fudge sundaes. Susie's dogs, Chester, the golden Lab, and Duffy, the black one, watch her every move, drooling onto her bare feet.

"Bullshit," Susie says when he tells her about Hollis and March. "I'd be the first to know."

"Well, you're probably the three hundredth to know," Ed informs her. He's a big, good-looking man who moved up here from New York City, and his only complaint about small-town life is that there isn't a decent bagel or a good cup of cappuccino to be found. He misses his daughter, an ill-tempered twelve-year-old, who comes up from New York for one weekend a month, legal holidays, and all of July. Ed has great blue eyes, and he cries at sad movies—God, even Susie's dogs are wild about him. If she let herself, Susie could get involved with him. And this is the reason she's ready to argue whenever she has a chance—to ward off anything deeper than what they already have.

"You know what I'm going to do?" Susie says, half in jest. "I'll call them both and get the real story."

Ed gets out of bed and stands between Susie and the phone. He's one of the few men Susie has known who look better without clothes than with them.

"Stay out of it," Ed says. "That guy is trouble."

The hot fudge is ready, but Susie doesn't bother with it, even though the ice cream she's scooped has started to melt. "You sound like you know something."

"I've heard rumors, that's all." Already, he's starting to back off. This often happens when Susie is reporting on local issues, whenever a source realizes he's said too much. "It's your friend's business, not yours," Ed adds. "Besides"—he really did have a great smile—"love is strange."

Susie has always wondered where Hollis was during those years he was away, but nobody else has ever seemed interested. *Out making money*, people usually joked. Or, *I don't know, but when you find out tell me—I'd like to be as rich as that bastard.*

Susie finds herself thinking about Hollis all that day, and into the next. She's got him so much on the brain, in spite of how she dislikes him, that she ignores her daily chores to focus on him instead. He's like some terrible puzzle, made up of equal parts flattery and contempt, and she's still trying to figure what bothers her most about him—the way he's manipulated the town fathers, with his wisely placed donations that have allowed him to buy up and redistrict most of Main Street, or the way he's maneuvered March back into his life—when she pulls up to her parents' house the following evening. It's a Wednesday, the night when Louise Justice roasts her famous rosemary chicken. Susie kisses her father hello, then goes into the kitchen, to watch her mother cook. She steals bits and pieces from the salad on the counter, then gets herself a cold beer.

"Hear any good gossip lately?" she asks her mother.

Louise has begun to fix plates of chicken and rice. "What are you after?" she asks drolly. "A good murder? Financial ruin?"

"Love," Susie says. "Or maybe it's more like insanity. I've been hearing all sorts of things about March."

Louise Justice spoons out the snap beans. When she's upset her hands always shake slightly, as they do now. "Tell March she's making a mistake," Louise says. "He's not worth it."

"Geez," Susie exclaims. "Did everyone in town know about this before I did?"

"Maybe you didn't want to know."

This statement from her mother brings Susie up short. Louise is right, of course. It's simply that Susie had no idea that her mother could be so insightful.

"You seem extremely sure that March is making a mistake," Susie says now.

They've brought the plates over to the table; any minute the Judge will come in from his study.

"I am."

Again, Susie is surprised, this time by her mother's certainty.

"For one thing," Louise says, "he killed Belinda."

"What?" Susie says. She tilts her head to search her mother's expression so quickly she can feel the vertebrae in her neck pop.

Louise has gone to get a glass of club soda for the Judge, which he always takes with a slice of lemon. Susie follows on her heels.

"Do you have any proof of that?" Susie's adrenaline is going like crazy. She is a reporter, after all, even if it's only for *The Bugle*.

"If I had the proof, don't you think I would have gone to the police?" Louise pours a glass of club soda for Susie as well. A good thing because Susie's mouth is now parched; as dry as dust. "But I don't need proof. I know. He did it."

Louise's hands are shaking badly as she returns the club soda to the refrigerator, but thankfully Susie doesn't see. Louise has always kept her suspicions to herself, which hasn't been easy, and which, she now realizes, was a mistake. People used to do more of that—look the other way—and Louise is as guilty as anyone else. The last time she saw Belinda was almost twelve years ago, only a few months before she died. They were both on the board of the Library Association back then, and there had been a meeting to discuss the coming year's cultural series. It was late when the meeting finally ended—Harriet Laughton had chosen to be difficult, insisting that her son, a rather boring botanist, be asked to lecture—and people were hurrying to get home. Louise was on her way to her parked car, when she noticed Belinda headed for her truck. It was a bitter, windy night, and the shutters which framed the library windows were banging against the bricks. Belinda was carrying an armful of papers and proposals, since she was then the association secretary.

"What a meeting," Louise said as she approached Belinda from what must have been her blind side.

Belinda was so startled that she dropped her pile of papers.

"I'm so sorry," Louise had said.

"It's nothing." Belinda was always polite; she'd been carefully trained by her mother, Annabeth. Why, you could probably wake her in the middle of the night and she would say *please* and *thank you*. "I got spooked." Belinda smiled gamely.

"Well, it's that kind of night," Louise had granted.

They'd both crouched down to gather the notes and proposals and that was when Belinda's sweater was pushed up above her forearm. She quickly tugged her sleeve back down, but it was too late. Louise had seen the line of bruises.

"I need iron tablets," Belinda had declared. "Anemia's the problem."

Once they'd gathered the papers, they both stood up. Louise remembers the chill she felt down her spine. *Something is not right,* she was thinking. She recalled seeing other bruises; although Belinda had the sort of pale, freckled skin which was susceptible to chafing and injury, there were too many instances when she'd been hurt. At a meeting the month before, Louise had noticed a mark in the shape of a butterfly on Belinda's cheek. The little boy, Cooper, had hit her with a toy truck, by accident, or at least that had been the explanation. When she sprained her wrist, and Harriet Laughton asked how it had happened, Belinda said her horse had bumped against her, and all that summer her wrist continued to pain her as she took the minutes for the association's meeting. Belinda had taken to wearing long-sleeved shirts in August; she had stopped looking her friends in the eye. All at once, in that parking lot, Louise was certain that she knew what the problem was, and what it had been all along. *It's him.*

"Well," Susie Justice informs Louise after hearing this story. "You have no proof whatsoever. Maybe she did need iron. Maybe she really was anemic, and bruised easily."

"All right," Louise says, as she goes to call the Judge in for dinner. "Fine. Think what you want to think."

"Mom," Susie says, following after. "You can't know for sure."

"There was the imprint of a hand on her arm. It might not have been clear, but I saw it. Do you want me to believe she did that to herself?" They can hear the Judge's footsteps on the stairs. "I know Hollis did that to her."

All through the meal, that story of Belinda nags at Susie, and when she leaves, she doesn't go straight home, but heads for Fox Hill instead. The trees wave their branches at her; the last leaves are falling, so many that Susie has to switch on her windshield wipers. Pulling up in front of her friend's house, Susie continues to have a sinking feeling. She should probably go home and mind her own business; only a fool listens to unfounded denunciations. After all, she wouldn't take one person's version of an incident if she were writing an article for *The Bugle*. But that one person is her mother, and Susie can't shake the feeling that Louise is right.

Susanna Justice is so deep in thought that she doesn't hear Gwen approach until the girl knocks on her window.

"Jesus, you scared me." Susie laughs. She swings her door open and gets out. Gwen has been walking Mrs. Dale's little terrier. "Is it a pain for you to have to take care of Judith's dog?" Susie asks as they head for the house.

"Sister's okay," Gwen says. She bends down and unclasps the terrier's leash once they're inside the hallway, then pats the dog on the head. "My mom's not here."

"Oh?" Susie says, taking off her coat anyway.

"She probably won't be back for a while," Gwen says. "She's out with you."

"Ouch," Susie says, following Gwen into the kitchen. "Sorry." She accepts the Diet Coke Gwen offers. "I hope I had a good time. Where was I, anyway?"

"She said you and she were going to a restaurant down in Boston. French and Cuban. You read about it in *The Globe*." Gwen gets some ice for their sodas. "My mother is getting to be a really good liar. She knows I know, but she won't admit anything. They're really good friends. They grew up together. I'm supposed to fall for that."

"If it makes you feel any better," Susie says, "she hasn't told me about Hollis either."

"It doesn't make me feel any better. But thanks for trying."

Gwen goes to the sink and spills out her soda. This morning, when she went to the Farm to take Tarot out to the fields, Hollis was leaving his house. When he saw her, he stopped in the drive-way and stared, his distaste perfectly evident. He hates her, that much is obvious. He wishes she didn't exist. It's a bother to have March be concerned about a thankless daughter, but there's more—Gwen realized this when she came home and caught sight of herself in the mirror. She could see how much she resembles her father, in the angle of her cheekbones, her thin, long nose, the set of her jaw. Those are his blue eyes which look back at her from the glass, pale as the sky.

Gwen has been phoning her father nearly every evening. They talk about the weather, about frost and rain, daylight and current constellations. They talk about the field trips he's been taking with his graduate students, the latest up to Oregon in search of Psoid beetles, which are decimating some orchards in that area. They discuss Gwen's school work and joke about the decrepit tomcat who lives in their garage and eats the tins of food they leave out for him, but coolly pretends not to know them. They speak of anything and everything, except what is happening to their family. They manage, however, to talk around it.

Are you happy there? her father has asked Gwen in a puzzled tone. *Do you want to stay? Do you want to come home? How is your mother?* he asks, always.

She lies to her father. Apparently lying must run in their blood, because it's getting easier for Gwen as well. *Don't worry, we'll be home soon. Definitely by Thanksgiving.* That's what she says, when in fact she knows her mother has already accepted Louise Justice's invitation for the holiday. What should she tell him? That she wants to stay on as much as her mother does? That the boy she's crazy about is her first cousin?

Yesterday when Gwen spoke with her father, she had an idea that he knew what was happening in spite of her lies. He listened, all right, but when she was done telling him how they'd be back before long, he asked if he should come see them. He could get reservations and be there by tomorrow, or the next day, or early the following week.

Gwen thought about the look on her mother's face that time she saw her kissing Hollis in his parked truck. She thought about the way her mother's eyes had closed, and how she'd arched her neck.

"I don't think so, Dad," she said to her father. "This might not be a good time."

Tonight, Gwen goes to her room at ten-thirty, to bed she says, but really to phone her father, and after that, to call Hank. She leaves Susie waiting in the kitchen, and she can't help but feel a tinge of satisfaction when she thinks how surprised her mother will be to find good old Susie parked in their house. It's nearly midnight by the time March does get home. There's a full moon out, and frost on all the fields. March lets herself in the door quietly, but the damned dog barks to greet her.

"Be quiet," March tells Sister.

March's face is flushed from the cold. They've stopped checking into that awful motel, and have begun to go to that funny little room off the kitchen March never even knew existed when she used to visit the Coopers. The room must have been meant for a maid or a cook; maybe it was Antsy—the cook responsible for all those delicious meals—who lived there. It's a dingy, chilly place, but that doesn't stop them any more than the knowledge that Hank is upstairs finishing his homework.

It has come to this: They don't give a damn about anyone but themselves. It's true, so March will just have to admit it. It's always been this way when they're together, and it's happening all over again. Why, at this point March isn't even certain she exists without Hollis. When she leaves their bed, in an attempt to get home and pretend to her daughter that their lives are still normal, that's the time when she feels as if she's entered into a dream. Everything seems gray and she's unsteady on her own, as if a strong wind could tip her over. If she stopped to think about what she was doing, she wouldn't believe it. Less than an hour ago, while Hank was studying for a math exam, and her daughter was left alone with a lie, March was down on her knees in that small room off the kitchen, not caring about anything but pleasing Hollis. The floor is old pine, and rotting, and now March feels tiny splinters in her palms and her knees. Hollis is a different kind of lover than he used to be. He was always sure of himself, but now he wants to be completely in control, and March doesn't fight that. In a way, it's a relief. March doesn't have to think when she's with him, or make a decision, or state a preference. She can tell, from the way he touches her, that he's been with a lot of women, too many, but she's the one he wants, and she always has been, and that alone makes her forget all reason.

"Stop it," March whispers to the dog when it jumps up to greet her.

"Sneaking in?"

Susanna Justice has been standing in the hallway, watching as March gingerly removes her boots.

"Good Lord," March says, clutching at her chest. She's wearing jeans and a pale blue sweater Judith Dale sent as a birthday gift years ago. "You almost gave me a heart attack."

"Here's the thing I'm upset about. Why is it that everyone in town knew about it before I did?"

"Knew what? That I was having a heart attack?" March takes her coat off and hangs it in the closet. By now, every word she says feels like a lie.

"That's not what you're having," Susie says.

So, March sees that Susie still has the annoying habit of judging others.

"Whatever I'm doing is my business."

"Don't you realize everyone is talking about you? Your love life is the main topic of conversation in town."

"And have you been defending me?" March says, with a bitter edge.

"I defended you to your daughter. Sort of."

"Oh, shit." March's cheeks are now flushed bright pink. "I told her I was out with you."

"Do you think she's an idiot?"

"Do you think I am?" March says.

"Actually, yes."

They both grin at that notion.

"I think you're insane," Susie hastens to add.

March's grin widens, the big smile of someone who no longer cares about sanity.

"I'm serious," Susie says.

"Overly so," March agrees.

March insists on making some tea; once they're in the kitchen, she fills the kettle, sets it on the stove, then grabs a bag of chocolate chip cookies and brings them to the table.

"You don't know the things people say about Hollis, March."

"Please." March bites off half a cookie. "They've always disliked him."

"I'm not talking about silly remarks about how he made his money." It's all so unsubstantiated Susie knows she shouldn't say more. As a reporter she should kick herself for passing on unfounded suspicions, but this is her oldest friend. In good conscience, she can't keep her mouth shut. "My mother thinks he may have had something to do with Belinda's death."

March looks at Susie, wide-eyed. "You've got to be kidding."

"Well, I'm not. She told me so at dinner."

"It's ridiculous. Does she have any proof? Did the police ever suspect Belinda's death was anything but normal?"

"My mom saw bruises on her."

"Come on. And for all these years your mother never said anything? And what if she did see a bruise? For all we know, Belinda could have had a boyfriend on the side who beat her."

"So you think she might have been beaten?"

"I think people hate Hollis—your mother included—just because he won't put up with their bullshit. Can you understand why he's so suspicious of everyone?"

Susie bites into a cookie. Louise Justice doesn't usually make false accusations, and Susie still feels something grating at her. "I'm worried," she says.

"You're always worried."

"I still wish you would have told me," Susie says.

"Well, I would've." March grins. "But I thought you'd disapprove."

"Who, me?"

"Yes, you."

They both laugh. No one, after all, could disapprove more.

"Stop worrying about me," March says. "You don't have to."

A friend is someone you tell the truth to, but Susie stops herself from doing that because the truth is, she's not going to quit worrying.

"I wish I could be happy for you," Susie says later, after they've finished their tea, along with the entire bag of cookies.

"Try to be," March says, as she walks Susie to the door, then out to the porch.

March throws her arms around her old friend, and they stand there for a while, even though the weather has taken a turn and is much colder than had been predicted. All along the stone fences, the bittersweet berries have become orange. People will soon be covering their beds with their heaviest quilts, their warmest blankets. Cats won't be forced out for the night, and those people in town who take their dogs for a late walk will see their breath form into clouds. Susie Justice will have to clear the frost off her windshield with the palm of her hand before she gets into her truck. As she drives away, she'll roll down her window. She'll bite her tongue and say no more; she'll simply wave to March, who's out there on the porch, dressed only in her jeans and her sweater, with no coat and no gloves and no protection from the cold.

FIFTEEN

RICHARD COOPER ARRIVED TODAY, IN spite of a storm that was rattling up and down the east coast. Ken Helm picked him up at Logan, and later that evening, at the bar of the Lyon Cafe, Ken tells people he would have recognized Richard anywhere. Sure, Richard's not a kid anymore, but he looks the same anyway. He's tall and thin, the way all the Coopers were, and he's just as distracted as ever, although he can certainly tell a good joke, Ken Helm will attest to that. Richard Cooper's got thousands of bug jokes he's picked up at entomology conferences. He's got a *Why did the beetle cross the road?* series which cracks up his students completely, although right now he tends to favor tick jokes. *What's the difference between a tick and a lawyer?* he asked Ken Helm as they were driving up on I-95. It's one he heard at a conference in Spokane last winter. *The tick drops off after it's sucked your blood.*

Richard's students appreciate him for more than his jokes. They respect him for all those aspects of his personality which most annoy March. He gets lost in what he does and can discuss a single topic, a variety of fungus-inhabiting Tenebrionidae, for instance, for hours. He's too kindhearted, and doesn't stand up for himself. As a graduate student, several discoveries he made in the field were claimed by his adviser, but Richard never cared about such things as who gets credit—it's the discovery that matters to him. It's doing the right thing. When he believes in something, he won't back down. He's tenacious as hell when he has to be, not unlike the trout-stream beetle, which will cling to anything, defying icy streams and swift currents in order to get where it is convinced it must go.

This clarity, this single-mindedness of purpose, is the reason why Belinda inherited Guardian Farm and Richard was left with nothing. His father was trying to teach him a lesson about obedience, and before Mr. Cooper could reverse his rash decision to disinherit his son both he and Richard's mother were killed at the turn onto Route 22. For all these years he's been away, Richard has only come back for funerals. His parents. His sister. His sister's only child. Now they have laid Judith Dale to rest in the same cemetery, and Richard plans to pay his respects at the grave site. But he doesn't have long to do so. It's late Friday afternoon when he arrives, and he has to present a lecture to his graduate seminar on Monday morning. He hasn't asked his neighbors to feed the stray cat living in his garage or bring in his mail. He has his return ticket for the noon plane on Sunday, and he's made reservations for March and Gwen as well. Just in case.

If luck is on his side, they'll all be out of here in less than forty-eight hours. Yes, it's true, he believes in fate. He's a scientist who happens to be convinced of the reality of destiny. His colleagues might mock this philosophy, but then let them explain why one sand beetle wanders into a spider's web while another passes by, unharmed. Love, it now seems, is not what Richard thought it would be. It's thicker and heavier and much more complicated than he would ever have imagined. He knows that his wife has been with another man, a man he happens to despise and holds responsible for his sister's death—and yet here he is, chatting with Ken Helm, insisting that Ken take the forty bucks he's offering for fetching him from the airport. Love has made him surprise himself. He would never have believed it possible, but it's turned out that he is a man who can walk up to a closed door on a murky November day, wearing his one good suit, and knock without hesitation, waiting while the rain comes down around him, even though he's not wanted. He can do this and not think twice, just the way he can spend hours watching a wounded cedar beetle and weep over its rare beauty, as well as its agony.

Richard is certain that other species fall in love—primates, of course, and canines—but he has wondered about his beetles. There are people who would surely get a chuckle out of the mere suggestion, but in Richard's opinion it's pure vanity to presume that love exists only on our terms. A red leaf may be the universe for the tortoise beetle or the ladybird. A single touch the ecstasy of a lifetime. And so, here he is, in love despite everything. It is he, stupider than any beetle, and far more obstinate, who has traveled three thousand miles, even though he fully expects to be turned away.

Gwen answers the door, and as soon as she sees Richard she throws her arms around him.

"Daddy," she cries, although he doesn't remember her calling him this before—it was Pop, he thinks, or Pa.

Gwen pulls Richard into the hallway, where a little white terrier jumps on his legs.

"Who is this?" Richard asks. He puts down his overnight case, then crouches to pet the dog.

"It's Sister." Gwen cannot believe how glad she is to see her father. He seems so real. So him. "She belonged to Mrs. Dale."

"Well, Sister," Richard says. The dog has politely sat down before him, and now tilts its head to listen when he speaks. "How do you do?"

They do like hell, if the truth be known. All of a sudden, Gwen is the one in charge of everything, like it or not. Her mother once saw to all of the chores, but no longer. March can't seem to deal with the trivial details of domestic life, they seem beyond her somehow, small but impossible tasks. If Gwen doesn't do her own laundry, she has no clothes. If she doesn't go food shopping or make the beds, no one else will. Once, while hurrying through the village on her way to meet her friend Chris, Gwen passed by some woman who had her collar turned up and a dreamy look on her face, and it wasn't until Gwen and Chris had ordered french fries and Cokes at the Bluebird Coffee Shop that she realized the woman she'd walked past was her mother.

Gwen is now responsible for herself in some deep, irrevocable way. There is no one to tell her what to do; for all intents and purposes, she's on her own. And although this is exactly what she once thought she wanted, her situation now brings her to tears.

"What's wrong?" her father asks, but how can she tell him?

"I'm fine," Gwen insists. "I'm just glad to see you."

"You look wonderful," Richard tells his daughter. Although seeing her so grown-up and so pretty without all that makeup makes him realize how much a person can change in a short period of time. Wasn't it only weeks ago that he worried constantly? That he feared she would return home with some new part of her body pierced and some new drug in her backpack?

Richard hangs his wet raincoat in the closet. His shoes are soaked, as are the cuffs of his slacks, but he will simply have to do. He can't make himself any more presentable before seeing March.

"Well?" he says when he turns back to Gwen.

"Well, what?" Gwen asks.

"Your mother. I'd like to talk to her."

I don't believe you would, Gwen thinks. To her father, however, she suggests that her mother's schedule is erratic.

"Then let's fix some coffee so it's ready when she gets here," Richard suggests.

The rain outside has become sleet, which hits against the window as though stones were being tossed from above. Coffee on a night like this isn't a bad idea. Richard has to duck to pass through the doorway into the kitchen. He'd forgotten how different the scale of these old New England houses can be; how wide the pine floorboards, how low the ceilings, how tilted the rooms from years of settling.

"Coffeepot?" Richard asks.

He used to cook when he first came calling on March. He and Alan's wife, Julie, had a great time of it, she as his amicable assistant, he willing to try any new recipe. Once they fixed pasta with a maple syrup topping; another time they tried something called bootheel pie, made out of turnips and celery and onions.

"Filters?" he asks.

Gwen sits on a stool, her legs pulled up. She has spent this afternoon with Hank, walking Tarot all the way into the village and then back again. When Hank kissed her, the horse tried his best to come between them.

"Forget it, buddy boy," Hank teased. "She's mine."

Just for that, Gwen kissed the old racehorse on his soft nose. His breath was surprisingly sweet, like new hay.

Hank had let out a groan. "I can't believe you did that."

"Would you ever lie to me?" Gwen had asked then.

"What are the circumstances? Is it that I know you're kissing a horse who has terrible breath? Or is it that I know there's going to be a nuclear war and we have only twelve hours to live, and I have to decide whether to ruin the last twelve hours of your life with fear, or let you enjoy the little time you have left?"

"Nuclear war."

Gwen had climbed onto the stone wall, then had pulled herself onto Tarot's back, where she stretched out, as though the horse were an extremely tall and comfortable couch.

"I'd tell you." Hank had grabbed the lead and they'd begun a slow walk back to the Farm. He didn't even have to consider; that's what impressed Gwen most. "What about you?" Hank had asked. "Would you tell the truth?"

Tarot had stumbled then, and Gwen had been forced to hang on to his mane; then she'd jumped off, so that Hank could lift Tarot's rear left leg and see to the problem. There was a tiny, sharp rock wedged into the frog of the horse's hoof, which Hank removed with a penknife. Gwen never did get to answer. Just as well, since she hadn't known what to say at the time. But now, in this kitchen, watching her father crouch down to search the cabinets under the counters for coffee filters, it has all become quite clear. It's not the lie that's the problem; it's the distance the lie forges between you.

"Daddy, don't bother with the coffee." This is what Gwen has to say, even when she sees the look on her father's face. "She won't be back until late. She never is." Gwen swallows; but it doesn't help. Words such as these always hurt when you say them. "She's with him every night. She may not come home at all."

Richard blinks, as if by doing so he could bring into focus a vision other than the one Gwen is offering.

"I'm sorry," Gwen says. She feels as though everything is her fault. She's only fifteen, why does she have to feel so damned responsible? She can't even tell her father about Hank, for fear he'll disapprove. When her father leaves the room, to make a fire in the fireplace, Gwen decides to finish the coffee he started, and she brings him a cup, with a little milk and a little more sugar, the way he likes it.

Richard gratefully accepts the coffee, and for one delightful instant he has the sense of being fortunate. She is a good girl, he sees that. Gwen pulls up a stool for herself beside the easy chair where he's settled. She's a good person.

Sister sits by the window and barks, and Richard finds himself wondering if Gwen is wrong about March, if perhaps that's her at the door now. The visitor, however, is only a rabbit, one who brazenly sits on the porch in order to escape the bad weather.

"We never had rabbits around here when I was growing up," Richard tells his daughter. "There were too many foxes for that. If you walked through the woods at night, you'd see them. Especially at dusk. At first you'd think you were imagining footsteps."

Sister has forsaken the door and come to join them, stretching out on the braided rug.

"Everything would be gray, even the horizon. And then you'd see it, all at once."

"A fox." Gwen smiles.

Richard nods. "Once in a while, in the winter, after a snow, you'd come upon a dozen or more of them, and then you'd know something was happening that no human could understand, or even recognize. They call it a foxes' circle, a meeting held as if there were a board of directors of the woods. I think about the foxes' circle when I do fieldwork. There's world upon world out there, with different rules."

"I wonder why they all disappeared."

"They found a single rabid specimen one season and that was the end of foxes on this hill."

It was the year when Hollis left town. Richard recalls that each time he came to call on March, he'd hear gunfire in the woods. He was grateful to Hollis back then; in leaving, Hollis had given Richard an opportunity he'd never guessed he would have. Funny the things you remember. Richard definitely remembers that March would smile whenever she opened the door and saw him. He knows he didn't imagine that.

"When I was really little," he says now, "maybe five or so, my sister found an orphaned fox. She kept the kit in her bedroom, secretly of course, because my mother would have had an outright conniption and made us all submit to a series of rabies shots if she ever caught sight of the thing. My sister kept an opossum one year, and then there was a crow with a broken wing that I found—she took care of that crow for months. My mother went crazy when she discovered wild animals had been in the house, but my sister was surprisingly strong-willed."

"Belinda."

"That's right." Richard regrets not telling Gwen more about his family, but for the longest time his personal history seemed extremely distant. Now, it's back. All he has to do is listen and he can hear gunfire in the woods. He can see the way the crumbs fell down on the ground whenever his sister reached for the stale bread she kept in her coat pockets, ready should she happen to discover some homeless or injured creature while walking in the woods. This is what Richard thought when she wrote to tell him she had married Hollis. Only this time the creature she'd chosen to care for was much more dangerous than an opossum or a crow or a fox.

"When the kit was nearly full grown, Belinda let it into the woods. But it kept coming back. You'd walk out the door, and there it would be. Or maybe it wasn't a fox at all." Richard places his coffee cup on the table and pets Sister's head. "Maybe it was one of those dreadful red dogs people say were bred from foxes."

"There are still some of those at Guardian Farm," Gwen says.

"Yes." Richard leans his head back against the soft fabric of the easy chair. He thinks this type of stuff is called chintz, but he doesn't know for sure. "I'm not surprised. There were always dogs hanging around, begging. My sister always set out food for them. She was much too kindhearted."

Richard has only begun to realize how tired he is, in spite of the coffee. He has a horrible sinking feeling in the pit of his stomach, which makes him think he should call Ken Helm and go back to the airport right now, but he doesn't. Instead, he falls asleep right there, in the chair. Gwen covers him with a blanket Judith Dale bought on a trip to Ireland taken with the Friends of the Library one summer. It pains Gwen to see her father sleeping in a chair, but what can she do? Shake him to consciousness? Tell him to flee? *Don't hurt yourself,* is what you say to a child, not a parent, and a man like Richard Cooper is not prone to take other people's advice, not once he's made up his mind.

There's a draft in the living room, and Sister curls up beside Richard's feet. On the mantel, the old clock March's father bought in Boston keeps time. The sleet continues until the roads are slick with ice and fallen leaves. It's so bad that by the time the first pale light of morning begins to break through the clouds, March has to inch along on the back road in the old Toyota. She is staying with Hollis later and later; this time, as she was leaving, he pulled her back to him. Susie thinks he's so evil, but he was concerned about March driving in such bad weather. People think they know him, but they don't. They don't know that he cries in his sleep, or that he needs to be comforted from the worst of his dreams, over and over again.

When March does finally get home, she has to carefully make her way up the frozen path, and hold on to the railing so as not to slip and break her neck on her way to the front door. She's not taken a coat. She's so hot these days; she's burning up. All she's wearing are jeans and a borrowed wool sweater of Hollis's. She hasn't bothered with underwear either; she's much too overheated for even the flimsiest silk. Inside, the house feels stuffy and close; there's the scent of coffee and of wet dog. There's something else too, a faint odor of regret which is sifting over the floorboards and the rugs.

As soon as she walks into the room, she sees that the man she's spent the last eighteen years with has come for her, and he appears exhausted by the effort. Richard looks so uncomfortable, folded up in that chair, in his best suit, which is now rumpled. The dog rouses and shakes itself from sleep, but Richard doesn't hear the clink of its collar. He doesn't hear March come closer, and crouch beside him. He's dreaming about her though, and in his dream she is surrounded by falling leaves, each one a brilliant yellow, as if fashioned from pure gold.

Richard doesn't wake until March takes his hand. As soon as he opens his eyes and looks at her face, he knows it's over. She pities him, that's what he sees, and pity is not what he wants.

"I don't suppose you'd like to fly to San Francisco with me on Sunday?" Richard laughs. He was supposed to keep this idea to himself until they'd spoken at length, but obviously he can't do that.

In spite of herself, March laughs. He never did like small talk.

"Should I take that as a yes?" Richard asks.

"It's not that I don't love you," March says.

Richard cannot help but wonder how many times this phrase has been spoken, and how many people who've recited these words have believed they were being kind. What makes a person love another? That's what Richard wonders, as March tells him that she'll be staying on, and that she never meant to hurt him. Are March's dark eyes the element that always gets to him? Is it the way her beautiful mouth twists to one side when she smiles?

Richard goes upstairs to grab a few hours of sleep in March's bed. When he wakes, the bright sunshine which blasts through the ice-covered windows is blinding. He gets his suit, having draped his trousers and jacket over a chair so he will appear presentable when he goes to the cemetery. He wants to look as though nothing is wrong when he goes downstairs and kisses his daughter good morning, when he speaks cordially to March and asks if he can use the Toyota in her driveway to run his errands. March has been crying; her face is all puffy and her eyes are red. Looking at her, knowing that she's been with Hollis and will continue to be with him, brings Richard immense sadness.

What would another man do? Carry her off, make demands, beat her until she gave in to him, stand there and cry? Richard Cooper is the same man he was before this happened to him. He's the man who leaves a check on the kitchen counter because he worries that his wife will run out of cash. He's the man who brings flowers to the graves of his loved ones, and says a silent prayer for each one. It's the same Richard Cooper who trades stories with Jimmy Parrish about racehorses who've been dead a quarter of a century or more over lunch at the Lyon Cafe, who calls for another round of beers and some chili-cheese fries, then makes certain he grabs the check before Jimmy can reach into his pocket for his own leather wallet. He's the man who drives to Guardian Farm late in the day and parks in the driveway where he has a good view of the house where he grew up, despite the uncertain November light.

When he sees Hollis slam through the front door, on his way to collect bills and circulars from a mailbox set out where Richard's mother's roses used to grow, Richard doesn't step on the gas and careen through the fence to run his rival down. Instead, he watches as some Canada geese pass by, high overhead. In the pastures there are still a few red dragonflies, the kind Richard used to collect when he was a boy. He used to keep them in a jelly jar, until he realized that whenever he caught one he damaged its wings, which marked it for death. That's what he thinks about now as he watches Hollis, who has lifted one hand to shade his eyes against the sun as he tries to figure out who's there, parked in March's car. By the time Hollis does understand who it is in his driveway, Richard will have already made a U-turn. There's no point in staying any longer. He'll leave a note for Gwen if she's not at the house when he stops to drop off this car, then call Ken Helm for a ride. He intends to trade in his tickets for a plane that leaves tonight. He'd just as soon sleep somewhere in midair, high above Chicago or soaring over the Rockies, as he would in someone's easy chair.

Gwen is in the barn when the Toyota makes that U-turn. She knows that her father will be gone before she gets back to Fox Hill. Standing there, watching him, she feels like crying. Maybe she should have insisted on going on his errands with him; maybe she should have tried to talk her mother into leaving. Gwen now considers herself to be a guilty party. She didn't say, *I want to go back with you*. She didn't take his side. Difficult as it is to admit, she wants to be here, saddling Tarot, meeting Hank later in the day at the library, where's he's working on his senior thesis. Traitor that she is, she doesn't run after her father. She lets Tarot eat sugar from her hand while waiting for Hollis to go back inside the house. That's one thing she'll do to honor her father—she'll avoid Hollis at all costs. When Hollis has finally slammed the door shut behind him, Gwen leads the horse out of the barn. She'd planned to walk him to the sunniest pasture, where the ice has already melted, but seeing her father makes her want to go miles away.

The footing is too slippery for riding, but Gwen doesn't care. She's completely unschooled and does everything wrong, but it doesn't matter with a horse like Tarot. He makes his way over the ice, then onto the packed dirt in the driveway. Gwen feels sure enough of him to give him his head, and let him take charge of matters. When he goes into the woods, right before the devil's corner, Gwen doesn't protest. Tarot walks quickly over brambles and fallen leaves; when they pass under low branches, Gwen ducks and rests her face against his neck. She can feel his blood, just beneath his skin; when he breathes, the air fills with smoke. He's like a dragon, ancient and fearless. He doesn't spook at anything, not when pheasants fly out of the bushes, not when they come upon a deer, drinking from an icy stream.

Gwen can only guess what they must have done to this horse to make him mean enough to kill two men. He was a machine, a winning machine. Hay in, shit out, and run like hell. Run so fast they can never catch you. She has seen marks in Tarot's flesh. He's been beaten, long ago, in another life that will always be a mystery. History is personal, Gwen understands that now. All you are seeing is what's before you, the rest is guesswork. Still, she believes that he was beaten with a chain, at least once. There's a circular indentation on his flank, and each time she runs her hand over that wound, Tarot throws his head back in a move so serious, so potentially killing, that Gwen's respect for him is renewed.

Now, as he jumps a fallen tree, Gwen holds on for dear life. She tells herself riding Tarot isn't any more dangerous than being on the back of Josh Krauss's out-of-control Honda roaring down the El Camino at midnight. All the same, she closes her eyes when they come to the thickest part of the woods, and when she opens them again, the Marshes are before her, all gold and brown. Herons rise from the grass. Ice covers the inlets. They're trotting through frozen mud now, over hermit crabs and minnows. Maybe it's the old apple tree which calls to the horse, or maybe it's the wild berries; either way, Tarot has come to graze in the Coward's front yard.

"Not here," Gwen tells the horse. "Let's go."

When Tarot refuses to move, Gwen kicks him, but she hasn't the heart to do anything more than tap, and Tarot doesn't even notice her boots against his flanks. He's come upon a pile of frozen apples, and Gwen had better settle down, since he's not leaving anytime soon.

The Coward sees the girl as she slips off the horse, and for a moment, he thinks it's Belinda out there, who used to ride this same horse when she came to visit him. Other people brought food and clothes—Judith Dale, of course, and Louise Justice occasionally—but Belinda brought him what he truly yearned for. Photographs of his son. School papers. Spelling tests. Paintings of boats and of starry nights. The first tooth his boy lost, which the Coward still keeps in a saltshaker beneath his bed. Locks of pale hair, retrieved from the kitchen floor after a haircut.

Belinda used to sit on his porch and cry sometimes; once, she spent the night, curled up on a blanket on his floor. She had hair the color of roses, and on the night when she stayed with him her lip was split open; it hurt too much for her to drink the water the Coward offered her. Although he knows that Belinda died years ago, she seems to have reappeared beneath his apple tree. The Coward pulls on his boots and hurries outside. He's ready to greet Belinda with a hug, but when she turns around he sees it's only the girl who was here before, the one who left him the old compass he was given on his twelfth birthday, when there was still hope for him.

"I'm not trespassing," Gwen says quickly. Maybe she's been crying about her father and maybe she hasn't been. This bright sunlight could bring tears to anyone's eyes. "It's this horse. He loves apples."

"All right," the Coward says in a surprisingly mild voice. Now he sees, there are indeed tears on this girl's cheeks. "Let him eat."

The Coward sits on the rickety front steps of his porch. The ice makes everything in the distance shine like diamonds. The Coward blinks in the light. He has always believed that if vodka looked like anything, it would look like ice. Gin, on the other hand, was pure, clean snow.

"You don't know me," the girl says.

She has come to sit beside him on the steps, which cannot be a pleasant experience, the Coward is certain, since he can't remember the last time he bathed. But in fact, his odor is no more offensive than marsh grass or old apples, slightly vinegary.

"I'm Gwen," the girl says. "My father is Richard Cooper. My mother is March."

The Coward appraises her. His niece, if what she's saying is true. Well, she does have the Cooper nose, straight and narrow, and those pale blue eyes.

"I don't take after my mother, if that's what you're thinking. But you're my uncle all the same."

"For all the good it will do you," the Coward says.

Gwen laughs. "Screwed-up family."

"You have no idea," the Coward tells her.

Gwen rests her chin on her hand and watches Tarot munch apples. It's actually beautiful out here, if you don't mind the isolation. If loneliness isn't a factor. Before she can say another word, the Coward has risen from the steps and is already heading for his house. He can't take too much of people. Five minutes is just about tops.

"Where are you going?" Gwen asks.

He doesn't want to think about his family. That's sorrow, plain and simple, and besides, he's got better things to do.

"I'm going inside," he tells the girl.

"To drink?" The horse has come near, so Gwen stands and reaches for the reins. "That's what you do, right? It's like your occupation or something, isn't it? Being a drunk?"

"Drunkard," the Coward corrects.

He squints against the glare of the diamonds in the Marshes. If he wants to, he can go inside and pretend there's no one beneath his apple tree.

"In case you're interested, your son doesn't drink at all. He won't even have a beer. Even if everyone else is completely wasted, he won't touch the stuff."

The Coward has reached his front door, but he doesn't go inside.

"You'd be proud of him," Gwen says.

Although the Coward's back is toward her, she knows he's listening.

"If you ever took the trouble to know him."

When the Coward turns to face this girl, she has her hands on her hips. Clearly, she's not the sort to back down from things. If she loves you, she'll fight for you, and that's what she appears to be doing right now.

"What makes you think I have a choice on that topic?" The Coward's voice sounds harsh.

"Because you do," Gwen says. "You just do."

The Coward watches as she leads the horse out of his yard, around the garden gate, then into the Marshes, where the ice has begun to melt in the thin afternoon sunlight. There's something hot in the center of the Coward's chest, so he sits back down on his porch. The floorboards are loose; beneath them is a den of raccoons. When the Coward walks across these marshes, to Route 22, and the liquor store beyond, that is his choice. In all these years, he has not stopped to think other choices were his to make as well.

Do what you want, do what you will, do what you have to, do what you think you cannot.

He feels sick inside. If he's having a stroke, then it's a suitable penance for all the ruin he's brought upon his tired body. If it's a broken heart, he deserves that too. Tonight will be so chilly he'll have to burn extra wood in his old stove, and the smoke will billow out into the Marshes like a flock of blackbirds. He'll drink ice and snow, he'll drink himself senseless, and he'll be surprised to discover that when he wakes the next day, on his hard, cold floor, he'll still hear that girl's words ringing in his ears.

PART THREE

SIXTEEN

HOW MUCH SNOW WILL FALL THIS WIN-
ter? That's what people want to know. How much
wood should be stored beside the front porch?
How much cash allotted to the Snow Shovelers'
Fund, which pays local boys to excavate driveways
and sidewalks for the town's senior citizens? Judgment is, there's a long, hard season in store, at
least among those who frequent the Lyon Cafe,
and this theory has been seconded by the patrons
of the reading room at the library as well. Just see
how high the hornets have built their nests, always a sign of deep snow to come. Sheep and
horses have especially thick coats for November.

Squirrels are still storing chestnuts. Warblers have already migrated south, moving through town much earlier than usual, forsaking their nests in the ivy.

Ken Helm has a mountain of firewood outside his small house. He's been chopping wood all summer and throughout the fall. His wife and two sons don't even notice the sound anymore, but they hear it in their dreams; a rhythmic hewing that echoes whenever they close their eyes. Susanna Justice drives out to order wood for the season, for her parents and for herself, as she does every year. It doesn't take much to heat Susie's little cottage, but she's heard this winter's going to be a killer.

"The Judge always gets his delivery first," Ken tells Susie after she's ordered two cords and is making out the check. "My favorite customer."

Susie smiles, but her mind is elsewhere. She's a bulldog all right; she can't let go, especially when she's got the sense that she's onto something. Yesterday she went into Boston to speak with the oncologist at Children's Hospital who was in charge of Belinda and Hollis's son, Cooper. Cooper was diagnosed with leukemia when he was four, and although the doctor refused to let Susie see the boy's records, he insisted nothing was out of the ordinary. Nothing out of the ordinary to get a death sentence for your four-year-old. Nothing out of the ordinary to be married to a man as distant and mean as Hollis, to hold your little boy in your arms all the way home from Boston after the doctor informs you of a diagnosis as cruel as that.

"Is Hollis still letting you cull through his woods?" she asks when she hands Ken Helm his check.

"I pay him good money for it," Ken says, defensively, as if she'd accused him of dealing with the devil. "I wouldn't take anything from him for free. I pay for the use of his land, but that doesn't mean I like him."

As soon as Susie hears that twist in Ken's voice, she knows he wants to tell her something. When she began working at *The Bugle*, it took a while before she understood that just because people don't answer directly doesn't mean they won't eventually tell all. Ken will talk, all right, if Susie asks the right questions.

"Were you using his woods back when Belinda was alive?"

Ken Helm has been accompanying Susie to her parked truck. Now, he stops.

"I didn't say anything about Belinda."

"That's true. You didn't." He knows something, all right.

"Is there something you wanted to ask me about her?" Ken holds his hand above his eyes to block the sun, but the result is, Susie can't gauge his reaction.

"It's probably nothing," Susie admits. "I heard some talk about Belinda and Hollis. Just gossip."

"What'd you hear? That he killed her?"

Jesus, Susie thinks. *Everyone does know.*

Ken stares straight ahead at the mountainous pile of wood beside his house. The line of his jaw seems unusually tight.

"That's right," Susie says, in an easy tone, not wanting to scare him off. "I heard he might have."

"That's not gossip," Ken Helm says. "That's a fact of life."

Susie's heart is racing. To calm herself, she shifts her gaze to stare at the woodpile along with Ken. It's taller than the roof of his house. Taller than many of the trees.

"Is there some proof?" Susie says.

Ken whistles through his teeth for his dog, a golden retriever who's strayed too close to the road which runs past.

"Anything at all?" Susie asks.

"The proof is that I know and everyone in this town who had anything to do with Belinda knows the way he treated her. She forgave him not seven but seventy-seven times. You'd see her face, and you knew. Whether or not he killed her with his bare hands doesn't matter. He's responsible for her death." Ken's dog trots over and Ken pats the retriever's head. "Just as I'm responsible."

Susie looks at Ken Helm, surprised at this assessment from a man she's always known, but has never thought to talk to before. "Why would you say that?" Susie asks. "What did you have to do with her death?"

"I knew what she was going through, and I didn't do anything."

Susie can't imagine that Belinda, who was extremely private and, although well liked by everyone, had no real friends, would ever confide in Ken.

"I was driving home one night, and I saw her in the road. I stopped, and she got into my truck. She said she'd hurt her arm, and I took her over to St. Bridget's. Now, of course, they've got a whole section of the place named after him, but back then when I said I'd call Hollis for her, Belinda got all panicky. I mean panicky. So I waited for her, and when the doctor was through, I drove her home." Ken's dog has gone over to the woodpile, probably searching for mice, and Ken whistles again, more sharply this time. "Her arm was broken."

"Did she tell you how it happened?"

"No, but after that, she came here sometimes. When she needed a ride to the hospital. I always did it, and I never said a word to anyone. Not even to my wife."

"You're not the only one responsible if everyone knew what was happening."

Ken shakes his head. "One time I was asleep, and I woke up for no reason, and when I looked out the window I thought there was a ghost out there. She was wearing something white, I guess that was it. She had the kid with her that time—he was only a baby and I figure she didn't want to leave him with Hollis. I can't say that I blame her. Nobody wanted to confront him, but we should have. We should have gone to him."

It is getting colder, even now, but Susie and Ken stand there, unmoving.

"'If your hand or foot should cause you to sin, cut it off and throw it away; it is better for you to enter into life crippled or lame than to have two hands or two feet and be thrown into the eternal fire.' Matthew 18:8." Ken Helm pauses to clear his throat. "It would have been a blessing if someone had stopped him."

They finally head toward Susie's parked truck. When they get there, Susie shakes Ken's hand before she opens the door. She has never before noticed that his eyes are green.

"It's the sun," he says, to explain why his eyes are watering, and of course Susie nods, even though the sky is filled with clouds and the light is hazy at best.

"Don't worry about the Judge's delivery," Ken says as Susie gets into her truck. "I'll make him a nice, neat woodpile."

On the way home, Susie stops at the Red Apple to pick up a few things—some yogurt, a box of fancy bakery-style cookies—but instead of turning left on Route 22 and going home to have lunch with her dogs, as she usually does, she turns right and drives to St. Bridget's Hospital. *Leave it be,* Ed keeps telling her, but how is she supposed to do that, especially now that she has that vision of Belinda dressed in white standing beside the woodpile in Ken Helm's yard?

Susie parks in the nurses' lot, and props her *Bugle* parking sticker up against the windshield. The bad thing about living in a small town is that everyone knows your business, but it's a good thing too, since it makes for connections which crisscross each other more often than the strands of a spider's web. Susie has known Maude Hurley in the billing department at the hospital for ages. In fact, she dated Maude's son, Dave, for quite a while, and remembers mostly that he was a terrific ice-skater and too perfunctory in bed. Maude, however, was a pistol, and Susie always enjoyed going to her house for Sunday dinners. Now, when she goes to the billing office, Susie brings the fancy chocolate chip cookies as an offering, but she doesn't need to bribe Maude for information.

"Honey, everybody knew about Belinda," Maude says.

But unfortunately, all of Belinda's hospitalizations date to the time before admissions were computerized. Try as she might, Maude can't call up anything on her terminal.

"That's that," Susie says, disappointed and starting in on the chocolate chip cookies herself.

"Not likely," Maude says, and she leads Susie down to the basement of St. Bridget's, to a room filled with ancient, mildewed files, suggesting that if anyone discovers her, Susie should say she's gathering information for the hospital's fiftieth anniversary.

Maude, Susie believes, would have made a great mother-in-law, and she gives the older woman a hug before getting down to work. It takes an hour and a half, but Susie finally finds what's left of Belinda's file. The file, however, covers only the last two years of Belinda's life. The upside, if one can call it that, is that even in that relatively short period of time there were four admissions. More than average, Susie would guess, but proof of nothing. Two of the entries are illegible, but the other two—"broken mandible," "fifteen stitches"—send chills along Susie's spine. What, exactly, she can do with this information, she's not sure, at least not until she notices Dr. Henderson's name at the top of the page in the listing for the patient's physician.

Susie eats from a container of yogurt while sitting in her parked truck; then she heads over to Main Street, where, to her surprise, Dr. Henderson agrees to see her, although he has a waiting room filled with patients.

"Are you writing an article about Belinda?" he asks when she brings up the name.

"I'm just interested."

"In?"

"The circumstances of her death, for one."

Susie would have guessed that Dr. Henderson, who's known to be cool and businesslike, would insist that the circumstances of a patient's death were privileged information, but he seems relieved to be talking about this subject. He takes off his glasses and leans back in his chair.

"Acute pneumonia," he tells Susie. "Which, of course, is absolute bullshit."

"Excuse me?" Susie says.

"She died because he let her die. I could have done something if someone had called me. By the time she was brought into the hospital—and then only because Judith Dale had happened to stop by and Judith had understood how desperate the circumstances were—Belinda's fever was raging and she couldn't breathe. She died of neglect."

"But she'd been your patient for years, surely you must have sensed something was wrong with her situation at home before that?"

"My dear, something's wrong in every situation if you look hard enough."

"Well, let me ask you this. Did you feel that some of her physical ailments, not the pneumonia of course, but the broken bones, the bruises, were caused by her husband?"

"It doesn't matter what I *feel*," Dr. Henderson says in his coolest tone. "Did I see him hit her? No. Did she ever confide in me that she was abused in any way? No. She did not."

Susie Justice can feel a pulse in the side of her throat.

"But she's dead," Susie says.

"That," Dr. Henderson allows, "is the sad truth."

That night, after Susie has told Ed Milton everything, he simply shakes his head. They're at his place, an apartment on the High Road, and he's cooking fettucini Alfredo, which smells even better because Susie is starving, in spite of the yogurt and the box of cookies she ate earlier in the day.

"All you have on him," Ed says, "is that he was guilty of ignoring her."

"Come on," Susie says. "It's like some secret that everybody knew, including that damned Dr. Henderson who always acts as if he was higher than God."

"Everybody *thinks*. If you ask me, she killed herself."

"How can you say that?" Susie can't wait for dinner and has gotten a jar of olives from the fridge. She stopped at home to get her mail and bring the dogs along with her, who seem oddly comfortable here at Ed's place. Best of all, Ed doesn't complain when two extremely smelly and slobbery canine specimens stretch out on his couch.

"She could have phoned Dr. Henderson herself. It sounds like she wanted to die."

"That's horrible," Susie says, but she is not entirely sure he's wrong. "So what do I do now?" she asks.

Ed Milton smiles. He used to hate it when cases didn't get solved; now he figures that some situations are simply beyond human control. "Belinda died twelve years ago, and it seems that legally Hollis had nothing to do with it. He probably smacked her around, but there are no comprehensive hospital records to back that up and no eyewitnesses. Basically, you have nothing."

"I don't accept that," Susie says, which may be the moment when Ed finishes falling head over heels for her.

"You don't have the makings for a criminal case," Ed says. "What you have, Susie, is a moral issue, and it's one which can't be tried in front of your dad."

Susie doesn't ask Ed's opinion about whether or not she should pass this new information on to March, who, it's quite clear, doesn't want to hear anything negative. This is not a new dilemma for Susanna Justice. Since that summer when she saw her father walk past the roses and knew he was in love, she has been wrestling with this puzzle: How do you tell an awful truth to someone you care for and wish to protect? She thinks about the nights when her father phoned home to say he had to work late, and the sinking feeling she had in her stomach whenever she took that message and had to report back to her mother, as if she and not the Judge were the liar.

Once, and only once, she tried to tell her mother. She was a freshman at Oberlin and home for the holidays. She was full of herself, and how much she had learned in a single semester. She was certain of everything a woman could be, all of which, of course, her mother was not. They had been wrapping presents at the dining room table, bickering over why Susie would not be allowed to move out of the dorm and into an apartment with her then boyfriend, when the argument had become heated.

"End of conversation," Louise had finally said. "Your father will not allow it."

"My father!" Susie had shouted. Why, he was probably with his mistress at the very moment they were wrapping his Christmas presents in gold paper. "Why should I listen to anything he has to say about morality? If you knew what he was really like, you'd walk out of here and divorce him!"

Louise Justice had gotten up and slapped Susie across the face. Louise had never hit anyone before, but she hit Susie so hard she left a mark on her cheek, making certain to silence her daughter before she could divulge anything more.

"You don't know the first thing about love," Louise Justice had told Susie that night. "And you certainly don't know anything about marriage."

This assessment is probably still true, Susie thinks as she takes off her clothes and gets into bed with Ed Milton later that night. She circles her arms around Ed and kisses him. Does she love him or not? How will she ever know? She loves the way he is in bed, she trusts his opinions, values what he thinks, yearns to see him at odd hours of the day. So what does all that add up to?

Look at the trouble love brings. Look at the mess it makes. Who knows what caused Belinda to marry Hollis—bad judgment or compassion or desire, maybe even loneliness. Who can tell why March would throw everything away for a worthless man, or why Bill Justice, the most honest man in town, would tell bold-faced lies every day of his life. There, in Ed Milton's bed, Susanna Justice suddenly needs to know if she's the only one so completely in the dark about such matters. Ed is honest; he'll tell the truth. His back is to her, and the hour is late, but she asks Ed anyway. *Have you ever been in love?* She's certain that he laughs when he turns to her, but in the morning she can't quite remember if he actually said, *Not before,* or if, perhaps, that was only what she wanted to hear.

SEVENTEEN

ON SATURDAY MORNING, GWEN HURRIES
to meet Hank at the coffee shop, so rushed for
time that she forgets to touch the Founder's knee
for luck as she runs past the statue. Hank left a
note taped to Tarot's stall for her to find when she
went to feed and groom the horse earlier, inviting
her to meet him for breakfast.

He's at a rear booth, and Gwen tosses herself
into the seat across from him. "What's the occasion?" She grins. "Is it your treat?"

"For once." Hank hands her a menu. "He's
actually paying me to do some work, so I figured
I'd take you out."

Gwen notices then, there's a cardboard box on the floor beside the booth. Inside are cans of paint and rollers.

"He's fixing up the house," Hank explains.

"Mr. Cheapskate? Hard to believe." Gwen peruses her menu. "Ooh," she says. "Banana-nut pancakes."

"He wants to impress someone."

Gwen puts her menu down. This is more than a date for breakfast. Hank has something he wants to tell her. "My mother?"

Hank nods, then orders for them both when Alison Hartwig, their waitress, comes over.

"He wants your mom to move in with him," Hank says when the waitress moves on. "He's planning on it."

"She won't." Gwen sounds sure of herself, but she has a funny feeling in her stomach.

"I'm painting the upstairs bedroom today," Hank says. "Linen white."

"Fuck him," Gwen says.

"Yeah, well," Hank murmurs, torn between the two of them.

"I'm glad you warned me," Gwen tells him.

Of course she can't eat when their food is served; the idea of living in Hollis's house makes her completely sick. She wanders through town when Hank goes back to finish painting, and sits on a bench in the town square beneath the bare linden trees. She has the feeling that she's on a train that's going full speed, and whether she stays on board or jumps off doesn't matter. Either way, she'll crash.

When Gwen gets back to Fox Hill in the afternoon, she finds her mother working at the kitchen table. It's cold in the house, and March is wearing two sweaters and two pairs of wool socks as she sets flat pieces of turquoise into a bracelet she plans to use as a sample piece at the crafts store in the village, and perhaps show to some jewelry stores down in Boston.

"It is freezing in here," Gwen says. She keeps her ski jacket on and zipped.

"I know. Something's wrong with the heat. Hollis came over to check it out, and the whole system may need to be replaced."

He probably broke it himself, Gwen thinks. Just the first of many good reasons for them to move in with him. "Maybe I should call that guy Ken and see if he can fix it," she suggests.

"No, don't," March says. "Hollis thinks Ken charges too much. He'll fix it himself."

Gwen bets he'll do precisely that. He'll fix it so they'll freeze to death in their beds if they stay.

"We're happy here, aren't we?" Gwen asks suddenly.

"Of course we are," March answers, startled by her daughter's serious tone. "We're fine," she insists.

Funny that Gwen asks if they are happy in this house; Hollis, after all, has been trying to convince March to move in with him. It makes sense of course, and yet she's hesitated. Mostly, it's true, because of Gwen, the same reason she hesitated all those years ago, in her garden. Maybe she hasn't been the best mother lately, maybe she's been thoughtless and selfish, but she still knows right from wrong. Or would it be so wrong to move in with him? Wouldn't it be more honest? More up-front?

Today when Hollis came to look at the oil burner, he didn't have time to stay. He told March he was fixing up the house at Guardian Farm, that she's certain to change her mind, and that he was, at that very moment, expecting a stonemason to arrive at his door. Already, he's had a cleaning service come out from the village to vacuum the rugs and wash the windows and polish all that old furniture Annabeth Cooper bought in New York. He even sent the dogs to the kennel to be bathed, and when they returned their clean coats were so red it was easy to understand how those rumors insisting they'd been bred from foxes had first begun. The refrigerator has been stocked with cream and salmon, fresh fruit and juices. Hollis hired Dr. Henderson's youngest daughter, Miranda, who runs a catering service, to bring him a month's supply of dinners that can be kept frozen until needed.

In truth, those dinners aren't all Hollis plans to freeze. He has removed the thermal coupling from the oil burner in the basement of the house on Fox Hill. No big deal, he merely wants to cut off the heating output and help make the place more unattractive. It's his house, and he would be well within his rights to insist that March move out, but he wants her to come to him of her own free will. Sometimes, however, free will requires a little intervention. Which is why Hollis is waiting at the barn the next morning when Gwen arrives. It is five-thirty when she gets there and she hasn't slept well; she doesn't even sense Hollis's presence until she's already given fresh water to Tarot, as well as to Geronimo and that stupid pony who always tries to bite her.

"What are you doing here?" Gwen asks when she notices Hollis in a corner.

"I own the place," Hollis says. "After all."

Gwen can't help but note how restless Tarot is with Hollis in sight. As soon as Hollis approaches, Tarot kicks at the wall.

"Kind of a waste to keep this old man," Hollis says. The contempt in his voice makes Gwen take a step closer to Tarot. Hollis and the horse are staring at each other. "Every once in a while I think about putting him out of his misery."

Gwen feels a chill. She can recognize a threat.

"He's not in misery," Gwen says.

"I've been thinking that we could help each other out. You and me. Believe it or not."

"Really?" Gwen's throat is dry. He wants her to become an accomplice to something.

"I'd like your mother to move in with me, and I don't want you to screw it up." *Like the last time,* that's what Hollis is thinking.

When you fucked up our plans without even being born. "In fact, I want you to think it's a great idea."

"Good luck," Gwen says. "Because that's never going to happen."

Gwen is totally freezing, but she couldn't leave if she wanted to. Hollis is blocking her way, standing in the doorway of the barn. There's a lamp right above him that casts a particularly harsh light. At this hour, he looks his age; he looks like an old man himself. He's the one who should be put out of his misery.

"All you have to do is be positive. Tell your mother you want to move. In return, I won't shoot him."

Gwen takes a deep breath. She hopes she can bluff him. "Not good enough."

Hollis stares straight at her.

"I want the horse," Gwen tells him.

Hollis laughs at that.

"I mean it. I want it on paper. A legal document that says I'm the owner."

Hollis can't help but smile. She's smarter than he would have guessed. Too bad she has no idea who she's dealing with.

"Fine," Hollis says. "My lawyers will draw up the transfer of ownership. I'll have it to you by next week."

"Fine," Gwen agrees, hoping only that she won't start to cry until she gets out of there. When she leaves, she runs. She's done it. Tarot is hers. She runs and she runs, but it seems to take forever to get away. She feels as if she's done a terrible thing, selling out her own mother for a horse, but she's done it, and she's not going to cry about it, at least not for long.

By the end of the week, they're ready to move. They have so few possessions the old Toyota's rear seat is not even filled. Like explorers in the New World, they travel light. Hank is waiting for them over at Guardian Farm, to help unload the car.

"I painted your room blue," he tells Gwen. It's the little room off the kitchen, which Hollis won't be using anymore.

"Thanks," Gwen says, gathering together her schoolbooks. "But I would have preferred you bombed it."

Gwen reaches for Sister, who's in a panic. The red dogs are all barking, and although the terrier yips right back, it's hiding behind a box of shoes and clothes.

"Come on," Gwen says to the dog. "Be prepared to enter hell." She shoos away the annoying mutts and carries Sister up to the house.

While March unloads the trunk, Hollis comes up behind her and circles his arms around her waist. March can feel the heat from his body, even in places where he isn't touching her. Funny, but she's thinking about the lemon tree in her backyard at home. She's thinking about the sound of gunfire all those years ago when the hunting ban was lifted; how you could find a trail of blood every time you went for a walk in the woods.

Hollis kisses the back of her neck and holds her against him.

"You're not going to regret this," he tells her, and March lets herself sink back against him.

When she follows Hollis up to the door, March doesn't dwell on how empty the house on Fox Hill looked when they left. She doesn't let herself get all caught up in guilt about how Richard will react when he comes home tonight and finds her message on his answering machine: She and Gwen will no longer be at the same number. Her words replayed on his machine will be calm, but there is no way to disguise their new phone number. It is, after all, one Richard has memorized; it was his when he lived at Guardian Farm.

There are lace curtains on all the windows in the bedroom where Mr. and Mrs. Cooper used to sleep, and the fresh white paint Hank hurried to finish on time is luminous in daylight. But daylight is not what matters here. They have their meals at the old kitchen table, they go about their business, but all the while, March is looking out the window, waiting for dusk, when she can go upstairs with Hollis. The blue satin duvet cover on the quilt is one Annabeth Cooper ordered from France, hand-stitched and amazingly silky beneath the skin, and the bed is larger than the old wooden bed March has at home.

On this bed, you dream things you can't discuss with anyone. Nights last longer on this bed; they begin before a suitcase is unpacked, before dinner is served, before morning, before noon. Always, she dreams she is falling and there's no way to stop. It's dream fucking that goes on here, the kind that overtakes you so that you don't bother to lock the door or make certain the window shades are pulled down. It's the kind of fucking that makes you cry out loud, makes you beg, then dissolve, that urges you to do what you've never done before. If someone knows you inside out, he knows when to start and when to stop. Don't think about the other women he's been with. Don't care if these women have felt absolutely certain they were the only ones, if he's told them he's never had it so good, not like this; if he's done it again and again. You know it's always been you, that's what he tells you, and that's what you believe. It's the way it was, isn't it, when you were so young the future seemed limitless, and it was impossible to tell where you ended and he began.

Don't think about the crows calling from the trees, or the sound of the front door slamming. What does it matter anyway? Let the dogs bark; let the hours pass by. It's all a dream, and it's yours, and it always will be. Give in to it, that's what he whispers. Don't bother bathing or combing your hair. Just do what he tells you, do it all night; go down on your knees and do it the way he likes it. Let it last an eternity, because, in all honesty, there's no going back. Doors have been shut, suitcases unpacked; days have come and gone and you're still here.

In the mornings, when March goes downstairs to make coffee, she doesn't say much. If she sees Hank or Gwen before they leave for school, she might offer to fix breakfast; she might stand at the window to wave goodbye, but her attention is limited. She cannot make sense of Gwen and Hank's conversations, or maybe she just doesn't want to. She stays in the dream. She used to be so orderly, but now she has to hand-wash her underwear, since she's run out of clothes. She's lost count of what day it is; she hasn't even bothered to change the sheets on their bed. And yet, she's convinced she needn't worry. Outside, there is wind and dreadful weather, but it can't hurt her. He'll tell her what to do and what to think, and after a while, if she stays here long enough, what to dream as well.

Since they've moved in, Gwen is the one who never sleeps. If she does happen to nap for a short time, she never has dreams, only black pools of unconsciousness. In the little bedroom painted blue, Gwen is camped out like a woman at war, ready to move on to the next battleground. She keeps her clothes in her backpack and her other belongings—books and makeup, even her alarm clock—in an orange crate beside the bed. She sleeps fully dressed on top of her blanket. There are circles under her eyes, and in only a few days, she's had so many cigarettes behind her closed door that the room stinks of smoke in spite of the recent coat of paint. Sister is holed up in the room with Gwen; the terrier only goes outside to pee, and even then Sister continually growls at the band of red dogs, who are far too curious and ill-mannered.

As it's turned out, this place is hell. *Oh,* Gwen would have said to Minnie, her old friend, if they were still talking, *what have I done to deserve this?* Chris and Lori think she's so damned lucky, to be living in the same house as her boyfriend. Wouldn't they love to be in her shoes? Well, as implausible as it might seem, not only have Gwen and Hank not taken advantage of the situation—in spite of how easy it would be to sneak into each other's bedrooms—Gwen has not even kissed Hank, not once, since she moved in. It's not that Gwen doesn't love him any longer, she does, more than ever. But she wants something pure. She wants the opposite of what her mother has, and, Gwen is well aware of what that is.

She hears them going at it, upstairs, on the other side of the house. At first she thought she was imagining the sounds. Shouldn't it be impossible to hear in a house as grand as this? Shouldn't the plaster walls be well insulated? Shouldn't there be some privacy? But she hears them, each and every night. Her mother's cries of ardor. His disgusting noises. When she can't stand it anymore, she gets out of bed and goes outside. She lets the screen door close behind her, but Sister usually noses the door open to chase after her. The nights are now so cold that all breath becomes smoke. In the barn, Gwen checks to make sure the horses' water hasn't turned to ice. She pats Tarot, and he nudges her sleepily, snuffling at her pockets for sugar. Sister hates horses, but despises the red dogs stretched out in the driveway even more, so the terrier follows Gwen into Tarot's stall. When Gwen pulls up a stool, so she can sit down and have a cigarette, Sister lies at her feet.

"Poor Sister," Gwen says to the dog, who wags its tail at the cadence of a friendly human voice. "You're not the bitch you once were, are you?"

There are pieces of straw in the dog's fur, and the creature flinches whenever Tarot shudders in his sleep. Tarot's lungs are watery and old and he makes a rushing sound when he breathes out. For two weeks running, Hollis has sworn that the purchase agreement will arrive at the end of the week, but Gwen is starting to get nervous. As soon as she finally does get ownership, she plans to get a safety-deposit box at the bank so she'll never lose the papers. She runs her hand over the horse's soft nose. She has the strongest sense that she needs to keep him safe, and for some reason, this gives her courage. When she has legal ownership, she'll leave. That's what she's decided, and although she hasn't had the heart to tell Hank, she believes that he knows. It's the way he watches her, as if she were already gone.

When Gwen can't keep her eyes open any longer, she carries Sister out of the stall and closes up behind her. There's a light on in the kitchen, and relief washes over Gwen. Hank has been waiting up for her with a fresh pot of coffee. They sit in silence, at two in the morning, as if they were an old married couple, drinking coffee and holding hands. They're trapped by circumstance. They can feel their situation chipping away at what they might have had.

Hank knows that if it weren't for the horse, Gwen would have already left. Her intention to leave Hank behind is not because she doesn't love him; it's because she knows he can take care of himself. On this night, however, they don't talk about how their future is unraveling; they don't think about all they have to lose. They go into that small bedroom off the kitchen and curl up together on the single bed, on top of the woolen blanket, arms entwined. If she could, Gwen would whisper that she loved him. If he could, he would vow that everything would turn out right. But that's not the way things are now, and they both know it. That's not the way things are at all.

EIGHTEEN

THIS YEAR, THE HARVEST FAIR, WHICH is always set out in the basement of Town Hall, is more crowded than usual, and March's booth—used clothing, the one she promised Regina Gordon she would run—has done a booming business—good news for the children's section of the library, to which all proceeds will be donated.

"I never thought I'd see you here," Susanna Justice says when she comes to look through a pile of old vests. She pulls out a double-breasted houndstooth which would look great with her brown corduroy slacks.

"Neither did I." March laughs. "I'm not the type."

They've been tentative with each other since March moved in with Hollis. Susie has taken everyone's advice and kept her mouth shut, but no one bothered to tell her that once she did, she wouldn't have much to say.

"Well," Susie says.

"Well." March grins. "You look great."

Actually, it's March who looks beautiful. She's wearing old painter's pants and a heavy red sweater she paid three dollars for this morning, bought from her very own booth. In Susie's estimation, March has lost weight. The angles of her face are more prominent. Her dark eyes more intense. March smiles when she catches Susie staring, and that's when Susie thinks, *It's love that's done this to her.*

"My mother is still counting on you for Thanksgiving," Susie says.

"That's so sweet of her, but I have Hollis to think about. He hates Thanksgiving. He thinks turkey's inedible."

"Bring him anyway." Susie actually manages to sound cheerful. "He can have a bologna sandwich."

Just because she's stopped pestering March doesn't mean Susie has given up her research concerning Hollis. She has been down to Juvenile Hall in Boston, but even with some strings pulled by a friend of Ed's on the force, she found nothing. It's as if Hollis never existed, or maybe someone simply wiped the slate clean, Henry Murray probably, with his ridiculously big heart and his faith in humankind. Still, Susie continues to feel if she only looks hard enough, she'll turn up hard evidence against Hollis, if not enough to send March running for cover, then at least enough to make her think twice.

"Even if Hollis doesn't want to favor us with his company, you can still come to dinner with Gwen and Hank."

"Easy for you to say." March laughs.

"Extremely easy." Susie is not laughing. "Nobody's telling me what to do."

"It's not what you think," March says. "He's not like that. You know me, Susie. Do you think I'd let someone boss me around? At my age?"

"Okay. I hope I'm wrong."

When Susie hugs March she notices the scent of lavender, a sad odor in Susie's opinion, one that marks the past and all things best forgotten. Most likely, there were traces of lavender cologne on the secondhand sweater March bought for herself, and the fragrance now clings to its new owner. In the end, what a friend wants for herself, that's what you have to want for her as well. Good fortune in all things, that's what Susie wishes for March, that and no mistake so terrible it cannot be rectified.

Susie moves on to used books. Just in time, March can't help but think; Hollis is approaching with two cups of hot coffee. You just have to know how to handle him, that's the piece Susie doesn't understand.

"Good old Susie-Q," Hollis says when he comes to March's booth and spies Susanna Justice nearby.

There are dozens of stands and far too many customers, at least to Hollis's mind. He's never been to a Harvest Fair, and he doesn't plan to come again. He's only here to keep an eye on March, probably a good thing since some guy is taking an awfully long time checking out an ill-fitting sports coat, soliciting March's fashion advice. It's Bud Horace, Hollis recognizes him now, the dogcatcher. Well, Bud's spending a little too long talking to March, and Hollis doesn't like that look on his face.

"Let's go," Hollis says to March when Bud finally pays for his damned sports coat and leaves.

"I think I'm committed to another two hours." March looks over her shoulder for Regina Gordon, who has everyone's schedule written down on a legal pad, but before March can spy Regina,

Hollis has already gone over to speak to Mimi Frank, who has taken the day off from the Bon Bon Salon in order to man the applesauce stand.

"How about it? Can you keep an eye on the clothing?" Hollis asks Mimi. "Personally, I think you have the energy to take care of two stands. I wouldn't say that to many people."

Mimi smiles up at Hollis; everyone notices how competent she is. "Honey, don't worry about it," she says.

"You charmed Mimi Frank," March says when Hollis helps her on with her coat. "That's hard to believe."

"Let's get out of here," Hollis says.

"We're gone." March is hoping for humor as they walk out of Town Hall, but somehow her words fall flat.

They don't have much to say to each other as they head for Hollis's truck; anyway, it would be hard to have a decent conversation with the wind blowing the way it is. When they reach the statue of the Founder, March pats his knee for luck. She has the oddest feeling that she dare not pass by the statue without giving in to this silly, superstitious act, as if on this blustery day she was, indeed, in desperate need of luck.

"Should we go to the Bluebird for lunch?" March asks Hollis.

"And see more of these idiot townsfolk? I don't think my stomach could take it."

After they've gotten into the truck, Hollis pulls her close and holds his face against hers and whispers about why he wants to be alone with her, how he wants to take her up to bed and show her how much he loves her, and March feels less jittery about the way he's been acting lately. But then Hollis starts talking about Bud Horace, and how Bud had better keep his dick in his pants. Did Hollis always speak this way? March truly can't remember. Did he always get angry so fast?

They're all pathetic, that's what he's saying now, with their moronic fund-raisers and their false cheer. He could buy them and sell them, he could do it in seconds flat; he could have them down on their knees and begging, each and every one, the members of the town council and shopkeepers alike, if he held out a big enough check. And where do they get off looking at him, looking at March? Where does that fucking Bud Horace think he's going to go with his used sports coat and his goddamned smile?

"Trust me," March says to Hollis when they stop for a red light. "I don't even know what Bud Horace looks like. Why should I? I'm only interested in you."

She kisses him then, hard and deep, but she has the nagging feeling that she's faking something. And worse—that she'd better. He's always been jealous, she knows that. Well, so has she. If he doesn't want other men looking at her, so what? It's because he loves her, that's all. It's because he cares.

She needs to concentrate less on the what-ifs and more on the here and nows. She needs to take pleasure in going day by day. Since they've begun living together, they don't go out very much, or at least March doesn't. She has set up a work space on the third floor, in an old guest bedroom, and she's begun to work on holiday presents: beautiful silver pendants, one for Susie and another for Gwen, luminous little things to slip onto silver chains, formed into the shape of crescent moons. March works when Hollis goes off in the mornings, to check his properties, and when he's at meetings in the evenings. She doesn't even realize how often she's alone until she's run out of silver, and has to ask Hollis to pick up more on his next trip into Boston.

But Hollis's next trip to the city falls on a Sunday, so all the shops will be closed, and March won't be able to get her silver after all. It's an emergency meeting with his lawyer, something about a hurricane and his property in Florida. March is still in bed and Hollis is in the shower on the morning he's to go to Boston, when the phone rings. It's early, and again March feels anxious—she's afraid the caller will be Hollis's lawyer, with bad news that will set him off. Or worse, that Richard will finally phone here. But when March picks up the receiver it's only Ken Helm, calling to let her know that the big chestnut tree over on the hill has blight.

"I can't promise we can save it," Ken tells her, "but we can try."

As they speak, March can hear Ken's wife and kids in the background. Ken will be lucky to have enough in the bank to pay his mortgage this month, and yet here he is, worrying about a chestnut tree on a Sunday morning.

March rolls over onto her stomach. It's warm under the satin quilt. She's only wearing panties, and doesn't want to get out of bed, especially not to go look at a tree, but Ken seems so serious when he speaks about the effects of blight.

"All right," March finally agrees. "I'll meet you there at ten. Right after Hollis leaves."

When March reaches to replace the phone onto the night table she sees that Hollis has been watching her. He has a towel around his waist and his wet hair is plastered to his head and the way he's staring at her makes her feel guilty, about what, however, she's not certain.

"Hey." March smiles. "Come back to bed."

He walks toward her without a word; he's amazingly quick, or maybe it only seems that way, but before March knows it, he's torn the blue quilt off and has grabbed her by her wrists, wrenching her to her feet.

"Who the hell was that?" is what she thinks he's shouting.

"Wait a second," March says.

He's really hurting her; any more pressure would probably snap her wrist bones.

"Hollis!" she says.

"Who was that on the phone?" He pulls her over to the dressing table, then shoves her against the mirror. The glass is icy cold against March's bare skin. "Who were you going to meet?"

"It was Ken."

"Don't fuck with me, March." His voice sounds completely empty.

"I'm not." Her heart is beating much too fast, as if she were scared of him.

"I mean it."

"So do I. It was Ken Helm on the phone." *Thank God it was only Ken*, that's what she's thinking. That is the one and only thought she can manage. "That old tree on Fox Hill is dying and he wants me to meet him to okay some work."

Hollis looks at her closely. He may not believe her yet.

"That's not your property. Why would he ask for your okay?"

"He probably thought it was too trivial to bother you with." March can feel herself sweet-talking Hollis. That's what she's doing, and it turns out she's good at it. Who would have guessed? She's not only a good liar, she is better than average at flattery. Already, Hollis is easing up on her wrists and she's no longer pushed against the mirror. She doesn't want to think about the way glass breaks, a jagged, unreliable shattering, so that you never can tell who will get hurt. "It's a stupid tree. That's all. He wouldn't have thought you'd be interested."

Hollis is still looking at her, but the situation no longer seems as dangerous. *Maybe it never was*, March thinks. *It probably never was*. He raises her wrists to his mouth, kissing first one, then the other, right at the most delicate spot, where the veins crisscross.

"I thought you went crazy on me," March says, relieved.

It turns out that her legs are shaking. They probably have been all along, but she doesn't realize this fact until he draws her closer to the edge of the dressing table. This is where Annabeth Cooper used to carefully apply her lipstick and rouge; she had three hairbrushes, all made of tortoiseshell, all imported from France.

Hollis pulls March nearer still, close enough so he can ease off her panties and fuck her right there, without saying a word, without asking.

"Listen," he tells her when he's done, "tell Ken Helm to do whatever he wants. I don't mind paying to save that tree."

When Hollis leaves, March stands at the bedroom window. He didn't hit her, that's all she knows. He wouldn't do that to her. She watches Hollis get into his truck and drive away. She knows what people say about Belinda, but she doesn't care. Hollis never loved Belinda, and she was a fool to marry him. This is what no one has ever understood, including Susie: He is different with March, and when all is said and done, he didn't mean to hurt her. He'd never do that.

She'll think about the yard at Fox Hill, that's what she'll do. She'll think about the nights when she and Hollis sat out there, searching for privacy and for stars. Whose tree is it, March now wonders, that chestnut so old there isn't another like it in the entire county? Does it belong to the man who owns the land where it grows, or the woman who looked into its branches every day for three years, or the person who can save it from blight? Does it belong to those doves who come back year after year to nest, or to the sky above, or to the earth in which its roots are settled?

March showers for a long time, hoping to get rid of those cold, blue marks Hollis left on her skin where he grabbed her and held on too tightly. When she faces the mirror she notices the white strands in her hair. She should go into town to the Bon Bon and have it colored, or buy a package of dye at the pharmacy, but she's simply in no mood for that. Instead, she pulls her hair back into an elastic band; she gets dressed in an old thermal undershirt of Hollis's and a pair of jeans, then pulls on her boots. What will happen to those foolish doves if the tree has to be chopped down? They should have been chased away in October; March should have shaken a broom at them until they were forced to flee from their own bad judgment.

When she's dressed, March makes tea and toast with butter, but she's really not hungry. The way he twisted her wrists hurt, and the way he fucked her hurt as well, but she's not going to think about that. Nothing happened, after all. Not really. It's just that some mornings you want breakfast, and some you don't. When Hank comes downstairs, still half asleep and uncomfortable in March's presence, she suggests he have her toast. As she washes up the few dishes in the sink, March can look through the window to see Gwen in a nearby pasture, exercising that old racehorse. From this distance they look so small, horse and girl both, like toys made of tin.

"Are you okay?" Hank asks when he brings his dishes to the sink. He insists on washing his own plate and coffee cup.

"I have to go over to Fox Hill and meet Ken Helm, and I guess I don't feel like it."

Hank offers to drive her over. He's had his license for ages, he explains, and he never gets to drive because Hollis doesn't allow him use of the truck. Hank has been saving every cent he manages to get hold of for a car of his own, although whatever he could afford wouldn't even be half as good as March's beat-up Toyota. As they leave the house, March tosses Hank the keys; then she grabs two letters she plans to leave for the letter carrier to pick up when he makes his delivery. One envelope is addressed to a jewelry shop on Newbury Street and the other to a craft store in Cambridge. March sent both shops photos of her bracelets, and neither has responded, so she's giving it one more try, suggesting to both that she display some of her pieces on a commission basis. At this point, March is seriously broke. If she wanted to buy a package of hair dye, she'd have to put it on Hollis's tab at the pharmacy. Last week she had to ask Hollis for ten dollars so she could give Gwen her weekly lunch money, and although he was more than generous, she hates to be one of those people who can't pull their own weight.

"Do you mind dumping these in the mailbox for me?" she asks Hank. "I'll let Gwen know we're going." As Hank heads for the mailbox, March walks toward the pasture, waving. "We have to go up to Fox Hill to look at a sick tree," she calls.

Gwen looks up and blinks. She sees Hank on his way from the mailbox to the Toyota. "We?" She's so used to her mother's recent detachment, her interest only in Hollis, that Gwen is too startled to do anything more than nod.

"We'll be back before you know it."

Hank has started the Toyota and now drives over to pick up March. "That threw her for a loop." March laughs when she gets in. "You and me together." March notices that Hank is too tall for the Toyota and has to scrunch down in his seat. He looks so serious and so young that March feels moved. He's shy and uncomfortable about making conversation and he hasn't had much practice driving. When he least expects it, he has to swerve to avoid hitting a rabbit, and they nearly barrel right into a stone fence.

"Sorry," Hank tells March.

"It's all right," March says. He looks amazingly like Alan, had Alan been sweet-tempered. "Those rabbits think they own the place."

Hank nods. It's awkward being with March, and he's relieved when they reach the house on Fox Hill to find that Ken Helm is already there. These woods were once filled with chestnut trees, but in forty years the species has been all but destroyed, and now it seems this old specimen will meet a similar fate.

"Drastic measures," Ken says grimly as they join him to study the tree. "That's what we need."

He'll cut off most of the limbs in the hopes of salvaging the trunk, even though he's doubtful that the tree can be saved. March tells him to go ahead and do as he sees fit, still, she worries about the doves who are peering down at them from their nest.

"They're going to have to move," Ken tells March as he goes to get his saw and ladder from his truck.

"I want to make sure nothing happens to them," March calls.

"I'll do my best," Ken says. "I can't do more."

Hank has been leaning against a small maple tree, looking at the empty house. He has almost no memory of ever living here, except for the day of the fire. He remembers more than most people would guess; that the fire seemed liquid, for instance, that it looked so pretty he wanted to reach out and touch the flames, but his mother wouldn't let him. She told him no.

"Let's go inside and see how the place looks," March suggests.

"I don't think so," Hank says.

"Oh, come on. Let's take a peek."

March goes on ahead, and Hank finds himself following. The house hasn't been unoccupied that long, but the pipes have been drained, and it's colder inside than it is out. Aside from a few big pieces of furniture—the dining room table, the couch—it's empty. They can hear an echo as they walk through the rooms, like the past coming right back at them. Hank goes to the doorway into the kitchen; he knows exactly what he's looking for. To the right of the frame, where the wallpaper is worn, he can see charred wood. He found this one day when he was visiting Mrs. Dale, and after that he always felt he had to revisit the spot, as though paying his respects.

"I'll be outside," he calls to March.

"That was a stupid suggestion of mine," March says later when she comes out to the porch. "You must be upset when you come here. You must think of your mother."

"I'm fine." Something has caught in Hank's throat, and he coughs. "But if it's all right with you, I think I'll stay here for a while and help Mr. Helm."

"Sure," March says, and she pats his shoulder when she walks by.

She feels sorry for him, Hank saw it in her face. Well, pity is meaningless, that's what Hank's been taught. It's what you do that counts, Hollis has always said, and in Hank's experience, Hollis is right. He remembers perfectly well the day Hollis came for him. They were living down in the Marshes and it was freezing cold;

there was ice in Hank's hair. His father had passed out and the fire in the coal stove had died; there was nothing but embers. He remembers how light spilled into the room when Hollis opened the door. Hank's father was on the floor, and Hollis rolled Alan's limp body over with his foot, then bent down to peer into his face. Hank was not yet five, but he already knew it did no good to complain; hunger and cold were the facts of his life, so he didn't say a word. He remembers, though, the look on Hollis's face, the absolute certainty there. How curious a man of conviction had seemed to Hank, how rare.

"Get what you want to take with you," Hollis had said. "Hurry up."

Because of Hollis's tone, because of the way he was standing there—and how tall he seemed and how completely confident—Hank never thought to question him. He got the stuffed bear the ladies from the library had given him on Christmas, and his wool sweater, and he didn't look back when Hollis closed the door. But now, for the first time, Hank has questions; it's what he's been instructed to do that's the problem. He's supposed to keep an eye on March: If she goes somewhere, he's to tag along, as he did today. If he sees her setting out mail for the postman, he's to grab it and hand it over to Hollis. When he raised the issue of March's privacy with Hollis, Hollis laughed out loud.

"You really think there's such a thing as privacy?" Hollis had said. "That's just some bullshit they hand out to keep people in line. If you love someone, you do what you have to. You don't think about what other people might say."

Well, Hank has done as Hollis asked, he has March's letters in his jacket pocket right now, secured when she went to say goodbye to Gwen. He's done what he's supposed to do, and when he hands the letters over Hollis will pat him on the back. Usually that's enough for Hank—just the tiniest bit of appreciation, a nod to a job well done. But this time is different. What Hank has done in stealing March's letters is wrong, that's the way he sees it. And the most awful thing is, once he's begun to question Hollis's motives on this, he has other questions as well, especially concerning Belinda.

"She was driving me crazy," Hollis used to explain, whenever he and Belinda would fight. "Some people have to be taught a lesson," he'd tell Hank. "You'll understand when you're older, when you've had to settle for what you never wanted in the first place."

Now, when Hank thinks about the way Belinda looked after they'd had a fight, he feels sick. He thinks about the sounds he thought he'd only dreamed when he first came to live with them. Frankly, he doesn't like the conclusions he's reached.

March calls out a goodbye to Ken and drives off, leaving Hank to help. Mostly, Ken needs the branches he cuts down to be sawed into pieces, then thrown into the bed of his truck, a job Hank is glad to do, since the work is almost hard enough to keep him from thinking.

"Good job, kid," Ken Helm says when they're done for the day. Ken will be back in the morning, to finish the job. "I guess I have to give you a percentage after I bill Hollis. Maybe I should charge him double."

Hank laughs. "It's okay." All the same, he's grateful when Ken Helm slips him a twenty. When all the dead wood has been toted away, they both shield their eyes and look upward.

"'Do not store up treasures for yourselves on earth, but store them in heaven, where neither moth nor woodworms destroy them, and thieves cannot break in and steal. For where your treasure is, there will your heart also be.'"

"That sounds like good advice," Hank says.

"It is." Ken nods. "Matthew 6:19. I didn't want to say anything to March, but that nest is going to have to go."

"I figured."

"Some people don't like to hear the truth."

And, Hank thinks as he watches Ken drive off, some people don't like to tell it. Hank, for instance, hasn't told anyone about the old man who has taken to following him. He didn't even notice at first, but for the past week or two he's felt someone watching him. He heard noises when he brought old Geronimo and Coop's ornery pony out to the pasture. A branch breaking. An intake of breath. He has taken to looking over his shoulder, even when he and Gwen are walking home from school on the deserted High Road. Recently, he'd begun to see bits and pieces of the old man. A footprint in an icy field. A thread snagged on some witch hazel.

Hank tried to train his eyes to look beyond what he saw. A twisted oak had hands. A stack of hay wore worn leather boots. Then, one day, Hank looked behind him on the road and there was the old man, thin as a stick, pale as winter, with an unkempt beard and clothes far too big for his frame. Hank felt panic rise in his throat. He had the urge to grab the old man or to run away, but he did neither. He kept walking, and before long he realized it was his father who was following him. He knew because the old man would not cross onto Hollis's property; instead he disappeared into the Marshes, without a sound.

What would be the point of having a father now? Hank's all but grown, he's managed without; he'd be embarrassed to be claimed by a pathetic drunk who doesn't seem to know when his boots are on the wrong feet. It makes no sense; not now. It's Hollis who raised him, Hollis to whom he owes his allegiance. All the same, Hank finds himself thinking of his father, the way he used to examine a bottle of gin before he began to drink, as if there was some promise deep inside. Well, there are no promises, that was the problem; not in drink and not in life, not now and not ever.

The door to the empty house is rattling as the wind picks up; March must have forgotten the latch. Hank is on his way to check when he sees the old man. He just won't stop. He's everywhere.

"What do you want?" Hank shouts.

The Coward is wearing a thick black coat Louise Justice brought him one year when the Judge grew tired of it.

"Stop following me around." Hank can feel his face flush with anger. He doesn't owe this guy anything, after all, not even courtesy.

The Coward is tall, like Hank, but he weighs perhaps a hundred and twenty pounds. He wants to say something, but instead he stands there, silent, his hands in his pockets.

"I want you to cut it out." Hank's actually sweating. Crazy, but he's nervous being alone with his own father, not that he thinks of him that way. "Okay? Do you understand what I'm saying?"

Hank wishes he could be nastier, but it's not in his nature. He could, if he wanted, blow this old man over with one breath. He could break him in two.

"Do you understand?" Hank asks, and for some reason he feels a burning behind his eyes, as though he might cry.

The Coward finds his son to be so beautiful it seems inconceivable that they could be the same species. Yet they are; they're flesh and blood. What he would not give to embrace this boy, to be a father for a minute or a day. But they are at a standstill, with nowhere to go. Here is the most difficult aspect of forgiveness: You have to ask in order to receive it. This, the Coward cannot do. He can stand there, on this cold November day, but he cannot ask for what he needs. And so it is his fate to wait in silence for another day, done in by his own fear, once again.

By the time Hank is done latching the door, the Coward has disappeared back into the woods. Since the hour when Hollis came for him, Hank has never looked back. But he's looking back now, and when he does he sees that the man on the floor they stepped over when they left that shack was consumed with grief, sick with alcohol. Hank can't help himself, he pities his father. He almost wishes he hadn't chased him off. Oh, he knows Hollis would consider this a weakness in him. Pity is for women, and babies, and fools. *Your father got what he deserved,* that's what Hollis would say.

No one gets what he deserves, that's what Hank is thinking now. Things happen, and sometimes it all goes wrong. An entire life can become a dead end. Hank considers this for a very long time, and by the time he's done thinking, he's no longer sure that Hollis has all the answers. Before he leaves, Hank goes to the garden shed for the ladder he always used for cleaning out Mrs. Dale's gutters. It's a heavy old ladder, but reliable and strong. He leans it against the chestnut tree and climbs up carefully. By tomorrow, Ken Helm will finish lopping off most of the branches, in the hopes that the blight will be stopped and new growth will begin in the spring.

For as long as he can remember, Hank has done as he's been told; a good boy, dedicated as a dog, thankful for scraps. A fact from Hollis was a fact indeed; no questions asked, and none need be. Now he's wondering if he's been misled, and if judgment is not such a simple thing. If he's a good boy, why did he steal the letters March meant to send? Why, on that day when Hollis came for him, did he not kneel down beside his father and kiss him goodbye, the very least any son could do?

As he goes higher on the old ladder, Hank is unsure of what he believes, but he does know one thing—everyone deserves at least this: fresh air, clear skies, the sight of the earth from the vantage point of an old tree. His hands tremble when he takes the nest, but he's careful as he comes back down the ladder. He places the nest on the ground while he carries the ladder over to a tall crab apple tree he helped Mrs. Dale plant a few years back. It was one of her favorites, an early bloomer with huge white flowers. Hank brings the ladder over, then grabs the nest, climbs up, and positions the nest into place. When he's back on the ground, Hank claps his hands together to clean off the dirt. He may not have accomplished much, but at least that's done. March won't have to worry about the doves, although, in Hank's opinion, she had better start to worry about herself instead.

N I N E T E E N

HOLLIS HAS BEGUN TO HAVE HIS DREAM about the horse again, that awful dream that always wakes him in the middle of the night and leaves him out of breath and sweaty and ready to run. He supposes that you cannot really murder a horse; that is something humans do to each other. You kill a horse, just as you would a cow or a sheep, but somehow it's not the same. It's uglier. It gives you nightmares, year in and year out and maybe even for the rest of your life.

If you are going to do it, Hollis knows, do it speedily and in the dark. Plan it out carefully, and be aware of what hours the grooms and the trainers keep. Make certain to get half your money up front, and be sure it's a great deal of money. After all, the owner of a dead racehorse stands to collect quite a bit from his insurance company. That's why he's paying you. All you have to realize is a single indelible fact: Just because you walk away after you've been paid doesn't mean you won't be dreaming about it afterwards, when you're no longer as hungry or as young.

Here's the thing about killing a horse—its screams are far worse than any sound a man can produce. Wear earplugs, work fast; be sure you're done and over the fence before they realize their pain. It's a lot of money for someone with no education and no training and no heart at all. It's a small fortune, if you can stand the way they scream when you shatter their cannon bones and knees with a hammer or a wrench. When you start to have bad dreams, go back and ask for more money from the owners. Don't call it blackmail; it's simply an extra payment for a job well done. After all, the horse wasn't running well, and that's what such horses are meant to do. Invest your money wisely, in land and condominiums and the market, and do it before you get hurt, because there will always be a horse who will fight for its life.

That is the one he always dreams about, the last one in Miami, a job so botched the owner never collected, even though the horse had been a Preakness winner and was insured for two million. Horses have hotter blood than humans, that's what Hollis believes, and he was covered with blood by the time he was finished. He had to stand in the shower for hours, and even then the cold water was a pale remedy. That horse, a white thoroughbred, had refused to go down. Hollis had blood under his fingernails and all over his boots; two weeks later, after he'd headed back to Massachusetts, he was brushing his teeth in the bathroom of his rented rooms above the Lyon Cafe when he found horse's blood in the rim of his ear. A single red thread which couldn't tie him to any crime, and could be easily scrubbed away with a damp washcloth, and yet that mark seems to have been a curse. He still does not like to look at himself in the mirror, for fear he'll see blood, and to this day he despises the color red.

That horse continues to follow Hollis while he sleeps. He runs in pastures that are as red as blood; he races through guilt and grief. Kill something, and it's yours forever. At night, you will be at your victim's mercy, but that's only temporary. Dreams, after all, are worthless things—Hollis knows that. They can't reach you on the street where you walk; they can only torment a man with a conscience, any fool who allows it.

Now that the dream is back, Hollis often gets out of bed in the dark. He leaves March sleeping, and goes to sit in Mr. Cooper's parlor, in the leather chair where Mr. Cooper liked to relax and smoke his cigars. He watches the light break through the sky above the Farm. Blood buys things and it always has. It was his dream to stand on top of Fox Hill and own everything in sight, and now he has made it all so real that if any trespasser comes by he'll find himself hauled off to jail. It's his, the acres of woodland, the houses, the fences, even this chair, where Mr. Cooper liked to read the Sunday paper, unaware that he was being watched through the window by a boy who owned nothing, not even the clothes on his back, which had been paid for out of the goodness of Henry Murray's heart.

"Everything you have I own," Alan Murray told Hollis when he came back from his father's funeral.

Well, he's fixed that, hasn't he? Sitting in the dark, Hollis thinks about his money. He thinks about the woman, asleep in his bed. Why is it he continues to feel so poor? Why is he waiting for March to bolt out the door? He's been worrying about Richard Cooper, who's not giving up so easily and who has taken to calling. Hollis has been hanging up on him, but sooner or later March will answer the phone, and that won't do. He'll see to it the way he's seen to the mail, so that March hasn't received any responses from the stores that want to sell her work. A woman who has her own money can leave you when you least expect it; she can walk off anytime.

Long before anyone in the house is awake, before Hank has fed the dogs, before Gwen has written a letter to her father or March has set about making a cranberry coffee cake to bring to the Justices' Thanksgiving dinner, Hollis has taken care of the phone lines.

"Must be some wire down," he says, when March tries to contact Susie to ask if there's anything else she should bring to dinner.

"Are you sure you won't go with us?" March asks.

"Dinner with those old coots?" Hollis grins. "I don't think so. I'll stick to frozen food."

Hollis has actually encouraged March to take the kids and go to dinner; their absence will give him the chance to look through her suitcase and her dresser drawers to make sure she hasn't managed to receive any letters from Richard before Hollis could retrieve the mail.

"I want you to have fun," Hollis tells March. "Enjoy yourself. Take Hank—he can eat the Justices out of house and home for a change."

"Remember," March says when they're ready to leave, "you can always change your mind and come for dessert."

"I'll think about it," Hollis tells her, even though he'd rather be tied into a straitjacket than have a meal with the Justices.

"Hollis isn't going?" Hank asks when March comes out to the car.

Hank is in the back seat, and March hands him the coffee cake. "He hates polite society. You know that."

"Well, I'm sure it hates him right back," Gwen says. She's sitting in the front seat, with Sister on her lap.

"You're bringing the dog?" March asks.

"I'm not leaving her here."

Hank looks over his shoulder at the house. "Maybe I should stay."

"Oh, no you don't," Gwen says. "Don't you feel sorry for him."

"It's not that," Hank insists.

Gwen smiles in spite of herself; it's exactly that.

"It's a holiday, that's all," Hank says.

"Well, you're coming with us," March says. "Hollis wants you to. One of the reasons Louise is getting a twenty-five-pound turkey is because I'm bringing two teenagers."

When they get to the Justices', Gwen and Hank take Sister for a walk, since March wants the dog to stay in the car during dinner. Actually, it's a pleasure for the two of them to be alone in the smoky air, because today everything smells like roasted chestnuts and burning wood and cinnamon wafting from the windows of the bakery, where they're working overtime to fill holiday orders.

"I wish you wouldn't be so concerned about Hollis," Gwen says as they walk past front lawns and fences. They've let the dog run on ahead through the last of the fallen leaves, those which haven't been blown away or turned into dust. "He still hasn't given me the ownership papers for Tarot."

"He will," Hank tells her. "He keeps his word."

"Yeah, right. I'll bet he does."

"He does," Hank vows. "You'll see."

Hank and Gwen take a longer walk than they'd intended, but the Justices' house is crowded even without their presence. Dr. and Mrs. Henderson are there, along with the Laughtons, Harriet and Larry—all of them so polite and stuffy that Hollis would have gone nuts in their presence. The Hendersons' daughter Miranda is there, free as a bird since her divorce last spring. Ed Milton has of course been invited, along with his twelve-year-old daughter, Lindsay, as has Janet Travis, the new attorney in town—since a resident of ten years is still considered a recent arrival—and her husband, Mitch, who teaches social studies at the high school.

"Where were you this morning?" Susie asks, after she's hugged

March and taken the coffee cake out of her hands. She can't help but wonder if March knows that some of the white in her hair has grown in; March looks older with her hair like this, and her face seems drawn. "I've been trying to call you to ask you to pick up some eggnog." Susie lifts the foil and peers at the cake. "Cranberry," she says. "Yum."

"I was home." March hangs up her coat and follows Susie into the Justices' kitchen. "Baking that cake."

"Well, I called and called and no one ever answered." Susie pours them each a glass of red wine. "Do you believe how many old folks are out there?"

"Ed Milton's not old." March samples the sweet potato casserole cooling on the counter. "He's cute."

"Don't get all excited," Susie tells her. "It's not serious."

Louise Justice comes into the kitchen, catching that last bit of conversation. "That's what Susie always says. You'd think she was a frivolous person, if you didn't know her better."

"Here's a drawback," Susie says. "His daughter hates me. If she keeps being so nasty, I'm going to be nasty right back."

"She's twelve," Louise says. "In six years she'll be off to college and you'll see her at Christmas vacation if you're lucky. And for now, she lives with her mother in New York. They moved to Roslyn, out on Long Island, this past summer, and Lindsay likes seventh grade a lot more than she thought she would."

Susie and March both give Louise a look.

"I didn't pry," Louise swears. "Lindsay volunteered the information. Which she would with you too," she tells Susie. "If you gave her the chance."

Louise now sets them to work. March is to ladle corn chowder from the pot into a tureen. Susie is to remove the oyster stuffing from the cooling turkey.

"I guess Hollis decided not to show," Susie says. "Surprise, surprise."

"He's opted for a frozen dinner and peace and quiet," March says.

"At least he let you come," Susie says.

"You wouldn't have wanted him here, considering how you feel. Both of you." March is looking straight at Louise.

"I told her about your theory," Susie admits to her mother. "About Hollis and Belinda. I'm sorry."

"I'm glad you did," Louise says.

"You are?" Susie is surprised and rather relieved.

"I am, although I know that March will make her own choices no matter what we say. Won't you, dear?"

"That's right," March agrees. "So I'd appreciate you butting out, unless you're willing to let me take over your lives."

"Touché," Louise says.

Susie pours herself and March more red wine, and gets some cold Chablis from the fridge for her mother. Louise nods and takes a sip of wine. Sometimes, in the old days, the Murrays would bring Judith Dale with them when invited to the Justices' holiday dinners. Judith would bring her special dishes: her apple brown Betty, her green beans with almonds, her onion soup with its delicious, thick crust. She worked well beside Louise in the kitchen, and Louise always told the Judge how lucky the Murrays had been to find Judith. Why, one year, before she knew anything, she sat Judith next to the Judge, and if she'd been more observant she would have noticed that neither of them spoke a word throughout that dinner, as if proximity and desire had made them mute. For all Louise knows, they may have been holding hands under the table all through dinner. She does remember how surprised and pleased she was when the Judge offered to help Judith clear the table, since he usually didn't think to attend to household chores.

"Are you okay, Mom?" Susie asks as she slips the bowl of stuffing into the oven to keep warm.

Louise has a house full of guests and she's standing there, doing nothing, with a glass of wine in her hand.

"Perfectly fine," Louise says.

She goes to help March take out the soup bowls from a high cabinet. Every time March reaches for a bowl that emerald ring which used to belong to Judith shimmers, as if it were made of some mysterious liquid. Louise tells herself she'd better snap out of her reverie and stop the self-pity; a ring, after all, is not a heart, it's not a soul or a husband beside you in bed every night. It's a rock that's only worth something in the first place because someone has decided to give it value.

The Judge now comes in. "There's the turkey," he says. His one holiday task: to carve. Louise has left out the knife he likes best and the large silver fork which belonged to her mother.

As usual, the Judge is wearing a suit and tie; he seems much too tall for the kitchen. He carves the turkey, teasing the women as they travel back and forth to the dining room, bringing out platters of food. He's the same man who's stood here in Louise's kitchen every Thanksgiving, but today something is different. The Judge's hands shake as he carves. It's a slight tremor, so mild no one would notice, except Louise.

When the Judge is done with the turkey, he goes to wash his hands. From the window above the sink, he can look into the yard. "Well, well," he says when he spies Gwen and Hank out there. "The reluctant guests?"

"They don't consider adults to be human," March jokes.

"I'll lasso them," the Judge says. "I'll offer food, that should do the trick."

As he goes out, a cold blast of air rips through the kitchen. The Judge is so tall he has to crouch to maneuver past the branches of a peach tree Louise planted in the first year of their marriage. This was the Judge's parents' house until the older Justices retired to Florida; Bill grew up here and Louise often thought of that when she was tempted to throw him out. She simply couldn't imagine him living anywhere else. And anyway, it's too late to think about such matters. What's done is done.

"You're sure you're okay?" Susie now asks her.

Louise moves her hand to her face, as if smoothing something out. Susie and March both look concerned. Louise must have slipped and shown them a bit of her pain. She must have let something through.

"A touch of the virus," Louise says. "Absolutely nothing."

The three women stand by the back door and look out. The terrier is in a pile of leaves, chewing on a stick, while Hank and Gwen whisper to each other.

"Everybody inside," they hear the Judge's voice call.

The dog starts running toward the Judge as soon as it hears his voice, and has leapt into his arms before the Judge knows what hits him.

"Wow, is that dog crazy about you," Hank says. "Look at her."

The terrier is making yipping noises as it licks the Judge's face.

"Stop that, Sister," the Judge says, but he seems extremely pleased to be holding this creature to his chest, in spite of the burrs in its fur and the mud on its feet.

At the door, Louise Justice turns pale. Clearly, this was their dog—his and Judith's—and now, in spite of the chilled wine, Louise has a mouthful of grief. Susie had begged for a dog when she was young, but the Judge had always said no. Too much hair and dirt and fuss.

"Mom," Susie says softly. She doesn't understand this—could it be that her mother knows about Judith Dale and the Judge? "Maybe you'd better get the dog out of here," Susie suggests to March.

"I'm sorry," March apologizes. She and Susie exchange a worried look. "I wasn't thinking. I'll put the dog in the car."

"No," Louise says. "Don't."

Outside, they can see that the Judge is crouched down; he's scratching the terrier's head. These girls in the kitchen, March and Susie, feel sorry for her, Louise is well aware of that. But what do they know about love? You make bargains you'd never imagine you'd agreed to, and you do it over and over again.

"I'm fine," Louise says. "We'll start with the chowder, before it turns to ice."

These girls think in black and white, love or rejection, yes or no. Louise watches the Judge as he makes his way to her back door and she feels the intensity of being together for nearly fifty years. She knows him completely, and not at all. She made her choices, just as March and Susie are doing. Young people believe that regret is something you will never feel if you simply do as you please, but sometimes it's a matter of degree. Would Louise have preferred not to have the Judge at her table? Would she have preferred to have raised Susie alone, or have some other man watching TV with her in the evenings, someone easygoing, someone whose affections she could be sure of?

"We're sitting down to chowder," Louise tells the Judge when he comes inside.

The Judge has muddy paw prints on his pant legs; the suit will have to be sent to the dry cleaner.

"Look at this mess," he says. When he brushes the leaves off his jacket, there's the tremor, in his hands.

"It's not so bad," Louise says, cleaning off the lapels. "It's a miracle fabric."

The Judge laughs. "I can always trust you to perform miracles."

"Hardly." Louise snorts. He was charming as a young man, so tall, so much fun in spite of his serious nature. She loved him then and she loves him still. Someone else might have left, but she stayed, and here she is, beside him.

"What's wrong with that daughter of Ed Milton's?" the Judge asks. "I've never seen a more sullen child."

He wasn't really there when Susie went through her worst times, at exactly the same age. Susie hated herself and everyone else, but the Judge was too busy to know. He was working, or over at Fox Hill, and maybe Louise was too quick to settle all of the daily details and problems before his car pulled into the driveway.

"The poor thing is twelve and she's worried that Susie will be a wicked stepmother," Louise tells the Judge. "I'm sure it will work out fine."

Hank and Gwen come in now, embarrassed to be late, worried about the dog.

"I'll leave my dog in the mudroom," Gwen tells Mrs. Justice. "If that's okay."

So it's her dog now. The Judge smiles to hear that, and Louise notices he has the look he always has when he's thinking about Judith.

"That's perfectly fine." Although Louise is addressing Gwen, it's the Judge she's looking at. "Whatever makes you happy."

By the time they finally leave the Justices' it's late and so cold they see their breath in the air. They have all overeaten, even Sister, who was slipped a plate of turkey and stuffing. It's a dark and beautiful night, dreamy and black, filled with the silhouettes of bare trees.

"Thanks for taking me with you," Hank says when they pull up to the Farm. "The food was great."

The dogs in the driveway rouse themselves and head over. Hank has brought them a bag full of leftovers which he sets down in the driveway.

"I can see why you like him," March says to Gwen.

Gwen's got Sister under her arm. Just being with all those normal people tonight has made Gwen realize how much she hates living out here. She watches Hank pet those dreadful dogs, the ones Belinda first took in out of pity.

"You don't see anything," Gwen tells her mother.

March stays in the driveway when Gwen goes inside. March has had several glasses of wine and she feels a little tipsy. She had fun tonight, something she hasn't had in quite a while. Finally, she and Hank walk toward the house together, and that's when March realizes that Hollis's truck is gone. They go inside and look around, but no one is home.

"If you're worried, I could take your car and look for him," Hank offers.

"No," March says. "I'm sure he's fine."

After Hank goes up to bed, March tries to call Susie, to talk about Ed Milton and his daughter, but the phone still isn't working. Maybe the wires have frozen; the house is cold, and outside the temperature is dropping. March makes herself a pot of tea and takes it into the parlor. She can view the driveway from here, and sometime after midnight she spies headlights when Hollis arrives.

"Hey," Hollis says when he comes into the parlor and sees March. He grins and takes off his gloves. "How was it?"

"Great," March says. She's relieved that he smiles, as if there was a right and wrong answer to his question and she's scored correctly. Since Hollis seems to be in a decent mood she dares to venture a question of her own. "Where were you?"

"Me?" Hollis sits down in the easy chair across from March. The cold is still on his skin and he rubs his hands together. "I took a ride up to Olive Tree Lake, to look at that development going up there and see if I want to buy into the project. Then I drove past the Justices', but the party must have broken up. I guess I missed dessert."

"And it was good too." March has the funniest feeling about tonight. Hollis isn't looking at her. He hasn't looked at her once. "You're sure everything's all right?"

"The only problem is how cold it is in here," Hollis says. "The burner's not doing the job."

"The phone's not working either."

Hollis goes to the fireplace and sets out some kindling and two logs. He bends down, one knee in the ashes. He has always found it best not to look at whoever he's lying to, although, in point of fact, nothing he's told March is an outright fabrication. He was up at Olive Tree Lake, true enough; he's simply failed to mention that he was there fucking Alison Hartwig. It wasn't as though he planned it. He drove down to the Red Apple to get a big bag of dog food, and there she was, buying eggnog and soda to bring home to her kids and her mother. He knew he was going to fuck her the minute he saw her; he knew it would be good to fuck someone he didn't give a damn about.

He has always been at March's mercy, and that's a problem. His own love for her is an agony. It makes him feel like a beggar, even now, and he can't have that. Let someone else beg. Let Alison Hartwig beg him to fuck her. At least it won't be him down on his knees.

March has come up behind him. She places one hand on his shoulder, and her touch makes him feel like weeping. But he doesn't. He's not even certain if he's capable of crying. People said that, when his son died—*Look at him, has he once cried?* Well, maybe he has no tear ducts, or maybe he's not human, but he can't do it, and what's more, he won't.

"I missed you tonight," March says.

Hollis reaches to take her hand then, but he's careful not to look at her. He keeps his eyes trained on the fire before him, and he doesn't dare let anything get in his way.

TWENTY

WHEN THE COLD COMES TO NEW EN-
gland it arrives in sheets of sleet and ice. In December, the wind wraps itself around bare trees
and twists in between husbands and wives asleep
in their beds. It shakes the shingles from the roofs
and sifts through cracks in the plaster. The only
green things left are the holly bushes and the old
boxwood hedges in the village, and these are
often painted white with snow. Chipmunks and
weasels come to nest in basements and barns;
owls find their way into attics. At night, the dark is
blue and bluer still, a sapphire of night. During
some winters, it is so cold that tears freeze before

they fall and a pony's breath may turn to ice inside its nostrils and lead to suffocation.

This year, December is so clear and icy cold the air itself seems as if it were a bell about to be rung. A Christmas tree is always put up on the first Friday of the month in front of Town Hall, beside the statue of the Founder, who, to ensure the festivity of the season, will be decorated with a wreath of ivy until the New Year. One week of frigid weather is nothing to a New Englander, but after two a person's patience can be tried. The Lyon Cafe always does its best business at this time of year. Some people say the surge in popularity is due to the hard cider served only in December, but the old-timers know it's because there's nothing better to do. The best there is at this time of year is cider and gossip, and at the Lyon Cafe, on a cold December night, it's possible to find both.

"Is everyone in the entire universe here?" Susanna Justice asks her mother when they step into the Lyon after a meeting of the library committee. Louise has attended as the secretary of the organization—a position she, thankfully, will be giving up at the end of the year—Susie, as a reporter who still has to go home and think of something interesting to write about the fund-raising drive in time for tomorrow's *Bugle*.

"Order the cider," Louise tells her daughter as she sets off to grab a table and Susie heads for the bar. There's some serious drinking going on at the Lyon, and the noise level is such that Susie and Louise have to sit close together at their table, with their heads nearly touching, in order to hear one another.

"I hope you're going to mention Harriet Laughton in your article," Louise says. "She's the heart and soul of the fund-raising committee. I wanted to ask March to join the committee, but I can never seem to get hold of her."

"I know. I couldn't either."

Susie had been calling and calling, with no success. When Richard phoned her to say he also couldn't reach March and hadn't heard from Gwen for several weeks, she went out to Guardian Farm, and she didn't like what she found.

"What do you want?" Hollis said to her when she got out of her truck. Susie was so startled by the hostility of his tone that she took a step backward; she shaded her eyes against the sun, the better to gauge his expression, but there was nothing to see. Just an angry man, staring her down.

"Actually, I want to see March," Susie had said. "Is that a criminal offense or something?"

All she got for an answer was the wind, flapping between them. A loose shutter on the house banged back and forth. Susie could practically see Hollis reaching inside himself for a way to get rid of her, a lie to tell. Funny how she'd never noticed before how much he'd aged; his posture was that of a young man, but that's not what he was anymore.

"What are you going to do, Hollis? Call the police and have me escorted off your property?"

Before he could respond, March came to the door. She ran out to hug Susie, then insisted on dragging her into the kitchen for a cup of tea.

"Why didn't you tell me Susie was here?" March said to Hollis. "You hate company, that's all there is to it."

She had thrown her arms around him, and Hollis had let her kiss him. For an instant, he seemed happy, there in her embrace.

"He's all bark," March said to Susie as they headed for the house. "Oolong." March had remembered her friend's favorite tea. "Right?"

"Right."

Once in the kitchen, Susie couldn't help but notice how streaked with white March's dark hair had become. March had stopped coloring it, and now simply drew it away from her face with silver clips. Hollis had come in after them, but after he allowed March to tease him about being antisocial, he withdrew to the parlor. Still, Susie had the sense he was listening.

"I'm worried about you," she told March after she'd been served a mug of tea. The house was cold and dim; March was wearing a heavy gray sweater that looked like one of Hollis's castoffs.

"You're always worried about me." March laughed. She explained that she would have been over to see Susie, but her Toyota had suddenly died. As soon as Hollis finished working on it, she'd come for a visit. "You don't have to worry," she'd insisted.

But sitting in the Lyon with her mother, Susie is still worried. "To tell you the truth, I wish March had never come back here," Susie admits as she and Louise sip cider in the crowded tavern. "What does she see in him?"

"Ah, love," Louise says with a surprising amount of bitterness.

Susie tilts her head and studies her mother.

"Didn't you think I knew?" Louise says. "How could I not?"

"Are you talking about Dad?"

"I didn't think it was a suitable topic for discussion. I still don't."

Louise checks the buttons on her sweater, as if something was undone. Clearly, even talking around the edges of the Judge's relationship with Mrs. Dale is tremendously difficult. Watching her mother, Susie feels extreme tenderness.

"Then we won't discuss it," Susie says.

"Fine." Louise takes her daughter's hand in her own. "That's settled."

"Unless you ever want to," Susie can't help adding.

"Susie," Louise warns.

"Fine. Next topic."

"Did you call Richard Cooper back and let him know you went to see March?"

"I did. He's all broken up about March leaving, but his main concern is that Gwen's living out there. I can't say that I blame him."

"I saw her down in the Marshes," Louise says. "That girl, Gwen."

"Are you serious?"

"I brought out some groceries and warm clothes sent by the library committee—there was a wonderful sweater, a hundred percent wool—and I put everything on the porch, the way I always do because Alan doesn't like it if you knock on the door. That's when I saw her."

"Inside the house?" Susie can hardly believe it. "I thought he didn't speak to anyone."

"Well," Louise says, "he's obviously talking to her."

In fact, Gwen has been going out to the Marshes most afternoons. Hank has so many chores to do, along with any after-school jobs he can find, as well as working on his senior thesis, that Gwen has too much time on her hands. She sometimes rides Tarot out to the Marshes, but usually she leads him, so he'll get a little exercise without having to carry her weight. Despite the cold, Tarot is content to accompany her; there are still some withered apples on the ground in the Coward's yard, and the grass is high and salty. The Coward has begun to tell Gwen about her family: How beloved her grandfather Henry was. How her other grandparents, the Coopers, were said to think so well of themselves they had to deflate their heads every morning or else they'd sail away on the strength of their own vanity. He has recounted a few small details about the fire, when his wife died, if only to suggest the reasons he has plunged into this life he now leads. The weirdest thing is, when he speaks about himself he uses the third person: *Alan Murray couldn't go into that house. He stood there and stood there, but he couldn't move.*

"So who are you now if you're not him?" Gwen has asked.

"I'm someone else," the Coward has told her, as if that information was as plain as the nose on his face.

That someone is often so far gone when Gwen comes to visit that he can't stand up. Once, she found him shivering on the floor. Another time, he was inches away from the smoldering ashes of his stove. Gwen knows where he keeps his liquor—the bottles are stored beneath the floorboards near his bed. On those occasions when he's not completely smashed, the Coward tells her what the village used to be like when he was a boy. Olive Tree Lake was so clear you could drink the water in a cup. Foxes trotted along back roads. Blue herons nested in the Marshes.

Gwen tries to bring the Coward treats, usually bread and butter, his favorite, but she doesn't chide him about his drinking. She knows how it feels to have somebody on your case, the way her mother used to be; it never does any good. It's cold in the Coward's house, and filthy as well, yet Gwen looks forward to coming here. Or perhaps it's the act of getting away from Guardian Farm she savors. Strange, but the Marshes seem real to her; it's the Farm that seems like a dream.

The phone lines have never been fixed, nor has her mother's car. No mail has been delivered for ages. Gwen has written to her father three times, and she still hasn't heard from him. She intends to ask if he'll send a plane ticket, so she can go home for Christmas vacation. She hasn't told Hank anything about her plan, and the secret has driven a wedge between them, not because of the vacation—that's nothing—but because if she gets ownership of Tarot beforehand, she'll borrow money from Susie Justice to have him trucked to California, and she won't use her return ticket to come back. She has to get out, that's what she's afraid to say out loud in Hank's presence. She has to do it soon.

Today, when Gwen goes to the Marshes the weather is so bad, with ice everywhere, that she leaves Tarot home. Sister follows her, though, and by the time they get to the Marshes, the terrier's coat is braided with ice. The Coward, however, is completely wasted. He took his weekly trek to the liquor store last night, then overindulged even more than usual. Gwen covers him up with an old quilt, right there where he lies on the wooden floor. She stays for a while, Sister beside her, though the house is cold and the Coward smells bad. She thinks about the life she used to have and how it doesn't even seem to belong to her anymore, and it helps her to understand the Coward's past. That's the reason he stays out here—everything he was has slipped away, and trying to retrieve it would be like diving into a bottomless pit.

Before she leaves, Gwen takes a piece of bread from the groceries Louise Justice has left, and crumbles it up for the mice. She leaves a note on the table: "I was here. You were plastered. See you tomorrow. Your loving niece, Gwen."

It is late in the day when Gwen walks back through the Marshes; the sunlight is pale and thin and already fading. Her boots make a path in the muck and ice, which Sister follows. A flock of starlings startles and takes flight when Gwen and the dog come too close. Out here, Gwen feels as though she's reached the end of the world. Every time she takes a step she can hear something break—hermit crabs, mussel shells, cattails. This spring she will turn sixteen, an age she has been waiting for for what seems forever. Why is it that spring seems impossibly far away, as if it were a goal she can only yearn for and never quite reach?

Gwen and Sister are both quiet when they get to Guardian Farm; they slip through the back door, but they're not quick enough. Hollis is in the kitchen.

"I thought you'd taken off and weren't coming back," he says.

He always makes snide remarks like this to Gwen; he must think he's amusing. Well, now that she's face-to-face with him, she might as well ask.

"No such luck," Gwen shoots back. Since she's already spoken to him, she decides to take the next step. "Did the papers come through?" Gwen tries to be casual about this, but deep inside she thinks herself a fool: she should have gotten ownership of Tarot before she agreed to move in.

"Papers?" Hollis says. He's having a cup of hot tea made nearly white with milk.

"Tarot? Remember? He's mine."

"Right, you weren't going to give your mother a hard time about moving over here, and I was going to sign over ownership of the horse."

"Right." Gwen breathes a sigh of relief.

"You believed that?" Hollis shakes his head as though she were the sorriest dolt he'd ever seen.

Gwen stands watching as he goes to the sink and rinses out his cup, then lays it neatly on the drainboard.

"I want those ownership papers," she forces herself to say.

"That's too bad." He's speaking to a bothersome fly, a gnat and nothing more. "Because you're not getting them."

Gwen can feel her face grow hot; she's been conned, that's what happened, and it was easy as pie for him to cheat her. Maybe it's the way he walks away, as though she were worthless, which makes her grab the teacup and throw it at him. It shatters on the floor to his left; it's Wedgwood and breaks into a hundred slivers.

Shit, Gwen thinks, when he turns and comes back at her. Instantly, she's afraid of him, though she hates herself for being so easily scared by the likes of him. He gets her by the arm before she can maneuver away. Sister begins barking, a hoarse frantic yip.

"You little bitch," Hollis says to Gwen.

"You'd better let go," Gwen says, as if she had any control here. "I mean it."

Sister's barking like crazy now, a growly sort of bark. Hollis is really hurting Gwen; it's as if he wants to break her arm or something. Gwen can tell he wants her to give up, and maybe, if she were smarter, she would.

"Fuck you," she says.

"Maybe what you need is a good spanking," Hollis tells her. "Maybe that would solve the problem."

When he grabs Gwen around the waist, Sister, who's been darting closer and closer, goes for Hollis's leg. The dog's teeth don't reach skin, but Hollis loosens his hold on Gwen so he can kick the terrier, who yowls and skitters off. Gwen breaks away and runs out of the house without thinking; luckily, the door flies open behind her and Sister can escape before it slams shut again.

As soon as she's outside, Gwen is running, and it's not until she gets far enough away that she allows herself to cry. She sits on a stone wall and cries until she sees that Sister has followed her. Then she crouches to pick up the dog, and starts walking again. She continues on the High Road all the way into the village. She's walking fast, so she carries Sister under her arm. The dog is still shaking, and it yelps when Gwen touches its side, sore from Hollis's boot. Darkness has settled by the time they reach the village; it's dark on Main Street and the streetlights cast a yellow glow. Gwen has less than a dollar in her pocket, and when she tries to use the phone booth outside the Bluebird Coffee Shop, a recorded announcement informs her she cannot make a long-distance call without a calling card number, something she doesn't have.

She continues down Main Street, past the building where her grandfather Henry Murray used to have his offices, past the library and the Lyon Cafe. In Gwen's opinion, the street where the Justices live is the prettiest in town; all the houses are white, and each yard is surrounded by a white fence. In the dark, the facades seem illuminated, as if starlight had been mixed in with the housepaint. Oh, what she wouldn't give to be a girl in one of these houses, with real parents and a bedroom up on the second floor. She would have wallpaper then, and a closetful of clothes, and someone who knew what hour she came in at night.

Gwen goes up to the Justices' front door, gathers her courage, and knocks.

"I really hate to bother you," she says when the Judge opens the door. She has no idea that her eyes are bloodshot from crying. "Would you mind if I used your phone?" Shock has made her unbelievably polite.

"It's March's girl," the Judge calls to Louise. He signals for Gwen to come inside, and once they're in the parlor he studies her. Gwen places Sister on the floor, and the dog cowers behind her legs.

"Been out for a walk?" the Judge asks.

Gwen realizes how muddy her boots are. She sits on a couch and eases them off. "Sorry about the mess." Her voice breaks then, and she has to look away.

Louise has come in from the kitchen and she and the Judge exchange a look.

"She wants to make a phone call," the Judge tells Louise.

"Help yourself," Louise says; then she guides the Judge into the kitchen to give Gwen some privacy. "What happened?" Louise asks him.

"Not the slightest idea."

"It's something to do with that man," Louise decides. "You wait and see."

Unfortunately, Gwen's father isn't home and she has to leave a message. She wants a plane ticket, which he can mail to the Justices', to be sure it arrives safely. She loves him and misses him, and there's nothing more to say.

"Did your phone call work out?" Louise Justice asks when Gwen comes into the kitchen, carrying her boots so she won't track mud in, the little dog following close behind.

"Not exactly," Gwen admits. "I might get some mail from my father delivered here, if that's okay."

"Perfectly fine," Louise says, although she wonders why that would be.

Gwen sits at the table, which is already set for dinner. There is a homemade chicken pot pie, biscuits, and brussels sprouts in need of butter. The sight of a real dinner fills Gwen's eyes with tears. There's hardly any food in the refrigerator at Guardian Farm; no one seems to care if they eat. Now that March's car doesn't work, Hollis has to drive her if she wants to go to the Red Apple market, or he and Hank go to the bargain warehouse up near Gloucester.

"Would you like to have dinner with us?" Louise asks when she sees the way Gwen is staring at the food.

Actually, she'd like to move in. She'd have first and then second helpings, with apple pie for dessert, then she'd go upstairs and sleep in the guest room, on clean white sheets, with the dog curled up beside her. The problem is her attachments, as if devotion were a downfall.

"I'd better head back," Gwen says.

Louise Justice can't help but think of that windy night, all those years ago, when she saw the bruises on Belinda's arm.

"Well, you're not walking," Louise decides.

"Really, it's not far," Gwen insists, but the Judge, who's come in for dinner, has seen the stubborn expression on Louise's face. He won't get dinner for another hour, that much is sure.

"I'll drive you." The Judge has made up his mind. This way he can stop at the cemetery, as he does two or three times a week.

They go out to the Judge's old Saab, with Sister leading the way.

"Give the front tire a wallop," the Judge tells Gwen.

Gwen looks at him, then grins and kicks the Saab's tire.

"Helps it to start," the Judge informs her.

The old sedan wheezes when the Judge gives it some gas, but it jolts into action, and they start for Route 22. Usually, the Judge doesn't like to come this way, but lately, he can't bring himself to drive on the old road that leads past Fox Hill. He doesn't want to see that house empty, and all its windows dark. When they make the turn at the devil's corner, the car skids a bit.

"Terrible spot," the Judge says. "Best avoided."

As soon as they pull into the driveway and the Saab sputters to a stop, Gwen grabs the door handle. She intends to say a quick thanks, and get out. She's ready to hold her tongue and watch her ways, avoiding Hollis at all costs. But the Judge is already getting out of the car.

"I think I'll come inside," he says. "Give my regards to your mother."

Before Gwen can stop him, the Judge is headed to the front door at a pace a younger man would have trouble keeping up with.

The dogs in the driveway are barking and Sister is growling as Gwen carries the terrier and races after the Judge.

"This probably isn't a good idea," she says.

"Oh?" The Judge has stopped to study her.

She can't tell him that she's afraid his presence will anger Hollis, and then they'll all have to pay the price. "You don't need to bother."

"It's no bother," the Judge says, as he goes up and knocks on the door.

Gwen doesn't want him inside, the Judge knows that. He has seen this over and over again in court. He cannot count the times he has heard that phrase "Don't bother" come out of the mouths of victims, especially in domestic disputes. When he first came to the bench he didn't understand the code people use, the ways a fact can be twisted and still manage to be the truth. *He didn't mean it, I didn't mean it, We didn't mean it,* and yet, it's done. After all the years he's spent in a courtroom, Bill Justice has acquired a lie detector implanted in his brain. And the funny thing is, after seeing how easily people tore each other apart, he could still come home and lie to his wife and persuade himself it was for her own good.

It's Hollis who opens the door, and he stops short when he sees the Judge. "To what do we owe this pleasure?" His tone is reasonably agreeable, not that that's the way he feels. "You're not selling Girl Scout cookies, I'll bet."

"I thought I'd bring Gwen home," the Judge says.

Gwen slips into the house, trying her best to be invisible. Hollis lets her by, but he doesn't open the door to invite the Judge in. If it were anyone else but Bill Justice at the door, he'd probably just slam it shut. Because it is the Judge, Hollis smiles gamely.

"Teenagers," Hollis says, assessing the Judge's face to see if Gwen has told him about their run-in and coming up with very little. The Judge, after all, is a poker player, a good game to know for someone in his line of work.

"I thought I could say hello to March," the Judge says.

"I think she's asleep," Hollis has the nerve to say, even though it's not quite seven.

This lie might have passed had March not heard the red dogs barking, then looked out her window and caught sight of the Judge's car. She's pulled on a sweater and come downstairs in her bare feet.

"It's so nice to have you stop by," she says to the Judge when she gets to the door. They never have company out here, and although March tells herself she doesn't miss a social life, she's inordinately pleased to see the Judge. "I've been meaning to call Louise. I never did thank her for that wonderful dinner."

March has her hair pulled back, and the Judge is surprised to see how white it has turned. She's skinnier than he remembered as well; could it be she's lost this much weight since Thanksgiving?

"I was just giving Gwen a ride home from town," the Judge tells March.

"Was Gwen in town?" March asks Hollis. "I didn't realize that."

Now the Judge knows what's wrong. March seems like a sleepwalker. *Wake up*, he wants to tell her. *Open your eyes.*

"Looks like it," Hollis says.

"Well, come in." March is still beautiful when she smiles. "Have some tea."

When the door is opened wider, the Judge can see into the kitchen. It is dimly lit and bare, as if no one lived there.

"With a cook like Mrs. Justice for a wife, the Judge certainly doesn't want our tea," Hollis says. "Isn't that a fact?"

Hollis and the Judge look at each other. Unless the Judge is mistaken, and he rarely is about such things, there is an attempt at intimidation beneath the surface. He's seen it before, at hearings and trials, and he knows precisely what this sort of man is trying to tell him. *Don't fuck with me. Don't even try.*

"Louise would love for you to come to dinner," the Judge tells March. "How about Friday?"

March looks at Hollis.

"That won't work out," Hollis says. "Friday isn't good."

March loops her arm around Hollis's waist. "I guess we have plans. Please tell Louise thank you anyway for the invitation."

"Well, we'll be in touch." The Judge nods. "We'll figure something out."

Hollis remains by the back door until the Judge has gotten into his car and pulled down the driveway. When the Saab turns onto Route 22, Hollis heads for the little blue bedroom where Gwen has been listening to every word through the thin plaster walls.

"What's wrong?" March says, following Hollis, not that he's listening to her. In his opinion she doesn't need to understand this; he can take care of the girl, after all.

Hollis stands in the doorway to the little room. Gwen is on her bed, a blanket wrapped around her, though it's flimsy protection. She feels all clenched up, as if she were expecting to be hit.

"If you ever bring the Judge out here again," Hollis tells Gwen, "you will seriously regret it."

"Wait a second," March says, confused.

"Let me handle this." Hollis cuts her off. "Do you understand what I'm saying?" he asks Gwen.

Gwen is going along with her plan of no resistance. She nods, agreeing to whatever crap he's spouting, grateful that the blanket is covering her and he can't see that she's shaking. Grateful that her mother is there, for March's presence seems to offer some immunity from Hollis coming any closer.

"I don't want him or anyone else on my property," Hollis informs March. "This girl needs to know that."

He's got that look on his face March knows far too well. He's in a mood, he won't back down; he's thinking only of the doors which were closed to him, not of how they're all open to him now.

"That's fine," March says. "The Judge won't come back here."

She counts to ten and by the time she reaches that last number, Hollis has gone outside to cool off. The screen door slams behind him, and there's an echo, cold wood against colder wood. They can hear his footsteps on the frozen ground on this quiet December night. They can hear the clatter of a typewriter as Hank works on his senior paper on the Founder, and a soft whining from Sister, who is hiding under the bed, fur darkened by dust. March goes to the window and sees Hollis out there by himself, looking up at the stars.

"He doesn't mean any of that," March says to her daughter. "Not really."

Gwen looks at her mother. She feels an odd tenderness, the way one might when finished with crying.

"Mother," she says simply, as if she were teaching sums to a six-year-old, "he certainly does."

TWENTY-ONE

SUSIE JUSTICE GETS HOME IN A HURRY, after a whirlwind trip to Florida. In six days she has been to Palm Beach, Fort Lauderdale, and Miami, then hop-skipped over to Orlando. She's writing a four-part series for *The Bugle* about vacation possibilities and retirement options, which will be chock-full of places to stay and eat and swim. She will not, however, mention in this cheery article how dreadful it is to come back to the cold once your trip is over, although she might suggest it's best to have the person who retrieves your mail while you're away take a look at your oil burner as well, as Susie's seems to have died during her absence, and she comes home to a stone-cold house, with pipes that are close to bursting.

Ken Helm is down in the basement, fixing the burner, and Susie is in her kitchen, still wearing her coat and her gloves, when Ed Milton arrives with a pizza and Susie's dogs, who have been staying with him for the past few days and who now follow on his heels, staring at him with adoration, since he was the one to most recently measure out their kibble.

"Wow," Ed says when he sees how red Susie is. Florida, after all, will do that to a blonde.

"I ran out of sunblock," Susie explains.

"I should have gone with you," Ed says. "I would have made sure you paid attention to the SPF."

Maybe his arms around her feel so good because it's freezing, or maybe she really missed him. "I wouldn't have listened to you," Susie murmurs.

"What is going on in here?" Ed asks. "It's freezing."

There is a metallic banging rising from the basement.

"Ken Helm," Susie explains. "Oil burner."

As much as she hates to admit it, she did miss Ed, and this makes her nervous. This is not the way Susie likes to run her life, mooning over somebody, thinking about making sure they get into bed as soon as Ken Helm leaves, even though she should be attending to the Florida article. She's going to have to find a getaways-to-Florida book at the library tomorrow, since she paid more attention to trying to track down Hollis's past than she did to restaurants and theme parks.

"The most interesting thing about Hollis," she tells Ed, as he opens the pizza box and they begin to eat standing up beside the counter, "is that nobody wanted to talk about him. His lawyer down there refused to see me. I went to this huge condo complex he owns in Orlando, and no one would speak to me. Not even the janitor. When I went to the racetrack he's part owner of down in

Fort Lauderdale, people clammed up so tight they wouldn't even tell me the temperature. It's like he doesn't exist, in spite of everything he owns down there, which let me tell you, is plenty."

"So, nothing?" Ed asks. He grabs another slice of pizza and begins to eat, eyes trained on Susie.

"I found one guy who let me take him out for a drink." She laughs when she sees the expression on Ed's face. "He was ancient, an old horse trainer who was still lugging around water and oats at the track. When I brought up Hollis's name, he said, 'Mr. Death.'"

"What's that supposed to mean?"

"He wouldn't say. But he did tell me that Hollis made his money by staying close to rich people, and by the time he was done, he was rich himself."

"Rich people with horses?" Ed asks.

"That's right. Do you think it was illegal gambling?"

"Susie," Ed says. "Don't go down this road."

Susie blinks. Ed thinks she's got something. The heat has kicked on, and the oil burner in the basement has begun to groan.

"Don't ever tell me to quit," Susie says. "I mean it."

"Okay. Then if you want to know what I think, I'll tell you. Insurance fraud."

"There you go," Ken Helm shouts from the basement. "It's working now."

"There was just a case of this over at the Olympia track. You've got an expensive horse that's not performing, the cost-effective measure is an accident or death and then you can collect your insurance payment."

"This is great," Susie says. "I got him."

Ed shakes his head. "You'll never prove it. Hollis's involvement in anything like that was all so long ago that by now, records will be tossed, even by the insurance companies, and everyone will have terminal memory loss."

"You're telling me to forget it? After all this?"

"Some people get away with things," Ed Milton says sadly.

"Well, someone should pay him back for everything he's done," Ken Helm says. He has come upstairs, dirty from crawling around in the cellar; the wall he's leaning against will have a film of black dust when he's gone. "Hey there, Chief," he says to greet Ed. "That should hold your burner for a little while," he tells Susie, "but you're going to need a new one, eventually."

When Ken leaves, Susanna Justice walks him to the door. "You're going to keep looking for something on him, aren't you?" Ken asks as he's leaving.

"I don't know," Susie admits. "I might give it up."

She doesn't have the heart to tell Ken that the sort of judgment he's seeking is not necessarily hers to set forth. Maybe she should have quoted the only passage from Matthew she can remember: *What I want is mercy, not sacrifice.*

That night, while Susie unpacks her suitcase, she can hear Ed running the water in her shower, and for some reason the sound gives her hope. She may decide to shock everyone in town, including herself, by marrying this guy. Marriage, after all, is a leap of confidence: We will be together, now and in the future. We are one, from this day forth. The Judge is thinking about such matters tonight as well, as he sits in his kitchen with a single light turned on. Marriage is many things to many people: a contract of convenience, a plight of truest love, an agreement made with a friend, or even with an enemy or, oftentimes, with a stranger you're convinced that you know. Can you love two people? The Judge has mulled over this possibility for more than thirty years, and still has no answer. The answer, of course, is based on one's interpretation of the nature of love, and the Judge considers himself to be too old and tired to expect any clarification at this point.

Still, he is thinking of Judith Dale tonight, as he often does at this hour, a time when most sensible people are already getting ready for bed. If he loved her would he have let her live the way she did, always waiting for what scraps of time he had, never having the choice to have a child of her own? But he did love her, that's the thing, and he continues to love her even now. When he feels this way, he often gets in his car and drives, so he can cry alone. Oh, how he wishes he could confide in Louise, who has, for all these years, been his dearest friend. The Judge gets his coat, and as he's about to go out the back door, Louise comes into the kitchen.

"This came this morning," she says, handing him a thick envelope addressed to Gwen.

"A plane ticket," the Judge guesses.

Louise nods. "I hope so. Why don't you drop it off on your way to the cemetery."

The Judge stands there, confused. Did she just say that?

Louise smooths the back of his coat, where it's bunched up. She's ready for bed, and her face is washed and clean; she looks a good deal like the girl that he married.

"Louise," the Judge says.

"I'll wait up for you," she tells him. She hopes that after all this time, he won't suddenly take it upon himself to apologize. She simply wants him to understand that she knows. That's all. "I'll fix us some tea."

The Judge drives out to Guardian Farm thinking that after all he's seen, people continue to amaze him. There's very little traffic on the road, and no moon tonight. The Judge parks and gets out, carrying the envelope from Richard Cooper. Now there's a man who's got a great deal to learn, and who doesn't seem to yet be aware of the difference between freedom and license. He should have come here with March in the first place. If there's one thing the Judge has learned after all these years, it's that only a fool tempts fate.

Gwen answers the door, wearing a heavy sweater; her hair is

uncombed and her eyes are sleepy. Hollis and March are upstairs, and Gwen's been fixing Hank some coffee; he's finishing his paper on the Founder tonight, probably pulling an all-nighter, since his senior thesis is due in the morning.

"I didn't ask you to come here," Gwen says straightaway when she sees the Judge. She steps onto the porch, pulling the door closed behind her. She's developed a nervous habit of chewing on her lip; when it bleeds she doesn't seem to notice. "He doesn't like company."

"Your father sent a letter," the Judge says.

"Oh," Gwen says, relieved. "Oh, good." She takes the letter and opens it while Sister noses at the door and comes to sniff at the Judge's shoes. "A plane ticket," Gwen announces, and then, surprised, she adds, "Actually, two."

"He's hoping against hope," the Judge says.

"I don't understand any of it," Gwen says.

"Well, you're among the majority, if you're talking about love."

"That's not what they've got," Gwen says, looking up at the bedroom window.

When the Judge heads for his car, Gwen slips the plane tickets inside the waist of her jeans, then picks up Sister and goes back inside. Hank is still at the table, papers spread out before him, but he's stopped working.

"What did he want?" Hank asks. Does he sound like Hollis? Lord, he hopes not. He's not jealous, but he is desperate. He gets this way whenever he feels he might be losing Gwen.

They can hear the Judge's Saab; it's so loud when it starts up all Gwen can do is pray Hollis won't hear.

"Nothing," Gwen says. "He just stopped by."

Hank feels a pain behind his eyes. Maybe he's lost her already.

"Shit," Gwen says when she hears something upstairs.

Hollis has slammed the bedroom door and is already coming down the stairs, cursing her. He's calling her a bitch before he's reached the first floor; no one's ever taught her a lesson, but that will all change now.

"What's wrong?" Hank says when Hollis comes into the kitchen, but even before the words are out of his mouth, Hollis is after Gwen, as if she were a mole he'd found in his garden and he had the right to grab her and shake her by the neck.

"Hey," Hank says. He gets up from the table so quickly that he upsets his cup of coffee, and liquid spills over his research materials.

"I told you I didn't want the Judge here," Hollis is saying to Gwen. "But you think you're too good to listen to anybody."

"I don't have to listen to *you*," Gwen says right back to him. She feels as if he could snap her spine if he chose to, but she doesn't care. How much she hates him is all she can think about at the moment.

March has come down from the bedroom, and she stands in the doorway to the kitchen. Now she knows how people freeze; she understands how that fire burned out of control before Alan could walk through the door. There is her daughter, frightened and shouting. There is the man she loves with his hands on her throat.

"I'm going to make you listen," Hollis is saying to Gwen.

"I don't think so," Gwen says. She can see Hank coming toward them, but that's not what gives her courage. She truly doesn't care if Hollis hurts her; she wants him to, because that would only serve to prove her right in her opinion of him.

"You don't want to do this," Hank says, getting in between Hollis and Gwen. "Don't do this." He's begging Hollis really; if he had to he would get down on his knees.

Hollis looks at the boy coldly, and then something clicks. "You're right." He goes into the parlor, where Mr. Cooper's gun is still in its case.

"Shit," Hank says when he sees Hollis go out the front door, the one no one uses anymore. Hank heads out the back, hoping he can cut Hollis off and talk to him. The red dogs come out of the shadows to greet Hank, but he jogs past them. He doesn't like the way he feels inside, the way his stomach is lurching. It's too quiet tonight; the air breaks like twigs.

"Now do you see what he's like?" Gwen is saying to her mother in the cold kitchen of the house. "Now do you believe me?"

March knows that when he gets like this, he always regrets it. Tonight, when she takes him into their bed, he'll cry. He'll tell her that he never meant to hurt anyone, and she'll believe him.

"Gwennie, you don't understand," March begins, but then she realizes that she hopes her daughter never will understand, and after that, how can she say more?

Gwen picks up Sister and slams out of the house. She races after Hank, and the closer she gets, the more she smells the bitter scent of hay. Already, the sound of the horses has begun to echo. When Gwen runs inside, Hollis is opening Tarot's stall, and Tarot is in a panic at his proximity. He kicks the stall behind him, and shakes his head back and forth. Hollis has the gun under his arm as he drags open the wooden door.

"Wait until tomorrow," Hank is saying. "You'll feel different then."

"Oh, really?" Hollis's tone is amused, even though his mouth is set in a thin line. "And you assume I'm interested in what the fuck you think?"

"It's late," Hank says now. It's not even ten, but Hank is willing to try anything to slow this down. His voice sounds comforting, but he's well aware that there's no comfort here. He puts his arm out, to stop Gwen from going closer. She is about to push him away, but then she looks at Hollis, and she knows she'd better stay put.

"Now you're telling me what time it is?" Hollis says, and his voice is so distant it sounds as if its point of origin was a million miles away. He has spied Gwen, who is shivering as she holds

Sister close to her chest. "You need to learn a lesson about what happens when things don't belong to you. You can beg," he tells Gwen, "but it won't do you any good."

Gwen can feel the cold air in her lungs every time she breathes. She can feel Hank next to her, the way his muscles are coiled, ready to do something, but unsure as to what that action should be.

"Come on," Hollis says. "Beg."

Gwen herself feels a weird sort of sensation inside her; it's as if something were being boiled.

"Please," she says.

Hollis considers, then shakes his head. "Not good enough."

Nothing will ever be good enough, that's the problem, Gwen sees that now. Some things are done rather than decided, and before she plans it out entirely, Gwen rushes for the door to Tarot's stall and swings it wide open.

"Go," she screams, but that's not necessary. Tarot moves so fast that Hollis has to jump aside, and by the time Hollis is thinking straight enough to go for his gun, his target is out in the open, running so fast the wind can't keep up, leaving a cloud of his breath behind. Hollis goes to the barn door and fires once, but by then Tarot has jumped the first fence in the field, and is bolting over the next. Hank and Gwen can hear him running, riderless and hot, on this freezing, black night.

When the horse arrives in the Marshes, the Coward is dreaming of snow. He opens his eyes when he hears a clatter, and sure enough, snow is falling and beside the apple tree stands Belinda's horse, pawing at the frozen ground, searching for apples.

The Coward has been sleeping in his coat and his boots; he goes outside and huddles near the horse and watches him eat. After a while, he gets a rope and ties the horse to the tree.

"There you go," the Coward tells the horse. "That's your bed."

The Coward gets himself a nightcap and sits on his porch until

Gwen arrives at his rickety, useless gate, her little white dog trailing behind. Gwen's eyes look strange and feverish and she has a purple bruise across her face. Hollis hit her only once, as she went past him leaving the barn, but he made certain to strike hard. There are broken blood vessels beneath her skin; he's left his mark for weeks to come.

When the Coward sees the way she looks, he has a funny feeling in his arms and legs, as though someone had set a match to his flesh. "What did he do to you?" he asks.

The girl looks straight ahead. Tears are falling from her eyes, but she's not making a sound.

"I won't let him get to this horse, if that's what you're worried about," the Coward says, suddenly much braver than he imagined he could be. He'd kill any man who came looking for this horse, or be killed himself. If he can stay sober long enough. That's the hitch, but there's no need to mention it to this lovely girl.

"Really?" Gwen says, because she's already realized she can't take Tarot with her and she can't stay. "You'd do that?"

"I would," the Coward vows.

A little while later, Hank comes looking for Gwen. He remained at the house until Hollis calmed down; it was, he believes, the least he could do. He might have leapt to protect Gwen when Hollis reached out and slapped her, but it was so sudden Hank was caught completely by surprise, or so he tells himself. Hollis doesn't mean to do these things; he's like a bomb, one which, if you don't defuse it straightaway, will go off when you least expect it. Surely, Gwen will understand this, and the reason for Hank's delay. Of course Hank hasn't sided with Hollis—it's simply a question of loyalty, not unlike a pledge you make to a country about to enter a foolish, wrongheaded war.

Gwen is sitting on the Coward's floor when Hank arrives; she's wrapped in a ratty wool blanket Judith Dale brought here years ago, trying her best to ignore how drunk the Coward has become.

"It's about time," the Coward says to Hank when the boy pushes open the door. "God, you are slow."

But fast or slow no longer matters, Hank realizes that as soon as he sees the mark Hollis left on Gwen's face. Hollis hit her hard, that's what Hank sees now, and he meant to. Certainly, Hank can try to explain it away, he can sit beside her and loop his arm around her and whisper how awful this is, how sorry he is, how Hollis probably regrets what has happened already, how he'd never actually go ahead and hurt Tarot, but none of this signifies anymore. Sitting there, more beautiful than ever, Gwen has made the decision to go.

God, you are slow, Hank keeps thinking as Gwen laces her fingers through his and rests her head on his shoulder.

"It's not your fault," she tells him, after the Coward has nodded off, and they are as good as alone. "It's just the way things turned out."

Hank laughs at that, a short harsh laugh that goes nowhere. He leans against the thin plaster wall where colonies of ants have lived for decades, perhaps for as long as a century. He closes his eyes.

Whose fault is it when love is denied? When youth is a curse rather than a blessing? Oh, if only there weren't other people involved; if only they were the last two people on earth, just them, opening the door to this old house, looking out at the deep, blue night and all those stars they'll never learn the names of, all those planets they can't even see.

They let the Coward sleep, and walk down into the Marshes. They hardly speak. What, after all, would they say? Wait for me? Don't hold this against me? Don't forget me, not tonight and not ever? Without language they can at least pretend they are the last two people, or perhaps the first, the ones who don't need speech. They need each other, that's all, for one last night.

They stay down in the Marshes until their fingers and toes are nearly frozen; then they come back inside, where they fall asleep side by side on the Coward's floor, close together, their breath even and deep. They are greedy for sleep and forgetfulness; one pure and perfect night of sleep, that's what they yearn for, but even that is too much to expect. Is it possible for two people to have the same dream? As Hank is sleeping on the hard, wooden floor he dreams of a hedge of evergreens in which there is a door. On one side of the hedge is the future, on the other side, the past. In Gwen's dream the hedge is made of thorns and the door has a lock and key. Someone is urging her to step through. *Go ahead*, they tell her, and when she does, the lock falls away. She can't look back, she knows that much; she doesn't dare. In his own dream, on the threshold of his gate, Hank can hear her footsteps in the distance, already fading.

In the morning, when the light is yellow and pale, and the Coward has begun to heat a big kettle of ice into drinking water for the horse, Hank steps outside onto the porch. By then, Gwen is gone.

"She went to Susanna Justice's," the Coward tells him. "She took the dog with her. She's going home."

Hank nods and sits down on the cold wooden steps of his father's house. He notices that the tide coming in sounds as if a million tears were falling. Perhaps it's the ice cracking beneath the rush of cold salt water. "I don't blame her," he says.

"Blame," the Coward says, "is a serious thing."

"Hey, when all else fails, blame yourself, right?" Hank tries to smile, but he feels too tight inside.

"If he comes for the horse, I'll kill him," the Coward says.

"Yeah?" This has to be a joke. "How do you plan to do that?"

The Coward watches a heron that is so far off it would look like a branch to other eyes. "My bare hands," he says.

Hank tries his best not to laugh. "You know what I'd try first?" he suggests. "Camouflage."

They work all the rest of the day on a dilapidated, filthy little outbuilding behind the house, which can serve as a barn. Hank hammers some boards over the holes in the wall and the Coward sets marsh grass over the roof. Today is the day Hank's senior thesis is due, but maybe he can get an extension.

"I can write you a note," the Coward says. "I'll explain everything to the school authorities."

"No way. Don't think anything is different between us," Hank warns the old man. "I'm helping with Tarot because of Gwen, not you."

"Of course," the Coward says. "And this is from Gwen, not from me."

The Coward slides the silver compass which once belonged to him onto the porch railing. Out in the tall grass, the stick that looks like a heron takes flight, slowly and beautifully in the last of the day's light.

"May you never be lost," Alan Murray tells his son.

TWENTY-TWO

MARCH IS NO LONGER WORKING ON HER
jewelry or expecting Hollis to bring back silver or
gold. She has taken the gemstones she'd hoped to
set into bracelets, the opals and the tourmalines,
and stored them in a canvas bag, kept in a dresser
drawer. Instead of working, she stares at the ice
on the window. She waits for night to fall. Sometimes she goes out beyond the fields. She walks
past the meadows and the split-rail fences; once,
she went as far as the cemetery, but she felt
frightened there. There were no leaves on the
trees, and the ground seemed so unforgiving and

hard. Worst of all, she thought she saw Judith Dale in the distance; she thought she saw her crying.

Now, March will not venture any farther than Fox Hill. That, at least, is familiar territory. She goes in the sleet and the snow, and maybe this is why she's developed a cough. It's an aggravating hack that won't go away, in spite of all the hot tea with honey she drinks. Fox Hill makes her sad, but she goes anyway. The mourning doves are gone. Hank's attempt to move their nest has failed; they're gone for good. When March peers into the windows of the old house, she cannot help but think of Judith Dale, and sometimes she looks over her shoulder, as if Judith might somehow appear.

Lately, March has been wondering why Mrs. Dale was not buried with the emerald ring, the gift of her true love. March has been thinking about this every day when she walks through the woods, and she believes she finally has the answer. Judith was not wearing the ring when she died; she'd already removed it, and set it aside. She was done with love. At least with the sort of love that has rules you have to abide by, and which, in the end, offers far less than you'd hoped for.

It's a very good thing that Gwen has gone. She would hate how dark it gets here, pitch-black by as early as four; she would despise how small their lives have become, how poor. On the holidays, there was no exchange of presents; even the gifts March fashioned have remained stored away. Louise Justice left a basket of eggnog and fruitcake from the library committee on their doorstep, similar to the one she left at the Coward's house. They are in that wretched group people in town feel sorry for, the pathetic creatures who don't even know enough to celebrate a holiday.

Well, Hollis at least still goes out; he's often at the Lyon Cafe, but he never takes March along. Other men might look at her. And, of course, the piece he never mentions: Other women might be annoyed by her presence. March is sincerely glad to hear him leave on those nights, as she is relieved when he gets out of bed in the mornings to go and check the boundaries of his property. Oh, he likes his property, yes he does. For weeks after Gwen left, he went out with his gun; he drove down every back road, yet he never did find the horse. March knows where it is, but she's not telling. She happened to discover its whereabouts one day when she was out walking, late, when dusk was settling and the light was so unreliable that at first she thought she was seeing shadows.

It was her brother, Alan, and the horse she saw, those two old bags of bones. Alan was gathering hay, which he cut with a scythe, then lifted onto the horse's back where it was tied with a rope. Blackbirds and gulls circled above the marsh, and the sound of the scythe echoed. March could feel her own heart beat in the silence; she held her black scarf over her mouth so her breath wouldn't freeze. She wished she could be like those blackbirds and fly far from here. She wished she could have cried out, *Save us from evil and from ourselves above all.*

Anything can fuel an argument between Hollis and March now. She looks at him the wrong way, she interrupts his work, she breathes; she's somehow not enough his. His ardor hasn't cooled, but often his flesh won't comply with his spirit's demands. When he can't make love to her he insists it's her fault. She never does as he says and she's taken to fighting back, which is foolish. She leaves the room, she slams the door behind her, behavior which only gives him all the more reason to go to one of the women in town who are so willing to pretend he belongs to them, if only for a few hours. When he comes home, he blames March even for this. She sent him into another woman's arms; she forced him to stray. Why does she do this to him? To them? After he's done berating her, he turns his fury on himself, and that, of course, is the thread that always ties March to him; that is the moment when she always goes to him and holds him. *No one will ever love you the way I do,* that's what he tells her then. *No one can have you, if I can't. Don't even think about leaving. I mean that. Don't even try.*

On New Year's Eve March is glad that Hollis leaves early. Let him go out and try to enjoy himself; she's tired and her cough is worse and she's grateful for some peace and quiet. Hank is supposed to go to a party, but at the last minute he decides to skip it. He's already wearing his good white shirt and has combed his hair, but it's Gwen he wants to be with, not his friends from school. He plans to watch TV and go to bed early, yet when he sees March in the kitchen, all alone, he can't abandon her. They drink tea and play five-hundred rummy, and then, in spite of himself, Hank gets restless.

"Let's go for a ride," he suggests.

March smiles up at her nephew. His sweetness always astounds her. "Go out with your friends," she says.

"Come on," Hank insists. "I've got my car."

March laughs at that since Hank's car, an old Pontiac he bought last week, has no heat and no back seat and is dented all the way around, from the previous driver. The rattletrap, they call it. The icebox.

"We'll go out and get one beer. Just for New Year's," he says. "We can't just sit here."

March grabs her coat and her long black scarf and hastily runs a brush through her hair. They get in the car, but they're freezing by the time they reach the liquor store; March runs in to buy them their bottles of beer so they can toast the New Year.

"Where do you think Gwen is tonight?" Hank asks March as they drive toward town.

"Probably with her dad," March guesses. "Don't worry, I'm sure she's not out with some other boy."

"That's all right," Hank says. "I want her to have a good time. I don't own her."

"Right," March says, opening her beer and taking a sip. "Nobody owns anybody. Or so they say."

A light snow has begun. Flakes catch on the windshield and

stick like glue. Hank switches on the wipers and they turn onto Main Street. They drive through town, counting the houses where parties are being held. When they pass by the Lyon, March has a funny feeling in her stomach. She's one of those women who no longer want to know the truth.

"Don't stop," she tells Hank.

They go on, all through the town. The defroster in the car isn't much use, and every once in a while Hank wipes off the windshield in front of him with the palm of his hand, or March cleans the glass with the tail end of her scarf. In very little time, everything is covered with a blanket of white. It is a beautiful night, so quiet the sound of their tires echoes as they drive on.

"You ought to see Dr. Henderson about that cough," Hank says when March starts hacking.

"It's the cold weather," March says. "I'm not used to it."

It feels so odd to be in the village; everything seems brighter and bigger than usual.

"Look at him." March laughs when they pass Town Hall. The Founder is covered in snow; only his nose is recognizable.

"I did my senior thesis on him, and I never realized he had such a big nose." Hank grins. "They probably should have named this town Noseville."

"Nostriltown," March suggests, as she finishes her beer.

"Schnoz City." Hank gets a particular hoot out of that one. "The football team at the high school could be the Schnozkickers."

March lets out a laugh. "They'd have big noses on the back of their jackets."

"Good old Schnoz City," Hank says affectionately. "Born and bred there."

They have turned down a side street, the one where Susanna Justice lives. Susie's little house is all lit up and music floats into the street.

"She's having a party," March says.

They pull over and park, then exchange a look.

"We could go in for a little while," Hank says.

"Have a drink and leave," March agrees.

March reaches into her coat pocket for an old lipstick, then peers into the rearview mirror so she can apply some color to her face. They walk through the snow, and go in through Susie's unlocked front door. It's hot in this little house, and noisy. There's the scent of cider and beer and pizza. As soon as Susie spies March, she runs over and hugs her.

"How come you didn't invite me?" March teases.

Susie is wearing a violet sweater decorated with rhinestones and a short purple skirt. She looks beautiful tonight, flushed and breathless and a little drunk.

"I sent you an invitation," Susie says. "I went out to see you last week, and Hollis told me you were sleeping, you couldn't see me. I thought he was lying, but what could I do?"

"Well, I'm here now," March says.

"Yes, you are." Susie smiles. "You know Ed," she adds when a good-looking man comes over to loop his arm around her waist. Susie's two Labrador retrievers are following him, eyeing the platter of mini-knishes Ed's been circulating.

"Sure, I remember," March says. "Thanksgiving."

"This guy must be starving." Ed nods at Hank. "He's started to drool."

They all laugh when they see how Hank is staring at the platters of food, as rapt as the retrievers.

"Come on." Ed guides Hank toward a buffet table which spans the width of Susie's tiny living room.

"Let's go into the kitchen," Susie says to March.

March nods and follows. She knows Susie's been checking her out; her clothes, after all, aren't nice enough for a party, and she didn't think to do anything about her hair, not even tie it away from her face. People seem to be staring at her as they head for the kitchen. She lives with the richest man in the county, and look at what she's wearing—worn corduroy slacks and a red sweater from the old-clothes bin at the Harvest Fair.

"You've got to try the pizza," Susie tells March. "It's made with pesto and feta cheese."

It's broiling in the kitchen—Ed and Susie spent all afternoon cooking pizzas with the oven turned on high—but March is shivering and she can't get rid of her damned cough.

"Have you seen a doctor?" Susie says as she pours March a glass of wine. "Because you should."

"You think I'm sick because I'm living out there with him," March says.

Susie puts down the plate she's already heaped with pizza and a salad Miranda Henderson brought over. "You told me not to judge," she says.

March smiles, and suddenly starving, she reaches for the plate of food. As she does, Susie sees a circle of purple bruises on her arm, leftovers of a disagreement they had last Saturday night when Hollis came home after midnight and refused to say where he'd been. *I'm not your servant,* he'd snapped at March, as though she were some harping wife. *I don't have to account to you.*

"Are you going to tell me it's anemia?" Susie asks.

"It was nothing."

Susie laughs; she can't help herself. "March. That's what they all say."

"No, it really was nothing," March insists. "We were arguing and he grabbed me. Believe me, if he ever hit me, I'd be gone."

"Eat," Susie suggests, and she stands there and watches March devour the pizza.

Someone in the living room has switched on the radio; there's already a countdown to midnight. Hank has made himself comfortable on the couch, so he can concentrate on eating. There's smoked salmon on crackers, bluefish pâté, marinated mushrooms,

French Brie. He's eating so fast and so much that Susie's dogs have switched their allegiance from Ed and are now stationed by Hank's feet.

"If you slow down," Bud Horace, the animal control officer, advises when he sits beside Hank, "you can fit more food in. The salmon is good, but you should try the pizza."

Hank is directed toward the kitchen, but it's hard to get through the crowd. He's doing his best to elbow his way past the bar set up in a corner near the front window when he sees Hollis's truck pull up.

"Fuck it," Hank says under his breath. He's the one who's going to be held accountable for this and he knows it.

Hollis comes in through the front door, wearing a black overcoat made of soft Italian wool, bringing in cold air and suspicion. He stops to greet two members of the town council, to whom he made sizable contributions, but his eyes flicker over the room. Before he can spy Hank, Hank makes his way into the kitchen.

"Hollis is here," he tells March.

March looks at him; then, without saying a word, she goes to the back door and wrenches it open. She's so panicked she doesn't even think to retrieve her coat. Hollis is probably walking through the living room right now.

"Wait a second," Susie says, grabbing March's arm and holding her back. "The man you're living with is here and you're running out the back door. Think about it, March."

"You don't understand," March says. She has said this so often it probably sounds ridiculous, but it's true. "He'll see my being here as a betrayal. He'll see me as one of you."

"Gwen left a plane ticket here. You could use it. You could leave—even for a little while. Take some time and think."

March has to laugh at that. You do not think about such matters; you fall into them, head over heels, without a safety net, without a rope.

That's what Hollis sees when he comes into the kitchen—March laughing at the back door—and that doesn't please him one bit. Earlier tonight, Hollis met Alison Hartwig at the Lyon; then they went over to her place—she had managed to get rid of the kids and her mother—but he let Alison know he had to be home before midnight. And then, after all that, when he got back to Guardian Farm, no one was there. Since that time, it's taken close to an hour for him to track March down. This doesn't please him either.

"Hey, Susie," he says, as though he isn't annoyed in the least. "Great party."

"Yeah, too bad you weren't invited," Susie says.

Hollis grins at that. "Aren't you afraid you'll hurt my feelings?"

"Nope," Susie says.

Hollis leans closer to March and kisses her. His lips are cold, and there's snow in the folds of his coat. "You're the most beautiful woman here," he says. "As usual." He notices Hank now, and wonders if perhaps the boy hasn't taken it too much on himself to think over matters that are none of his business. "I didn't expect to see you here," he tells Hank. "You'd better head out."

Hank looks at March, uncertain as to what he should do.

"Go on," March insists. You can't even tell that she's nervous. She laughs, then has a sip of wine. "Find some folks your own age. Just don't freeze in that car of yours."

"Sure," Hank mumbles.

"Hey." As Hank is about to pass him by, Hollis puts a hand on his shoulder. "Don't tell me you've been drinking."

"Just a beer," Hank says. "One."

"You don't want to go in that direction," Hollis says. "Considering your background and all."

It is the worst possible thing Hollis could say to Hank and he knows it—the threat that he might take after his father. March can't quite believe she has actually heard right.

"He had one beer," March says. "I bought it for him. That doesn't mean he's an alcoholic."

"Maybe I'll stick to Coke." Hank grabs a can from the counter. "It's probably not a bad idea."

"We'd better head out too," Hollis tells March after Hank has left.

He says it easily, but he doesn't mean it that way. Nothing is easy with Hollis. March looks at him closely. The evidence is in his eyes. That's where the anger is.

"You could spend the night," Susie says to March. She's not fooled by Hollis's pleasant manner, and she never will be.

Hollis laughs. "Aren't you girls a little too old for pajama parties?"

March hugs Susie. "Thanks," she says. "Another time."

"You can come back whenever you want to," Susie tells her, low so that Hollis has to strain to hear. "You know that."

By the time March gets to the front door, Hollis is waiting with her coat and scarf. There's confetti in the air and slow music playing, but Hollis pays no attention. He holds open the door for March, then lets it slam once they're out of the house.

"Don't ever do that to me again," he says as they start down the snowy walkway leading to the sidewalk. They can still hear voices from the party drifting out of Susie's place. Hollis is so furious that the air around him pops. "You should have been there when I got home, but you weren't, and that's the problem."

He grabs her by the arm, to make his point, to make certain she's listening and to reel her in, closer.

"I don't like an empty house," he says, in a voice so mean it's barely recognizable.

March hears Susie's front door slam as another guest leaves the party. Some man has stepped out onto Susie's porch and March is mortified to think of the tableau which greets this stranger: an angry man, a woman who looks frightened, snow falling, ice on the herringboned brick path.

"What are you looking at?" Hollis is facing the stranger, whom March now recognizes as someone who works at the paper with Susie. The sports editor, she thinks. Bert something-or-other. Whoever he is, he was about to take his gloves from his overcoat pocket—he's already got his car keys in his hand—but he stopped when he saw Hollis holding on to March.

"Hey, buddy," he says to Hollis, his voice soft, as though he were talking to some maniac. "Come on. Ease up. It's New Year's Eve."

March blinks back her tears. That's how they look to him: A couple on the edge. A woman who's about to be hurt somehow. And maybe he's right. When it comes down to it, who is she anyway? The woman she thinks she is or the woman she appears to be?

"What did you call me?" Hollis says. He lets go of March and takes a step toward Susie's front door. He used to talk this way to Alan and his friends when they followed him home, those boys who tossed rocks and curses just above his head. *Buddy* is just another way to say he's nothing, and he doesn't have to listen to that. Not anymore.

March is breathing frigid night air, but she's burning up inside. What she wants is for Susie's guest to go back to the party—then she and Hollis can walk away from this without any permanent damage. She wants that so badly she can taste it, but the taste is bitter, a cold soup made of stones.

The door behind the stranger opens again, and light floods the walkway. Two women, leaving Susie's party, are laughing, but the laughter falls onto the ice and onto the sidewalk, where it cracks open into silence.

"Honey?" one of the women calls when she sees Hollis and the stranger facing off. It's the sports editor's wife or his girlfriend, March realizes this from the measure of concern in her voice.

"Honey?" The woman blinks several times, as if what she is seeing right in front of her eyes couldn't possibly be so.

"Let's go," March says. Now she's the one to grab Hollis, but he jerks away. When he turns to her, she would swear he doesn't know her.

"Are you telling me what to do?" Hollis asks.

Susie's three guests are watching in silence; all anyone can hear is snow falling.

"Please." His favorite word in the world, and March knows it. "Please," she whispers, so that those people watching don't see that she's begging.

When they get to the truck, Hollis steps in front of March, and for an instant March thinks he's going to open the passenger door for her. Then she sees the look on his face and she lurches away, so that her back is flat against the door. In spite of herself, she cries out. Her eyes are closed when he slams his fists through the window on either side of her head; she hears glass falling as though meteors were raining from the sky. March cries out again, then hunkers down to protect herself, until she realizes what has happened. She's not the one he aimed to injure. He has purposely crashed through the glass, and when he withdraws his hands from the shattered window they are covered with blood.

"Oh, no," March says when she sees what he's done. She rises to her feet. If this is what love can do, they'd best give it another name. There is blood on the concrete, and in the snow, but Hollis doesn't seem to notice; that's what's scaring her most of all. He pulls her to him, with all that blood on his hands.

"I would rather hurt myself than hurt you," Hollis says. "I never want to hurt you."

"I know that," March tells him.

"Hey!" the man on Susie's porch shouts. "Are you all right?"

They are so far from that, March doesn't waste her time answering. Her attention is riveted on the way blood spreads. It's on her boots; it's pooling beneath her feet.

"I know you didn't mean it," March says.

Those guests leaving the party are still watching from the brick walkway, uncertain as to whether or not they should intervene. It is still possible to hear the festivities inside the house. Someone must have told a joke, because several people are laughing, and the laughter circles upward. In spite of the snow, March can see stars in the sky, the way they used to when they dragged the ladder out to the chestnut tree and climbed as high as they could.

March takes her scarf and tries to clean the glass out of the gashes in Hollis's hands, but there's too much blood, and Hollis's blood seems far too hot in the chilly air. March can't stop shaking; it's as if she had some rare disease for which there's no definitive diagnosis. Maybe it's terror, maybe it's regret, maybe it's only the cold night, the last of the year.

"It's all right," Hollis tells her, but it's not. He wraps the scarf around his hands. "See?" he says. "It's nothing." But that's not true either.

March's mouth is so parched that her lips hurt. Hollis insists on driving, even though the pressure from the steering wheel must cause him pain. They take the back road home, although the snow has made for treacherous driving. The gears of the truck grind; the tires slide over patches of ice. All the way there, March tries to see him in the same way she had before, but she can't. No matter what she does, no matter how she tries, there's a man of more than forty with bleeding hands who is driving too fast and who still has no idea of what he's done to them.

When they get to the house, all the dogs are seeking shelter on the front porch. The snow is coming down harder. Hollis unwraps the scarf from his hands and washes up in the kitchen sink. When he's done, they go upstairs to their bedroom. They don't have to speak. Hollis, after all, is tired, and frankly March is too. As Hollis unlaces his boots, March watches him. He looks so old tonight, so completely worn out. Would she even recognize him if she met him on a crowded street? Would she know him at all?

Looking at him now, March sees that the boy she loved, the one who kissed her in the attic and promised to love her forever, is no longer inside him. That boy is separate. He's taken on a life of his own. There he is, sitting at the foot of the bed, moving aside so Hollis can pull down the quilt and get in between the sheets. March lies down beside Hollis, but she keeps her eyes trained on that boy, the one she loves beyond all time and reason. Just as she suspected, he's tired too. He rests his beautiful head, then closes his eyes.

March tries her best to be quiet; she doesn't cough, doesn't move. She listens for the sound of Hollis's even breathing, and soon enough there it is, slow and easy. The boy she loves is now curled up on the extra quilt, lonely, the way he'll always be, with or without her. He told her once he did not trust the human race and he never would. He told her he never meant to hurt her, and that, she knows, is true.

Although it's not easy to leave that boy on the edge of the bed, March grabs her clothes and her boots and goes downstairs to dress in the dark kitchen. There is the teapot on the rear burner of the Coopers' stove; there is Hollis's black coat, where he left it, thrown over a wooden chair. There are his gloves, on the shelf, and the glass he last used to drink water, rinsed out and drying on the drainboard. Everything March sees is a shadow in the dark, even herself: her scarf, her hand turning the doorknob, the way she shivers when she feels the cold against her skin.

She slips out the door so quietly that the dogs curled up on the porch don't hear her pass by. When she gets to the very end of the driveway, she turns to look at the house. If she didn't know better, she would swear that a girl with dark hair was standing in the place where the roses used to grow. If she didn't know better, she'd hesitate. Instead, she turns and runs.

At first, she counts her steps the way she used to, but after a while she stops counting. She paces herself so she won't become exhausted; she avoids the road and goes through the woods. The air is so cold it snaps; the clearing sky is filled with stars. March hurries; she's going so fast that she might have missed seeing the foxes if her coat hadn't been snagged by a branch. When she turns she spies them in the meadow, more than a dozen foxes, all in a circle, just as Judith Dale had told her. Here was a meeting of the last specimens on the hill, the descendants of those few who managed to escape in the year when open hunting season was declared.

Judith Dale used to swear that at gatherings such as these, each fox would rise on his hind feet and walk about, just like a man; if you listened carefully, you could hear each one speak, in measured and somber tones. What you overheard might change your life and rearrange all you once believed you knew for certain. A fox's secret was one worth knowing, worth waiting for, worth its weight in gold, or so March had always been promised. But Judith Dale was wrong, and now March is glad to discover that she was. These creatures are nothing like men; they haven't a word to say, and no secrets to tell. When March leaves, several of them follow for a while, as though they were dogs—not that she needs their guidance. She knows the way, after all. She's been here before.

IT'S FREEZING IN HANK'S DREAM ON THE MORNING when it happens, that first bright day of the year. He is dreaming about a tree of ice—leaves, trunk, and branches—when he hears the crash. In his dream, the tree falls to pieces, shards of crystal that can cut like knives. That's when he gets out of bed; he goes to his window and witnesses the last few instants of what is happening, as Hollis's truck skids into the devil's corner.

Hank pulls on his jeans and races downstairs; he slams out the door and runs down the driveway in his bare feet. The snow cuts into his skin, but he runs faster. At the edge of the driveway, the red dogs gather together, afraid to go farther. The crash is so close that Hank can smell gasoline. There is Hollis's pickup, on its side, and the newspaper delivery truck crossways, blocking Route 22. Before Hank can round the corner, Hollis's truck bursts into flames. The driver of the other truck is sitting in the road, shaking, as the roar of the fire rises higher and ashes fall down, like thick black snow.

"He just kept going," the driver of the delivery truck says when Hank pulls him to his feet and guides him farther from the fire. They stand there and watch the flames. The road is so burning hot it's melting patches of ice. By the time the EMT and fire trucks arrive, whatever snow remains has turned black.

There's soot all over Hank's clothes and in his eyes. For days afterwards, he will find ashes, in the strands of his hair, under his fingernails, in his eyelashes. He doesn't tell March the true date of Hollis's accident. He waits several days before he sends the telegram. He doesn't want her to think that Hollis was chasing her, flooring the gas on that icy morning so he could track her down at Logan before her plane took off. Maybe he was after March, or maybe he was simply in a hurry to get to the Lyon Cafe and find somebody to take her place. But there's another possibility, and it's one Hank believes: Hollis simply couldn't bear to wake up and find himself alone. There was a time, once, when Hank was nine or ten and woke in the middle of the night, when he made his way downstairs and he saw Hollis at the kitchen table. Hank stood there in the doorway and watched, and he thought he would never in his life see a lonelier human being, not if he lived to be a hundred.

Perhaps this is the reason Hank stays with Hollis at the funeral parlor. Someone should be there, and in all honesty, Hank can't imagine being able to sleep even if he were to spend the night in his own bed. There's a room to the left of the chapel, and this is where Hollis is. Hank picked out his clothes: A pale gray suit. One of the good white shirts Hollis favored, tailored in Italy. Black boots, hand-polished. A dark blue tie, the color of still, deep water. Hank chose the coffin as well, the most expensive one available, fashioned of cherrywood and brass. Though Hank himself prefers plain pine, he knows that Hollis would have elected to show people in this town that he had the best. Regardless of whether or not anyone appears at the service tomorrow, Hank has seen to it that he has received exactly that.

The room beside the chapel is poorly heated and the lights are turned low. Hank tosses down the duffel bag of clothes he's brought along, then positions himself in an overstuffed chair. It's not unusual for people to spend the night here. They don't want to let go; they want one more chance to make it right. For those who believe in paradise, such a night is wrenching. For those who believe in a single worldly existence, it may be the longest night they ever spend. All the same, Hank is there for the duration, he's not about to leave, although in many ways the man in the coffin doesn't resemble Hollis. It's not only his physical aspect which seems so altered, by fire and reconstruction, it's that Hollis would never lie down like this, so mild and meek.

The later the hour grows, the more chilled Hank feels; at last, he covers himself with his coat, and he falls asleep that way, sitting up, his long legs stretched out, his breathing the only evidence of human life until Alan Murray comes to pay his respects. Alan wears the Judge's recycled overcoat and a pair of boots Judith Dale left him one winter when the snow was particularly deep. He has tied back his hair with a rubber band and clipped his beard with a pair of nail scissors. Although he has a pint of gin in his pocket, he won't have a drink until he begins the walk home.

He passes by his son, asleep in the chair, and goes to sit on the wooden bench facing the coffin. It is gratitude which has brought him here and kept him sober, at least for these few hours. Without thinking, Alan bows his head. For the day Hollis came to take his son, he is grateful. For every meal Hollis fed the child, he is more grateful still. For every dollar spent, for every night of sleep, for blue jeans and socks, for shoes and books, for cups of tea, for milk, for pie, for companionship, for curfews, for duty, for love.

Hank wakes from his uneasy sleep and blinks when he sees the old man. The chapel is now so cold that a film of ice has formed on the inside panes of window glass. Outside, the night is as blue as a lake and much deeper than any river. If your soul were free, it would be the sort of night to rise up.

"You're staying with him?" the old man asks.

"Sure," Hank says. He runs a hand through his hair; still, some strands stick up like stalks of wheat. His face is pale in the dark, his skin ashy.

"It's good that you're staying," Alan Murray says. He can feel the weight of the bottle of gin in his pocket. His circulation is shot, so he rubs his hands together.

"Oh, yeah?" Hank says dryly. "What do you care?"

"I don't think anyone should be alone in circumstances such as these." Alan nods to the coffin. "Even him."

Alan stands and buttons the Judge's overcoat, which billows out on his thin frame. His posture is terrible; he smells like hay. His throat closes up when he looks at his son, the way another man's might when looking at stars. "Get some sleep," he advises.

It's advice well taken, and Hank does manage a few hours of restless sleep. In the morning, he changes his clothes in the men's room. He wears a black suit he took from Hollis's closet, good wool, quite well made, but much too small for Hank's build. He is fully prepared to be the only mourner, considering how people in the village felt about Hollis, but as it turns out, he isn't alone at the funeral. Several women attend the service. Each comes in by herself, and unless Hank is mistaken, several are crying. There are no flowers decorating the chapel; nothing like that. The coffin is now closed, as Hollis would have wished.

When the service is over, Hank stands on the steps of the funeral parlor. From here, he can see most of Main Street: There is the bakery, which is right now baking cinnamon bread. There is the library with its tall, arched windows, and the Lyon Cafe, which is always dark and shuttered at this time of day. Hank loosens his tie and unbuttons the top two buttons of his white shirt, but he keeps on the jacket borrowed from Hollis, even though it doesn't quite fit. He heads down Main Street, then gets into his car, which is already packed with his belongings. He's going to stay with the Justices until the end of the school term. After graduation, of course, he's free to go where he chooses. He will not remain at Guardian Farm. He decided that right away, and it made no difference when the Judge told him he was Hollis's only heir.

Hank's friends would think him insane to give it all away, but that's what he's done. He's donated all the land to the town; a trust has already been drawn up. The income from Hollis's properties in Florida will pay for all the upkeep on the Farm, the gardeners and the caretakers, even the kibble for the red dogs. The trust will underwrite the Library Association and the Snow Shovelers' and Firemen's Funds and provide hay and oats for Tarot for as long as he lives, just as it will pay for Alan Murray's tab at the liquor store on Route 22. After all, who is Hank to sit in judgment of his father? Who is he to measure another man's sorrow? Hank is indebted to Hollis, and he always will be, but he knows what happens to a man who won't give up those things it's impossible to hold on to. He knows what can happen to any man who won't let go of his pain.

Although Christmas vacation is over and Hank's friends have all gone back to school, Hank won't return to classes until tomorrow. Instead, he now drives over to Fox Hill. He flips on the radio and keeps the window open, in spite of the cold, just as Hollis used to. He parks near the quince bushes, then gets out and climbs as far as he can go. From here a man can imagine he's looking out at the whole, wide world. He's the king of everything, of sky and cloud. This is where Hollis will be laid to rest, and the gravediggers, who are traveling over the dirt road right now, will have to be paid extra to deal with the brambles and the ice. Hank had to do battle with the town clerk to get permission to bury Hollis here, and thankfully, the Judge came to his aid and eased his petition through the corridors of Town Hall.

In truth, what harm can one grave do up here? Why, it's almost heaven, it's so clear and clean. Years from now, children in town will talk about the New Year's Day when there was black snow. They'll say the devil reached out and took what belonged to him; they'll avoid that intersection where the grass still refuses to grow. But Hank knows better, and on the first day of every year he will always make certain to say a prayer for those to whom he wishes peace, both the living and the dead.

BY ALICE HOFFMAN
ALSO AVAILABLE IN VINTAGE